FORGED IN FIRE AND BLOOD

WHIT JORDAN

ISBN: 979-8-9911876-4-0 (Paperback)
ISBN: 979-8-9911876-5-7 (eBook)

First Edition: October 2025

Book Cover by Maple Projects
Map by Inkarnate

Bibliobean Books
PO Box 162
Franklinton, NC 27525
www.bibliobeanbooks.com

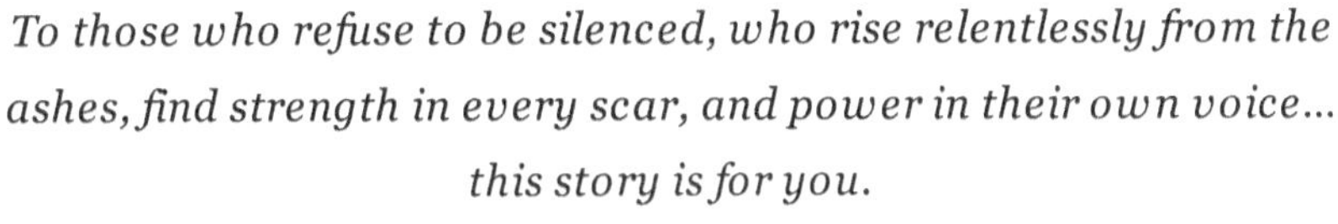

To those who refuse to be silenced, who rise relentlessly from the ashes, find strength in every scar, and power in their own voice...
this story is for you.
May you always give tyranny hell.

 Content Warning

This work contains themes and depictions that may be distressing or triggering to some readers, including but not limited to:

- Physical abuse and torture
- Psychological trauma and PTSD
- Sexual assault
- Death and grief
- War and violence
- Suicidal ideation
- Corruption and possession
- Child endangerment and death

Please take care of yourself while reading. Your well-being matters more than finishing a story.

Pronunciation

Characters:

Brynn (brin)

Eowyn (ay-oh-win)

Cia (see-ah)

Ronan (roh-nan)

Roimh (romh)

Renoa (ren-oh-a)

Perri (peh-ree)

Mideton (mid-ton)

Britta (bree-ta)

Parela (pah-rey-la)

Drescher (drey-sh-er)

Finnick (fin-ick)

Mahurin (ma-hur-n)

Muris (mur-iss)

Kailiao (kai-lee-ow)

Clans:

Tiene (tee-in)

Riacán (ree-uh-kahn)

Cerwei (sir-way)

Nua (noo-ah)

Róisín (roh-sheen)

Fuath (foo-ath)

Oéngus (oh-en-gus)

Places:

Reikhaven (rike-hay-ven)

Reik (rike)

Tuathinne (too-ya-thin-uh)

Ravndal (rah-ven-dah)

Agderian (ag-deer-ee-uhn)

Agderia (ag-deer-ee-uh)

Vaniran (van-ire-an)

Brucoll (brew-kol)

Inevar (eye-ne-vah)

Other:

Draíocht (dray-oak)

Rüin (roo-n)

Laioses (lay-o-see)

Eadom (ay-dom)

Mirákhi (mee-rah-kee)

Gaia (guy-ah)

Dagda (dahg-duh)

Seidré (say-dray)

Beireoir an bhais (b-yor-irr on bahs)

Part 1

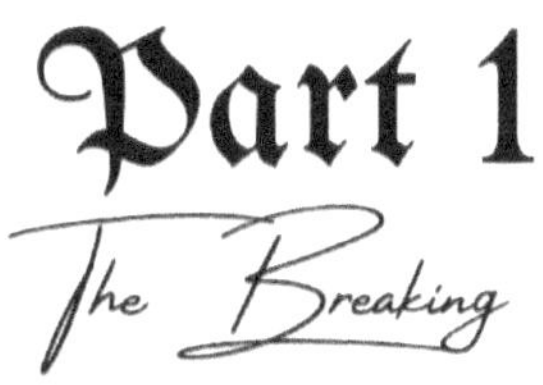

A child, chosen by Eadom, born of Light,

Shall bear the weapon forged in fire,

And broken in blood.

The Chosen shall unite the Laioses,

And bring Death upon all who bear His name.

Guard the Chosen until the darkness breaks—

And what was lost shall restore again.

Chapter 1

Star-burst shaped saltite stones hang uniformly with overwhelming decadence from the high vaulted ceiling above me. I smile faintly and imagine how they will shimmer, taking on a life of their own once the sun begins to set. A soft shuffle of footsteps echoes across the alabaster floor behind me, drawing me from my thoughts. I turn slowly, offering a bright smile to the wrinkled face and warm honey-brown eyes bowing humbly before me.

"Mideton, my dear friend, what a lovely way to greet the morning." I gesture toward the array of servants arranging holly along the mammoth hearth in the center of the Great Hall. "You've truly outdone yourself this year."

His weathered cheeks tint with the faintest shade of pink as gratitude softens the deep lines of his face. "You are far too kind, milady. It was your vision that gave life to this splendor."

I look away, lightly clearing my throat against the sudden tightness forming there. The frozen southern wind howls threateningly against the frosted glass wall before me, as if sensing the discomfort threading through me. I shiver at the sound of wailing that echoes within my mind.

"Please be sure to bring in extra logs," I say quickly, too briskly. "The next few evenings will be quite cold."

Mideton bows his head, but not fast enough to hide the flicker of hurt in his eyes. "Yes, milady. As you wish."

I nod, resisting the urge to reach out and gather his gnarled hands in mine. His hands look as if they were carved from the very stone beneath us. My chest aches as I glance up at the stoop of his once-proud shoulders. He had stood tall once, like an iron pillar...but now he seems as if he may collapse at any moment. Yet, never once in my years within these walls has Mideton ever faltered in his duties.

I tear my eyes away, focusing instead on the servant's draping strands of golden fabric across the beams of the hall. They work carefully, mindful not to brush against the delicate saltite stones above. I bite my lip, already envisioning the gaudiness that will reflect from the golden canopy once the stones begin to glow.

I startle as Mideton's hand clasps mine suddenly, though they are comforting and familiar. His whisper settles over me like warm wool. "It's not too extravagant for Lord Roimh, milady," he says with a reassuring squeeze.

I return his soothing pressure, offering him a grateful smile before quickly pulling back, glancing around to be sure we were not being watched. Another gust of wind rattles the glass behind us and the shrieking crescendos in my mind, clawing at the edge of my reason. I squeeze my eyes shut, willing the nausea to subside and force my breath to steady against the threat of unraveling.

"Here, milady." Mideton's voice is low, urgent. He presses a steaming cup of tea into my hands. "This will help with the headaches."

I sip slowly, allowing the honeyed Valerian warmth to melt its way through my bones. The shrieking softens, caged again in some hidden place. I glance past the cup to the looming tree line of Reik Forest, barely visible beyond the fortress walls. The darkness feels aware. Watching. A chill crawls through me.

"I hear them," I whisper to Mideton. "The trees."

His color drains in an instant. Alarm flashes across his face. He steps closer, clasping my arm in a grip far stronger than expected. When he speaks, his voice is like ice against my ear.

"Speak not, milady. The stones have ears...and they bleed such atrocities."

I recoil slightly, startled by the ferocity of his fear. But when I meet his gaze, it is not anger that I find. Only worry. Deep, fathomless worry, etched into every fine line of his face. I offer him a small nod of understanding, and his shaky hand quickly drops as I straighten my shoulders.

"I must go," I say. "The queen's seamstress expects me. Please oversee the hanging of the ivy...and be sure the wild berries and floating candles are placed along each table."

I turn, gathering the folds of my woolen skirt. I pause halfway to the door and gesture to the northern corner of the

Great Hall. "The musicians should be stationed there. Make sure they're offered refreshments through the evening." I pause, lowering my voice. "Quietly, of course. Despite his Lordship's opinions of the townspeople, we must show them kindness."

Mideton nods conspiratorially. "You are as kind as you are generous Lady Brynn. Never forget that. May the Dagda bless you this Yultane."

I flush, heat creeping into my cheeks. He winks, then turns and barks orders with a force that banishes all signs of age from his posture. A general among foot soldiers. I smile crookedly at the image of Mideton on a battlefield, fearless and shouting, the savages of Ravndal scattering before him. Someone I would not want to face across enemy lines.

As I make my way down the hall toward my chambers, his compliment lingers in my thoughts. Yultane tradition calls for benevolence. My decision to hire musicians from Reik, rather than Agderia, had come with a cost. I rub my throat absently, lips tightening. The cost had been steep. A chest of gold to feed each of their families through the winter...and certain *stipulations* Lord Roimh insisted upon in return. My stomach churns at the memory.

I round the final corner, pausing before the heavy wooden door of my bedchamber. I inhale slowly and square my shoulders, bracing myself for the flurry of corsets, fabrics, and lace that I am certain awaits. The hum in my mind pulses gently now. Distant. Masked. I step into the chaos the royal seamstress, Birdie, has no doubt prepared for me.

Chapter 2

I stare at myself in the mirror while my silent voice screams from within, my skin shrieking in disgust. The dress is an absolute abomination. Light blue, net-like polyester mushrooms out from my waist and each of my short arms. Yet, Birdie is under the impression the dress needs more. I am not one to doubt the artistic talent of the royal seamstress, especially with the reputation Birdie has among the court, but this is excessive.

"Birdie, I do believe if you add any more to this dress, it will swallow me whole."

The plump raven-haired woman hisses, "Lady Reikhaven, you mustn't question an artist in the process of sculpting her creation."

She pulls tightly on the corset, and I sharply inhale as pain lances through my ribs. I force a meek smile in response. I remain silent throughout the remainder of Birdie's fussing. It is safer that way. I have long since silenced my voice; better to let it fade than risk *her* hearing it.

Hilde.

The queen.

Her whispers nest in the corners of my mind like smoke. I don't know if she's placed them there or if fear has, but sometimes, I wonder if there's a difference.

"Oh, Lady Reikhaven, I do believe my work here is done. You look exquisite!"

Birdie's face beams as she steps back from me, taking in her handiwork. I gather the voluminous skirt, the dress rustling in protest. I placate her with a smile, pretending it is everything I want in a ball gown, though my short stature offers little reprieve for the billowing fabric. I twirl my soft auburn hair nervously between my fingers and study my reflection. I am not willowy thin like most ladies of court, an opinion my husband shares often and with disgust. The evidence of both my children marks the plumpness of my stomach. The corset, thankfully, offsets the sagginess of my breasts. I study the light splatter of freckles on my face, wishing I could scrub them from my porcelain skin. At least Birdie has made my turquoise eyes shine, hopefully distracting from the rest.

"Thank you, Birdie. Your work is quite...extravagant."

Birdie's eyes sparkle eagerly. "Nothing but the absolute best for the queen's favorite."

I silently cringe, wincing at the compliment. Queen Hilde has a way of sucking the very air out of a room, like a phantom of death. She is the last person I would ever choose to spend time alone with, even if she is the Queen of Agderia. I frown at the memory of my time at court as I stare absentmindedly at the shell of the woman before me. Cold wrinkled fingers press against my warm cheek and draw me from the haunted memory.

"Do not frown, Lady, it makes you look unraveled and does nothing but emphasize the wrinkles on that pretty face," Birdie exclaims, patting the offending creases around my mouth.

I stare up at her, attempting to mask my annoyance. She is draped in a quilt of colors and textures. Her dress of velvet is embroidered with golden thread, lace spills from her sleeves, and brooches are pinned to her bodice like jeweled barnacles. A bird-cage shaped hat rests atop her head, the black netting fluttering as she moves. Her once dark hair is now streaked with gray, the years creeping in unmercifully. A flicker of irritation crosses her powdered face as she meets my narrowed gaze. I smile sweetly, hoping to avoid another lashing from her sharp tongue. Birdie owes no loyalty to me, only to my *benevolent* benefactor.

I bite the inside of my cheek, remembering why the queen sent Birdie in the first place. With the Laioses threatening the border, what better way to ensure I remain loyal to the Crown. After all, the traitorous blood flowing in my veins may answer the call of the savagery it yearns for. I drop my eyes in humble obedience and pray to the Dagda that Birdie cannot see past my carefully laid mask into a heart that longs for freedom.

"Good girl!" she says, her smile thin and humorless. A smile that never reaches her dead eyes. A common trait among those closest to her royal majesty.

The words echo in my skull, reverberating not just from her lips, but from a deeper place. As if the queen herself has spoken them from within me.

A cold shudder tightens around my core. I touch my face lightly, searching my eyes in the mirror for any hint of that same emptiness. Years within the palace walls, and now Reikhaven, have left wounds deep in my soul. And yet, somehow, my eyes still shine. Still burn with life.

The humming in my mind shrieks as Birdie sharply sucks in air. A flurry of fabric and thread erupts around me. She moves quickly, retreating as if she too hears the screaming in my head. Her orders to the maidservant are laced with venom. The door slams behind her, and I am left in silence.

The silence is worse.

The dress tightens around my lungs. The tentacles of its fabric snake up my throat. I claw at them, my nails digging into my own skin as the room spins. Tears blur my vision as I stagger to the water basin, frantically washing the crimson from beneath my fingernails. I tug the fabric from my body. It falls in a heap to the floor. I stand in the cool air, bare and gasping.

And *free*.

"What in the bloody hell is that?" Cia asks teasingly, nodding toward the light blue mound crumpled against the floor.

"Torture," I croon back, quickly dressing in my woolen skirt and white tunic.

I watch with amusement as the wraith of a woman glides into the room. The sunlight from the bay-side window disappears into the black depth of her shoulder-length hair. She snickers as she flops lazily into the plush, straight-back chair across from me, draping her legs over the chair's arm. A mischievous grin spreads across her face as she helps herself to the raspberry tea cakes.

"It looks like it came from Lady Tuathinne's closet of horrors," Cia says, plopping a cake into her mouth. Her lips stain brightly against her warm golden skin. "I hate that I will miss the show."

My laughter fills the room at the thought of Cia in Agderia's finest, rather than the forest green breeches and loose tunic she always wears.

"I'd rather leap from the veranda into the icy Gaiad Sea than spend an evening with Agderia's elite wearing a fisherman's net of ugly blue."

I roll my eyes and pour honeyed tea into two cups. "It's a *gift* from the queen."

Cia snorts, reaching for sugar cubes. "The queen is an idiot."

The teapot clatters against the silver platter as my eyes widen in horror. I glance toward the door and hurry across the room, shutting it quickly. I turn to her, fear sharpening my whisper.

"You mustn't say these things. The stones have ears."

She shrugs, unconcerned, and continues her sugary feast.

"Cia, please," I plead. "Promise me you won't speak like that. Not here. Roimh will have your head."

Her brooding eyes fix on mine, smoldering with rage. "I'd like to see that arrogant ass try."

My shoulders sag as a sudden chill tightens the air. I busy myself with the hearth, stoking the fire. The flames lick and roar to life. Their dance of light thunders in my ears and I am swallowed within the warmth. That is until Roimh's voice mockingly invades my tranquility.

Ladies wear dresses and finery, not pants as if they are men.

I rub my cheek, a phantom pain flaring where Roimh's rage once struck. I force myself to look away from the flames and toward Cia's impassive face. She is the only woman in Reikhaven bold enough to defy Roimh. Her coin buys her certain liberties, but those liberties will last only so long. Roimh's little ravens are always listening.

Cia rises and moves toward me. She clasps my hand and leans her forehead to mine.

"Brynn, you deserve more than this. You deserve to live without fear."

The truth in her voice guts me. I squeeze her hand, blinking back tears. My soul longs for peace, yet fear has woven itself into every thread of my being and paralyzes me into submission. It toys with the heartstrings that bleed within my chest for a peace that surpasses my understanding.

A soft knock and childish giggles break the moment. I smile. The wounds in my heart seal with each infectious laugh. Freshly scrubbed faces greet me as I open the great wooden door.

"Mamma!" Ophele cries, reaching for me, her golden curls bouncing.

"I apologize for the intrusion, milady," Sarmien says, bowing deeply. She eyes Cia with caution. "The children wanted to see you before you left for Reik."

I gather Ophele in my arms, steadying her. Though nearly eight, her legs remain weak from the fever she suffered shortly after birth. I tousle Olan's sandy hair as he races his half-grown frame toward the sweets.

"Leave them with me, Sarmien. Take a moment for yourself. I'll have Britta fetch you when it's time to leave."

Sarmien curtsies, delight scrunching her pointed nose, and darts down the hall, no doubt to the young guard she secretly adores. The door latches shut behind her.

"Bet you can't fill all these chocolates in your mouth," Olan dares, grinning at Cia.

Cia grins back. "Challenge accepted, Little Lord."

Ophele plays with the ends of my hair while I watch chaos unfold. I kiss the top of her head and comb her golden curls through my fingers. I breathe in their joy, desperate to hold it a little longer.

"I won!" Olan shouts, chocolate falling from his mouth.

"Only because of that big mouth," Cia says, tickling him.

The sun casts long shadows across the walls, dancing with their laughter. I watch, entranced by their movement. The warmth in my stomach returns as I watch their darkened leaps and twirls along the bookshelf and chamber walls. As if nothing in this world matters more than the joy within the shadows. For a moment, I forget the fear that festers inside of me every waking moment, and I soak in the happiness that encompasses every inch of the room. That is until Britta arrives.

Her sudden and unannounced arrival jolts me abruptly from my trance. Olan protests loudly. My heart aches for more time with the boy who is slowly becoming a man. Resentment simmers beneath my skin and eats away at my throat. I silently vow to find a way around Roimh's cruel restrictions. Cia meets Britta's stiff posture with a glare and gently helps Ophele stand. The shadows in the room stretch darker until the room is encompassed in their wrath. Britta flinches as Cia brushes past her, dragging a furious Olan behind her.

At the doorway, Cia points at the blue monstrosity. "Please report back on Lady Tuathinne's dress. I'm not sure it could top *THAT* monstrosity."

Britta hisses her contempt and quickly moves toward the door. Cia rolls her eyes and disappears down the hall, her dark hair trailing like smoke. I watch her go, longing to follow on whatever adventure Cia is sure to partake upon. But I instead turn to Britta's waiting gaze and prepare for the short trip to Reik.

Chapter 3

The sun hides behind thick gray clouds as I step onto the cobblestone courtyard in the center of the fortress. Wind whistles in contempt against the aging stone walls, and I pull my woolen cloak tighter. I bite my lip, regretting the lavender-dyed chemise I chose to wear. The pendulous sleeves whip in agreement against my skin with every gust. Britta will fuss about my hair tonight, frizzed and knotted from the cold, but I haven't the heart to tame the wildness living in each strand.

Metal grinding against whetstone slices through the bustle of men in formation. I glance up toward the turret at a raven's caw. Its wings beat the air with menace as a whisper coils in my ear. A shiver ripples down my spine, and I quickly glance away, pulling the cloak protectively around me.

"Your horse, Lady Reikhaven," a sandy-haired lad says, approaching with a crooked smile.

I exhale in relief. "Thank you kindly, Finn," I say, shakily taking his hand and mounting the mare.

"It is but an honor, Lady." He grins boyishly and for a split second I am reminded of Olan.

I brush my silken gloves against the mare's chestnut mane. Each stroke calms the voice whispering in my head. I smile politely, aware of Drescher's narrowed eyes on our exchange. I clear my throat, nervously finding my voice.

"Good day, Captain. Thank you for this escort."

His hazel eyes, cold and unimpressed, rake over me. "You will follow orders today, Lady."

A fire sparks in my gut before I can stop it. Fiery words dance across my tongue before I can clamp my mouth shut.

"It is I, Lady of Reikhaven, who will be giving the orders today, *Captain*."

The courtyard falls still. An overwhelming sense of fear weighs down upon me in an instant flood of regret as Drescher's face reddens like Vaniran's iron-rich cliffs. His snow-white warhorse snorts as he yanks the reins and wheels threateningly toward me. I flinch, heart slamming in my chest as he approaches, but he veers away, cantering toward the gate. I silently curse my loose tongue, vowing to keep my distance from the captain as much as possible should the fire on my tongue betray me again.

I urge my mare forward, heat rising in my cheeks under the weight of watching eyes. I swallow back the growing fear rising as I dig my nails into the palms of my hands, holding the reins tightly. The fire inside me dies beneath the cold realization that there will be consequences. I stare down at the muddied slush beneath my mare's hooves. Surrender. It's what life has taught me since my arrival as a babe to the great Agderian capital. Always surrender. No matter how much it bloodies your soul.

I try desperately to remain stoic as I trot through the gate, but I wilt like a flower weighted with morning dew. Panic drowns me, tightening my chest with a desperate wail of my lungs for breath. Ahead, Drescher barks orders to the scouts flanking us. He turns back, scowling. I avert my gaze. He shouts at Finn, commanding him to take my left flank. I glance around uneasily. There are too few of us. Why would Roimh send so small an escort? I settle on Drescher's presence being explanation enough. Roimh trusts his blade.

Drescher came to Reikhaven not long after I arrived as Roimh's chosen bride. The fortress buzzed with rumors of his disgrace. A castoff of Lord Tuathinne's mercenaries with a temper and taste for blood. I've kept my distance from the silver-haired brute whose eyes were always a little too violent and a little too watchful. His scarred neck, torn ear, and hawk-like stare make my skin crawl, but Roimh quickly elevated him. Made him Captain of the Guard and his most trusted official. It was through Drescher that Roimh's reputation darkened from respected to feared.

I breathe in the scent of wet earth, relishing the icy sting in my lungs, and allow my gaze to drift beyond the hills. Freedom waits there. A life untouched by duty and fear. A life I have longed for and will never be able to seek. The hour scurries by, lost in my longing, and before I know it, the hills give way to the salty air that lingers just ahead.

I look up as the clouds part slightly, leaving behind snowflakes that kiss my cheeks. My eyes dart to the wooden rooftops, dappled with pale light, that appear ahead. I glance back one last time toward the rolling hills before slipping on my mask of nobility for all of Reik to see; leaving my hope to die with each dutiful plod forward.

Shops line the cobbled road, their signs swaying in the breeze. Drescher's horse presses through the crowd, his hand resting on his sword's hilt. The noise of the street grows. Peddlers shout their wares of spices, fabrics, and meats. My senses drink in the vibrant pulse of the little town. I cling to the scent of sweetened perfumes and cooking meat. Bearded men in colorful robes offer skewers of venison and rabbit. I nod politely, my stomach growling, and guide my mare through the press of bodies. Children with cherry noses weave through the crowd, giggling. A sharp pang tugs at my heart, missing my own. Lustful stares greet me with curious glances and whispers follow me as I pass.

If only the Gaia would grant me wings.

The newness of my presence fades as we near the livery at the end of the road. Reik Forest looms nearby, its soot-colored trees casting long, grasping shadows. I hum quietly to drown out the whispering wind. The lanterns flicker in answer as if warding off the dark.

"Sure, is a pretty song, Lady."

I startle, nearly toppling from my saddle and into the

muddy puddles of broken cobblestone below. Finn catches my arm with surprising quickness, steadying me before I tumble. I clutch his hand breathlessly.

"Th—thank you. I—" I plant my feet on the ground and step away from the forest's reach. "Must be fatigued from the journey," I murmur.

His light blue eyes linger on me curiously.

Drescher approaches, his voice sharp, eyes calculating. "We leave at eykt."

I nod, feigning agreement. Three hours of freedom.

I lower my lashes and say sweetly, "I'd like to visit a few shops before we head to the harbor, if that pleases you, Captain."

He grunts, and his annoyance lingers heavily between us. The scouts peel off toward Cia's tavern a few paces from the livery yard in search of ale and willing bodies to hold. My breath catches slightly, hopeful that Cia's plan works. Audun Slade may brag of the beauty among his courtesans, but according to Cia, it is Sasha who holds Drescher's attention.

Let him be distracted. Let him follow her. Let me be free, if only for a moment.

As if on cue, the dark-haired beauty steps from the growing shadows of the tavern entrance, pouring ale into waiting cups. Her lilting laugh rings through the crowd. Drescher turns sharply, eyes narrowing at the sound of her voice. I smirk inwardly at the source of his sudden rage.

Sasha laughs as a man with long amber hair kisses her

hand. She glances toward Drescher, biting her pouty lip. His jaw clenches and his hand drifts to the hilt of his sword. Ale spills to the ground as Sasha's suitor pulls her close, their bodies nearly flush. Drescher trembles, his temper barely contained.

I step forward quickly and smile sweetly. "Captain, I'll visit Parela's shop for tea. You're welcome to the tavern while you wait. I'm certain you'll return before I finish."

Drescher tears his eyes away from Sasha with effort. His voice is cold.

"You will not leave Parela's until I return." He nods toward Finn. "The lad will suffer if you disobey. And you, milady, will endure Roimh's punishment." He briefly pauses. "Perhaps a contest—whose bruises will fade first, *milady*?"

I instinctively rub the back of my scalp and freeze. The smugness on Drescher's face says it all. He knows. Roimh must have bragged. I glance at Finn. The tightness of his jaw betrays his knowledge too. Shame burns my throat, and I hurry to blink away the tears that threaten. Drescher snorts and turns away. There's no pity. No outrage. Just indifference. Her Majesty's favoritism wavers under the temperament of a Lord who sees me as expendable. My vision blurs and I quickly blink away the evidence of my brokenness. I gather my skirts, avoiding Finn's gaze.

I hurry across the cobblestone and through the parting crowd, whispers blooming behind me. My pace quickens as I abandon decorum and run for sanctuary. Finn silently follows, matching my frenzied pace.

Relief washes over me as Parela's shop comes into view. A bright oasis of silk, fur, and damask against mossy stone walls. I slowly catch my breath, inhaling the cranberry-laced ivy that winds elegantly around the door frame. Finn gently nudges me inside to the privacy I desperately need and shuts the door.

The smell of lavender and honey calms my nerves as I drift through the racks of fabric, lightly fingering the soft silk. Audun Parela is as famous for her sharp tongue as her sewing needle. Rumors say Birdie once attempted to assassinate her to claim the role of Royal Seamstress, only for Parela to kill the mercenary with fabric shears. I fell in love with her quick wit and blunt words upon our first acquaintance, which has led to an unexpected comradery between myself and the spunky dressmaker.

At the back of the shop, I find her hunched over a mannequin draped in emerald silk. Her glasses hang from her nose and a pin rests between her lips. Her salt-and-pepper bun is a storm of curls.

"You look beautiful today, Parela."

"Child, the Dagda will have your tongue for that lie." She glances up, then smiles. "Though it does warm my heart to see you, my dear."

She sets the pin and sweeps over to kiss my cheek, holding me at arm's length.

"Your hair looks atrocious," she says with a click of her tongue.

I laugh. The windy ride from the fortress ruined the curls

Britta worked so hard to tame. She gestures toward a corner chair, away from any window shoppers who may sneak a peek inside. She pours a cup of hot rum tea and presses it into my chilled hands.

"Sit. I'll braid it while you tell me about those heathen children."

I sink into the chair, recounting Ophele's antics and Olan's carving obsession, as her fingers work through my hair. A soft chuckle comes from Finn, who stands guard at the front of the shop, with the mention of Ophele setting winter moths loose in Sarmien's hair. I tell her of the Yultane ball, the menu, and the preparations I have made that cater to Roimh's fancy. When I get to the capon and eel, her fingers go still.

The mood shifts as she draws a long breath.

"When?" Her voice trembles with fury. "When did he hurt you?"

I bow my head as Finn shifts uneasily at the door. "A little over a week ago."

She says nothing. Her braiding continues as if she didn't see the bruises along the back of my neck. I hold back tears, my body slumping under the weight of silence and shame.

She suddenly stops again and kneels in front me, gently lifting my chin.

"You do not lower your head for anyone, Child of Light." She smooths away a tear escaping down my cheek. "No matter what lies you have been told or what evil has filled your precious head. You, my dear Brynn, come from the ancient blood of Seidré. Remember that. No matter what happens, remember these words."

My heart stutters and I suck in the perfumed air around me. "How is it that you know of my bloodline? Hilde...the queen I mean, she...she forbade anyone beyond those in her closest circle to know my true lineage. How is it that you know I carry traitorous blood?"

A strangled cough reveals Finn's eavesdropping as Parela's eyes flash. She recovers with a soft smile and pats my cheek.

"There will be time for answers one day." She claps her hands together with struggling enthusiasm. "Now, let's see if we can sneak you away from that brute of a Captain."

The corners of my mouth twitch happily in anticipation as she moves through the shelving and beyond the wood-grained countertop toward the front of the store. I follow, still breathless as she flings fabric in her search. A tarnished copper mirror catches my eye, the golden flames caved into its frame seeming to dance in the lamplight, glistening for my attention. I stop before it, entranced in the way the flames race up each side. I take in the reflection staring back at me, touching the braided loops in my hair and tracing the tightened braids at my temples until they rest mingled within the loose hair trailing down my back.

A slow burn in my stomach rumbles awake, something foreign, but alive. I gasp in surprise, clutching the warmth that grows. Parela grins as she comes up behind me. I glance at her, ignoring the strange sensation that stirs and quietly say,

"They look like the warrior braids from the stories my nursemaid, Aylah, told me."

Her lips twitch. "Do you know why warriors wore them?"

I laugh. "They're just stories."

Parela scoffs and wraps a plum silk scarf embroidered with lavender around my hair. "You must see through the shadows of what you have been raised to believe, Brynn. For all our sakes."

She adjusts the veil over my face, concealing the familiar freckles that gather along my cheekbones and continues, despite my incredulous stare. "Braids are worn for protection. A symbol of balance among the gods of the Gaia and the intertwining of Dagda's creation. It is said the power of the Ancients lives within each woven cord." She stands back and happily admires her handiwork. "Your eyes are stunning, my dear, absolutely stunning!"

I glance at my reflection and smile. Only my eyes show, the sparkling bright blue dances with anticipation against the flecks of green. I can blend in within the crowded street and hopefully make it in time before Drescher returns.

I hurriedly make my way across the shop to where Finn stands ready, Parela trailing dutifully behind. I stop cautiously at the door, checking for eager eyes. To my relief the curiosity or morbid fascination of the Lady of Reikhaven is fleeting, and they have gone about their trading and selling as usual.

I hug Parela tightly. "Thank you, for your kindness. For everything."

I step back and glance at Finn. His wide grin reveals his eagerness for our act of rebellion against Drescher's command. I search his eyes, looking for any sign of regret he may have for agreeing to accompany me. "Drescher may return quicker than anticipated. Are you willing to take the punishment for disobedience?"

Finn's grin only widens with acceptance. "Life would be boring without a little disobedience." He winks and opens the door wide, stepping out onto the cobblestone and disappearing into the crowd beyond.

Parela nods at Finn disappearing into the crowd. "Run along, my sweet. Be free. If only for a moment."

I slip into the crowd, barely able to contain my squeal of delight as flutters of excitement dance through me with each step I take.

Yultane decorations sway above in a plethora of reds and greenery; decorations grace each storefront throughout the town. Spices from Inevar fill the air. I breathe in the scent of smoke and the earthiness of clove, cumin, and wormroot—only found in the Brucollian swamp lands. The square is packed with open stalls of vendors. I pass by a colorful tent of red and blue, the fabric tightened against four slim posts at each corner. My mouth waters with the smell of freshly baked pastries dusted in sugar and displayed in baskets upon a makeshift table.

I move slowly through the crowd, enjoying the bustle around me and the solitude it brings. I stop at a tent where a boy sells roasted chestnuts. His dark hair curls around his ears. With a conspiratorial wink I pay him double. He reveals a toothless grin. His voice is thick with an Inevarian accent as he says, "Hap'y Ultane, missus."

I nod politely as he hands me a fresh sack.

Children dart past me as I admire each booth I pass. A glass blower molds a pitcher with fascinating craftsmanship. A heavily wrinkled man with a long black beard denoting his Brucollian ancestry shouts praises of his exotic spices. His long beard jangles with metal trinkets with every movement. I frown slightly, wondering if Roimh is aware of vendors selling smuggled goods from Laioses territory. My mood shifts and I look nervously over my shoulder for any sign of Drescher. I freeze. A man with golden eyes watches me intently.

My blood chills and my breath quickens. I tug the veil tighter over my freckles and hurry into the crowd. I hastily look for Finn as I weave in and out of the townspeople, fighting the urge to call out to him. I glance quickly behind me and let out a sigh of relief. My pursuer now lost in the sea of faces surrounding me. I relax slightly and decide to finish with the task at hand: Yultane presents for the children.

A necklace shines brightly at the last stall that leads to the docks despite the abundance of clouds above. Relief floods within me and I hurry across the street. Two birds, one stone. The docks for Olan's gift of a sailor's glass and Ophele's gift of something exquisitely made. The necklace is like a beacon, drawing me through the crowd. The closer I near, the greater the whisper in my head eagerly surges.

I stand mesmerized before the stall.

The necklace dangles delicately from the intertwining horns of small Elkan antlers. At its center rests a white opal stone, cradled by seven interlocking circles that bloom like the petals of a golden flower. Each petal bears a symbol too small to read and I marvel at the hands that could have etched them. I reach out, longing to run my fingers over the artistry.

"Beautiful, isn't it, missus?"

I jerk back as a wafer-thin woman calls out from the shadows of the booth.

I shakily reply, "Quite beautiful."

The woman moves nimbly toward me despite her frail look. My skin prickles and I take a cautious step back, avoiding her pox marked face.

She ignores my reaction. "Tis a design of old. Of a time not known to mankind as it is now."

Her shaky hand lifts the chain. I reach to help, and her icy skin brushes mine. Her eyes widen. The whisper angrily screams. I stumble back as she grabs my wrist. I gasp, stunned at the strength in her feeble-looking fingers as her milk-white eyes pierce my soul.

"You are not who you seem."

I choke with the race of my heart, scrambling to maintain my ruse.

"How much for the necklace?"

She releases me, her eyes gleaming. "Keep it. It was yours before. It will be again."

I furrow my brows in puzzlement and my eyes dart down to the chain dangling from my now closed hand. Finn returns to my side, and I glance up only to find no one before me.

I look to Finn and ask, "Did you see her?"

"Who?"

I sigh heavily, quickly losing the enthusiasm I once had for my little outing.

"Never mind. I have one more stop and then we can return to Parela's."

I walk cautiously toward the docks. My encounter with the woman awakens a sense of dread that creeps up my spine as the salty breeze tries desperately to snatch the veil from my face. The stale smell of salt and fish thickens as the wooden planks replace stone, the crowd growing smaller with each step.

Regret fills my stomach as I near the first of the ships waiting along the harbor dock and the jeers of sailors unloading their goods. I should have just sent Finn to complete this task. I stiffen my spine and lift my head in defiance at their taunting. Finn swears quietly behind me.

I muster the little courage that remains within me as I stand quietly before the first ship docked. The Sea Lord. It is Reik's largest ship and used by the Master of Ships himself during supply runs. I watch as a lad of no more than sixteen hefts a large barrel down the gangway. I clear my throat and force my voice to be strong as I call out to him.

"Pardon me. Could you direct me to the Master of Ships?"

The lad stares at me, shifting the barrel uncomfortably in his outstretched arms. I repeat myself slowly, unsure if he understands what I am asking.

"Da Cap'n be yonder in da tavern, missus."

A man dressed in tattered clothing and hair hanging in a stringy ponytail down his back swaggers behind the lad.

"I see. Could you help me then?"

The man's eyes linger over me, his greedy smile revealing a gaping mouth of black. "Depen un wat yur ask'n." He licks his tongue with beady eyes and sneers.

Finn steps forward. "You will answer the lady respectfully or I will cut out what's left of your rotten tongue."

The man moves so swiftly that his only tell is the distinct flash of metal. I take a step back onto the sandy cobblestone road as he nonchalantly rolls the razor-like knife across his knuckles. He points the blade at Finn.

"Nun I cut a smile in dat purdy lil face uh yurs first, *boy*."

The lad sets the barrel down on the dock and interrupts the cold war, turning to me.

"What do you need, missus?"

"I have business to discuss."

The lad's eyes narrow suspiciously. "What kind of business?"

I let out a frustrated sigh and sharply say, "I need to

purchase a looking glass. I am willing to pay whatever price."

The slimy man with a tongue of rot snorts in response. The lad ignores the outburst and nods behind me. "Ask him yourself."

He marches toward us; an imposing force wrapped in fiery gracefulness. His gray cloak waves in the wind of his wake. His crimson hair falls just below his broad shoulders like subtle waves that refused to be tamed. His luminous skin, lightly kissed by the sun, stretches tightly across his sharpened cheekbones and strong jaw, which is now sharply clenched in an imposing frown. The smoldering golden flecks of his eyes set against a deep gray that looks like storm clouds rolling behind a sunlit horizon.

I hurriedly whisper to Finn. "Where is Lanthe? Why is he no longer the Master of Ships?"

Finn grins. "He is honorable, milady. No need to fear."

I relax my hands slowly though the unease continues to creep up the back of my neck. Finn abandons my side and cheerily calls out the man's name.

"Eowyn!"

I watch as they clasp arms like old friends. The man's stormy eyes flick to me and burn through me as he leans down to Finn's ear and whispers. Finn's shoulders stiffen and he lets go. He brushes past me for the lad setting a wooden crate atop the lone barrel. Eowyn's voice thunders with a clear urgent command.

"Igor, hurry to the tavern. Audun Cia has a barrel she

needs loaded before we set sail. Take Finn with you."

The pair run off. Much faster than I believe necessary. My heart thunders in my chest as the broad-shouldered man rushes to me. A low rumble is the only warning as a burst of gray clouds my vision.

I slam hard into the sandy cobblestone.

A scream rips from my throat.

I choke on sand and smoke that fills my lungs.

Stone pelts. Splintered wood stabs.

The earth explodes...again and again.

Eowyn wraps my body into his. A protective cover from the fiery hell coming for us. Callous hands rip me from the ground. I am lurched to my feet. My ears ring and the world muffles around me in a suffocating haze. Something wet trails down my forehead. I swipe it away, but still another trail comes. I look down at my hands. My eyes blur against the bright red smearing my fingertips. I'm bleeding. I'm bleeding. I blink slowly and look around me. A thick wooden splinter protrudes from Eowyn's thigh.

Men scramble along the broken dock. Blood pours from gaping wounds and missing limbs. Someone reaches out from the bay. Half of his face is gone, all that remains is muscle and shattered bone. I look away, unable to bear the sight of him sinking to the bottom of the darkened water. Eowyn grasps the splinter and yanks. Blood spurts to the ground with a pulsating release. My stomach turns violently with the sight.

I crawl to him, blinking against the smoke blurring my

eyes. I snatch the veil from my head and kneel in the puddles of blood and pieces of flesh littering the ground. He ties the veil tightly above his piercing wound. He looks up at me with a flicker of sympathy in his golden eyes.

The bay erupts with a fiery roar. Men scream in pain as the burning water swallows them whole and races for the fleeing ships. All succumb to the fire's rage and the shadowy depths below.

Bile rises in my throat. Teeth swim among the ripples in the bloody puddle at my feet. I remain frozen. My mind screams and yet I cannot move. Eowyn pulls hard on my arm, his fingers digging into my skin. My protesting feet stumble forward. I slip on the broken plank...no, not broken plank.

Bodies.

Eowyn snatches me toward the market, his sense of urgency drums through me with every beat of my frantic heart. A crowd gathers along the harbor entrance; their eyes filled with horror and shock at the carnage behind us. I do not look behind me, the roar of flames and the cries of the dying too much for my mind to bear. A piercing scream erupts from the center of the market. A scream that silences with the gurgle of death. Eowyn pulls me to him as my blood turns cold.

The crowd erupts with chaos. They scramble, push, and shove each other to escape whatever suffering it is that comes for them. They run past us, trampling each other as they seek refuge in the flaming wreckage. It is as if Death corrals them like cattle.

A woman holding a small child shoves me hard to the ground in blind desperation. I claw at the running legs of those around me, scrambling for anything that will raise me up from the pandemonium dressed in the stain of blood.

Eowyn picks me up before a boot can plant squarely into my jaw. He roughly throws me over his shoulder. I beat my fist across his back in blind desperation as he runs straight to the haunting war cries bellowing from the town square.

This is how I am going to die. Sacrificed on the altar of savagery.

He sets me against the wet stone of an alley, now soaked with blood and salt, along the harbor sea wall. Waves lap eagerly over the stone wall and into the alley way, leaving bloody sea foam as an offering. The air thickens with the cries of pain and death. Of children wailing. Flesh tearing. A deep, haunting cry vibrates through the town as the Laioses sing their death song.

My heart pounds as Death nears.

The Dagda will save no one today.

Eowyn presses me tighter against the stone, shielding me with his body. I wince as my back grinds into the jagged edges of the wall—edges sharpened by the brutal winter storms of the Gaiad Sea.

Seeing my pain, Eowyn shifts his weight away and lifts the hood of his lambskin cloak. Seconds crawl by as the sound of flesh striking bone echoes through the shadows. Splash after splash echoes off the stone walls, each one sharper than the last. I freeze mid-struggle against my captor as realization strikes with sickening chord. The splashes are bodies, striking the bay from the windows above.

My blood hums as I slowly lift my eyes to the man above me.

A perfect ring of unnatural gold burns within his storm-flecked irises. Amber and gray swirling together like a winter sunset. He blinks and the golden glow in his eyes vanishes as if imagined it.

I gasp and his rough, calloused hands clamp over my mouth. All I taste is salt. Something primal stirs awake inside me as my panic surges. Every instinct in me thrashes. Screams. Blood floods my tongue as I bite down, tearing at his flesh.

He jerks back with a grunt, his hand recoiling in shock. His gaze flares, not with anger, but something else. I press myself tighter into the stone despite its wicked bite. The warmth inside my gut surges forth and cracks open with a trickle of release that flows sharply through my body until my flesh burns hot.

Chapter 4

My body awakens with the flames licking inside my blood and I drive my knee hard into Eowyn's groin. He doubles over with a grunt as I tear free from his cloak. The breath leaves my lungs at the sight awaiting me.

Men, if they can still be called such, move through the smoke and ruins like shadows carved from nightmares, clothed in fur and bone masks that leer from their faces. Their bare arms are slick and gleaming with the splatter of blood. They move through the cowering townspeople like animals hunting down easy prey. In their wake, Death stalks.

There will be no escaping this horde.

Silent tears trail down my cheeks as I watch a wolf tear into its prey. The sound of flesh ripping, wet and jagged, echoes through the alley as a woman is gutted by Elkan antlers near the entrance. I whimper and shake as those same antlers glide mercilessly across the throat of another. Fear claws at me, dragging me under its cold, choking tide.

Eowyn pulls me into his arms, wrapping me in the dark

folds of his cloak. He silently shields me from the savagery beyond our hidden refuge. I bury my face against his chest and inhale the smoke that clings to him, my shaky sobs muffled. The flames that once ignited my body yielding to the horror filling my mind.

These are my people.

Slaughtered in the streets and I...remain hiding. Too cowardly to move. Too afraid to watch. I am Lady of this territory and yet...I have done nothing.

I pull back and stare down at my hands. At the blood streaking them that is not my own. The blood that will now haunt me in the night and stain my dreams.

The skin-crawling scrape of bone against stone echoes down the alleyway toward our hiding place. Eowyn shoves me behind him with a guttural growl. I cry out, catching the edge of his cloak before the stone can bite my face.

I cower behind him, breath frozen in my lungs as a sun-bleached bull mask emerges from the shadows. Its curled horns are razor-sharp, and its jagged teeth are fixed against the cheeks of the towering man beneath. The eye sockets are hollow, twin abysses that swallow all light. Blood drips from his hands, trailing down with each deliberate, echoing step.

I stifle a sob and scramble back as he growls low, beastly. Eowyn stands firm, remaining defiant despite no weapon in his hands. My eyes dart between the death that advances and the man who shields me.

A soft, golden light flickers against the mask's bone-white

surface, casting it in a terrifying glow. The beast halts. His head turns slowly. The black void of his gaze settles on me. I reach for Eowyn, my desperate fingers clutching the back of his arm hard.

The antlers lift.

Then, like a curse, the words fall from the masked man's lips, thick with the ancient tongue of Seidré...

"Beireoir an bhais."

Bringer of death.

My head spins. My knees weaken as the world blurs around me. The voice chants inside of my skull, whispering the threat over and over. I clutch my ears and collapse with a strangled sob. I rock back and forth as if it will somehow make it stop.

Eowyn growls low and vicious. The masked Laioses steps closer, dragging the Elkan antlers along the stone. A predator toying with his prey.

Three thunderous blasts of a horn echoes across the sky, and the masked hunter freezes mid-step. The sound pierces my soul, leaving a sickly silence in its wake as bile scorches my throat. I watch through blurry eyes as the masked man turns and slinks into the shadows beyond the alleyway, into the eternal black of Reik Forest.

A sob claws from my chest as Eowyn lifts me into his arms. My head pounds with every agonizing movement as we leave the protection of the alley and into the bloodied aftermath that lies waiting. I bury my head into his shoulder, willing the smell of smoky redwood to silence the urgent whisper awakened by the masked man's threat.

Eowyn sets me down gently on trembling legs as we enter the town square. All around us, the survivors weep. A fractured song of mourning that rises beneath the ash.

We pass what's left of the vendor tents. Woven baskets of Inevar spice are burnt, shattered, and blood-soaked. The Inevarian man is pinned to the pillar of his stall. I gag, clutching my mouth. Bone juts from his eyes. Blood spills from his open mouth where his tongue once was. Each step we take crushes me beneath the weight of death.

We pass the dark-haired boy. He clings to his dead mother. His eyes swollen with tears as his little body desperately tries to shake her awake. The sack of chestnuts drowns in her blood. I step toward him, my maternal instinct surging, when a voice cuts through the smoke like a blade. Loud, harsh, and too familiar. I flinch, turning to face the mountain of a man charging toward me.

Drescher.

Eowyn steps quickly away, leaving me to face Drescher's wrath alone.

I rush forward on weak legs, afraid of inciting more fury. I know the look in his eyes, the kind of rage that doesn't bloom in public but instead festers behind fortress walls.

His gold cloak, torn and ash-stained, trails behind him like a dying banner. A long gash slices from his left eye to the bridge of his nose, a violent reminder that he faced Death and won.

I reach him just as the sound of thundering hooves shakes the square. A familiar fear grips me. A fear that overpowers and destroys the terror that has flowed within me since the first fiery explosion. A fear that I have learned to cower before on bloodied knees.

Drescher grabs my arm, hard. He bends it brutally and yanks me close. A performance. A perfect display to show the arriving lord that his captain risked life and limb to protect his wife. I grit my teeth, forcing my spine straight with the last of my strength just as Roimh's calvary floods the square.

Like daggers across my skin, I feel them. His eyes.

He observes the destruction of the town like a child bored with his toys. I lower my gaze, my soul shrinking inside me. His voice cuts cold and clean as steel.

"Burn the bodies." He nods toward the harbor to the charred ships and drifting flesh. "I want a full report as soon as you are finished."

Drescher bows his head. "Yes, mi'lord."

Roimh's voice bellows. "Double the guards. I want scouts at the forest line. Every able-bodied man. No one sleeps tonight." He turns to me. "*Wife.*"

His gloved hand thrusts toward me. I quickly obey, lowering my head further. My fingers touch his and my stomach turns. Drescher lifts me into the saddle and Roimh wraps his thick arms around my body like a noose. I bite back a cry as his grip crushes against my ribs. Without a word, his dapple-gray mare spins dizzily and races toward the fortress.

The rolling hills I longed for earlier are now a blur, a smear of ice, withering grass, and smoke beneath a screaming sky.

The fortress walls rise ahead as the sun begins its slow descent. Roimh does not speak. The tension is a silent warning to my senses. It is enough to keep me upright in the saddle, even as exhaustion claws at me. My thoughts churn with terror and heartache. The fear of what awaits fills my chest with the sickening shroud of dread as we ride through the fortress gate and into the courtyard. Fear clouds everything. Even Roimh.

He swings down from the saddle with a thud and stalks off without a word. His boots strike the stone angrily as he barks orders at every soldier in his path. Mideton hurries toward me, his face going pale at the sight of my bloodied dress and matted hair.

"Are...are you alright, milady?"

Sorrow wells within his aging eyes. I collapse into his arms without thinking, my legs buckling as the last of the adrenaline leaves me. He catches me with surprising strength, wrapping his frail arms around my trembling frame. I press my face into his shoulder as he helps me up the stairs. Tears sting my eyes, but I don't cry. Not yet.

"Let's get you inside. Britta will get you cleaned up. Some hot broth will warm your bones."

I let my weight sink into the safety of Mideton's arms, my head resting against his shoulder as we walk through the fortress toward my chambers. The longing to crawl into bed, to wake from this nightmare, grows with each step. But even sleep will not free me. The stench of blood and burning flesh still clings to my senses, leaving no escape from the horrors now burned into my memory.

Mideton leaves me in the care of Britta whose gentleness after such trauma nearly breaks me. I bite back tears at the memory of the boy and the roasted chestnuts as she carefully removes my soiled dress. Her golden-tawny fingers move quickly, undoing the last of the braids Parela had woven so urgently.

Steam curls through the washroom as I lower myself into the bath she has drawn. The heat should soothe me but instead I feel impossibly heavy. I scrub until my skin burns. Every inch of me is raw, desperate to shed the marks left by this terrible day.

The water turns red with the blood of others.

I lurch forward and vomit into the waiting bucket. I scramble from the bronze tub. Britta silently kneels beside me, smoothing my hair back and wrapping my shivering body in a fresh cotton cloth. I say nothing as she helps me to the corner of the room, and I sit on the wooden stool, trembling.

Flashes of Elkan antlers, haunting masks, glowing eyes, and the death stare of those dying in their own blood cloud my mind with the sound of the bloodied water hitting the frozen ground below. I watch with ragged breath, barely registering that Britta has refilled the tub. The stone floor is bitter beneath my feet as I stumble across the washroom.

She gathers my ruined dress in her arms and gives my hair a final, tender pat. I lower myself into the fresh warm bath, sinking low. I let the water rise above my shoulders and baptize the filth clinging to my soul.

I draw my knees to my chest and stay there until the water cools. Until my silent grief erupts from my chest in sobs I can no longer hold back.

And over it all...echoing through my blood and bone...

Beireoir an bhais.

Bringer of death.

Chapter 5

I sit at the small table closest to the fire, wet ringlet curls trailing down my back, as deep streaks of pink and orange bleed through the great windows facing the western hills of Reikhaven. The hearth's warmth offers a fleeting reprieve from the growing chill in my bones. I sip at the warm broth Britta left behind, devouring it in a quiet hunger. A curse slips from my lips as the bowl wobbles and sloshes onto the parchment scattered across the table. I blot the spill in a panic, whispering a prayer to the Dagda that I haven't ruined a scroll that survived the Great War.

My station as the queen's favorite afforded me the finest Agderian education. Her Majesty ensured that every detail of Agderian history...and the pageantry of court, of course, was drilled into me by militant tutors and carefully chosen governesses. I can only assume she desired a well-rounded ambassador of sorts. One who was conditioned to believe that love must be earned through obedience, and desire sacrificed for devotion to the crown.

Only Aylah, my gentle nursemaid, ever offered true affection within those cold palace walls. On the eve of my twelfth name day, she sat me down in the quiet dark of my tower room and spoke life into the hushed rumors whispered among the townspeople. Great truths, long buried, that stir once more.

Bathed in the pale moonlight, I watched with bated breath as she slowly unraveled the cloth headdress she always wore so dutifully. I remember gasping at the sight—deep kisses of fire scorched the creamy skin of her neck and ear, where long black hair no longer grew. Her voice had trembled as she recalled her childhood in Ravndal, before the Great War, and the fire that scarred her. A Laioses without the gift of the Dagda. That, she told me, was the only reason Queen Hilde allowed someone with traitor's blood so close to the daughter of Seidré.

Much of what I know of Ravndal's history, I learned only through the filter of Agderian bias. Stories of Eadom, the Great Star, falling from the moon's grace into a pit of nothingness. Of Mirákhi, the Great Darkness, overwhelming Eadom's light— though Eadom proved a formidable foe. Their power clashed endlessly, shaping what we now call the Dance of Draíocht. From that celestial dance, Gaia, and all life upon her was born. It is here that Agderian and Ravndalian histories begin to differ, subtly, at first. At least until the Great War.

Weeks turned into months. Our lessons grew more dangerous. Aylah began smuggling ancient scrolls beneath the cover of darkness, some so fragile they crumbled at the edges. From them, she began to teach me the old language of Seidré. By day, I would steal away to the shadowed corners of the castle, pouring over the hidden scrolls she had tucked into my mattress the night before, desperate to understand the blood that bound me to a forgotten lineage.

Our lessons ended abruptly.

One morning, after I spent a particularly long night in the queen's chambers, Aylah was summoned. She never returned. Not a word was spoken of her again. Even now, a sharp sting blooms in my fingertips at the memory. I rub them absently, trying to shake the phantom ache that still lingers.

Every few moons, the queen would press her clawed fingers into my skin, tasting my blood with a strange smile. She claimed it was to keep me safe, to assure the Draíocht hadn't tainted me. But there was something in her eyes that turned hollow in those moments, and I would return to my chambers foggy headed, sometimes sleeping for a day...sometimes two. My memories of Aylah come and go like the flickering of candlelight. The harder I grasp for them, the quicker they fade. But no matter what, Aylah's teachings have always remained carved deep into the marrow of my soul.

I stoke the fire, now burning low in the hearth, and move to the tattered remnants of my past. One bloodstained cloth catches my eye. I lift it gently and hold it to the light, smoothing its creases with trembling fingers. The ink is faded, nearly gone, but the ancient words still whisper through the weave.

When the branch is severed, the root will bleed. Two lights fall so the flame will rise.

The wooden chair protests as I lean back, puzzling over the crude translation. The sound of boots echoing through the stone corridor washes any sense of exhaustion from my body. I hastily gather the scattered scrolls and cloth scripts in my arms and drop them haphazardly into the hold beneath the table. I quickly set the loose board back in place and conceal my hiding spot with the edge of the fur rug.

My mouth dries as the heavy oak door flings open, slamming against the stone wall with a deafening crack. I flinch beneath its wrathful echo, but I have no time to react before Roimh barrels toward me. My back hits the wall hard in the narrow space between the hearth and the bedposts.

His pointed nose presses cruelly against mine. Thick fingers clamp around my upper arms, locking me in place beneath the weight of his bulging, darkened eyes. His untethered rage spits venom across my face as he shouts.

"You common whore!"

My entire body tenses. I turn my head, desperate to shrink away from the hate curling off his breath. My silence only fuels him. His fingers dig deeper, and pain flares through my arms. Then, as quickly as he struck, he retreats. My body sags with fleeting relief.

The back of his hand slams into my face. I taste blood as I hit the floor. My ears ring with a shrill scream that I realize is my own. Blood spills warm and wet from my nose. My vision narrows to shadow and shape. A hand in my hair jerks my head back. His breath is hot and cruel against my cheek.

"You will learn to obey me, Brynn, or—" My scalp burns as he tightens his grip. "—I swear to the Dagda, I will dispose of you. You've fallen out of favor, my dear. Or have you been too blissfully unaware...in your *condition*?"

He throws me down and turns away, staring out the window. I scramble backward, curling into myself. My hand trembles as they brush my swollen cheek. Every beat of my heart pulses through the bruises blooming beneath my skin. He turns again, his eyes gleaming with disdain at the sound of my whimper.

"You ran from Drescher to parade through the market... with one of my own guards. A guard who is now mysteriously missing after an attack on my town." His voice drops, quieter now, more dangerous. "The queen will have my land, my title, and my head if you die before fulfilling the promise she was given." He spits the words like poison. "You. The orphan girl. The one with a whore's blood in her veins. Once that promise is fulfilled, you'll be worth nothing. You, Brynn, will be no one."

The control over his anger is like shifting sand. Tears slip down my cheeks. He grabs my jaw roughly, forcing my gaze to meet his.

"You have embarrassed me for the last time, *wife*."

The room spins with the horror of him…of what he is. I try not to tremble. Try not to cry. But my soul cowers beneath the weight of his loathing. He releases me only when he is satisfied with my silence. Then, without a word, he turns and leaves. The silence that follows is deafening.

I collapse inward. A thousand pieces of me fracture beneath the surface, each one heavier than the last. The sorrow in my chest is cavernous. I can feel it spreading, suffocating, certain that I will never breathe freely again. Violence is no longer reserved for closed doors.

When Britta enters, her face lowered in guilt, I understand what I hadn't dared admit until now. I am no longer safe within these ancient walls. There will be no hero coming to save me.

Chapter 6

Britta's silence offers little comfort as she helps me from the cold floor. In her silence, Roimh's words echo louder than any scream. I fight the urge to bury myself within, to silence the ache in my bones and the shame in my blood. My heart scrambles for some excuse...any excuse...for his rage. Anything to soften the sting of his voice and the bruises on my skin. But the truth rings louder than my denial. I will never be enough. Not for him. Not for anyone.

I sink heavily onto the edge of my feather-stuffed bed, Roimh's final words choking the breath from my chest.

You have fallen out of favor...or have you been too blissfully unaware in your condition...

My thoughts circle around the cryptic threat like carrion birds. The rumors of my chronic headaches and bits of hysteria from the voice whispering with the trees have reached him. But what did he mean? What promise? The questions dig deep, but no answers rise. Only fear.

Britta kneels before me and pulls a tiny jar from her apron

pocket. I brace myself for the familiar stink of soured cabbage and the cold sting of the ancient cream passed down through her ancestors. Ginger, yarrow root, and the milk of lee beetle... strong enough to heal the worst of Roimh's artistry.

I gag as she dabs the bitter ointment across my busted lip, my eyes watering with the tingling burn. Britta's warm, olive-toned fingers move with practiced tenderness, her eyes refusing to meet mine. She slips the jar back into her pocket like a guilty secret, well-hidden from prying eyes. Roimh never questions how my face heals so quickly. I think he prefers it that way...a blank canvas, one he can shape with fury again and again.

I watch in silence as Britta places a cup of honeyed wine laced with poppy on the table. Her eyes flick to mine, softened with sympathy. She reaches out to smooth my hair, fingers gentle as falling snow. Her lined face, her silence...they speak louder than any apology. I feel the unraveling begin, the war of grief and rage tightening in my chest. I blink back tears.

"Thank you, Britta", I manage, voice hoarse. "That will be all for tonight."

She offers a kind smile and pats my hand reassuringly before quietly exiting the room. I listen to the fading echo of the door closing. Alone again.

I reach for the cup and lift it to my lips, but the image of Finn's face flashes in my mind like a scream. I spit the wine back into the cup, bile rising in my throat. I cannot forget him. I *will not*. He may be gone, but if there's even a sliver of hope, I must plead to the Dagda for his safety while there's still breath in my body.

Throwing open the heavy cedar chest at the foot of my bed, I pull out the warm fur cloak and wrap it tightly over my nightdress. I pull out a bolt of woolen fabric and wrap it around my head, careful not to disturb the salve burning against my bruises. I fumble to imitate Parela's technique, praying it hides me well enough in the moonlight.

With only the silver light of the moon to guide me, I slip through the fortress corridors, careful to avoid the gaze of passing guards. My breath fogs in the air as I cling to the shadows, slipping unseen past the frostbitten garden walls and into the waiting snow. I crouch behind frozen hedges, heart pounding, until the rhythmic crunch of heavy boots fades into stillness.

And then I run.

The temple looms ahead, its bones broken, its soul forgotten. The Temple of the Dagda—once a place of wonder and worship, now abandoned to ruin. The whispers in my mind stir like restless spirits at the sight of it, faint cries rising in urgency with each step across its crumbling threshold.

The lobata vines claw at the stones, curling over shattered pillars and into the hollow spaces where stained glass once glowed. I stumble through the wreckage, my breath catching in my throat as I climb the cracked steps and enter the ruin. I expect rot, mildew. Instead, I am greeted by the familiar scent of vanilla and nightshade. A pulse hums in the stone beneath my feet and the tips of my fingers ache with memory. The whispers become wails.

Roimh would never dare step foot here. He scorns the old ways. Scorns the Dagda. The people of Agderia have turned too, trading their reverence for the divine in exchange for the brittle safety of the queen's shadow. The tithe, the loyalty, the faith—all poured into her coffers while the Creator's temples withered.

Still, the smell draws me forward, laced with memory and...something else. I taste the bitter ghost of ginger and gag, spitting onto the floor. Britta's salve. Even here, it rots my senses.

I pull the woolen hood from my head and let the moonlight wash over me. Shattered glass sparkles like fallen stars, scattering colored light of violet, crimson and jade across the marble floor. Each broken piece reflects what once was with an ethereal radiance.

I step lightly toward the altar at the far end of the sanctuary that overlooks the angry sea beyond. The black agate glistens proudly under the fractured moonlight. Carvings along the floor guide my path, each a memory of what once was. The Dagda shaping land and sky, beasts of tooth and talon, storms and seed. All that roams the Gaia and the skies above. I pause before a toppled column etched with seven knotted cords. One of flame. Another of water. No beginning, no end.

When the branch is severed, the root will bleed. Two lights fall so the flame will rise.

The words, half-remembered from Aylah's scrolls, echo through me like a drumbeat. I press my fingers against the cord of flame, cold stone biting my skin. A scuff of feet breaks my reverie.

"Pardon my intrusion, missus."

I whirl, voice trembling. "W-who is there? Show yourself."

A child steps from the shadows. Filthy, thin, eyes sunken with hunger and frost. Her voice is sweet as a lullaby.

"Come. The Dagda awaits your sacrifice."

A thousand warning shriek in my head. Yet concern softens my spine.

"You're freezing. Come with me. I can find you a warm bed. Food. Safety."

She tilts her head. Laughs. It curdles my blood. "Agderian royalty, offering kindness? Have your people not taken enough?" Her gaze drifts to my bruises. "Love has not been kind to you." I flinch as she gestures toward the altar. "You have a sacrifice to attend."

I purse my lips together, mustering what little courage remains in my heart. With weighted steps, I move past the child and up the crumbling steps to the waiting point of penance. The Gaiad Sea roars to life, its large rolling waves crash hard against the sandy cliff, its salty spray rising high into the sky and tumbling down in droplets against the frozen vines wrapping up the broken frame of towering windows.

Flecks of bright green glow under the rays of moonlight shining upon the black agate stone before me. The candlelight flickering across its glass-like stone gives the altar a hauntingly frightening radiance. I kneel before the altar and whisper desperate words of hope, protection, and resurrection. I beg for mercy. For Finn.

A breath warms my ear and with it, the scent of iron and clove, sharp as memory. A flash of red silk. A golden clawed finger. The queen's veiled smile.

"Sacrifice is forged in fire and blood."

I scream and reel back. The child lunges. We crash in a tangle of limbs. My head cracks hard against the marble floor. A shard of turquoise glass protrudes from my palm. She grabs my wounded hand, slamming it against the altar. Agony explodes through me. My blood ignites. My veins shimmer with icy starlight. My screams shake the air around me as the stone drinks eagerly from my palm. Rage burns through the pain and I swing hard. My fist connects with her jaw, and she crumples beside me. I wrench my hand free, my body slick with sweat and chest heaving. My blood sears like fire beneath my skin.

My battered arm slips from the altar like dead weight, my head lolling to the side. My throat burns raw. I try to swallow, but the smoke clings like ash to my tongue. Each movement sends agony rippling through my bones as I force myself to stand. The room tilts, a dizzying spin of shadow and ruin. I stagger, grasping at a crumbling column before the floor tears itself out from under me.

The stone rises and falls like a tide. I collapse to my knees, bile rising in my throat. I swipe the back of my bruised hand across my mouth, wincing as blood stings the cut on my lip. Everything hurts.

The altar pulses through the haze like a living thing. Dull at first, then glowing, a heartbeat made of fire and hunger. I wince and turn away, but the sight sears in my mind. I blink furiously, searching for the girl's crumpled body. The creature. The child. The wraith.

A hollow throb beats behind my ribs. My chest tightens. Panic coils like smoke in my lungs. I gasp, but no air comes. Just salt. Fear. The heavy, suffocating knowing that I am not alone.

The edges of my vision fray to black. I stumble down the steps of the ruined altar, each one steeper than the last until there are no more steps and only open air. I crash to the floor of the sanctuary and crawl through the debris. My body trembles with each inch forward. The stone gives way to earth, the earth to brittle frost, then to snow.

The frozen garden welcomes me like a grave. I collapse, my body shuddering as warmth bleeds from me into the frozen roots of the ground. Somewhere beyond the pounding in my skull I hear footsteps. A soft crunch through the snow.

The scent of smoke and redwood overwhelms me as strong arms wrap around me. I am lifted, my limbs limp. I try to speak. To cry out. But no sound comes. My head falls against a shoulder that feels too familiar. I cannot see his face. Just the deep hood drawn low, hiding everything but the edge of his jaw and the wind-worn cloak that billows behind us. I curl my body into his warmth as he carries me swiftly through shadowed halls. Stone arches blur above me as the world tilts and dims.

I moan softly, my bones aching, as I am laid gently onto the softness of feathers. Chilled liquid sloshes against my dry lips. A calloused hand tilts my chin, coaxing my lips to part. I shudder as the coolness slides down my raw throat, coating the wounds inside with honeyed wine and numbing my pain with poppy.

The sound of fabric rips through the hush. I force my eyes open, blinking through the haze. A hooded figure kneels at my side; his face bowed in shadow as he wraps my wounded palm.

I try to move away, to demand who the hooded man is, but my poppy-laced limbs refuse to obey. My voice is lost somewhere in the cavern of my pain. My eyes flutter, too heavy to hold open as the man rises.

His calloused hand, warm and rough, brushes my cheek. He tucks a loose strand of hair behind my ear with a touch so familiar it stings. His touch lingers, and for a flicker of a moment, I think of eyes like storms on a golden horizon. A quiet, broken whisper slips through the veil of my fading consciousness.

"I'm sorry."

I fight to open my eyes, desperate to glimpse the face

behind the voice, the weight of his guilt heavy in that single phrase. But he is already retreating, his silent steps swallowed with the crackle of fire in the hearth. Numbness wraps me warmly in her embrace and carries me gently into the nightmare that awaits—the lingering scent of smoke and redwood blanketing me.

Chapter 7

Panic claws at the edges of my mind. Something is wrong...unnaturally wrong. Shadows coil and slither around me, and I instinctively wrap my arms around my middle. A chill prickles down my spine. I spin, searching for light...for any sign of escape from this consuming dark. But there is nothing. Just the crush of silence pressing in around me. The air thickens. My breath shortens. The darkness closes in, suffocating me.

I drop to my knees, burying my face in my hands. Then...

A crunch.

Dry leaves underfoot.

I jerk my head up, tears streaking down my cheeks. A path stretches before me, smeared in crimson. It goes on and on, endless and haunting. I reach for the dark red strewn across the forest floor...

Not blood.

Leaves...

They crumble into dust in my hands. The shadows twist

behind me, but ahead...ahead a brilliance grows, distant and fading. It blooms at the edge of the void.

I turn from the glare of the light, heart thundering, and face the endless forest of snowy white trees surrounding me. Rot gathers around the base of each trunk. It creeps up the bark like veins of ink. Blackened filth clings and splits the pale wood. It peels in long, tattered strips that hang like mourning shrouds. I follow the lines of decay upward. The canopy above twists in a web of limbs and dying leaves. No...Not branches.

My brow furrows. I squint, trying to focus, but the light behind me pulses brighter, flashing like a warning. My breath stumbles. Cold washes from my head to my gut. An unease scrapes its claws down my spine.

Bones.

The trees are made of bones.

Whispers curl through the air. Their low, dissonant notes claw at the corners of my mind. Not imagined. Real. I hear them. My head snaps up. My eyes dart wildly.

The bones sing.

A bitter, mournful melody seeps from their hollow cores, vibrating in the air around me. Their voices stroke my skin like ash, my skin prickles in their wake. My arms glow faintly...reddening with a heat blooming beneath the surface. Flame flickers through my veins.

I gasp, bent over, clutching my stomach as fire crawls upward from deep inside me. I sob into the silence. Dagda, please...please have mercy.

Sweat stings my eyes. The air tastes of smoke and salt. I wipe my brow and turn, desperate for the light again...for some shred of salvation...

But it's changed.

A flicker moves just beyond its edge. A shape. A shadow. Phasing in and out between the dying trees. My heart drops. The crunch of ash draws closer.

I run headlong into the glare. Into the nothingness that the light offers.

The forest groans around me. Shadows shift like smoke. Whispers rise into a shrieking crescendo.

"Amhai Rohnaith."

Chosen One.

Soul crushing terror grips me as their haunting song howls through the trees. I push harder down the never-ending path, my lungs screaming, my legs throbbing with every jarring step. Survival. It drives me with raw, primal desperation. A cry rips from my throat as a predator closes in.

I glance over my shoulder and nearly stumble as it chases me through the dark. Hooked horns slice through the canopy, ancient bones disintegrating to ash in its wake. Neither man nor beast, the monster belongs to Aylah's bedtime stories... creatures born of Mirákhi...made to destroy the children of Eadom.

But those were stories.

And this is a dream.

Isn't it?

The beast lunges and the earth behind me tears open. Rot rolls toward me in a tidal wave of black decay. It splashes against my leg and I scream, agony blooming as my skin blisters beneath its cursed touch.

I am going to die.

This is my penance.

Death has come for me.

I trip, hitting the ground hard. Ash explodes around me, choking the sky...clogging my throat. I claw at the air, gasping...drowning in nothing.

The monster roars in triumph above me, towering on legs of stretched sinew. Its gray-white muscles pulled light like glistening silver. Its face lowers.

A bull's skull...bleached and bloodied. Razor-sharp teeth drip fresh crimson.

I scream...scrambling...slipping...kicking at the ash.

Please, I beg...let me wake...

The beast halts, its head jerking upward as a raven cries out from above...its caw sharp and angry. The light ahead flares, blinding in its brilliance. The ground rumbles beneath me, vibrating through my bones.

I throw my arms over my face, shielding my eyes. My ears ring from the force of it. Even with my eyes closed the light burns through...hotter...brighter...closer.

I open my eyes, blinking rapidly against the light that

floods my vision. The path ahead is silent. Still. Not a trace of the creature remains. No rot, no claw marks, no bones turned to ash.

Nothing.

Only the light.

I stagger to my feet, heart pounding in my ears, and slowly turn toward the source that saved me. My breath catches in my throat.

Before me looms the Great Wheel of Gaia.

Aylah's stories flash through my mind. Tales whispered by candlelight of a wheel that binds life and time...ever-turning... never-ending. A sacred relic of Gaia.

The ash-dusted wood groans as it turns slowly. Solemnly. Rüin markings cover every inch of its surface...not symbols etched on the wheel, but markings of the wheel itself. As if the wood and the power are one.

I step closer, hypnotized. I count the spokes protruding from the center of the wheel. Seven. I step closer, the world around me forgotten...lost to the quiet pull of the markings. Each spoke bears a symbol, etched with a reverence that hums beneath my skin. Elegant vines curling into bloom, robust flames licking upward, crashing waves frozen mid-surge, a scattering of bright stars, airy swirls of wind, and an eternal knot fashioned upon a tree's trunk.

But one is different.

Black as a starless night.

Its carvings writhe like living shadows...shifting and

indecipherable.

Dread slithers through me, and I tear my gaze away, heart pounding. The air around it whispers with venomous hunger...watching...waiting...

My senses dull with each turn of the wheel. Thought, sound, breath...everything fades. All that matters are the spokes.

Time. Life. Death.

Nothing exists without the wheel.

A dreamy smile tugs at my lips as my eyes catch on the spoke carved in flame. It is beautiful...dangerously so. Licks of orange and gold swirl up the battered wood, dancing around glowing Rüin markings. I ache to remember what they mean. Aylah would have my hide for forgetting.

I sigh, leaning back on my hands and reluctantly tearing my gaze from the flames. Only then do I notice the slender, bony fingers turning the wheel...each rotation slow and precise. My breath catches in awe.

Three women work the wheel in silence, clothed in veils as fine as spider silk. Their long white hair flows freely to the bareness of their feet. Light threads from each of their hands, casting shadows across their naked forms and illuminating the world around me. I am entranced. Lulled from my fear.

The threads shimmer with stars...tiny points of light flickering with secrets. I watch, dazed, as they twist together into a tapestry of the Fates' choosing. I reach for them without thought...the warmth in my belly rising...the fire inside me purring to life...

Their heads turn slowly in unison. Their eyes lock on mine.

My trembling hand drops. The hush thickens. And then, their voices rise...one note, three tones...blending like the wind through bone.

Chosen One.

Life Taken Away.

Life Restored.

I fall to my knees, screaming as fire erupts in my veins. My hands claw at my own flesh, digging into my arms, my chest...anywhere to stop the burn. The flame roars beneath my skin, consuming me from the inside out. I sob, throwing my head back. I beg for mercy.

A voice.

Familiar.

Close.

It whispers in my ear...words that pierce through bone and settle in my soul.

"Beireoir an bhais."

Cold steel bites into my skin. A sharp breath gurgles as warmth spills down my chest.

I collapse into the ash, choking on the blood that fills my throat. My fingers twitch, reaching for the wheel spinning endlessly above me. The stars blur. My vision darkens. My blood pools beneath me.

And still, the wheel turns.

Its ancient spokes creak with indifference. The Rüin markings ignite in blinding blue, bathing me in cruel light as the wood hungrily drinks my sacrifice. My eyes grow heavy...

And the wheel does not stop.

My death is nothing but that of a thousand more.

I am nothing.

No one.

Chapter 8

My ears perk at the murmur of hushed voices beyond my chamber door. I open one eye groggily and brush a spiderweb of auburn hair from my face. My heart drops as the haze of sleep lifts. I sit up with a gasp, clutching my neck, lungs greedy for air.

I'm alive.

It was just a dream. A hallucination.

A twisted trick of exhaustion and wine.

Sunlight streams through the tall, frosted window overlooking the Gaiad Sea. I fall back against the mountain of pillows, dazed. My gaze lands on the goblet of wine sitting on the bedside table. My fingers rise slowly to my cheek. The sting is real. The pain echoes. The memory clings.

Did I make it to the temple?

Or did I fall asleep before I ever left?

I reach for the goblet with my left hand and freeze. The bandage is still there, wrapped tight around my palm.

A lump forms in my throat. My lungs seize.

Pain ripples up my arm.

Terrified, I fling the quilts aside, the cold air biting at my legs as I scramble to uncover the truth.

My voice splits the morning air as I tumble from the bed, legs buckling beneath me. The wooden chamber door slams open against the stone.

Cia rushes in and I stumble into her arms, sobbing uncontrollably. The room seems to darken with my anguish as she wraps me tight, bracing my shaking body against her own.

"Shhh, shhh...you're alright," she whispers, voice tight with panic. "What happened? What did Roimh do?" She pulls back, her breath catching at the terror carved into my face. "Brynn, please...just tell me what to do."

I try to speak, but my voice catches in my throat. Britta hurries in behind her, wide-eyed and breathless. Cia guides me gently into the creaking chair by the icy window, dropping to her knees in front of me. She clasps my trembling hands in hers. Britta rushes to the hearth, coaxing the embers to life. Shadows lurch wildly across the stone walls as warmth finally spills into the room. I swallow hard, my voice barely more than a whisper.

"Th-the bed."

Cia crosses the room in a blink, Britta trailing closely behind. Through frightened tears I watch the color drain from Cia's face as Britta gasps and cutters curses under her breath. Cia snatches the quilt from the bed. A cloud of ash billows in the air. Bones rattle against each other in anger at the disturbance of their refuge among the quilt. The room shifts.

Cia stands frozen as Britta snatches the sheets from the bed. The moment the fabric tears free, the whispers in my head erupt...sharp, shrieking. I crumple in my chair, hands flying to my ears as the voices claw at my mind. Britta rushes to the hearth and tosses the cursed remnants into the flames. The fire roars to life...blue and blinding, and the shrieks intensify. Pain explodes in my skull. I scream as ghosts in my mind wail in agony. It feels like my eardrums rupture, like my head is splitting apart.

Britta stumbles backward from the hearth with a horrified gasp. Cia moves at once. I double over in the chair, teeth clenched, eyes squeezed shut as visions assault me—my death, the turning wheel, the whispering bones.

I snap my eyes open. My breath catches.

Ash covers my feet.

Terror seizes me. I tumble from the chair, screaming. I claw at my legs, desperate to ride myself of the gray grit. My bandaged palm rips open in my frenzy. Blood seeps through the fabric, pooling crimson into the soot.

"Get it off! GET IT OFF!!"

Hands catch mine—firm and steady—wrestling them away before I can do more damage. I thrash like a wounded animal, sobs tearing from my throat. Cool water splashes over my skin. Rough hands scrub the blood and ash from my feet. I collapse backward into Cia's arms, too weak to resist.

She holds me tight, her breath steady against my ear. Her

soft murmurs work like balm across my panic-stricken mind. Britta kneels before me, face tight with unspoken worry as she works. Her eyes flick up briefly, then shift behind me to Cia.

Cia's arms tighten around me. I cling to her like driftwood in a storm.

Britta finishes cleaning the last of the ash and stands slowly, her jaw tight. Without a word, she begins overturning furniture. She yanks down one of the tapestries from the stone wall and tosses it aside. Cia helps me into the chaise near the hearth. The blue flames burn low behind me as she pours a goblet of wine and presses it gently into my trembling hands. She kneels before me, her fingers moving carefully over the bloodied gray fabric wrapped around my palm. My heart thuds painfully. She won't meet my eyes.

Cia never shows fear.

"Wu-what are you doing?" I whisper.

"Totems," she says softly.

My brows knit together. "Totems?"

Britta's voice drifts from the shadows, her tone thin and hollow as a grave wind. "Dark instruments, milady. Used in the practice of the Draíocht to weaken its victim."

A chill runs up my spine. Cia's jaw tightens. Her eyes flash with restrained fury, tongue poised to strike.

"Britta," I say gently, before Cia can speak. "You talk of a power only given to the Laioses' gods. A power that no longer exists."

The shadows deepen around us, flickering with the fire's

dying breath as if the room itself bristles at my denial.

Cia rolls her eyes. Though she is annoyed, there is a sorrow behind her gaze. She tucks the fur blanket tightly around my shoulders and takes my hand again, pressing it between both of hers. Her grip is warm. Urgent. Pleading. She's only ever pleaded for one thing.

For me to leave Reikhaven. To flee the monster who haunts its walls.

The white flecks in her dark, catlike eyes glint like glass. "What Britta speaks of isn't the Draíocht the Gaia gave the Dagda and their children. That was life-giving. Balanced." Her voice dips. "This Draíocht is bought with blood."

My breath catches. I snatch my hand from hers, nausea blooming in my gut. The flicker of disappointment in her eyes pierces me, but she says nothing. She rises without protest and joins Britta in her search, rifling through corners and crevices for the supposed totem. I sit frozen, staring at the hearth. The blue flames crackle low and wild, a fading echo of the voice that haunted my dream.

Chosen One.

I sit in stunned silence, my gaze sweeping across the wreckage of my chambers. Smoke clings stubbornly to the crisp morning air, curling in soft tendrils that veil the mess in an eerie hush. I avoid looking at the hearth—its blue fire long extinguished— though its presence pulses in the corner of my eye.

Perched on the chaise, I draw my legs tightly to my chest,

the sting of raw skin grounding me. Britta has gone to fetch warm broth and herbs for my feet, and the waiting stretches endlessly.

Across the room, Cia leans against the stone wall beside the open window, the icy wind tousling her cropped black hair. The uneven layers frame her sharp, angular face—a portrait of strength and restraint. Her golden-brown skin glows faintly in the morning light, and her eyes, always so sure of themselves, seem lost now...fixed somewhere deep in the gray swell of the Gaiad Sea. She turns at last, her voice low, almost too gentle for usual steel.

"What did you dream?"

My mouth dries bitterly as the mask I wear each day crumbles, fear hollowing its way into the marrow of my bones. I swallow hard. Hesitantly...brokenly...I begin to speak. The words taste like ash as I recall the horrors that filled my night; the wraith-like child, the altar, the man in the cloak, the nightmare.

With each detail I utter, the room seems to darken, the air turning sharp and cold as if the shadows themselves are listening. My voice wavers when I speak of the monster born of bone and rot, of the whisper that cut through my soul like a blade, of the wheel spinning hungrily as it drank my blood.

Cia listens in rigid silence, her jaw clenched tight, the angles of her face sharper now beneath the weight of my confession. When I finish, she turns from me and begins pacing, her arms crossed over her chest. She moves with practiced calculation—

more soldier than friend. Without a word, she crouches before the hearth, stacking kindling with tight, deliberate movements. The silence presses in like a held breath. Then, the fire catches. Bright orange tongues of flame curl upward, dancing shadows across her skin. The white flecks in her dark eyes catch the firelight as she turns to face me, her voice low and horse.

"Do not tell anyone of this. Anyone." She casts a quick glance toward the open chamber door, then locks her gaze onto mine. "I'm serious, Brynn. You must keep this to yourself. Roimh. Britta. No one. Do you understand?"

Her intensity steals the breath from my lungs. I nod slowly, my heart racing in alarm, the weight of secrecy settling over me. I lean forward, my voice trembling.

"But what of the wraith? The totem? The ash and bones?" I hesitate. "What am I to think of this, Cia? What am I becoming?"

An inner struggle betrays itself in the furrowing of her brows. Her jaw tightens. She sighs heavily and sinks to the floor at my feet. I watch her warily, frustration mounting as her eyes slowly scan the room—everywhere but at me. The silence stretches unbearably. My cheeks flush with the heat of my rising anger that boils beneath my skin.

"Speak plainly, Cia." My voice cuts through the quiet like a blade. "What are you hiding from me? You speak of blood magic and the gods as if you are one of...them."

The words hang in the air. A sickening feeling coils in my gut. Cia's head snaps to face me, her eyes dark with something unreadable. Sorrow? Guilt? Her lips twitch into a half-hearted smile, but there's no humor in it. Only distance.

Before I can press her further, the door creaks open and Britta bustles into the room with arms full of herbs and steaming broth. Cia rises slowly, the moment vanishing like breath in the winter air.

Her voice is carefully even, too soft. "I will speak to Mideton. Inform him of Brynn's...unexpected fatigue and need for convalescence."

Britta huffs as she kneels beside me, efficiently setting to work. "She will still have tea this afternoon with the visiting lords' and merchants' wives. *He* will expect it."

"Fine," Cia snaps. "Then I will accompany her."

The room stills. Britta nods approvingly, but my blood flares hot. Anger wails within me, loud and unrelenting. I stand suddenly, pain biting at my wounded feet, but I do not falter.

"I am no child to be governed over," I say, voice low and sharp. "Both of you would do well to remember that."

Britta bows her head in shocked submission. But Cia...she grins, wicked and slow.

"There's a fighter in you, Brynn." Her voice softens. "You would do well to remember that."

The shadows of the room dance along the stone wall as Cia moves effortlessly to the door. She pauses, casting a wink and haughty smile over her shoulder before disappearing to the echoing corridor.

I sigh and turn my attention to Britta and her incessant fighting over my battered feet. I regretfully sip the warmed bone broth as she dips torn linens into a milk bath that smells strongly of low tide and salt rot.

"Britta, how in the name of the Gaia is this supposed to help?" I grumble, nose wrinkling.

She laughs and croons, "Ahh, hush now, child. Just relax. Everything will be as it should soon."

My jaw tightens. "That answers nothing. Answer me, Britta. How does this help? How does the foul-smelling ointment you apply on the nights when tempers flare mask the swelling and the bruises?"

Her fingers still against my feet. Her smile falters. Alarm flashes across her eyes.

"You ask too many questions, milady," she murmurs, her voice barely above a breath. "Questions that will get us both killed."

I set the bowl on the floor and reach for her damp, work-worn hands, clasping them tightly. "Please. I must know. I am tired of secrets and lies. Tell me what you know."

She pulls her hands free with stiff resolve; lips thinned to a single pale line. My hope falters. I close my eyes, pressing fingers against the ache growing behind them. Silence stretches. Then, her whisper slices through the stillness.

"What I tell you mustn't leave this room, milady."

I meet her eyes, a quiet nod my only answer. She studies my face, my pleading gaze and trembling hands. Her words come out in a rush, the words slipping out like a confession.

"The Draíocht...flows freely within the Gaia. Everything birthed from its soil can be used, should you know how."

My chest tightens. My skin prickles with growing unease. This cannot be. Everything she has confessed contradicts everything drilled into Agderians from birth. The Draíocht sleeps with the gods. Even Aylah said so.

My voice cracks like dry parchment. "How? The Draíocht sleeps with the gods. Everyone knows that."

Britta gently touches my cheek, her thumb brushing the faint bruise from Roimh's slap, now fading with the light of the rising sun. "Nothing is ever as it seems, mi'lady. You ought to know this by now."

She turns from me, bustling about the room to clean the evidence of the morning. I'm left in silence, tangled in my own breathless thoughts, every heartbeat a drum against my aching skull.

When she finishes, she plants her hands on her wide hips and declares, "Let's get you into bed. You need rest before entertaining those squawking hens."

The thought of crawling back into bed makes my stomach lurch. I glance toward it; the memory of the ash and bones still etched into my vision.

"I'll stay here." I force a smile. "At least for now."

She purses her lips in disappointment but nods with understanding. Relief floods me. My body softens against the velvet cushion beneath me. But I do not close my eyes...not yet.

I keep my gaze on the flickering hearth, counting each breath to calm the rising tide in my chest. Britta tucks a warm blanket over me, careful not to disturb my milk-soaked feet. Her footsteps retreat across the floor, and I am lulled to sleep by the gentle crackle of the fire.

Chapter 9

Sweat drips upon heated metal with a hiss. I swing the hammer hard against the darkened metal, the sharp ring of impact echoing like a balm across my troubled soul. The noise from the tavern fades into a hollow murmur. Nothing exists but the glow of the ancient symbol burning beneath my crosspeen hammer. A firm hand clamps down on my arm. Instinct flares. I twist and swing.

"Cia! Stop!"

I blink, my breath sharp. The hammer halts mid-arc, trembling in my grasp. Gray eyes blink back at me beneath auburn hair slicked to a too-familiar brow. The hammer drops with a thud to the sand. In one breath, I pull the blade from my boot and slam Eowyn against the cedar pillar behind him. My dagger hums at his throat, hungry for a fight he doesn't deserve.

"Gods, Cia!" he growls.

"Your procrastination," I hiss, pressing the blade until it kisses his skin, "is proving to be quite the bloody fucking annoyance, brother."

His face falls with a heavy sigh. It's the same fight that has been escalating for weeks now. The longest we have ever been at odds with the other. He lifts his hands in muted surrender, and I slowly release my grip, jaw clenched in bitter disappointment. Stepping back, I toy with the knife in my fingers, its weight familiar and cold. I watch him through narrowed eyes as he rubs at the light stubble shadowing his sharply cut jaw. He looks older than he did even a week ago. Worn down by the same dread gnawing at me.

"What's happened now?" he asks, voice low.

I glance around at the bustle of the town square, the ever-present loyalists slinking about like well-fed dogs.

"Not here," I mutter.

He nods, already guessing more than I've said. I dip the still-glowing symbol into the barrel of water at the edge of the blacksmith's shed. Steam hisses as the metal cools. I pocket the crude creation and slip into the shadows cast by the forest trees.

Damp earth and rotting leaves fill my lungs. The weight of my chest eases as the darkness folds around me—steady, quiet, a welcome reprieve.

I roll my eyes at the crunch of leaves behind me. Loud as a rutting stag. All that training and Eowyn still moves like a soldier trying to be a scout. I wait for him on a fallen log, sunlight filtering through the canopy in weak, patchy streaks. The weight in my chest tightens again, worse than before.

I miss her.

The one who would understand the weight of doing nothing.

It was supposed to be simple. Protect the prophecy. Protect our people. Years of strategy, of sacrifice, of secrets piled upon secrets...and all of it to bring us here. To the breaking.

But I never imagined it would feel like this. Like betrayal carved into bone.

Brynn.

Sweet, stubborn Brynn. Gentle light in the middle of all this rot.

I got too close. Gave too much of myself. Now I'll be forced to watch the prophecy play out...knowing full well the cost.

Miserable fool.

"You're in a foul mood," Eowyn mutters as he breaks through the tree line, brushing cobwebs from his tangled hair. His face is sour, his tone worse.

Gods, he looks so much like Ronan.

My gaze flickers toward the border, aching for the strength of his arms, the scent of leather and smoke that clings to him. I shove the feeling down deep into the well of shadows inside me.

I push off the blackened log, teeth clenched. "We have to tell her."

Eowyn blinks, folding his arms across his chest. His incredulous look grates more than it should. I breathe, deep, trying to calm the cold building in my lungs...it doesn't.

"Bloody damn, Eowyn! We can't just sit here twiddling our thumbs while Hilde, the gods, and who knows what else *toy* with her."

His frown sharpens, the dimple in his unshaven chin deepening. "What do you mean Hilde is toying with her?"

I sigh loudly and dramatically. I *want* to provoke him. I revel in the look of apprehension on the poor bastard's face.

"Oh, I don't know," I sneer. "Maybe the same way the gods are toying with *you*. Or do you always trust cryptic witches who lurch out of alleyways muttering death threats?"

His shoulders go rigid. Guilt pricks, but I'm too angry to care. His eyes flash with a flicker of flame as he snaps, "I told you. Like I told the others. The hag warned of death if we took her then. The bombs went off early. Too early."

"Yeah, well, *I* did my part," I spit. "I had her children. We could be in Tiene right now, safe, ahead of all this madness—if you'd just followed the plan."

His temper erupts. "*Your plan failed, Cia!*"

The impenetrable cold hits before I know what I've done. A blast of shadow bursts from me, slamming into Eowyn's chest. He flies across the clearing, crashing into the trees with a thud that stills the forest.

I stagger back, breath catching in my throat. He doesn't move.

"Eowyn!" I rush to him, heart hammering. "I'm sorry...I didn't mean...I don't know what..."

He groans, and I drop to my knees beside him, frantic hands checking for breaks. He grins. That wolfish grin of his that makes you want to punch him and hug him.

"The Draíocht is awakening," he rasps.

I pause and grin back, offering my hand. The shadows curl inside me.

"Yeah, well. I was *getting* to that...before you decided to be an ass."

He rises slowly, brushing bark from his tunic, and pulls me into an embrace. His hand presses the back of my head, his forehead resting against mine—a gesture older than either of us.

"Tell me everything," he says, voice warm and steady.

The ring of embers in his gray eyes glow bright.

Chapter 10

The warmth of the afternoon sun spills lazily into the parlor, gilding the white marble floor and catching on the lumine-stone veranda just beyond the double glass doors. Golden light drapes across the room like a silk veil. Opulent. Intentional. Roimh's hunger for such picturesque affluence left the town of Reik overtaxed and starving for three winters, all in pursuit of that golden glow.

The women gathered around the white oak table marvel over the room's splendor, their voices lilting with praise. All I can see are hollow-eyed children in threadbare clothes and mothers scraping together what little they can to survive.

I shift in my seat, uneasy beneath the watchful crimson eyes of the beast adorned on the velvet tapestry above the hearth. The sigil of Reikhaven. The Great Bear of Agderia. The monster within the shadows. The beast behind closed doors.

I sip my lukewarm tea and force a smile, feigning polite interest as the wife of Roimh's distant cousin prattles on about absurdly lavish Yultane gifts. Audun Elendil intends to bestow upon her insufferably spoiled daughters more than either one deserves. Lady Renoa's hawk-like gaze fixes on me with unsettling precision. I reach for a tea cake to avoid her scrutiny, but the movement only feeds her. Her eyes gleam, and a thin, knowing smile curls her thin lips.

"Lady Brynn," Renoa croons sweetly, "Lord Tuathinne spoke of the bombing at the bay. He failed to mention you were injured."

I instinctively draw my bandaged hand back into my lap, cradling it beneath the folds of my gown. A lump catches in my throat as the conversation stalls. Curious eyes pivot toward me like hounds scenting blood.

The door slams open with a bang, saving me. I exhale in quiet relief as every head turns toward the noise. Renoa's malicious smile falters at the sight of Cia's less than graceful entrance.

I hide my smirk behind my teacup as Cia forces her way between myself and Elendil, Mideton scrambling to place the wicker chair. Cia drops into it without even an ounce of grace, sprawling like she owns the room. Elendil winces, her powdered face puckering as if Cia's presence might stain her lace cuffs. Renoa regains her composure, though her voice now carries a steely edge.

"Lovely of you to join us Audun Cia. Lady Brynn was just about to share how she came upon that rather unfortunate wound before your...robust appearance."

Cia flashes a syrupy smile that doesn't reach her eyes. "*If*

Lady Brynn wanted to share such a traumatic experience," she calmly says without blinking, "it should be on her terms. And not served as gossip for those bored of their own husbands, *Lady* Renoa."

I nearly choke on a sip of honeyed tea, my eyes widening as silence descends. Renoa's jaw tightens, and her already pointed nose sharpens.

Cia plucks a tea cake from the tray and pops it into her mouth with theatrical delight. Across the table, Lady Odette of Vaniran hides a laugh behind her embroidered sleeve. Her chocolate curls bounce with barely restrained amusement.

Elendil, eager to distance herself from the tension and align herself publicly, speaks up with a self-righteous huff. "The Laioses have grown dangerous. They burned a village just beyond our estate's border. Bloodthirsty savages, the lot of them."

The room suddenly dims. The golden afternoon light losing its warmth as the women nod gravely, murmuring their agreement like a prayer.

Elendil's words embolden Renoa, who pounces with renewed glee. "Lord Tuathinne did mention your rescue, dear. From the worst of the attack, wasn't it? By the Master of Ships himself, no less. Lanthe's long-lost brother...Eowyn, I believe?"

I grit my teeth, digging my nails into the soft flesh of my uninjured palm. Renoa's smile deepens, feeding on my discomfort like a vulture circling carrion.

"We were all quite troubled to hear of the attempt on your

life," she says sweetly, her gaze sweeping the table of women. They shake their heads with practiced sympathy before Renoa turns her eyes on Cia. "Though it seems with the company you keep, Lady Brynn, misfortune is bound to follow."

Cia stiffens. Her fingers dance precariously close to the diamond-encrusted tea fork beside her saucer. I reach for her with a steady hand, my touch landing softly on her chilled forearm. The light in the room subtly brightens. I square my shoulders and fix my gaze on Renoa, my voice calm but firm.

"Lady Renoa, if you're insinuating Audun Cia is anything less than the brilliant businesswoman and loyal friend she is, then I must conclude it is *you* who brings unsavory company to this table."

A stunned silence follows. That is until Lady Odette lets out a sharp laugh and slaps her palm against the table with a clink of glass. Renoa's face turns purple with rage, her expression twisting as Elendil stares between us, aghast. Renoa rises abruptly, trembling with unrestrained fury.

"I do hope little Ophele has not inherited your...crude sensibilities," she spits, her voice dripping venom. "Tuathinne requires a certain finesse you clearly lack."

I freeze.

She watches me squirm with a predator's delight before delivering the final blow. "Ah, so Roimh has yet to share the delightful news of your daughter's betrothal to my handsome son, Baron."

The wicker chair creaks beneath me as I sit back, the blood

draining from my face. My pulse roars in my ears.

"She is only seven," Cia snaps, her voice low and dangerous.

"Yes, well," Renoa replies brightly, "the engagement will be formally announced once she comes of age. Though perhaps arrangements should be made for her to reside at Tuathinne next year—" she narrows her eyes at me, "—to unlearn some of her mother's...ghastly decorum."

She turns away, ignoring Odette entirely, and commands, "Come. It seems Lady Brynn is unwell and in need of rest."

The click of heels and swish of velvet skirts fade into the distance, leaving the parlor silent and airless. I sit frozen in the golden light, its warmth now a mockery. A tear slips down my cheek.

"Do not show that miserable cunt any weakness."

I fall apart despite her insistence, burying my face in my palms as the sobs break loose.

"How—how could he do this? My sweetest, dearest Ophele. Handed over to those...monsters." I look up at Cia, her expression carved in stone, my own voice cracking with despair. "He didn't even have the decency to speak with me. He decided her future without a word. Without a thought for what this would do to her. To me. To Olan." My breath hitches. "He silences me, Cia. Again, and again. He takes and takes, until there's nothing left but a shattered soul."

Cia kneels in front of me and gently wipes the salty tears from my cheeks.

"I don't know how much more I can bear," I whisper, my voice raw with exhaustion.

The white flecks in her dark eyes shimmer to life as she squeezes my trembling hand. But before I can say more, she rises and strides to the door. She calls for Mideton, her voice sharp.

He appears almost immediately, the color draining from his face as he catches sight of me. His graying eyes dart between us while Cia mumbles something low and urgent. My brow lifts at the sudden flare of his voice.

"He will not agree to this," he hisses.

I go still, gripping the wicker chair as if it might anchor me. Cia leans against the doorframe, arms crossed in stubborn defiance. My vision blurs for a moment as my eyes adjust to the sudden shift of light in the room. Mideton curses beneath his breath and glances at me. The pain etched on his face is so deep, I half expect him to collapse under the weight of it. He turns away, retreating down the corridor. My heart races. I move to follow, but Cia holds her ground, the air between us thick with urgency.

"What did you say to him? What is he so afraid of?"

Cia pushes off the doorframe and stalks to the cherry wood cabinet beneath the bear tapestry. Her hands rummage noisily through its contents.

"Where does the bastard keep the rum?"

"Cia! Answer me. What is going on?"

She slams the cabinet door shut, the sound sharp in the

heavy silence. "Guess we're doing this without the help of a bloody damn drink," she mutters.

I huff, foot tapping against the stone floor as impatience sparks in my chest. She ignores me. Instead, she grabs my hand roughly and drags me through the glass doors onto the veranda. Cold, salty wind lashes my face, tangling the emerald-green skirt around my legs. The only comfort is the warm kiss of sunlight across my cheeks.

The wind howls around us, stealing the softness from Cia's voice as she speaks.

"I made you something." She pulls a closed fist from her pocket and places it into my hand. "This will keep you safe...at least until I can do more."

Her nose crinkles with unease as I stare down at the unexpected gift, confused. Cold metal presses into my palm, quickly warming against my skin. A necklace, crude and roughly forged, curls in my fingers. The edges of the blackened metal are jagged, sharp enough to draw blood if held carelessly. My thumb glides over the three-pronged symbol carved into its face. A symbol I recognize from Aylah's ancient scrolls.

I glance anxiously over Cia's shoulder, checking the parlor for any watchful eyes that might have followed us. I lean in, voice barely above a whisper.

"A Rüin? Cia, you will be killed for treason if anyone finds out you made this."

She closes my fingers tightly around the pendant. "Let me worry about that. This will keep you safe. That's all that matters."

I open my hand as she points to the two crossed prongs with urgent precision. "These are the horns...symbols of strength and protection. They'll ward off anything that means to harm you." Her small finger moves to the center prong. "And this...this represents the Gaia and the Draíocht she will offer freely...when the prophecy is fulfilled."

My stomach tightens. "Prophecy? What prophecy? Why are you speaking in riddles?"

She offers a strained smile, a tremor of anxiety in her voice. "I'll explain everything once Mideton returns. But please, Brynn, whatever happens...whatever is said...you must know I've only ever fought for what's best for you."

The sunlight gleams off the blackened metal in my hand, and for a heartbeat, the surface seems to shimmer...swirl with motion. A rush of whispers flutters through the salted wind, brushing against my skin like breath. I quickly close my fist, shoving the Rüin deep into my skirt pocket...and the ghosts it stirred with it.

"I trust you, Cia. Always."

Her lip quivers slightly before she quickly looks away. Whatever war is raging inside her unsettles me completely. Cia has always been my strength. To see her shaken...so vulnerable, is terrifying. I pull her into a warm embrace, hoping to calm whatever storm is rising in her chest.

The glass doors behind us creak open, and Mideton clears his throat with a gravelly rasp. She pulls back at once, brushing her sleeve across her cheek to hide the evidence. He holds out a thick woolen cloak, his voice strained through clenched teeth.

"You must go now. Lord Roimh is off visiting Audun Slade with Lord Tuathinne." He levels a sharp glance at Cia. "She must be back before the setting sun."

Cia snatches the cloak with a scoff. "Yes, yes, I heard you the first time, old man. I'll return her before his highness stumbles back from whoring. Gods willing."

My jaw tightens, and my heart splinters a little more at the reminder of Roimh's latest indiscretions. I take the cloak without protest, tugging the hood up over my hair. Mideton rolls his eyes and steps aside as Cia barrels past, dragging me in tow.

The metal Rüin in my pocket sears hot against my thigh as we sweep past Roimh's blood-red sigil...the Great Bear. Its carved eyes glint like embers, following us with silent, snarling judgment. Cia tightens her grip on my hand and leads me down the corridor, fast and unrelenting. I glance back once and meet Mideton's weary eyes and gentle smile. But already, dread is coiling in my gut, crawling up from the soles of my feet as we rush toward whatever task Cia deems too urgent to wait.

We slip through the corridors, keeping to the shadows, careful to avoid any wandering eyes that might question why I'm leaving the fortress without an escort. The scent of roasting pig and duck wafts through the halls, making my mouth water as we pass the kitchens. Inside, the staff is a flurry of movement, preparing for the evening feast.

I stifle a laugh as Cia swipes a hunk of cheese and a heel of crusty bread from a silver platter. The burly Master Cook from Inevar would flay her alive if he caught her pilfering from his carefully arranged tables.

The sound of waves grows louder as we reach the crumbling staircase carved into the cliffside—its tone worn smooth by salt and countless winters. I clutch the rails as I descend carefully, the wind tugging at my cloak. Cia moves like a shadow down the sand wall, already waiting below with impatience etched into every step she paces.

"Where are we going?" I call, breathless from the climb down.

"Come. We don't have much time."

I follow, obedient but uncertain, the sand shifting treacherously beneath my feet. The fortress disappears behind the rocks as we make our way along the shoreline toward the distant town of Reik. The sea glitters beside us, catching the light like shards of broken glass. My heart drums with unease.

The sun dips lower on the horizon with every step. I glance back at the vanishing cliffs, Mideton's warning echoing in my mind.

We won't make it back before nightfall.

Cia stops so abruptly that I crash into her back. She lets out a loud and haunting whistle, like that of a whippoorwill. I pull my cloak tighter around my shoulders as another bird call answers beyond the sandy dune ahead. She squeezes my hand

and offers a reassuring smile before we scramble over the dune together.

At the crest, I hesitate.

Nestled between sun-bleached stone and lapping waves is the blackened mouth of a sea cave, half-concealed by towering boulders. The tide hisses against the rocks like a warning. Above the narrow entrance is a jagged hole, as if the sun has burned through the stone over centuries. I gasp as small figures scramble into view, barefooted and eager hands clamor across the rocks and shifting sand. Children.

Cia beams as she digs into her leather satchel, pulling free the pilfered scraps of cheese and bread. The children squeal with delight, swarming around her, clutching at the meager offering like a feast. I take a cautious step forward as my heart twists.

"Who are they, Cia? Why are they hidden...and starving?"

She doesn't answer right away. Her eyes scan the children, her jaw set tight.

"These are the refugees from the village Elendil mentioned earlier," she finally says, voice sharp. "The one supposedly burned by the Laioses."

I blink in shock. "But if not the Laioses, then...who?"

She turns to me with a hard scowl, the wind catching the edge of her cloak as she waves the children back toward the shadows of the cave.

"I can bring them to the fortress," I plead. "They'll be safe. Fed. I can find them homes..."

"No," she cuts me off coldly. "No one can know they survived."

My face wrinkles in confusion, lips parting to speak when a mountain of a man steps from the mouth of the cave. I freeze as I stare at the fury carved deep into every line of his face. I instinctively take a step back, heart thundering in my chest, every part of me ready to run.

"Don't worry," Cia says lightly. "He looks mean, but he's a softy at heart."

There is absolutely nothing soft about the behemoth storming toward us. Each side of his shaved head is inked with dark tattoos, curling like smoke down to his thick neck. The crimson hair left atop his head is braided into three tight rows that hang to the nap of his neck. A wild, bushy beard frames his square jaw, barely masking the scowl that darkens his features. His voice booms across the clearing, gravel rough and full of fire.

"Have you lost your bloody mind?"

Cia shrugs, unfazed. Her face breaks into an easy laugh. "Probably. Still too early to tell."

He reaches her in three strides and sweeps her into his massive arms. Despite the thunder in his voice, there's a gentleness in the way he holds her. His gaze never strays from me though, sharp and unwavering. Suspicion smolders in his striking green eyes, but something else lurks beneath it... familiarity. As if he's seen me before.

He presses a kiss to the top of her head and mutters into her hair, voice low and rough with tenderness. "I've missed you."

She wriggles free, grinning up at me like a misbehaving child caught red-handed.

"Brynn," she says brightly, turning toward me, "I'd like you to meet Ronan."

He offers no greeting, just a nod and a hard stare that could split stone. His lips thin. His jaw tightens and when he speaks it's a growl aimed past Cia's grin.

"He's going to be pissed."

Cia smirks, her fingers idly twirling a piece of his beard. "Yeah, well when is he not?"

Ronan snorts and shakes his head, his large, calloused hands brushing gently against her cheek.

"Do what you must," he says quietly. "I'll keep the little rascals at bay."

She yanks him down by the beard, and his head dips willingly as she presses a soft kiss to his sun-warmed cheek. From behind his tall legs, a honey-eyed girl with windblown golden hair peeks out shyly. I kneel to meet her curious gaze, offering a gentle smile.

"Hello, my name is Brynn. What's yours?"

Her small voice carries a sweet, sing-song lilt.

"Lyla."

She steps out slowly, clutching the fabric of Ronan's pants as I extend a hand. "It's very nice to meet you, Lyla."

She beams, flashing a gap-toothed grin just as Ronan steps

between us, blocking my hand from hers.

"She isn't going to hurt the child," Cia snaps, exasperated.

His eyes stay locked on mine, cold and searching.

"That remains to be seen," he mutters.

Cia rolls her eyes and grabs my hand with a firm grip. "We're going into the cave. Keep the children out, you overprotective ass."

The sun sinks lower, and our time away begins to tick with urgency. The hairs on the back of my neck stay raised the entire walk to the cave as Cia mutters under her breath about men and their bloated egos. I don't dare look behind us, not with the memory of that towering man's glare still burning in my mind.

We scramble over the slick boulders guarding the cave and step onto the damp, sandy floor littered with traces of those who've taken refuge here. Worn blankets, scattered bedding, a few comforting toys. Ghosts of hurried flight cling to everything.

Cia gently sets a rag doll on the ground before perching on a small boulder. She offers her hand without a word. I grasp it and pull myself up beside her, silently wishing I were in breeches instead of this gods-damned skirt. Brushing the sand from my legs, I sit and wait—again—for the brooding woman beside me to finally explain why she's dragged me across half the coastline.

Minutes pass. My patience thins.

"Why are we here?"

She tucks a stray lock of black hair behind her ear. "Just wait. You'll see."

I sigh and glance up through the jagged hole in the cave's ceiling. A faint trickle of water echoes from somewhere deep inside. I shift uneasily as the sun sinks lower in the clear blue sky.

Cia sits motionless, serene despite my rising anxiety. The last rays of daylight spill through the cave entrance, casting a soft golden glow across the stone walls. It feels sacred. Like the cave itself is holding its breath, waiting.

I gasp as vibrant blue symbols painted into the stone erupt into radiant light, casting the cave in a pulsing, ethereal glow. The Rüin markings cover every inch of the damp walls, alive with something ancient and unseen. For a moment, I wonder if it's these symbols that have shielded this place from Roimh's ever-reaching hand. My fingers slip into my pocket, curling tightly around the crude necklace Cia gave me. I cling to the fragile hope that it, too, might offer protection.

Cia's voice cuts softly through the reverent stillness.

"You asked about the prophecy. About the Draíocht." She gestures toward a mural where a tree spreads across the rock face, its thick trunk branching into seven limbs. "From the Gaia came seven clans, each bearing the blood of a god."

I follow the sweep of her hand to another painting: a ritual, flames curling around a circle of robed figures

"I assume you know of the Rite. Of the Draíocht's return to the Gaia after the ritual failed."

"Yes," I murmur. "A queen and her lover destroyed the source. Sacrificed it. That's why the Draíocht returned to the Gaia, as the Dagda intended."

Cia stares at me, slack-jawed. "By the gods, no," she breathes. "That is not at all what happened."

I blink, startled by her vehemence, but she glances to the cave mouth where the sunlight is fast retreating.

"I don't have time to explain it all now. Not yet. But I will." Her voice lowers with a fierce promise. "Soon."

She hops down from the boulder and walks to another tree painted along the wall. This one is grotesque in form, its lines jagged and broken. Five branches stretch strong and proud, but two hang limp at the trunk's side, withered and barely clinging to life. "This one," she says, pointing to a sunlit limb, "represents your lineage." Her finger drifts to a branch shrouded in shadows. "And this one...mine."

"Like the sun and the moon," I whisper. "Day and night."

Cia nods, a faint smile ghosting her lips, though sorrow darkens her eyes. "The Great War destroyed our home. Our people."

She moves to stand beneath another mural, where ancient script crowns a towering tree glowing with vibrant blue light. This tree pulses with life. Its seven branches healthy and whole, intertwined like melodies in a song. Each branch teems with delicate details: flowered leaves, winged creatures, tiny beasts crawling the winding limbs. I'm drawn to it by some unspoken force, my fingers aching to trace the glowing lines.

I scramble down from the rock, the hem of my skirt catching my boot. I stumble forward, just catching myself before I fall face first in the sand.

Cia snickers and clears her throat pointedly. "If you are quite finished with the dramatics..."

I blow a stray auburn curl from my face and glare at her in mock offense. She just winks and turns back to the mural. The air grows still as her fingers graze the ancient writing, and my skin prickles as she begins to recite the words above the Tree of Life.

A child, chosen by Eadom, born of Light,
Shall bear the weapon forged in fire,
And broken in blood.
The Chosen shall unite the Laioses,
And bring Death upon all who bear His name.
Guard the Chosen until the darkness breaks—
And what was lost shall restore again.

She turns just as I step up behind her, the flickering blue light casting an otherworldly glow along the curve of her cheek. The cave hums with quiet power, but it's the stillness in her eyes that sends a shiver through me.

My fingers tighten around the necklace hidden in my pocket, the cold metal suddenly too heavy to bear. The prophecy hangs between us like a blade balanced on a ledge.

Words echo in my mind.

Chosen.

Death.

The darkness breaks.

Cia meets my gaze, calm despite the weight of what she's revealed. Her voice is light, almost teasing.

"Well, you wanted to know the prophecy," she says. "So, there it is."

I scoff, my jaw clenching. "And what exactly am I supposed to do with that?"

I gesture toward the glowing tree, frustration rising like bile in my throat.

"Your prophecy is just another riddle. Another half-truth wrapped in riddles and shadows...like everything else that comes out of your mouth lately."

She crosses her arms and grinds her teeth, clearly holding back the tongue-lashing she wants to give. After a tense beat, she throws her hands up with an exasperated huff.

"I give up!' she snaps. "You're as blind as they come, Brynn. And honestly, I can't tell if it's willful or just plain ignorance." She storms past me, then spins around, her restraint unraveling with every breath. "One day, you're going to have to choose what side you're really on. And gods, I hope you choose character over loyalty...because right now, your loyalty is drowning your character."

The silence that follows rings louder than her outburst. I

remain frozen in the center of the cave, reeling.

Her footsteps fade.

My heart aches with a loneliness I can't swallow. In twenty-seven years, I've had only one true friend. And now, as the distance between us stretches into something jagged and real, I can't help but wonder if this...this loss...is what finally breaks me.

Maybe she's right.

Maybe I've been clinging to loyalty like a lifeline, blind to how it's poisoned everything it ever touched. A loyalty drilled into me as a child. A loyalty that's done nothing but strip me raw.

I exhale shakily, staring up at the fading light dancing on the walls. In the hush that follows, I wonder how to hold on to the only world I've ever known...when standing in the glow of truth has never felt so hollow.

I leave history behind as I step from the mouth of the cave toward the crashing waves of the sea. I feel more lost now than I ever have. I don't belong anywhere...not in Agderia, where I've spent most of my feeble life, nor in Ravndal, the territory of my birth. Roimh's bitter words echo through my mind.

You are nothing. You are no one.

The setting sun bleeds across the sky in a blaze of orange and pink, staining the gathering clouds with deep shades of violet. Light and darkness converging, entwined in one final spellbinding creation. I step into a growing pool of seawater at the cave's entrance. It rushes around my boots, cold and sharp as it seeps into the seams.

Cia stands atop the golden dune, staring out at the vast sea. The salted wind tears around her small frame, dragging shadows along the ground like greedy fingers. Her cropped raven hair whips behind her, revealing the slight, elegant point at the tips of her ears. The fading sunlight catches her skin in hues of burnished bronze, like honey dipped in shadow. She looks like a memory come to life. A ghost of my past, come to claim what's left of me.

Ronan steps away from his silent watch at the cave entrance, his voice low and rough behind me. "She loves you. She wouldn't be fighting this hard if she didn't."

A surge of emotion rises, love pushing against the weight of fear, threatening to drown me. I struggle beneath it, my voice breaking with truth.

"As I love her. More than you could ever understand."

He exhales slowly, something gentler softening his sharp features. "Then go to her. Mend what's broken." He pauses beside me, his towering frame casting long shadows in the waning light. "Cia fought the same fight you're in now. Torn between loyalty and love. She won." His gaze turns down, the faintest ache beneath his words. "But this..." he gestures to the cave, the children, the setting sun, "...it opens wounds she thought had long healed. Again, she's forced to choose. And today, she chose you. Love for you over loyalty to another."

His green eyes meet mine, hardened with quiet warning. "A

choice that might break her."

My heart slams in my chest. I glance toward Cia, wind-blown and waiting. A lump catches in my throat as my heart sinks like stone. Memories flicker—her laughter in moonlight, her arms wrapped around me in grief, her voice steady when mine faltered. She has picked up every shattered piece of me, time and time again.

My voice steadies, the decision already made. I lift my chin and meet Ronan's unflinching stare.

"I will not break her."

His features ease, a ghost of a smile playing at the edge of his beard. A quiet breath of relief settles between us.

"See that you don't," he mutters, his voice rough with warning—and something like hope. *"Beireoir an bhais."*

I stumble back, heart hammering in my chest as blood rushes to my head. Every instinct scream to run but I can do nothing but stare, paralyzed, as recognition roots itself deep in my bones. My eyes flick to the massive one-bladed ax slung across his back and the Elkan antlers hanging lazily at his thigh, then back to the narrow eyes that pierce straight through my terror.

I scramble backward, clumsy with panic, dragging my feet toward the safety of the dune. Fear claws at me with every frantic step. By the time I crest the top, breathless and shaking, the sun is nearly drowned beneath the sea. Cia stands alone at the edge, unmoving. The distant roar of the waves calms her in a way that feels otherworldly, as if the ocean itself is holding her steady.

We say nothing at first. Together, we watch the last strands of sunlight vanish beneath the horizon, surrendering to the hush of night. When I finally speak, my voice fractures with the weight I can no longer carry.

"You're a Laioses, yes?"

She swallows hard, her silence more telling than any answer. Then, slowly, she shakes her head. I glance back at Ronan, my lip trembling as I bite it. When I meet her gaze again, the fear between us is thick, tangible. Webbed. Knotted. Ancient.

I clear my throat, the words coming out trembling and unsure.

"Do you want me to leave with you? To join the rebellion? To take the side of the Laioses because of some prophecy written in dust centuries ago? Is that why you brought me here...to prove you're not bloodthirsty monsters?"

The whites of her eyes catch the rising moonlight, a quiet glow in the shadows. Her voice is barely a whisper, but it cleaves straight through me.

"Yes."

Fear of the unknown coils tightly around my heart. The fear that this choice, this night, might unravel me completely. That I'll end up more broken than ever before. And yet, something warm stirs deep in my gut. It rises slowly, calming the frantic beat of my heart as I look at the hope laid out before me.

A life free from pain and heartache.

A life filled with adventure, with peace.

A life where my children are not pawns to be traded into the aristocracy I've grown to despise.

I reach for her hand and give it a firm squeeze. "I trust you. I will always trust you."

She holds me back just as tightly, her eyes shining with unshed tears as she says softly, "There are things I cannot tell you...for your protection. And things we don't yet know. Can't yet understand. Fate is fickle. And the gods...the gods are restless." She leans forward, pressing her forehead gently to mine, one hand at the back of my head. Her voice trembles, low and raw. "I will do whatever I must to protect you." She pulls back slightly, her fingers trailing a loose strand of hair from my cheek. "But you must make a choice, Brynn. Soon."

I cup her damp cheek, my thumb brushing away a tear as I smile. "I will always choose you, Cia. Always."

Her grin blooms, wide and cheeky, as she loops her arm through mine.

"Well then. Come on. We've got plans to make. Dreams to fulfill." She glances up to the sea of stars slowly awaking and mutters under her breath, "Assuming Mideton doesn't kill me before the night is over."

I cast one last glance at Ronan, retreating into the cave like a hen gathering his brood.

"We really need to talk about your taste in lovers, Cia. Pretty sure that one still wants to kill me."

She turns her head and laughs, pulling me along the moonlit shore.

"Don't mind him. He worries too much."

But I stop short, resisting her tug. "He called me 'bringer of death' in the ancient tongue, Cia. *Twice*. Once during the attack on the harbor and again tonight. You may want me to come to Ravndal, but how can I trust that he...or others like him, like the Laioses who attacked the harbor...will ever accept me as I am."

She frowns, the spark of moonlight glinting in her eyes as she exhales her frustration into the salt-stung night. "There are far more who *do* accept you than those who don't. The Laioses protect their own, Brynn—always. No matter the cost." Her voice softens but remains firm. "If Ronan truly believed you a threat, you wouldn't have left that cave tonight. He would've held you until the clan chief returned. But he let you go. That means something." She takes a breath, her tone sharpening. "You're not safe behind those stone walls, no matter how gilded they seem. Roimh is selling your daughter, corrupting your son, and slowly beating the life out of you. The queen's reach stretches farther than you think. But there? With us? You have a chance. A *choice*."

Her voice pierces through me, every word slicing clean through my defenses. Truth, it doesn't knock. It carves. It strips you bare. Leaves you standing in its wake with nothing to hide behind but yourself.

We begin the long climb back up the winding, weather-worn steps. I walk in silence beside her, each step heavier than the last. My thoughts race ahead me, conjuring every possible outcome that might follow if I leave this life behind. Every possibility. Every cost. And yet, the question coils around my soul like a living thing.

Am I brave enough to go?

Chapter 11

We hurry through the empty corridors in mutual silence. The shadows slip alongside us, cloaking my presence despite the torchlight flickering along the rugged stone walls. My mind races in step with the frantic beat of my heart. Memories come for me, loud and unrelenting, until I am drowning beneath their weight.

The subtly sweet smell of nightshade lingers in the air, the gravel of the castle garden crunching beneath my slippers with every tentative step. I stiffen, clutching the leather-bound book to my chest as a second pair of footsteps follow behind mine, slow and deliberate.

A smooth, familiar voice calls my name, and butterflies flutter to life in my stomach. A smile tugs at the corner of my lips, and I bite down on it, giddy and flustered all at once.

I draw a breath to steady myself and turn, head bowed, eyes lowered. But when I finally lift my gaze, my heart stutters. There he stands—Audun Roimh—with his charming smile and those bright hazel eyes that always see more than they should.

I lose sense of myself as he steps closer, his nearness stealing the breath from my lungs. The book presses sharply into my ribs, its cover shielding the secrets within. Secrets that would betray me if ever uncovered. But he doesn't see it. He never does. He reaches for a loose strand of hair that has fallen across my cheek, brushing it back with deceptive gentleness.

"Breathtakingly beautiful," he murmurs.

I blush, the warmth rushing to my face as butterflies become a frenzy within. "Thank you kindly, Audun Roimh."

His smile deepens as he lifts my trembling hand to his lips, pressing a kiss to my knuckles like something out of a fairytale.

"I have a gift for you," he says.

He slips a small journal from his jacket pocket, bound in soft leather and gilded with delicate golden leaves.

"For you," he says, "to write of your adventures."

The leather-bound book pressed to my chest softens beneath the loosening grip of my fingers as I stare, wide-eyed, into the depth of adoration in his gaze. I reach out slowly, accepting his generous offering. My thumb drifts over the tiny golden leaves embossed on the cover, their edges glinting in the waning light.

"You are far too kind, Audun Roimh," I murmur, glancing at the withering garden around us. The ivy is dry, the roses *brittle on their stems. A shiver dances down my spine. "Though I'm not sure I'll have many adventures behind these castle walls."*

His grin widens, too polished, too sure. He lifts a hand to my face and traces the freckles scattered across my cheek as if he's memorizing them.

"Don't you worry that pretty little head," he says, his voice dripping soft as silk. "I promised you the world, didn't I?"

The sun slips free from behind a curtain of clouds, casting golden light over his hair and crowning him in princely wonder.

"I always keep my promises," he says.

Our courtship began in a fever of passion and endless hope. A hope for a future unbound by the trappings of court and the queen's iron rule. Promises whispered in the shadow of the day and dreamed of in the dead of night. Promises that now lie shattered at my feet, buried beneath bloody fists and hateful words.

I once believed I had won the greatest of gifts in Roimh's affection. He was the prize of Agderia, the man all the ladies of court longed for—the handsome Audun of Reik. And somehow, impossibly, he was mine. I never thought myself worthy of his attention, and yet he chose me.

If only I had known.

I was spun into his web of treachery and deceit until every last drop of me was consumed by his pursuit of a life he could never afford—a life bought and paid for with slivers of my battered soul.

Through our marriage, Roimh was crowned Lord of Reikhaven and given full access to the dreams he never dared speak aloud. Dreams that slowly devoured the innocence that once filled my heart. I fell helplessly in love with a man incapable of loving anyone more than he loves himself. I gave and gave, offering pieces of myself in hopes that one day, he might love me for me.

But year after year, hope shriveled beneath the weight of silence. My voice was caged, my wanderlust stripped away and replaced with the slow ache of life not worth living.

Now I stand amid the wreckage of a future that will never see the light of day. I cannot look beyond the shards—only a broken mirror reflecting the pain and regret. Echoes of a woman still struggling to find her worth in a world that insists she has none.

My gaze tugs toward Cia's profile. She presses her lips tight, her eyes staring ahead with quiet intensity. A faint smile pulls at my mouth, my chest swelling with something soft and warm. She is my safe place. The one who sees the hidden bruises of my heart and heals them with quiet truth. She has risked so much by revealing her true self to me. And still, she risks even more...our friendship...her safety...for the sake of my own humanity.

I blink away my tears as a strange warmth blooms in my stomach. It rises and coils, burning with sudden urgency.

Before I can make sense of it, I'm shoved hard against the cold stone wall.

A gasp catches in my throat, cut off by the icy press of small fingers against my lips. The torchlight dims. My breath hitches. Cia's eyes gleam—two silver moons in a darkened sky. She quickly shuts them, strands of silky black hair falling like a curtain to shield her face from view.

Shadows thicken around us, curling like smoke. I struggle to breathe through the silence, the darkness pressing in so tightly I feel I might suffocate. Whispered voices creep closer, slipping through the black veil like a blade through cloth.

Cia's touch is cold against my skin, but steady. I tremble and close my eyes, bracing myself against the sound of Renoa's voice. It slices through the silence like broken glass, sharp and too loud.

"Perri has received several ravens since we arrived," she says. The click of her heels echo off the stone, each step drawing nearer. Her voice dips into a rasping whisper, "Each one sealed with the royal crest."

A startled gasp follows...Elendil's. High-pitched, disbelieving. "The royal seal? From the queen?"

Renoa snarls, "Quiet, you fool!" A pause. The faint jingle of jewelry, as if she's glancing warily around. Her voice sharpens to a hiss. "These stones have ears."

Elendil falls silent, skirts rustling as their footsteps fade slowly into the dark.

Cia grabs my hand before I can draw a breath. We run,

stumbling, breathless, my heart hammering in my chest. The corridor rushes past in shadowed streaks, and when I glance behind us, I swear I see it...the torchlight dying one by one in our wake.

Stifled giggles spill through the wooden door of my chambers as I smooth my frizzed hair and brush the sand from my woolen-skirt. Behind me, Cia casts a backward glance, clearly more tempted to pry open the waxy seal of Lord Tuathinne's letters than face whatever mischief my children have managed in our absence. My exhaustion gives way to joy as the heavy door creaks open, and I am greeted by the sweetest surprise.

"Mamma!" Ophele cries, walking unsteadily toward me.

I bend and catch her in my arms, my heart unraveling at the feel of her tiny arms thrown tightly around my neck. I breathe in her sugary scent as she buries her face against my chest. My throat tightens with tears I dare not release.

"My little bird," I whisper, pressing a kiss to her golden curls. "Oh, how I've missed you."

Lifting my gaze, I search the room for the sandy-brown haired boy who holds the other half of my heart. I open my arm with a hopeful smile.

Olan shifts uncomfortably, a reluctant glimmer in his eyes. He walks to me slowly, wrapping his arms around me with the stiffness of a boy who now believes he is too old for affection. I hug him tighter anyway, anchoring myself to the warmth of his body though my heart aches.

Yet another thing Roimh has taken from me...Olan's childhood.

His temper flared after Olan's tenth nameday, cruel and unrelenting. For nearly three years, I have watched a father strip the joy from a boy who was once all light and wonder. A dreamer. A child with his mother's wanderlust and a heart eager for adventure. A boy who meets the world with kindness, regardless of title or station. A boy who is nothing like his father.

I tried escaping once, desperate for a safe haven after one of Roimh's drunken assaults. Drescher discovered us, hidden among the boards of blacksmith's wagon. Olan was sent to train with Drescher at the age of ten. Sarmien was hired through Mideton to care for them both. Frost had only just begun to lick the ground when the blacksmith was brought out in rags. I can still hear his tearful screams with every bloody lash, the whips slicing through flesh and exposing his ribs. Any access to either is given solely with Roimh's approval now.

I clear my throat and blink back the tears as I take in the table overflowing with sweet cakes, sugared berries, and warm loaves of bread. Steam rises in lazy spirals from clay bowls of duck and cabbage soup.

"What a wonderful surprise, my lovies." I turn to Sarmien who is busily pouring lemon-flavored water into iced goblets. "You are so kind, Sarmien. Thank you."

Her hazel eyes twinkle with pride, though a blush creeps across her round cheeks. "It was Olan's idea, milady. A picnic supper to celebrate Yultane." She nods toward the freckled-faced boy, whose face flushes a deep red. He tries to suppress a smile and fails.

"He organized everything. I just helped a bit."

Ophele lifts her chin with mock indignation. "Hey! I helped too, you know!"

I arch an eyebrow in mock surprise and lunge, fingers tickling her sides until she dissolves into laughter. "Did you now? What a fine help you were, my clever girl."

She grins and squirms away, catching her breath as she smooths the wrinkled front of her dress. "I put the napkins on the table and didn't eat any berries before you got here. Not even one. Ask Sarmien."

Sarmien chuckles. "A true show of restraint."

Ophele flashes a toothy smile before exaggeratedly plopping on the chaise, her blond curls bouncing in the firelight. I glance at Britta, who stands quietly in the corner, dabbing the corner of her eye with a kerchief, hope welling with her tears.

"Britta, I'd like to freshen up so I can enjoy this lovely feast." I turn to Cia with a smile. "You'll stay and eat with us, yes?"

Olan's head snaps up with an eager grin. Cia's bright laugh ripples through the room, warming the corners still steeped in shadow. I leave them behind and hurry to the bathing chamber, eager to wash away the grime of salt, sweat, and sand. My skin sighs beneath the cool kiss of water as I splash the day from my face. I run soaked fingers through my tangled hair, braiding it loosely over my shoulder while Britta fastens the whale bone buttons down the back of my burgundy dress with practiced ease.

Mideton's voice filters through the door, grave with warning. Cia's reply is sharp and cold as ice. Afraid of a confrontation, I step quickly into the room. Mideton is already retreating, his face tight with restraint. Sarmien's expression is ghostly white as she fills Cia's bowl and goblet with trembling hands.

I move to stand behind Olan and run my fingers through his tousled hair, a quiet comfort more for me than him.

"Sarmien," I say gently, "the children will stay with me tonight."

She hesitates, wide-eyed and stammering, "B-but Lord Roimh..."

Olan speaks before I can answer, his voice sudden steel in the room.

"Dagda curse the day he keeps Ophele from Mother the night before Yultane."

Cia chuckles, grinning as she playfully punches his arm. "The tiny lord has spoken."

I clap my hands with a smile, attempting to lift the tension that clings through the air. "Yes! Now let's eat and then..." I widen my eyes dramatically. "...presents!"

Ophele squeals and I sit next to her on the chaise, wrapping her in my arms. Her fingers curl affectionately around the end of my braid. Her joy wraps around my heart like a balm, softening every edge. Sarmien offers a warm smile and bows her head as she slips quietly from the room. Britta trails behind her with a gentle nod and the promise to return with nightclothes for my little guests. Olan flops into a chair with a smug, satisfied grin. He greedily devours the steaming duck soup and thick slices of buttered bread.

The nearly full moon glows high in the sky, casting silver light across the frosted windows of my chambers. The night wears on, but I bask in the cozy warmth blanketing the room. Olan listens with wide eyes as Cia gives sage advice on swordsmanship. His spoon hovers midair, forgotten in his hand.

I sit back and watch, mesmerized, as Cia's lithe body shifts into motion. Her movements are a quiet dance of footwork and grace balanced with power and precision. Her shadow twists across the wall under the flickering amber glow of the hearth, echoing her every movement.

I should have seen it sooner, recognized her for what she is. A Laioses. Fierce where others bowed. Reckless where others hesitated. Her hatred for Queen Hilde has always run too deep, her defiance too natural...too earned. There's always been a mystery to her, something untamable, though somehow, I've always felt safest within her shadow.

A knock sounds at the door. Britta enters with the children's nightclothes and begins clearing the table. Mideton steps inside, arms laden with packages. Cia is at his side in an instant, the grin and twinkle in her eye could melt ice.

I raise an eyebrow and laugh. "What is all this, Cia?"

She turns to the children, eyes bright, and says with theatrical reverence, "Happy Yultane, little rogues! May the Dagda give you strength, the Gaia offer you provision, and the Fates grant you mercy through every season."

Ophele scrambles from the chaise, rubbing her sleepy eyes as a greedy smile spreads across her face. She lets out a delighted squeal as she snatches the smallest parcel from Cia's hands. Her fingers work quickly to unwrap the golden thread binding the lilac fabric.

I laugh, my heart light with joy. "I see you've been quite busy." I nod toward the growing pile of gifts. "And I imagine Parela has been as well."

Cia only winks, sprawling lazily into a nearby chair. She sips her wine and watches the chaos unfold with a look of quiet satisfaction. I sip from my own goblet, the spice wine warming me from the inside out. Guilt creeps in as I watch the joy on their faces. Ophele's necklace sits tucked safely in a drawer beside my bed, but all I could salvage for Olan after the chaos at the harbor were a bag of roasted chestnuts, a worn book of sea adventures, and a promise that one day soon, I would give him the looking glass he's always dreamed of.

Cia leans close, her voice low and playful. "Go on. Check the drawer near your bed."

I blink surprised and cross to the barnwood nightstand. I open the drawer and gasp, staring at what rests inside. Nestled next to the deep emerald-green lace that cradles Ophele's necklace lay a looking glass of exquisite craftsmanship unlike anything I've ever seen.

Tentacles of a sea monster wrap elegantly around the coral-red leather that encases the tubes of forged brass. Along the longer lens, waves crash against the hull of a brave ship locked in battle, its sails straining against the pull of the beast's reach. A perfect rendering of strength against all odds, of courage in the face of monstrous fate.

I glance back at Cia, her eyes dancing. Her voice is smooth as silk as she says, "Compliments of the Master of Ships."

My chest swells with emotion. I turn, bearing the gifts in each hand, and step forward with a tearful smile. "Happy Yultane, my little doves. May the Dagda bless each of you."

Ophele claps her hand in giddy delight, bouncing unsteadily on the balls of her feet as I present the necklace.

"Ooooh! It's so sparkly!" she squeals, grabbing it with careful reverence. She holds it high in the firelight like a treasure plucked from the stars. "Can I wear it now, Mamma? Please, please, please?"

Her excitement fills the room like sunlight, and I can't help but laugh as I kneel to fast the necklace around her neck. She grips my arm and twirls dramatically, the icy opal glinting with each spin. Olan steps forward more slowly, his eyes wide with disbelief as he stares down at the looking glass.

He reaches for it with hesitant hands, brushing his fingers along the coral-red leather and forged brass. His bright blue-green eyes shimmer with unshed tears, wonder etched across his face. I gently cup his chin, grounding him in the moment.

"Never let anyone keep you from the desires of your heart," I whisper. "Be fearless in your pursuit of adventure, my son."

He throws his arms around me and pulls me into a firm embrace. I blink, surprised at the strength in his limbs. Gone is the little boy who once chased butterflies in the garden and leapt into muddy puddles without care. In his place stands someone on the cusp of maturity. I cling to him, afraid if I let go, he'll vanish into manhood before I have the chance to memorize the last echoes of his childhood. The hearth crackles behind us. Cia clears her throat, giving Olan a quiet moment to wipe the tears from his cheeks.

"Gather round, you two," she calls, voice rich with mischief. "I have a tale to share."

I brush a hand along Olan's cheek, smiling softly, then glance at her as I guide Ophele to the chaise.

"What tale will you spin for us tonight, my dearest friend?"

Cia takes a sip of spice wine, her lips curling into a wicked grin. "A tale of the gods."

A chill traces the length of my spine as the children clamor around our storyteller. The room dims beneath a blanket of flickering shadows. Cia ignores my worried glance as I take a seat near the hearth, desperate for the flames to drive away the cold dread that curdles in my stomach. With a haunted voice and eyes glowing like twin moons, she weaves a story from my childhood I had long buried.

"Long before Agderia ever formed," she begins, her voice

low and melodic, "the children of the Gaia and her lover, Dagda, roamed the earth. Each child was blessed with the blood of their creators. They were tasked with the honor of guarding the Draíocht gifted by Eadom the Ancient and to keep it free from the darkness that crept across the land. But darkness is a patient entity. It swallowed the gods, one by one. And when they fell, so too did the gifts they passed down. The world grew cold. Winters came and went, and the children of the gods forgot the power that slept in their blood. They hid from the wrath of the Bloodless."

Olan's bros pinch together. "Who are the Bloodless?"

Cia dramatically groans. "You're just like your mother. Questions upon questions."

She shoots me a pointed look and continues, "The Bloodless are those born without the gods' touch. Powerless."

Ophele lifts her chin, squaring her tiny shoulders with righteous pride. "Pappa say stories are for idle hands. He says the gods are dead."

Cia's nostrils flare, her voice sharpens. "Yes, well your father is an—"

I clap my hands, cutting her off before the word leaves her lips. "That's enough stories for tonight. Gather your treasure and get ready for bed. The sun will rise soon."

Cia rolls her eyes but says nothing. The children grumble their disappointment, dragging their feet as they corral their gifts into lopsided piles. The warmth of the moment slips through my fingers like grains of sand as Roimh stumbles through the doorway.

My heart seizes. The chair behind me crashes to the floor as I shoot to my feet. He reeks of wine and salt, his gaze unfocused, lips curling into a smile that never reaches his eyes. Without hesitation, Cia rises. She tucks Ophele against her chest with one arm, the other sliding protectively in front of Olan. Her posture shifts, tight and poised like a blade drawn from its sheath.

Roimh stumbles over his own feet, catching himself on the doorframe with a muttered curse. I lunge forward instinctively, grasping his arm to steady him before he can fall flat onto the floor.

His breath is warm and sour against my cheek as he slurs, "I have a present for you, wife."

I force a bright laugh, gently guiding him toward Cia's empty chair. "How thoughtful! Why don't we sit down first, hmm?" I glance toward Cia, my eyes silently pleading. "Audun Cia," I say through a thin smile, "would you be so kind as to escort the children to Sarmien?"

Roimh's voice cuts through the room like a whip, "They stay."

I flinch as Ophele edges further behind Cia, her small frame trembling. Cia's eyes burn bright in the firelight, the white flecks in the onyx of her irises nearly glowing like stars on the verge of collapse. I force myself to look away from the fear on Olan's face.

Roimh fumbles in his pocket. He belches, tossing

something toward me with a smirk. A brooch clatters across the stone floor, the sharp brass glinting as it rolls to a stop on the fur rug. I stoop quickly and scoop it up. The weight of it is heavy in my palm. The crest of Reikhaven stares back at me, etched in ruby and brass. The snarling bear's teeth is sharpened into a grotesque growl. Blood-red gemstone eyes glint with menace. I paste a smile to my face and lift my head.

He sees it.

The flicker of disappointment.

Of revulsion.

His eyes narrow, fury flashing across his face.

Pain explodes through my ribs as his boot crashes into my chest. The air is torn from my lungs as I fly backward, slamming against the bed frame. My skull cracks against the wood. A scream tears through my mind but never makes it to my lips.

Before I can breathe, he's on me. His knee plunges into my stomach with a crushing weight. A flash of steel gleams in the firelight. Cold metal presses against my throat.

Olan screams. It's a raw and terrible sound.

I can't take my eyes off the face hovering above me. A stranger. A monster. His face is twisted with hatred; his gaze filled with murder. I understand then, with absolute clarity...he means to kill me.

I whimper beneath him, suffocating under the crushing weight of his knee. My lungs burn. My ribs scream. My eyes dart through the haze of pain...searching...pleading...for Cia.

She meets my gaze, her face stone, her eyes ablaze. She presses a trembling Ophele into Olan's arms, her lips brushing his ear in wordless whisper. He nods and turns away toward the wall, forcing Ophele in front of him and covering her ears. Cia moves. Silent. Deadly.

There's a flash of silver and then she's behind Roimh, a predator poised above its prey. The blade glints in the firelight and slices into the flesh of his neck. Her voice is death incarnate.

"I relish it every night...the feeling of my blade slicing the flesh from your body. The stink of your blood soaking the stones of this cursed fortress. Release. Her. *Now.*"

Roimh snarls at me with molten rage. His hand trembles against the hilt of his blade, but slowly, he eases the edge from my throat. I gasp as his knee lifts. Air floods back into my lungs in ragged gulps.

He stumbles to his feet and whirls at her. Cia stands calm, the shadows gathering at her back like smoke curling from a flame. She twirls her dagger through her fingers, unimpressed, unbothered, and unmoved.

Roimh's voice bellows, thick with fury, "How dare you speak to me, you bloody whore!"

The shadows stir. They crawl from the corners of the room, inching toward the children, wrapping protectively around them like a dark cloak.

I scramble across the floor, each movement agony, but I force myself to keep going. Olan clutches Ophele so tightly her tiny fists tremble. I gather them both, huddling behind the cover shadow, shielding them from the storm. The air thickens. Firelight flickers.

Cia hasn't moved. Her blade hovers, poised at Roimh's stomach. Her lips curled into a snarl, her whole body taut with barely restrained fury. Roimh steps forward, pressing into the tip of the dagger until a bead of blood stains his shirt. Without breaking eye contact, he stoops and snatches the brooch from the floor. He slams it into the table. Wood splinters. Shards skitter to the floor like thorns.

He doesn't speak again. His boots thud like drumbeats in my chest as storms for the doorway. The shadows of curtains slowly leeching into the floor.

I remain frozen, ears ringing as Roimh turns to me. A dark stain blooms at the center of his fawn-colored tunic, the red spreading like poison. He sneers, his eyes wild and lips curled in hateful delight.

"YOU will pay for this." His gaze cuts to Cia, and his voice drips with triumph. "With the price of *her* head."

My knees weaken. The room spins as the door slams. I gather my weeping children into my arms. I kiss their tear-streaked cheeks and murmur the same lie over and over, "You're safe now."

Behind me, Cia moves. The heavy scrape of a trunk against stone. The rattle of chairs being stacked. Her voice grunts with effort, "I'm staying here tonight."

Ophele sniffles against my chest. I smooth her damp curls

and press a kiss to her brow. "See? Audun Cia will stay with us. All is well, my little dove. We're safe." I turn to Cia, offering a watery smile and a conspiratorial whisper. "Do you think we might coax her into telling us more stories?"

The corner of Olan's mouth curl with his smirk. "Maybe Cia will finish this time."

Ophele bursts into a fit of giggles as Cia sticks her tongue out at him, the sparkle returning to her eyes. I usher them both into bed, tucking them safely beneath the heavy quilts as Cia stokes the fire in the hearth. The warmth spreads slowly through the room, chasing out the chill still clinging to my skin.

Once the flames catch, Cia settles cross-legged at the foot of the bed, her fingers painting vivid shapes in the air as she speaks. Her voice is rich with drama, her eyes alight with mischief. Stories spill from her lips: tales of fjords and glaciers, of trolls and towering giants, of a clever mouse who steals cheese from the farmer's cupboard, and a sly fox who tricks a water dragon into giving up her glowing scales.

Ophele yawns loudly, curling deeper into the blankets, but Olan's eyes snap open as the tone of Cia's voice shifts, low and reverent.

"Every year," she says, "as the leaves of fire and smoke give way to the silence of midwinter, the gods awaken for those who still believe. The veil thins under the winter moon. And in those hours, the slumbering gods of Elye may return...guided by the Fates to protect their children from the darkness and the schemes of the Bloodless."

Olan's voice is thick with sleep. "Are the Laioses the Bloodless?"

Cia's face darkens instantly. Her head turns toward me; eyes narrowed in contempt. She mutters a string of sharp words under her breath. She exhales hard and turns back to him.

"No, little Lord," she softly says. "The Laioses are the ones who remember. Who still live by the old ways...the true ways. Each clan honors the god from which their bloodline came. They protect the Blessed. And yes, even the Bloodless."

I lean forward slightly, caught off guard by how different this version of the story is from the one I've always known. The queen has always painted the Laioses as savages. Her proclamations thundered through the Kingdom after the Great War: The Laioses are enemies of peace, corrupted by a stolen power that never belonged to them, extremists stuck in their bloodlust. She outlawed the use of Draíocht and all of those bearing its power in the name of Agderian safety. Any who remained within the kingdom were sentenced to certain death in the brutal mines of Tuathinne.

The whispers among the servants used to terrify me. Whispers of hidden bloodlines. Whispers of Draíocht. Whispers about me.

I glance at my hands, rubbing the tiny scars along my fingertips where she bled me under the light of each full moon.

"Then why do the Laioses attack Agderians if they're sworn

to protect?" Olan mumbles through a yawn.

Cia's mouth twitches into a grin. Her catlike eyes narrow with amusement. "Protection comes with a price, little Lord. The Laioses pay it with sharpened horns and strengthened shields."

He nods, as if that half-answer satisfies something within him. His eyes give up their fight and flutter shut. Cia rises silently from the bed, stoking the fire with slow, measured care. The silence between us stretches awkward and heavy. The flames rise with a sudden crackle, casting shadows across her sharp features. Her face is carved in grief as she turns to me. Her voice is quiet. Broken.

"Love doesn't live here anymore, Brynn."

I swallow hard, battling the tight burn rising in my chest. My teeth clench against the wailing of my soul. The truth of her words echoes like a melody. It takes every ounce of strength not to weep for the agonizing death of my hope.

Cia watches me closely, the firelight flickering against the sorrow in her eyes.

"After tonight," she murmurs, glancing toward the door, "I'll need to remain unseen. I won't be allowed back." Her gaze sharpens. "I need an answer."

I gently untangle Ophele from my arms and rise, joining Cia at the hearth. I clasp her hand, shivering at the coolness of her skin. My voice waves.

"I'll go." I glance at my children nestled together in bed, then back to her. My spine straightens. "We will go."

Relief softens her features, and her eyes shimmer like the moonlight pouring through the frost-glazed window. My heart aches at the peace radiating from her. It is as if some long-held breath within her has finally been released. Something deeper passes between us. A knowing. A vow unspoken.

Cia leans her forehead against mine, her palm cradling the back of my head. For a moment I am reminded that she is my home. She steps away and begins to pace the room with purpose, her steps somehow assisting her formulation of a plan. I watch from the bed, exhaustion pulling at me.

"I'll speak with the Tiene Clan Chief. We'll find a way to get you out."

I jolt from the edges of sleep with a hiss. "No! We leave with you. Only you. I won't be used as a pawn for your cause."

She curses under her breath, sharp and frustrated. "I cannot get you all out alone. I'll need help."

My jaw tightens. "Fine. But once I'm out...I'm free. I *choose* what path I take."

Her frown deepens, the furrow between her brows shadowed. "Give me a few days. I'll send word when I've made a plan. Pack only what you and the children can't live without."

I blurt out, "Do you carry the god's blood, Cia?"

She jerks her hand from mine as if scalded. Her eyes narrow, sharp and piercing, her entire posture suddenly guarded. I flinch at the shift in her energy. Coiled. Defensive. Dangerous. She blinks rapidly, as if pulling herself back from a ledge. I have no time to consider why my question garnered such a reaction as the atmosphere in the room suddenly shifts.

Black, fog-like shadows tear free from the walls like a tapestry being unraveled. They slick across the cold stone floor with an eerie grace, drawn to her like mist pulled by breath. My heart pounds wildly as I watch, frozen in place. The whites of her eyes vanish, swallowed by inky black. Then...light. From the center of each darkened eye, a pale brilliance shines, twin full moons suspended in endless night.

My breath turns to mist. The air grows dense, chilled, as the shadows draw near, casting a cold that seeps through my bones. I cannot move. I cannot speak. I can only watch.

Cia lifts her hand slowly, delicately, with a strange ethereal grace. Her fingers curl through the air, coaxing a ribbon of darkness to swirl and dance along her skin. It tenderly wraps around her like a lover. Her features soften. The sharpness fades and in its place is a soft, warm, peaceful smile.

My chest tightens at the sight of it. My understanding solidifies. She is not just a weapon of shadow, this power within her is a song only her soul knows how to sing.

I gasp as her fingers slowly uncurl.

Perched in her palm is a tiny fox, no larger than my pinky. Its body is made of shifting, ghostly shadow, its eyes glowing a vivid, impossible blue. It blinks at me curiosity, shaking its wispy form as it releases soft trails of shadow into the air. With a playful pounce, it nuzzles her hand and begins to dance among the fog drifting around its tiny paws.

"*Draíocht.*" Her voice is breathy. "The power given by the gods to create...to protect. Not to destroy." A single tear slips down her cheek. "This is what it means to be Blessed."

"It's...it's beautiful," I whisper.

I reach out, tentative, awed by the ghostly fox as it dances through the air before me. The moment my fingers graze the shadows, a sudden burst of heat ignites in my stomach, white-hot and blinding.

I double over with a strangled cry, flames licking through my chest like molten metal. The pain is unbearable. I collapse from the bed, curling tightly against the cold stone floor. My body convulses as the heat radiates outward. Tears blur my vision, mixing with the sweat that pours from my face. I can't breathe. I can't scream. I burn.

Icy droplets spatter across my skin, sizzling against the heat that roars beneath my flesh. I suck in a gasping breath, licking at my dry lips, desperate for anything to soothe the raw agony scalding my throat.

Muffled sounds clatter in the distance. Footsteps. Glass.

The roots of my hair cry out at the tender touch of cold hands against my head. Cia's pained voice slowly comes in clearer.

"You're okay. Everything is okay. Drink this."

Through blurred vision, I catch the faint shimmer of indigo as she lifts a clay flask to my lips. The bright violet of the liquid pulses in the hearth's light. I groan as she tilts it further. I swallow the putrid liquid slowly, shivering as its unnatural coolness coats my tender throat. The fire in my body settles to a cauldron of warmth and then...nothing. I blink, dazed, as an icy heaviness blankets my body. My mind numbs to the world around me with the gentleness of the liquid's lullaby.

Chapter 12

I stalk through the shadows of the alley, waiting for the oyster wagon to rattle past the cobblestone square. The stench of brine and rot wafts nauseatingly through the air. I pull my cloak tighter over my head to mask the sulfuric burn as the guards on patrol shuffle by the harbor entrance. Incompetent fools. I roll my eyes at their lazy gait, their dull eyes blind to the danger lurking among them.

I glance up. A single candle flickers in the open window above Parela's dress shop. Good. He's waiting.

The patrol disappears toward the tavern, and I slip from the alley. My footsteps make no sound as I cross beneath the waning moonlight. The stone wall bites into my fingertips as I scale it, careful to avoid the bell rigged above the shop door. I heave myself over the window ledge and land with a soft roll into the warmth of the room—silent, poised, ready.

"You've gotten lazy, little sister."

The hiss of a blade slices through the air in answer. It embeds into the wooden mantel with satisfying finality.

Eowyn's eyes narrow at my smug grin as he lifts the severed lock of braided hair between two fingers.

"You just had to prove a point."

"Lessons must be experienced, dear brother." I purr, patting his cheek with my sweetest smile. "Next time I will take your flesh instead."

I snatch the bottle of whiskey from his hand and drop onto the worn chaise with a heavy sigh. Reaching into my boot, I pull out the empty flask and toss it onto the table between us. It clinks against the wood before rolling to a stop. I take a long swig from the bottle, welcoming the familiar burn that does little to dull the pounding in my head.

Eowyn stares at the flask, then back at me, his eyes narrowing as the pieces click into place.

"I had to use it tonight," I mutter, coughing through another mouthful of fire.

He snatches the flask, bringing it to his nose and inhales sharply. The faint stain of purplish liquid clings to the inside. He staggers back, his face draining of color. Without a word, he hurls the flask across the room. He turns to me, fury vibrating through his voice.

"What have you done?"

I lean forward, setting the bottle back on the table with deliberate care.

"What had to be done," I say, inspecting my nails.

"Bloody damn Cia!" he snaps. "I'm not here to play cat and mouse. How did you even get the drink of death? Who did you use it on?"

I look up at him, cool and unbothered, though my jaw tightens. "You know good and bloody damn well who I used it on."

His breath catches. "No."

"She was about to ignite, Eowyn," I hiss. "In the middle of that cursed fortress. For all of Hilde's eyes to see."

He slumps into the chair opposite me, stunned in silence. I offer the bottle again. "Drink up." My voice drops. "You're going to need it for what comes next."

The heaviness within me lightens as I recount all that today has brought forth. The shadows at my feet curl with amusement, giggling at the way Eowyn's face darkens as I speak of our visit to the cave—knowledge Ronan apparently chose to withhold. Likely to spare me. The big buffoon.

My heart sighs, longing for the comfort of those bear-like arms around my waist again.

Eowyn abruptly rises and moves to the hearth, staring into the flickering fire as if it holds answers. Its warmth glows along the walls, cutting through the cool shadows that press close around me, stirred by my desire.

He clears his throat as I step forward. My shadows settle reluctantly as I reach for his shoulder and speak low.

"I had Muris smuggle in the Queen's Death when Brynn started showing signs that the prophecy might come to pass. A backup plan, in case things didn't go the way *you* expected."

His head turns slowly, eyes rimmed with restrained pain.

His voice is soft, but it lands like a stone.

"It's a death sentence, Cia."

My lips thin at the quiet scolding. "It bought us time," I bite back. "Time we *needed*."

I step away, retrieving the bottle waiting dutifully on the table. I spin it in my hand, then flash him a sheepish grin.

"Besides, I'm fairly certain the Guard will be combing the town at first light, sniffing for my blood."

Eowyn closes his eyes and pinches the bridge of his nose. "What did you *do* now?"

The rim of the bottle muffles my laugh as I take another swig.

"Oh, you know...just threatened to gut him. Right there in that bloody fucking fortress of his."

His gray eyes flare with fury, and the hearth roars its response. Tiny fireballs leap from the flame like sparks from a forge as he explodes. "You *did* what?"

My eyes widen in alarm as the wood surrounding the hearth begins to singe, releasing a high-pitched shriek. Eowyn whirls toward the flames with a curse just as two thin ribbons of shadow lash from my palms, curling through the air. They strike the fire and snuff it out in a breath, smothering the hearth in their inky black coolness.

Smoke billows thick around us, suffocating the room in choking plumes. Parela is going to raise immortal Hel tomorrow. Silence stretches long and taut between us as the haze begins to settle.

I've known Eowyn long enough to recognize the kind of silence that isn't anger but...shame.

I stay still, letting thin wisps of shadow curl lovingly around my body, relishing the feel of their touch once more. They cling to my ribs like a lullaby. Eowyn doesn't share in my joy. Instead, he moves swiftly to the window to check for any noise or wandering eyes below. Without a word, he draws the sword of his birthright from its sheath. The long blade gleams faintly in the moonlight, cold and quiet.

He drops into the window chair with a heavy sigh, then pulls a whetstone from the pouch on his belt. The scraping of stone against steel slices the quiet. I move to the chaise and sprawl among the silken pillows, waiting.

Scrape. Scrape. Scrape.

And waiting.

Scrape. Scrape. Scrape.

The tension coils too tightly in my chest. I pop up with flailing arms and exasperation. "For the love of Eadom, say *something!*"

"Come here."

I move toward him, muttering obscenities with every step. "What do you want, Eowyn? Throttle me? Fight me? Do something other than this incessant brooding."

He glances up at me, the candlelight catching the strand of red that falls over his face. There's a flicker of joy there, teasing in the depths of his smoke-gray eyes.

"Shut up and just watch."

I cross my arms and scowl at him, rolling my eyes dramatically.

I watch as his calloused hands push the whetstone delicately down the length of the blade. My breath catches in my throat.

The seven Rüin marking etched into the heart of the steel glow a bright icy blue with every pass of stone against metal. One by one, they flare like starlight drawn from deep water.

My heart hammers in my chest, something ancient within me answering the call. Each stroke of the whetstone down steel ignites a flare of Draíocht—a live pulse of it, dancing along the sharpened edge of the Sword of Tiene.

Eowyn looks up with tears in his eyes, and it takes everything within me not to leap into his arms, overcome with joy.

It's happening.

The Fates have finally heard our plea.

But the moment is short-lived. A whisper curls from the back of my mind—a voice older than bone, dark and knowing.

A breaking. Blood for blood.

I steady myself and clear the grief from my throat. "She's ready to leave, Eowyn."

The light in his face dims. The air shifts. The joy between us snuffs out like a candle in the wind.

"We'll do it once we get the children out of that cave and across the border," he says gruffly, sliding the glowing blade back into its sheath with a metallic hiss.

My eyes drift toward the fortress shoreline. Toward the place where the other half of my heart waits.

"When?"

"The men are already in position, waiting in the Dark Forest. While the Lord plays prince among thieves tomorrow night, we'll make our move."

I exhale hard and curse myself for not stealing one more night in Ronan's arms. "I'll need to make myself scarce as the day progresses."

Eowyn nods, his broad frame rising to its full height. He steps forward, lowering his forehead gently to mine.

"We'll get her out, Cia. I promise."

I draw in a ragged breath. "And then what, Eowyn? We just pray to the gods she doesn't die? We save her just to sacrifice her?"

He pulls back and glances away, jaw tight. His voice is hard, emotionless. "Make preparations. If all goes as planned, we will be in Tiene within a fortnight." He turns to me, his face softer, "The Fates may be fickle, but they are not cruel. They do not burn stars just to watch them fall. "

I nod once, solemnly, and slip back out through the window just as the first golden rays of morning split the horizon.

The sun casts its fire across the bay as I hurry over the cobblestoned square, careful to doge the sleepy-eyed patrols. My cloak whips at my heels as I make for the livery. For the first time in what feels like forever, a smile breaks across my face. With each step, my heart thunders louder in my chest.

We're going home.

Chapter 13

Breathe in through your nose and out through your mouth.

And smile. Be sure to smile.

My slight pout softens into a pretty smile, one that doesn't quite reach my eyes but placates any curious onlookers. Polite nods and hollow laughter slip past my lips as I greet the affluent crowd gathered in the great hall.

I hate this.

The absurd celebration of wealth by the wealthy.

I make a beeline for the nearest frosted windowpane overlooking the Dark Forest and nearly trip on the sweeping fabric of my dress. Grimacing, I scan the room for Roimh, my heart stuttering in my chest.

Dagda, help me if he saw.

My flushed cheek finds comfort against the cool glass. I exhale a soft sigh as a chill runs down my spine, a sharp contrast to the suffocating heat radiating from the hearths burning at either end of the room. My breath fogs the window while streams of rain chase each other down the pane in erratic paths.

Despite the festive atmosphere behind me, my mood mirrors the weather...gray...brooding...unsettled. I stare out at the distant line of shadowed trees, waiting for the familiar whisper to stir in my mind.

Silence.

I should find comfort in the knowledge that I am not, in fact, losing my mind.

And yet...

A part of me longs for the whisper to return. It has been a part of me—that voice—distant and hollow enough that I can never hear it clearly but always there...always waiting.

I still can't make sense of the changes rippling through my body since discovering Cia's identity. I feel untethered, powerless, exposed...at the mercy of whatever the Fates choose to cast my way.

Roimh's voice cuts across the room like thunder, booming with laughter and drawing the attention of everyone near him. I jerk my cheek from the window and turn in time to see the ladies of the court fawn over him. Their smiles drip with flirtation. His drunken grin is an open invitation.

He struts through the crowd like a crowned king, drunk on admiration, while everything I once held sacred—love, respect, understanding—is tossed into the blaze of his making like soiled rags.

My gaze shifts to the feasting tables, overflowing with

savory meats and steaming breads. A shrill voice rises above the musicians tucked into their shadowed corner. A small grin tugs at my lips.

Lady Tuathinne's hairpiece bobs like a peacock mid-parade. The orange and gold plumes only emphasize her beak-like nose and wide, gossiping mouth as she flits about the room.

But the moment passes.

I grit my teeth and step away from the fogged window, reminding myself of the responsibilities that chain me to this place.

My clumsy foot catches in the overwhelming cascade of blue tulle, and I stumble...helplessly face-first...toward the alabaster stone floor that glimmers like starlight beneath me. Before I make a complete spectacle of myself, strong hands catch me.

A firm grip steadies my elbow, holding me just long enough for my balance to return. Embarrassment floods every inch of me, seeping from my skin like heat as I keep my eyes down and fumble at the fabric tangled around my ankles.

"I...I'm terribly sorry. I wasn't paying attention to where I was going."

I freeze as calloused fingers tilt my chin upward.

I find myself staring into smoke-gray eyes. He holds me closer than he should, and my heart stutters in response. Flecks of amber and gold flicker to life in his irises—like firelight filtered through morning fog, Autumn sunlight caught in the haze.

"Eowyn..." His name escapes me, barely a breath, as heat tightens in my throat beneath the weight of his gaze.

I tear my eyes away and clear my throat, grasping for composure. "I mean Master of Ships." I nod politely, voice steadier now. "Happy Yultane to you. I hope you've managed to find some refreshment?"

He says nothing at first. Instead, he offers a deep green handkerchief, embroidered in golden thread. I glance down and notice red wine staining my skin like bruised petals. My cheeks burn as I take the cloth from his hand, careful not to meet the fire still smoldering in his eyes. His voice settles into my ears, low and warm.

"No apology needed, Lady Reikhaven."

I hold my breath as I raise my head and return the handkerchief.

Strands of red-copper hair fall loose across his face, settling along the sharp edge of his jaw. The dimple in his chin deepens with a quiet smile, and for a moment, the clamor of the ball fades into silence. The glint in his eyes, the flecks, like tiny rolling flames, pull me in.

A warmth stirs in my belly, roused from its slumber. The same warmth I felt in that nightmare, standing at the foot of the Wheel of Gaia.

His scarred hand brushes mine as he gently pushes the handkerchief back toward me.

"It's yours," he says softly. "Consider it a token of my admiration."

"Why would you admire *me*?" I ask, breath catching, my chest tight with the pounding of my heart.

His face softens, touched by something almost like sympathy. "I've heard many in Reik speak of the Lady of Reikhaven. With respect. With gratitude." He nods toward the musicians in the shadowed corner. "Your fairness is well known among the townspeople."

I blink, unsure how to respond. A thousand thoughts tumble behind my eyes, but one surfaces and steadies me.

"Thank you...for the looking glass," I say quietly. "Olan won't stop talking about it. He keeps asking if it's magic."

His smile deepens. "Perhaps it is."

I reach for a passing tray of refreshments to distract myself, my cheeks hot beneath his unwavering gaze. I lift a golden chalice to my lips, welcoming the rosemary and honeyed wine as it soothes my dry throat and the fire igniting beneath my skin.

"Why, there you are, my wife," a too-familiar voice calls out. "Care for a dance with your husband?"

I jolt, nearly choking on the wine in surprise.

The handkerchief crumbles quickly to the floor as I turn toward the bone-chilling voice behind me. Eowyn steps forward slightly, concealing the fabric beneath his boot. Roimh stands close, the edges of his smile too sharp, his beady eyes gleaming with a jealousy that simmers just beneath the surface.

I force a bright smile and nod, turning sideways to offer the chalice to a passing servant.

"Eowyn, is it?" Roimh drawls, voice thick with disdain. "It seems you're well acquainted with my wife. I assume the hefty sum deposited into your account was sufficient payment for the protection you offered at the docks?"

Eowyn doesn't flinch. "Aye, Lord Roimh. Your generosity knows no bounds."

Roimh's eyes flick between us like a predator assessing a threat. I keep my gaze down, resisting the urge to look up at Eowyn's stance beside me—his calm, unshaken presence a quiet defiance.

Roimh snorts and jerks me close, his fingers biting into my arm. Pain blooms beneath his grip, sharp and immediate. I blink hard, willing away the tears that sting my eyes.

The flames in the nearest hearth burst upward, roaring violently. The stained-glass windows overlooking the Dark Forest rattle in their frames. Screams erupt across the hall as guests near the fire recoil, several already singed by the sudden blaze.

Roimh's face darkens, his round features sharpening into something cold and rigid. His jaw sets like stone, eyes hooded and gleaming with fury. He snaps his fingers toward the musicians tucked into the corner, and despite the panic, their instruments strike up a lively tune.

The dissonance is nauseating.

Mideton rushes in to manage the chaos, ushering the most hysterical away from the hearth. Meanwhile, Roimh offers the

Master of Ships a dismissive nod, bidding him farewell.

He turns, dragging me toward the center of the room like cattle to slaughter. My heart pounds as I glance back, searching desperately through the blue of spinning gowns and drunken stares for Eowyn.

No trace of him remains in the growing sea of faces.

Roimh spins me before him with a smile stretched too tight, then leans in close, his voice low and gritted between his teeth.

"You're quite distracted tonight, Brynn."

He pulls me hard against his chest. I stiffen instinctively, words fumbling from my lips in the shape of an apology. His fingers press into my spine, bruising, as his breath, thick with wine, floods my ear.

"Do not embarrass me tonight," he whispers, voice edged with steel. "Or there will be consequences."

I swallow my fear. Deep. Hard. And fasten the mask of Lady Reikhaven to my face.

To the room, we are perfect. A vision.

His delicate, adoring wife—meek and composed. His porcelain doll. The mother of his heir, waiting dutifully to fulfill his every ambition.

He spins me once more, a silent acceptance of my compliance. And with it, a coldness settles into my soul, extinguishing what little warmth still lingered in my chest.

I avoid his scrutinizing gaze as the song carries on, our

movements precise, our smiles practiced. We dance beneath the watchful eyes of courtiers and merchants, playing our part flawlessly.

But inside me, a storm brews.

I keep my focus narrowed to my breath. Steady. Measured. Controlled. Terrified he will see the truth behind my eyes. The sorrow. The fear. The growing fire that refuses to die.

For the remainder of the night, I remain at his side, barely breathing. Noblemen and merchants wealthy enough to receive invitations vie for his attention, and we glide through the crowd with the ease of royalty. I perform my role beautifully. I laugh when expected. I fall silent when required.

No one notices the scream building inside me.

No one sees the agony behind the mask.

No one hears the voice crying out at the man beside me—at the violence hiding in the tilt of his hand, the cruelty woven into every careful smile, the danger in every word left unspoken.

The pounding in my head reaches a fevered frenzy as the night draws to a close.

I am so tired...

Tired of pretending.

Tired of hurting.

Tired of being *Lady Reikhaven.*

I am exhausted by a life I no longer wish to live.

The musicians play the final notes of the evening as Lord

and Lady Tuathinne descend upon us like birds of prey.

Lord Tuathinne's eyes rake lazily over me, his voice oozing as he croons,

"Lady Brynn, you are quite stunning tonight." His gaze lingers hungrily on my chest. "Roimh, what a gift she's become."

My jaw tightens. I shift, the revulsion crawling across my skin like ants. The pleasantries in Roimh's voice drip with venom, and I know from the chill behind his smile that he felt my discomfort...and that I'll pay for it later.

"She is quite the reward, Perri. Quite the reward indeed." His tone is syrupy sweet. "But not as lovely as your Renoa."

Lord Tuathinne doesn't look away from me. He watches the rise and fall of my chest, eyes gleaming with certainty of possession. Roimh lifts Renoa's hand and presses his lips to her knuckles. She flashes a seductive smile, more predator than guest.

My stomach twists. I lower my head, unable to bear the hunger in Perri's violet eyes.

I am no longer a person to him. Just a prize.

A possession he means to have...by any means necessary.

Renoa's high-pitched voice slices through the air, sharpening the ache behind my temples. Her smile is a flash of teeth, neither warm nor kind.

"Why, Lady Brynn," she purrs, "you look positively fatigued. I'd be *delighted* to retire while our husbands swap stories of their youthful transgressions."

The wariness her presence stirs crawls up my spine.

I remember Agderia.

I remember the court.

I remember her.

The girl who made sure I understood that, queen's grace or not, I was *nothing*.

A filthy refugee from Ravndal.

A mistake the crown had pitied.

And now here she stands, wrapping her thin arms around mine, parading us from the great hall as if we were childhood friends instead of old enemies.

I nod meekly, deflated, dragging the weight of my insecurities with me as we slip into the night—twin masks of charming nobility that hide daggers behind smiles.

I am grateful for the silence as we make our way to my chambers...at Renoa's request.

But the quiet does not last.

As we pass the golden veranda, her voice cuts through the stillness like a blade.

"I'm not sure what all Roimh has told you," she begins, voice low and measured, "but the threat of Ravndal has stirred quite the frenzy in the Capital." She walks slower, words thick with implication. "Rumors along the border speak of ghost warriors. Phantoms who leave nothing behind but blood and bone. Death rides before them on skin-crawling horns."

She stops just short of my chamber door, her words soaking

into the chilled air like fog. The flickering torchlight casts long, warping shadows across the stone as she turns to face me, clutching my hand. Her expression softens, almost mournful in the golden glow.

"There are tales of what those savages do to women and children," she whispers. "Horrid things. Things the queen is trying so very hard to keep from spreading further than the border." She shivers, drawing closer. "As you know, Tuathinne lies closer to the Capital than Reikhaven. An alliance with the strongest military force would ensure protection—not only for your children, but for all of Agderia." She pauses, her eyes gleaming. "At least, that's what Her Majesty wrote in response to Perri's petition...for Ophele's betrothal to my Baron."

Her words hit like a blow, a reminder I wanted to forget.

Shock.

Horror.

Both twist within me, sharpened by the gleeful delight in her gaze.

The hallway tilts. My vision narrows. My breath stutters. Panic claws its way up my chest as the floor beneath me pitches forward violently.

Renoa's grip tightens around my hands. Possessive. Triumphant. Her smile grows, curling at the edges with satisfaction as my knees begin to buckle.

Something is wrong.

Dagda, please.

Help me.

A sharp, searing pain blooms at the tip of my index finger. Familiar. Terrifying.

I choke back a cry as bile rises in my throat, the sting burrowing into my skin like venom.

The world tilts. The hallway spins in a violent blur. My legs collapse beneath me, and my vision swims with tears I cannot blink away. Muffled voices reach my ears—urgent, distorted, frantic. And then...

A scream.

A scream only I can hear.

A scream tearing through my skull as everything goes black.

Soft hands wrap around my waist, gently pulling me free from Renoa's tightening grip. I close my heavy-lidded eyes as the scent of fresh juniper and lavender surrounds me, grounding me.

I am safe.

I sag into Britta's embrace, her strong arms tightening protectively around my waist. Her warmth wraps around me like a blanket pulled from the hearth, holding me upright as my mind floats somewhere behind the veil of reality.

But pain drags me back.

A sharp, rhythmic throb pulses through my pointer finger, echoing the frantic beating of my heart.

I lift my hand through the haze, blinking slowly until I see it...a thin, bright stream of red trailing down my porcelain skin.

My body begins to shake, the taste of ash rising thick and bitter on my tongue.

She will always find me.

Tears sting my eyes as I turn to Britta, her face pale and stony with fury. She cups my chin, her thumb brushing away a silent tear from my cheek.

"Remember the fire within you, Brynn," she says quietly, her voice a tether in the storm. "You come from a great line of warriors." She leans in and softly says, "Your torture is birthed from *her* fear."

I lean into her touch, fragile and desperate, closing my eyes against the childlike wail clawing its way out of my soul.

"Help me to bed, Britta," I whisper, voice cracking. "Before the weight of it all buries me."

We move slowly down the corridor, my body aching with each step. The pain in my finger throbs with every heartbeat, a cruel reminder of the queen's hold over me.

I am her tool.

A pawn in her relentless game for godly power.

I am nothing. No one.

The wooden door to my chamber creaks open, the sound echoing the hollowness in my soul.

I sleep fitfully.

Memories rise and fall in my dreams like ghosts beneath ice. The winter moon lingers above, casting its pale glow through the frost-kissed windowpanes when a sound drags me from the haze.

My eyes flutter open. Disoriented, I rub at them and squint into the shifting shadows on the wall, cast by the low-burning fire in the hearth.

A chill prickles along the back of my neck.

Something is here.

A voice, thick with drink, purrs from the shadows near the bathing chambers.

"Hello, Brynn."

Terror blooms.

I shrink deeper into the feathered mattress, clutching the white fur blanket to my chest like a shield. My body trembles, breath-catching in my throat as the shape in the dark moves forward.

He steps into the firelight.

Too fast.

Faster than I can react.

Fear swallows me whole. My voice rises to scream.

It's crushed as he snatches a fistful of my hair.

Pain spikes across my scalp, white-hot and blinding. His breath, rank with whiskey, coats my skin as he presses close.

My nightdress clings to me in twisted, wrinkled folds, a second skin soaked in dread. His voice rasps against my ear.

"On your knees, before your lord, Poppet."

His tongue forces its way into my mouth, thick and invasive, plunging down my throat with sickening force.

I struggle, twisting beneath him—panic wild in my chest.

His teeth bite down hard, tearing at my lips. I cry out, the taste of blood flooding my mouth.

Fueled by whiskey and rejection, his rage explodes.

A fist slams into my face, and the bones beneath my skin shatter like glass.

Stars burst across my vision. I crumple to the floor, clutching my jaw.

Dislocated.

Broken.

Pain cleaves through me like a blade, and still his fists keep coming.

Flesh and blood. That's all he wants.

Tears streak down my face, hot and stinging as they slide through the cut his signet ring carved into my cheek. I curl into myself, knees tucked tightly to my chest, becoming one with the fur rug beneath me—praying for it to end.

I wait for the next punch.

A voice erupts from the shadows. A witness.

"Roimh!"

A man steps forward from the same darkness Roimh emerged from, seizing his shoulder with a laugh too loud for the horror in the room. "Come now. Let's leave the girl and find some of Sade's whores in town. We wouldn't want to ruin Brynn's pretty little face now, would we?"

Roimh doesn't move.

He stands over me, breathing hard.

When he finally speaks, his voice drips with venom.

"Your value only comes from what is given to *me*." He crouches lower, hatred glittering in his eyes. "If you will not give it freely...then I'll take it. You are *mine*, Brynn. My property. It's best you remember that."

A sickening crack ricochets off the chamber walls as Roimh's boot slams into my ribs. Agony explodes through my side.

My soul wails into the dark void within me.

He stumbles across the room, his rage unchecked, and kicks a chair at the small round table. It crashes violently into the wall, splintering into fragments that scatter across the floor like the shattered pieces of my heart, torn by sorrow's merciless hand.

I try to breathe, but each gasp cuts deeper.

Slowly, I lift my head, heavy and trembling.

Lord Tuathinne crouches before me.

My body flinches instinctively, a groan escaping my bloodied lips as his hand grips my chin, the dislocated bones scraping with burning agony, and tilts my trembling face toward the firelight. The pain in my fractured ribs sears with every breath, each movement threatening to cave in my chest. My heart gallops wildly, trapped inside a body too broken to run.

His eyes gleam—deep violet, darkening with desire.

"So tragically beautiful," he murmurs.

Revulsion surges through me. I try to inch away, my bones screaming in protest, but I am too weak as his cold fingers intimately trace my exposed thigh. His voice is thick with desire.

"Next time, *Poppet.*"

A trail of blood streaks across the white linen of my nightdress, his fingers having lingered far too long against the peak of my chest. I stay still, eyes clamped shut, silently cowering as he rises to his feet.

I do not move.

I do not breathe.

Not until the echo of his footsteps fades down the corridor and the weight of his presence finally lifts.

Wretched, heaving sobs threaten to tear from my throat and shake my broken body. I lay on the floor in silent agony, afraid to move or breathe, as pain and heartache erupt like wildfire through my chest. I lie on the cold floor, surrounded by blood, breathless and numb. The strength I once held flickers beneath the shattered slivers of my resolve. A coldness creeps against my skin like frost. Ruthless. Hungry. Snuffing out the last flickering flame inside me.

I curl against the bloodied fur rug, trembling, my body a broken shell as my soul mourns the light I may never see again.

I wait.

For the rise of the morning sun.

For anything that might still be left of *me*.

Chapter 14

My agony whimpers pitifully as gaunt hands clasp my arms with trembling care. My knees buckle beneath the weight of pain blanketing every inch of my body. My swollen, blurry eye searches the dim light...desperate...pleading.

A broken cry tears from my throat as I'm gently pulled to my feet. I instinctively clutch my ribs. The world spins. The torment swells.

Every movement sends waves of fire through me. My skin protests, raw and torn, as dried blood cracks beneath the movement of wrinkled hands lifting my drooping head. I blink through a curtain of tears, through the one eye not yet swollen shut, and find Mideton's face hovering near mine.

He surveys me with grief-stricken eyes, taking in the damage, the marks of brutality carved into my skin like a hunter's prize. His voice breaks the silence, low and trembling, yet somehow still steady.

"Britta—warm a bath. Quickly."

He kneels beside me, his palm supporting the base of my

skull as he calls behind him. "Help her bathe. Then fetch the healer." His voice hardens with urgency, though sorrow fractures every word. "And be discreet. We still have guests. If anyone asks about Brynn's absence," his jaw clenches, "tell them she has fallen ill and is sequestered to her chambers."

He hesitates before softly adding, "And Britta...tell Sarmien to keep the children away."

A breath. A crack in his voice.

"They mustn't see this."

Mideton holds me close, cradling my broken body against his own frailty. Each step toward the bathing chambers sends a jagged bolt of pain spearing through my ribs.

I gasp. My knees threaten to buckle.

With agonizing slowness, I am eased down onto the wooden stool beside the bronze tub, steam curling into the air like a ghost. I cry out softly as he brushes the blood-matted strands of hair from my swollen face, each tug pulling at the roots with a fresh wave of torment. He chokes back a sob, barely able to keep it contained, and murmurs through the tremor in his voice,

"You're safe now, Brynn. It's okay. You're safe."

His words echo through me, filling the hollow place where my strength once lived. Britta moves swiftly in the background, her footsteps a quiet rhythm as she fills the tub with steaming water.

Mideton gives my hand a soft squeeze and rises with slow reluctance. He lingers, gazing down at me with a look so full of sorrow it's as though he carries the weight of my pain on his shoulders.

Then he leans in.

A gentle kiss presses against my bruised, throbbing forehead. And though he says nothing more, the gesture is balm enough. I close my eyes. I needed that more than words. Through blurred vision, I watch him step away, moving to the door with quiet resolve. He pauses just beyond it, standing guard like a sentinel of grief.

Britta approaches, her arms steady, her presence a fortress. She helps me rise slowly, every moment steeped in care. My nightdress is soiled, torn and bloodstained. She says nothing as she cuts it away. But her eyes…. Dagda, her eyes…they fill with tears she refuses to shed as they roam over the marks of cruelty.

She helps lower me into the bath, the heat wrapping around me like a long-lost embrace. My skin prickles with the first touch of relief, the ache in my ribs and jaw easing just enough to breathe again. I sink deeper, until the water cradles me.

But no warmth can reach the cold lodged in my soul. I close my eyes, chasing peace.

Instead, I find *him*.

The echo of his voice lingers, brutal and venomous.

Mocking.

Triumphant.

Haunting.

And though my body is clean, I feel no purity.

Only silence.

The gentle caress of water distracts me from my torment, trickling down through the blood-matted strands of my hair. Britta hums softly, a mother's lullaby born from habit. Her voice is light and warm, casting a fragile peace over the room. Her hands are tender and reverent.

The water turns red, baptizing me in the remnants of my own suffering.

Commotion stirs beyond the chamber walls, shattering the fragile calm. I tense. My breath snags.

He's coming back.

Terror overtakes me as voices rise angry and urgent. I shake as they grow closer, my pulse quickening in time with the pain pulsing in my ribs. Britta stiffens behind me.

Without hesitation, she moves to stand between me and the door, a trembling shield against whatever fresh horror is about to enter.

The oak door slams open, crashing against the stone with a deafening crack. Smoldering eyes of violence land on me, dark and deadly, but not his.

Cia.

Her mouth falls open in shock. Her chest rises and falls with fury barely contained. Through gritted teeth she hisses, "I am going to bloody kill him."

Shame claws at me. I lower my gaze, unable to withstand

the rage mirrored in her face. She takes in the damage of my bruised jaw, broken body, and the red-stained water. When she speaks again, her voice deathly calm.

"Why is he still breathing?"

Mideton's eyes narrow, torn between diplomacy and the truth he cannot say aloud. Britta looks as though she might bolt, wide-eyed and trembling like a frightened fawn.

I clutch the edge of the bronze tub, my fingers slipping against its curve. I try to speak, try to soothe and stop what's coming, but the words dissolve beneath the pain choking me.

I watch in horror as Cia moves—so fast it's as if she slices through the air.

In seconds, her slender fingers wrap around Mideton's frail, wrinkled throat. He slams into the stone wall with a sickening crunch; his breath knocked from his lungs.

Her voice is a blade, sharpened by fury.

"Tell me where the bastard is."

I whisper through the throb of pain, through the terror that coils in my gut.

"Cia...please...stop."

She doesn't let go.

Mideton's face turns purple, his mouth gasping open as she slowly turns her head, meeting my helpless gaze. Her head whips back to him, her nose nearly brushing his. Her voice is venom—low, furious, final.

"You're a bloody coward. Your hands are just as bloodied

as that sniveling shit's. Both of you. Get. Out."

Britta stumbles back, her eyes wide with fear, carefully navigating around the violent storm radiating from Cia's body. She disappears out the door without a word.

Only then does Cia release Mideton. She shoves him hard, and he stumbles out into the corridor. I flinch, afraid he'll fall and shatter like glass. He pauses once at the door; his ghostly face twisted in guilt. The weight of her words has struck its mark.

I clutch the edge of the tub, wincing as the door slams shut with a force that makes the stone walls tremble.

Cia turns back to me. The darkness that once boiled from her…gone. What replaces it is something far more devastating.

Tenderness.

She moves to my side and kneels, her voice thick with grief as she dips the sponge into the bloodied water and gently presses it to my fractured face.

"Brynn…" Her voice breaks. "My sweet, sweet friend. I'm so sorry. So very sorry."

The sponge trails across my skin with reverent care.

Her voice hardens—not with rage, but with conviction.

"He will pay for this. He will pay for all of it."

Neither of us speak as Cia continues to bathe the shame and hurt from my wounds. I sit there…numb…while she empties the deep red water and replaces it with fresh warmth. The room fills with steam again, but I can't stop shaking. The silence reminds me of another bath where the water turned red like the blood in the streets of Reik.

The chill that overtakes me now feels deeper. That day I feared the world outside. Now, I fear the man I call husband. The true savage that wears a lord's smile.

I don't see Cia's fingers move until I *feel* it—

A sharp, agonizing pop.

My jaw snaps back into place.

My eyes roll, nausea twisting through me as I choke on the pain.

She says nothing as she quietly begins wrapping my ribs in clean linen. The fire hisses and pops in the hearth, casting orange light across the stone, but its warmth cannot reach me. I shiver uncontrollably, the ice in my veins untouched.

My voice trembles as it breaks the silence, pushing through the pain in my swollen mouth.

"Cia...if he catches you here, he'll kill you. Drescher... looking."

Cia shrugs, brushing tangles from my damp hair. "That's nothing for you to worry about." She stops brushing and turns to face me. "I'm nearly finished with preparations. We'll have one chance at this, but it will be worth it, Brynn. So worth it."

Her eyes move over my wounds, her voice softens. "Send word through Mideton when you're healed enough to travel." She leans in, her breath warm against my wet hair. "Your future no longer lives here."

I reach up and gently cup her cheek, nodding through the pain.

The well of numbness inside me quivers and slowly drains. In its place something powerful stirs.

Hope.

It starts low in my chest, then rises, roaring like the sea beneath a stormy sky.

Cia helps me to the bed. I lower myself slowly, teeth clenched. I quietly, painfully tell her everything. Every detail of the night's terror. Every shadow. Every wound.

She listens, steady and silent, as she fluffs the quilt over my legs. The blood-soaked fur rug is gone, replaced with one of speckled sheepskin.

A small, silent mercy.

A soft knock at the chamber door startles me. My breath catches in my throat as I turn wide-eyed to Cia.

Her face is stone—unmoving, unafraid. Not a flicker of fear crosses her features. With practiced ease, she pulls the gray woolen hood over her head and moves to the window. Winter wind spills in from the sea as she cracks it open.

The door handle shifts with a slow, deliberate lift.

No.

My heart pounds, each beat screaming at the sight of her still inside the room. If she's caught here, it will mean her death. Paralyzed terror leaks from every inch of me and I curse the brokenness of my body for not being able to shield her.

Still, Cia remains utterly unbothered.

She steps into the windowsill, wind snapping the hood from her head as stray tendrils of hair whip across her flushed cheeks. She turns to me and winks. Then like a bird taking flight she...leaps.

The door creaks open just as she vanishes from view, plunging three stories down toward the snow-covered ground below. I hold my breath, trembling, but all I hear is the wind.

Chapter 15

I pace the cramped room, vibrating with untethered rage.

He's late. As usual.

Though he'll say he's *always on time when it matters.*

"Well, this matters," I snap, loud enough for the fidgety shadows to hear. They twitch in agreement along the apartment walls, dancing like nervous whispers.

"Hello, little sister," a voice purrs from the doorway leading up from Parela's fabric shop below.

I spin on my heal, practically hissing, "What the bloody hell took you so long?"

"Wouldn't you like to know?" he drawls, lips twitching in that insufferable, mischievous way.

I roll my eyes and hurl my empty wine cup at his stupid, smug face.

He laughs, snatching it midair with infuriating ease before plopping onto the ottoman. Without hesitation, he pours himself a drink into the very cup I just used as a weapon.

I tap my foot impatiently while he performs his little show, pompously savoring each sip. He wipes his mouth on the back of his hand with a belch that makes me grimace.

"Now," he says, kicking his boots up with a lazy grin, "what's got you in such a mood? Even your shadows are afraid of you." He nods toward the quivering darkness curling along the walls. "Come now, Cia. What's so important you had to drag me from the docks?"

I sigh, and the rage inside me twists, yielding to something deeper.

Grief.

"She's been beaten again," I say quietly. "Worse than before. Beyond sadistic this time." I swallow hard, the image of Brynn's face flashing behind my eyes. "Her face is so bloodied and bruised...you wouldn't even recognize her."

He straightens, the tension in his body shifting like a drawn bow. His jaw clenches so tightly I half expect it to shatter.

I watch him carefully. The shadows in the room still, poised to move should his temper spill over. Eowyn has never turned his fury on another...not intentionally. But it takes tremendous control not to let your emotion dictate the power running through your veins. The Draíocht doesn't just live within us—it remembers the gods it came from.

And it behaves like them.

Tiene, god of fire, was infamous for his wrath. Villages reduced to ash by the mere wave of his hand. Entire coastlines swallowed in flame because someone dared provoke him.

I square my shoulders, steadying myself. My own control

teeters close to the edge. A coldness washes over me as I speak the next words, each syllable iced with fury.

"Lord Tuathinne stood in the shadows...and watched... while Roimh beat her face into a bloody pulp."

His eyes darken with deadly promise, and I feel the heat ripple from his deathly still form. I silently thank the Gaia I hadn't lit a fire earlier—Parela's shop would've gone up in flames within seconds.

Instinctively, I reach for his shoulder.

Agony rips through my fingertips the moment I touch him. I grit my teeth, hissing against the searing pain. My shadows rush forward, racing for the raw skin, wrapping around each fingertip with a protectively cold embrace.

"He..." My voice breaks. I force it out. "He threatened to rape her. Said he'd let Roimh watch." I swallow the bile rising in my throats. "He wiped her blood on the breast of her nightdress."

The rage shuddering through him is palpable. His knuckles whiten, fists clenched so tightly they tremble. I let the silence linger. Let it crackle. I know better than to interrupt his fury.

He turns and walks to the hearth. The logs alight beneath his hand, bursting into flame. I do not breathe as the fire feeds on his rage, flickering violently, eager to consume. He stares into the flames for a long, brittle moment. Then slowly, he turns.

His eyes glow with molten heat.

"I saw how she looked at him during the ball," he growls.

"How jumpy she was. Like a caged animal in a room full of wolves." His jaw tightens. "She even cowers when he walks past. It's subtle…but it's there."

Finally.

He sees her as I have seen her for the past year. A woman imprisoned. A woman stripped of freedom, used for the blood in her veins. A woman given every luxury but denied the most basic of human decencies. Kindness. Dignity. Peace.

He stalks across the room, each footstep heavy with the weight of his wrath, an unspoken judgment cast on the kingdom that allows this to happen. He pours another cup of wine, trying…failing…to drown the fire inside him.

"I stayed long enough to gather intel from the drunken fools," he mutters. "I wasn't planning on making a scene…" He pauses, mouth twitching with guilt. "But she tripped over that gods-awful costume."

A grin tugs at my lips. "You helpless idiot," I murmur. "So, it *was you* who scorched half the ambassadors?"

His eyes narrow. The dimple in his chin deepens as his mouth twists—not in amusement, but in memory. In rage.

"I want to burn this entire town to the ground," Eowyn snarls. "I want to cut off Tuathinne's cock and feed it to Roimh while they both beg for mercy. I want to crown that spoiled tyrant with the fire of my sword."

I lean back in the chair with a satisfied smile and lift my cup in solidarity.

"Gods, I *do* love it when you go feral, brother." I raise my brows, grin widening. "Let's level the town to ash. Let them whisper for centuries of the bloodthirsty Laioses and the mighty clan chief of Tiene. Give that evil bitch a taste of what's coming."

Eowyn snorts, dragging his fingers through the stubble thickening across his jaw. I sigh and pick up the needle dagger waiting on the table. I twirl it between my fingers, trying to ease the sudden unease rising inside me. A shift in the air.

An omen.

A sixth sense, gifted by Fuath, God of Shadows. The only reason I've stayed alive this long.

Before I can speak it aloud, Eowyn's voice breaks the tension, low and haunted.

"The gods are stirring, Cia." He leans forward, elbows on his knees. "I saw what happened in the Temple of Dagda. With Brynn."

My hand stills. The dagger freezes mid-spin.

His voice grows quieter, but no less grim. "Whatever was waiting for her there. Whatever wanted her blood on that altar...it wasn't born of Eadom."

Dread blooms like ink through water, staining every thought.

"She was dragged to that altar like a lamb for slaughter that transformed like a Werebeast."

A slow grin spreads across my face despite myself, the image vivid in my mind. Brynn, the quiet prisoner, shattering the chains they forged around her.

"She fought it," he continues. "Fought until her body gave out." A heartbeat of silence. "Afterward, I couldn't shake it. For days. So I sent a raven to Cerwei." He reaches into his coat and pulls out a blood-stained scrap of cloth. He thrusts it toward me, his eyes smoldering. "Eire, their clan chief, sent this in reply."

I snatch it from his hand, heart thudding. Scrawled in blood are words that silence everything else in the room.

The Draíocht awakens with the Child of Light.
The Gaia gives to the One willing and broken.
Death comes with the Darkness.

The blood drains from my face, and the unease within me wails to a fevered pitch. I swallow hard and turn wide-eyed toward Eowyn's furrowed expression. The shadows coiled along the corners of the room rise around me like sentries, responding to the storm raging beneath my skin. I whisper the word like a curse as the shadows recoil.

"Mirákhi"

The name hangs in the air like a warning, thick and vile.

The Serpent. The Ancient beneath the stars. The one Eadom bled to bind. The Unseen One. The one even Fuath will not name.

The one the queen serves.

I nearly jump out of my skin as the window overlooking

the town square reverberates with a sharp bang.

Eowyn shoots to his feet, dagger in hand. I thrust the blood-marked scrap into his open palm. It disintegrates into ash at the heat of his touch.

We turn together, shoulders squared, as I inhale sharply and call the shadows into form. A solid wall of inky black ripples out from me, shielding the room like armor. We move forward as one, silent and sharp.

I let a narrow sliver of sunlight filter through the shield, thinning it into a gauzy gray mist. Blood paints the glass in streaks, racing down the pane as if in flight. I curse under my breath.

Eowyn growls and thrusts the window open. Heat slams into me, knocking the breath from my lungs. He reaches out and lifts the limp corpse of a raven from the sill. Its neck is twisted at an unnatural angle, one talon clenched around a shard of bone.

He yanks the bone free. I watch as the shadows around me dissolve like smoke, collapsing to the floor with my fleeting hope.

Eowyn turns; his face carved in stone. The bone slips from his hand and clatters to the ground between us.

"Tell me," I breathe.

His voice cracks. "It's Ronan. They're being hunted."

I drop to my knees, the floor cold against my skin as sorrow bellows from deep within me. No tears fall. I let fear surge through me, stoking the furnace of my blood and the darkness of my soul.

I will *not* lose him.

I will *not* accept Death's decree.

I rise, trembling but whole, as the shadows seep from my skin. Tendrils of midnight answering my call.

Across the room, Eowyn watches with the eyes of a god— smoldering, ancient, *furious*. Smoke thickens around us, feeding the heat in his voice.

"Tomorrow is fated—"

I grin wickedly, my voice a blade wrapped in shadow.

"Not finished."

Chapter 16

I wince, muffling a cry as the healer prods at my broken ribs. Her frown is sharp enough to freeze the depths of the Gaiad Sea. She forces the bitter tea of poppy down my throat without a word of comfort. Britta's growing scowl is the only warmth in the room. She is my one solace beneath Roimh's violence and the healer's silence.

The healer has tended to my wounds too many times to count. And every time the old woman greets me with the same expression...cold...indifferent...as if my pain is a stain on her day rather than a cry for help.

I watch her limp toward the door, her bony hand leaving behind only a curt word for Britta and a small jar of poppy seeds. Nothing more than ritual. Nothing more than dismissal.

The chamber door clicks shut. Britta lets out a long, audible sigh and turns to me with fire in her graying eyes. Her expression is steel. The poppy seeds are forgotten the moment they hit the waiting table.

She reaches into the secret pockets sewn into her skirts and pulls free the Draíocht-laced salve. Without hesitation, she slathers the thick, pungent balm across my bruised and swollen face. A warm tingling spreads beneath my skin as the Draíocht begins to knit the broken pieces back together. The pain begins to dull.

I close my eyes and desperately try to imagine that the magic can reach deeper. That it might mend the black hole tearing into the center of my soul. But some wounds leave more than bruises. And there are no salves for those.

I am jolted from my longing by the icy sting of the same milky slave Britta once used on my legs. She says nothing, but her quiet care stirs something deep within me, some buried yearning. Her touch is how I imagine my mother's might have felt. Gentle. Present. Safe. Oh, how I wish I could turn back time. Just for a moment. Just to feel my mother's hands.

Britta lays a linen strip soaked in the milky salve across my swollen eye, then turns her attention to my ribs. She rips away the healer's harsh binding and begins rewrapping them with fresh cloth soaked in her own remedy, one soaked in care and not obligation.

Sleep tugs at the edges of my mind, but I fight against it, grasping blindly for her hand. My voice cracks, low and panicked.

"Britta. The drawer. Please. I need the necklace from the drawer."

She pauses, puzzled by the sudden request. I cannot explain, not now, that it's the only thing keeping the darkness at bay. A tether. A ward. A promise of Cia's protection. Britta senses the urgency in my trembling fingers and squeezes my hand gently before slipping away. The soft scrape of wood is followed by a sudden gasp that rings loudly in the dim haze of my mind. I force one eye open, heavily lidded and blurred. Britta stands frozen beside the drawer, her hand lifted. The crude Rüin necklace dangles between us like a charm—rough, jagged, and holy.

A sudden, heavy knock on the door sends us both into a panic.

Britta slams the drawer shut and slips the necklace into her hidden pocket just as the door creaks open. I fight to stay upright, my poppy-laced mind swimming in syrupy dread.

The warmth in the room drains instantly.

Roimh steps inside, his face a mask of shame and carefully measured regret. He freezes at the sight of Britta. She dips her head and hurriedly gathers her supplies, casting me one last, desperate glance before vanishing through the doorway.

Everything inside me screams to go with her. To flee with the last sliver of safety tucked into her pocket. But I remain rooted, frozen beneath the weight of exhaustion and fear.

"Brynn. Poppet," he murmurs.

I flinch at the nickname.

His grip tightens slightly around the item in his hands as he crosses the room with careful, practiced steps. I clutch the quilt tighter around me, pressing my panic deep into the shadows of my soul. I do not move as he lowers himself onto the edge of the bed at my feet.

There's a softness to his face. A deceptive tenderness that twists the knife deeper. The man I once imagined him to be flickers in his eyes, and I hate myself for how fiercely a part of me still yearns for that illusion. For the childlike hope that refuses to die, even now.

"I'm so sorry, my love."

He reaches for my hand.

A wave of ice crawls up my arm.

"I don't know what got into me," he says, voice low, rehearsed. "It must have been the whiskey."

He clasps my limp, unresponsive hand and adds gently, "You know I love you. I would never hurt you on purpose. I just...wasn't myself."

Pain shoots through my jaw as he reaches for my face. I swallow the whimper threatening to rise as his fingers, cold as stone, graze my bruised cheek.

"I'll make this right," he whispers. "I swear to you, I'll be better...to you, to our children. I'll be the man you deserve. Just give me a chance."

His words are like poison wrapped in honey—soothing the wounds he carved, even as they fester. My shattered heart strains toward his promises, aching for something to believe in. But my mind, bruised and battered like the rest of me, remembers the truth.

He places a leather-bound book, wrapped in a pretty indigo ribbon, onto my lap. A gift—bought with my own blood.

My mind screams in betrayal as his lips press lightly to mine.

He leans back, smiling brightly—as if I've already forgiven him. Forgiven the beast.

Curse this traitorous heart, trapped in its endless cycle of pain, remorse, and ready absolution. I *must* break the shackles it still clings to.

He rises, sandy-brown hair lifting with the movement, and turns his back to me. Hands clasped behind him, he strolls toward the window that overlooks the dying garden below. The room's air shifts with his mood, and dread slithers through me. Have I angered him again without realizing?

"There have been disappearances in the border towns," he says, voice cool. "The queen has ordered Lord Tuathinne and me to stop the savages from taking more of our people. Olan will ride with us."

Terror jolts through me. My heart thunders as I try to stand, try to protest, but the poppy drags me down. It pins me to this bed...to this fortress that has become my prison. I lower my gaze in mute submission as he spins back, irritation carving lines across his brow.

"He is no longer a child, Brynn. He must learn his place as heir to Reikhaven."

He approaches, studying the bruises his hands created. I want to shrink away, to escape his scrutiny, but I cannot move.

"The healer says the swelling will fade in a few days. By the time I return, you'll look as you once did. You shouldn't scar." He grasps my chin, tilting my face to the light. Revulsion flickers in his eyes. "Hopefully, by then, your face won't cause me pain."

The sting of his words is a blade, sharp and precise, slicing clean through flesh until I am filleted down to bone. A body. Nothing more.

Hope shatters beneath the weight of his cruelty, drowned in a hurt too vast to swallow. Still, I offer a tender smile, despite the tears that gather and blur the world around me. Death has come for our love. A quiet burial amid the bloody remnants of my heart.

I sink back into the pillow, head throbbing with every heartbeat, as he leaves without another word. The book sits heavy on my lap, a mockery in its ribboned prettiness. I stare at it with burning rage before flinging it across the room. It thuds against the stone and lands in a heap; pages splayed like broken wings.

Britta bursts in, eyes wide with panic. She sees the book, then me. Whatever she finds in my face steals the breath from her lungs. Before I can speak, before I can even try to explain the ways my shattered soul is screaming, she's already moving.

She gathers me into her arms, and I fall apart.

The sobs tear through me, violent and raw. My body trembles against hers, the pain in my ribs sends shock waves of agony through me as she whispers soft words into my hair. Her hand strokes the back of my head, gentle as rain. I clutch her tighter, burying my face in her chest, desperate to stay in this place of safety. In this fragile, fleeting moment where the world cannot reach me.

When the sobs soften into trembling breaths, she pulls back to wipe the tears from my cheeks.

"Olan," I whisper miserably, the name catching like glass in my throat.

Panic flashes in her eyes before she catches herself. My chest heaves with another sob.

"He'll be okay, Brynn," she says firmly, her voice a tether in the storm. "I'll make sure of it."

"H—how? Roimh is taking him to the border. They won't know...won't see him as mine. They'll see him as Reikhaven. They'll see him as the enemy. Britta, they'll kill him."

She pulls me into her arms again and begins to rock me, her voice a steady hum against the storm rising in my chest.

"You let me worry about this. Mideton and I will get word to Cia. She'll make sure he's safe."

I nod in agreement through my sobs.

Cia will protect him.

She will fight Death himself if she must.

The spiral of pain and fear coils itself inside me like a serpent, tightening...but I clutch to that thought as Britta rocks me gently. Over and over, I whisper the words against her shoulder, a mantra between breaths. *She will protect him. She will protect him.*

We stay like that, clinging to one another, until the distant blare of a horn cuts through the quiet.

Roimh is gone.

"Now," Britta says softly, brushing my damp hair from my face, "let's get you another draught of poppy. You need to sleep. Your body needs to heal."

I nod again, even though everything in me begs to stay wrapped in her arms forever. I am starving for affection. Ravenous for the safety she offers.

She rises and moves about the chamber, preparing the tea with practiced hands. I watch her through heavy lids as the warmth of the fire flickers against the stone walls. When she returns, she presses the cup into my trembling hands. I drink it eagerly, already craving the sweet nothingness it promises.

From the hidden pocket of her dress, she retrieves the necklace.

"This will protect you until I return," she murmurs, slipping the crude chain over my head and settling it gently against my throat. Her fingers linger there a moment, warm and secure.

"I've informed the ladies of the court that you're abed with exhaustion. No one will disturb you. And Mideton..." her voice lowers, "he'll stand guard, just in case."

I reach for her hand and clasp it weakly in mine, the weight of sleep crashing into me. My body is too tired to fight it. My eyes roll back, and the darkness folds me into its arms.

But this time, I am not afraid.

No matter what horrors may come.

No matter what the nightmares show me.

I am loved.

184

Chapter 17

A day has passed since I begrudgingly left Brynn's bedside. Freezing rain cuts through the crimson canopy above, worsening my mood and drenching me as it falls from the towering Bloodsworn trees. They are still in full bloom despite the winter wind now slicing through their once protective leaves.

Of course, the Gaia wouldn't make this easy.

I snort, rolling my eyes at the thought.

Whack.

A sharp branch snaps across the side of my head in reply. I hiss, ducking quickly to avoid a thicket of thorns that seem to lunge toward me with sudden malice.

"I get it!" I shout over the thunder of hooves beneath me. "Alright, sorry!"

Eowyn's laugh bellows beside me. I throw him a murderous glare as I yank thorns from my woolen hood. The branches ahead retreat, swaying gently again, the Gaia begrudgingly accepting my half-hearted apology.

Our horses begin to slow as a faint glow breaks through the edge of the darkened forest. My heart kicks harder, thudding with a mix of dread and expectation.

We dismount in silence beneath the tree line, the border to Ravndal stretches eagerly just ahead. My heart drums restlessly, yearning for the sandy dunes and familiar heat of the Wasteland that beckons beyond.

An ear-splitting screech tears through the hush.

The shadows inside me rise, wailing in fury.

My hand flies to the Elkan-hide hilt bound in corded leather, drawing the curved blade from its fleece-lined sheath. The steel sings, and the Rüin marks etched along the edge pulse with a black that seems to drink the light. Unyielding. Endless.

Eowyn meets my gaze with a grim nod.

I drop into a crouch, stepping heel-to-toe through the brittle underbrush. Behind me, his blade hums to life, its fiery heat casting a flush of warmth along my spine. I break left, flashing him a cheeky grin before I go. His eyes are like twin embers mirroring the flames dancing along his own Rüin markings.

The Draíocht in my blood thrums with urgency, a rising storm as we part ways, flanking whatever chaos waits ahead.

Anger rises from its familiar depth and boils over at the sight of broken bodies littering the ground. The Draíocht in my blood lets out a deafening roar at the spider-like creature atop the flailing body of a young woman as she fights against its poison-laced legs that are sharpened into jagged talons.

Nylar.

The name sends a chill ripping down my spine.

What are they doing this far from the bogs of Brucoll, their rotting kingdom of mist and marsh?

I scan the mangled bodies strewn across the clearing, searching desperately for any sign of Ronan. Another scream, raw and soul-shattering, shreds through the air. My gaze snaps to the Nylar as its gaping, dripping jaws descends toward the woman's throat.

Without thinking, I bolt.

I tear through the tree line, fully ignoring Eowyn's shouted command to hold. I run headlong into the clearing with a snarl, my vision red with fury. The Nylar turns at the last second, its blood-slick mouth curling back, the hundreds of eyes atop its swollen head narrowing in on me. Two elongated fangs flare outward in anticipation.

I laugh.

Not out of joy, but madness. The creature thinks I'm prey.

But I am no offering. I am death wrapped in shadow, and I have come to feed.

It screeches, high and piercing, as it charges on massive legs that pound the earth. Venom flies from its gaping mouth in globs of spit that hiss as they strike the ground. I weave through them, growling at its pitiful attempt to stop me.

The black fibers of its body tremble with fury as it suddenly rears, standing on three of its six grotesque legs. It towers above me like a creature crowned in rot.

Then it strikes.

Talons like hooked blades crash downward. The ground quakes beneath their weight. I drop low, sliding across the blood-slicked grass. My blade arcs overhead, the curve of it gleaming like a crown of death. I aim for the place I know it cannot defend.

Screams of agony rip through the air as my blade carves through the Nylar's flailing fangs, slicing clean down the soft flesh of its underbelly. Blood, thick and black as pitch, pours from the wound as its towering legs give out one by one.

I howl in the face of death.

The Nylar looms above me, its fangs rattling a bone-chilling song as it presses me into the unyielding stone. My raised blade hisses, trembling under the steady drip of venom.

I mutter a prayer to the gods, any that might be listening, as the shadows within me surge forward, cloaking me in a barrier of living night. The Nylar recoils, then drives its fangs into the first layer of shadow. The shield shrieks in pain, recoiling from me in ragged wisps.

I brace myself.

The creature gathers its strength again, raising its grotesque head to strike. The shadows around me flicker weakly. Before the creature can reach me, a guttural bellow tears through the air. A roar so deep and raw that it awakens my soul.

Ronan.

I would know that cry of fury anywhere.

My smile widens as I lock eyes with the hundreds staring back at me.

"Death awaits you," I whisper.

Sand and pebbles rain down from the boulder above, dusting my short dark hair in white. The Nylar's bloated body arches back, flailing like a stallion refusing the reins. It rears high, shrieking, and its monstrous legs slam into the ground in search of balance. I step forward from the rock with measured precision, each move deliberate. The songs of my ancestors' thrum through my blood as I strike...twisting...spinning... carving a deadly dance beneath its bulk. My blade sings, and with each loop and slash, I sever its strength.

The Nylar's left side buckles with a sickening thud, my blade having found the delicate joint behind its foreleg. It stumbles, desperate to rise, but I'm already gone...moving out of reach before it can lash out.

Ronan's voice echoes through the clearing with a fierce roar and it pounds against my ribs like a second heartbeat. I look up and see him balanced atop the writhing back of the Nylar, ax raised high, every line of him carved in defiance. Sunlight breaks through the low-hanging clouds, casting him in gold like a god descending into war.

A savior among darkness.

My savior.

Our triumph is short-lived.

The sound of pounding hooves and screaming children rises

from the southern hilltop, echoing across the plateau. I spin toward the cries just Ronan brings his ax down on the Nylar's head. It lands with a sickening *thud*, the creature's body going still.

I stand, frozen in horror as the refugees from the caves, begin to crest the hill in a panicked wave, their faces twisted with terror as they flee toward us. My heart plummets. Lyla stumbles among them, struggling to keep her footing as she scrambles down the slope. A calvary is thundering in full charge behind them.

From the opposite tree line, Eowyn erupts on horseback. His blade burning with fire, the steel wreathed in living flame. His eyes blaze a molten orange beneath the green hood of his cloak, the wolf-bone mask fastened tight over his face.

My skin prickles.

He looks like a living effigy of the god his bloodline was born from.

Did he know? Is this why he waited?

The questions rise, unrelenting, but I shove them down. There's no time for answers. I shift my weight, bracing for impact as I unsheathe dagger after dagger. The ground quakes beneath me, thunderous with the charge of hooves.

Ronan leaps from the Nylar's carcass, horn in hand. Three sharp blasts echo across the plateau. Its low, haunting notes splitting the air.

The warband of Tiene bursts forth from every edge of the field, their war cries a feral song, their weapons gleaming as they charge for the enemy. Ronan lands beside me, his presence towering, solid. My heart steadies, the comfort of fighting beside him wells deep within. I brush my pinky against his. A fleeting moment of intimacy amid the chaos. He glances down, black Nylar blood crusting his face, and smiles.

My stomach flutters.

"Flirt with me later, Ronan of Tiene. I have bodies to dismember."

He snorts, the corner of his mouth twitching.

"After you, Cia of Fuath."

I grin, running headlong into the storm, my heart light as a feather.

Finnick's blond hair glistens red as his blade lodges deep into the skull of a Tuathinne solider closing in on the children near the wooden bridge that connects Ravndal to Agderia. Finn was our closest spy within the Guard, warning us ahead of time of any movement of Roimh's small army along the border. The dock explosion created more complications than anticipated, thanks to Eowyn's decision to leave Brynn behind instead of stealing her away as planned. The young Laioses rejoined the warband, his cover blown to smithereens like that of Roimh's merchant ships.

I launch toward them, where lads barely grown stand tall, fighting with the fury of Tiene in their heart against an onslaught that never seems to end.

All around us, chaos reigns.

Men weathered by time, women clutching infants, children

screaming in terror all surge toward the border bridge in waves, desperate to escape. I scan the crowd, searching frantically for Lyla. But she's not there.

I freeze in place, battle haze shifting into something sharper, more frantic. I drink in the madness around me, desperate for a flash of golden hair. Behind me, my shadows rise in warning. A poisoned arrow whistles through the sweat-slick strands tucked behind my ear, close enough to sting the air but not my skin.

I whisper a breathless thanks to Fuath.

A second arrow comes fast and I drop low, the shaft slicing just above my shoulder. I spin into a crouch, a snarl curling from my lips as I face the one aiming to kill me. A Goliath stands there, reaching for the twin blades at his sides. His face is marked by old pox scars, twisted and raw, enhancing the venom that burns in his dusk-colored eyes.

No words pass between us.

Only the hunger for blood.

I stay low to the ground, drawing strength from the Gaia, each breath synced to the pounding rhythm of his heavy-footed approach. A predator in wait. I count the beats, watching...patient...ready.

Sweat gleams along the pox-scarred ridges of his face as he raises both blades high like a fool, exposing the vulnerable softness of his gut. With a rebel's cry, I launch from the ground, shadows unfurling like wings at my back. My curved blade drives into his belly, ripping through muscle and intestine, vibrating against the bone of his spine. In one swift motion, the dagger in my left hand finds his throat—silencing the scream before it can rise.

His blood coats my face in a hot spray as I rise slowly from the carnage of my own making. I spit on the twisted mask of death frozen across his features.

Agderian scum.

Suddenly, the ground splits open with a scream from the hilltop. Trees tremble and fall as wave after wave of the Banshee's wail crashes through the air, a sound so sharp it carves into bone. I clutch my ears, the warmth of blood pooling in my hands. The shadows close around me, tight and protective. Fuath's cocoon anchoring me in a sea of darkness against the Banshee's assault. Sight is lost to shadow. Sounds turn to nothing but pressure. I thrash within the shroud, desperate to see, to find the source of the scream that's tearing the Gaia apart.

I grit my teeth as a second wave of sound tears through the air, flattening the billowing grass beneath me. The soil shudders free from its roots, dirt, and stone erupting around my feet. Strong hands seize my arm and instinct takes over. I flick the dagger in my grip, slicing through the blanket of shadow surrounding me.

Pain flares, searing hot through my arm.

I freeze.

Eowyn.

The shadows recoil from his flame, retreating into the pores of my skin, Sight floods back to me in a rush of blinding light. I blink hard, eyes adjusting to the sun breaking through a sky once cloaked in storm.

The air reeks of blood, smoke, and death, but there is no time to mourn. The warband regroups, limping into formation, shields locked tight in a wall of defiance as they advance up the hill. Towering above them, all I see is Ronan, his ears stuffed hastily with strips of cloth, his eyes locked on the horror ahead.

I follow his gaze.

Two men stand at the hill's summit. One holds a blade to Lyla's throat. The second restrains a struggling boy in one hand and grips a scepter of black onyx in the other. At the scepter's crown, a deep violet stone pulses with unnatural light.

The Draíocht within me screams, a visceral, wrathful sound. The stone is no ordinary gem. It radiates *death*.

"Cia! Move!"

Eowyn's shout breaks through the haze clouding my thoughts, snapping me from the stone's allure. I don't hesitate but run headlong into danger, all sense of self-preservation abandoned. The Draíocht howls within me, confirming what I already know. The scepter will unleash rot and ruin if I don't stop it.

I vault over the dead, boots pounding across the torn and bloodied earth. Faster. Closer. I must reach them.

I must save my people.

A coldness seeps into my bones as I near the figures standing like sentinels above me. Roimh holds Lyla with a blade to her throat, his sadistic grin deepening with every one of her frightened tears. Rage flickers inside me, sharp and immediate. Lord Tuathinne grins down at my snarling face, lifting a hand to beckon me closer. Taunting.

Sweat stings my eyes but still, I climb.

The boy writhing in Perri's grip thrashes like a caged animal, blood streaking his bruised face from a cut along his cheek. He looks at me and I freeze. His pleading gaze slices through me, carving open something deep and old.

Olan.

The spark inside me erupts into wildfire. My shadows explode outward, no longer waiting for permission. They surge with a will of their own, born of blood, grief, and wrath. I drop to my knees, fingers digging into the soil, and pull the strength from the bones of ancestors.

The shadows strike.

Perri and Olan are thrown back as the wall of night slams into them. The scepter flies from Perri's grasp, tumbling to the grass. The violet stone dulls instantly; its power severed from his touch. But my heart...my soul...wrenches as Olan's small body crumples, unmoving to the ground. I scramble up the rest of the hill, deaf to Roimh's furious shouting, blind to the flame that streaks past me.

I do not stop.

Roimh crashes to the ground, releasing Lyla as he clutches his face. My feet carry me past them, straight to the body. I fall to my knees, gathering Olan into my arms. My hands tremble as I smooth the crease in his brow and press trembling fingers to his throat.

Searching.

Hoping.

Praying.

For the rise and fall of his chest. For the flicker of a pulse beneath his skin. For a miracle in a world that gives none.

I let out a jubilant cry, lifting my face to the sun, breathless with gratitude as my fingers feel the steady pulse in his neck.

Thank you, Dagda, I whisper.

My joy curdles as Eowyn yanks me to my feet, forcing me to abandon Olan's limp body in the grass. He gathers Lyla, sobbing and shaking, into his arms. His voice bellows across the plateau.

"Retreat! Now!"

I blink back tears as he drags me toward the dying cover of the tree line, the weight of the moment crushing every step. I glance back and freeze.

Perri stands tall amid the wreckage, the scepter once dulled now clutched in his fist, pulsing with a sickly violet light. The glow of the stone mirrors the gleam in his eyes.

No.

It cannot be.

The Draíocht inside me screams, recoiling from the abomination radiating from the Lord of Tuathinne like a sickness given form. His gaze shifts, slow and menacing, toward Ronan who raises with the warband for the bridge. Terror claws its way up my throat.

"Ronan!"

Perri slams the scepter into the soil. The ground convulses violently.

From the base of the staff, a thick, oily-black substance bubbles up and begins to spread. Hungry. Unnatural. The violet stone brightens as the corruption widens, devouring everything in its path.

I wrench free from Eowyn's grip and dart into the shadows of the trees. Darkness wraps around me like armor as I scramble up into the branches, breath shallow, limbs shaking. From my perch, I watch in horror.

The warband retreats, led by Muris, racing for the rendezvous point in the distant mountains of Cerwei—*without Ronan.*

He remains behind. The sun gleams cruelly off the blade of his heavy ax as he swings at the ancient wood of the border bridge. The oily-black magic creeps closer, inch by inch, like a living thing thirsting for him. I whisper desperate prayers to the gods.

The blood magic—spawned from Perri's cursed scepter— spreads with a rotted hunger, devouring the dead, leaving behind only ash and bone.

Ronan roars.

The sound vibrates through the trees, through *me,* like thunder beneath skin. With one final swing, the bridge shatters and collapses into the gorge below.

I shield my eyes as the sun bursts through the overcast sky, pouring golden light down on where he stands alone. The grass around him ignites—fire blooming in a perfect ring at his feet. Each lick of flame pushes back the encroaching black.

The darkness recoils.

Tiene.

I whisper a breathless thanks to the god of flame.

I descend, clambering from my hiding place as Drescher and what remains of the Guard rush for the waiting horses in the shadows of the forest. My body aches, each step heavier than the last. I scan the clearing, but Ronan is gone and with every heartbeat, a hollow sorrow settles deeper into my soul

Please be alive.

I watch in disgust from the base of the tree as Perri yanks the scepter from the ground, triumph shining in his eyes like poison. He holds it aloft with glee, basking in the ruin he's carved into the land.

Out of the fifty refugees, only ten remain alive. The rest—claimed by the greed and wickedness of Agderian men. A cry builds in my chest, but before it can escape, Eowyn's sparrow-like whistle cuts through the silence.

A command. A summons.

I tear my gaze from the carnage and retreat...like a coward.

Each step toward Reikhaven feels like a nail driven through

my feet, anchoring me to a weight I can no longer bear. I feel heavier than I have since I fled those bloodstained walls of the Capital as a girl.

Back then, I thought I had escaped the god's cruelty. But now, with each soul lost, each cry unanswered, I see it for what it is.

I am no hero.

Just a martyr in this cruel game of the Fates.

Chapter 18

Pillowy snow clouds blur the soft glow of the morning as I stand at attention atop the wet stone parapet above the iron fortress gate. An icy wind screams down, slicing through the green wool of my dress and sending a chill through my bones. I pull my fur cloak tighter, but the meager warmth against my skin does nothing for the ice settling in my chest...the slow freeze of a heart turning to stone.

It's been days, and he's coming.

His greasy blond hair, matted with grime, whips wildly in the wind as he approaches the gate. My breath escapes in a trembling cloud, vanishing into the gray sky, as the iron chains below groan and clank with the weight of the rising portcullis.

Then I see them.

My eyes widen in horror.

Dozens of men...without the red cloaks of the Guard.

A ragged caravan, limping home.

I rush forward, gripping the icy stone wall to steady myself as my soul plummets to the soles of my feet. My vision blurs. I choke back a cry, fighting the bile rising in my throat.

My Olan.

Slumped over the horn of his saddle, his face hidden. He doesn't look up. Doesn't *see me.*

My skin prickles. His eyes remain fixed on the ground, unmoving beneath the wind's howl. He won't meet my gaze. Something is wrong. Terribly, terribly wrong.

I search Olan's body for any sign of injury, but find none. A heavy fur cloak drapes over his slumped shoulders like a false shield of protection. My nostrils flare as I bite the inside of my cheek, grounding myself...desperate not to unravel.

Perri rides just ahead, holding the reins to Olan's horse as if he's dragging a prisoner to justice. My breath stutters. Roimh follows close behind, his cheek marred by a fresh, seared gash. The wound oozes down the side of his once-beautiful face. His hazel eyes lock onto mine, and he offers a smug half-smile as his dapple-colored warhorse carries him through the gate.

I look away, unable to endure the weight of his gaze.

Behind him, the remnants of the Guard stumble forward in silence. Some limp. Others stagger, blood crusting over their wounds. The truly injured bring up the rear, supported by comrades or dragging their broken limbs on their own. Their ghostly faces are hollow and distant. Violence clings to them like smoke.

They are not whole.

Each face is a mirror, reflecting their own nightmares; the battlefield following them home. Dread settles like lead in my bones

I race down the spiraling tower steps, feet striking stone in a frantic rhythm, heart hammering louder than the wind that screams through the walls of the fortress. When I burst into the courtyard, snow dusts the stone in a thin, deceiving hush. The soldiers mill about in disarray, parting slowly as I pass. In the center, Roimh sits tall atop his horse, waiting like a warden. I scan the courtyard, and my heart seizes mid-beat. Olan's fur cloak disappears into the fortress, shepherded quickly by Drescher's massive frame.

I'm so focused on reaching Olan before he disappears that I barely register Roimh's presence. There is sharp thud of boots striking the cobblestone behind me.

I freeze.

The sound cracks through my focus like thunder, and I nearly slip on a path of ice as I whirl around to face him.

Roimh.

The man I once loved.

His lightly tanned skin now looks ashen, stretched thin over sharp cheekbones. His eyes are hollow. Haunted. His steps hold a different weight—colder, emptier. It's as if he stared death in the face and came back...less than whole.

My breath catches, but before I can form a single word, he kisses me. Hot. Desperate. A brutal tangle of tongue and teeth. The frenzy in his touch ignites something buried deep within me. My traitorous heart pounds, responding to the familiarity of it. His arms crush around my waist as his body presses hard against mine. I quietly thank the Dagda and Britta's medicinal salve for healing my body enough that the pain of his embrace is minuscule.

Foolish heart. Stupid, aching heart.

My mind screams—*No. No. Not this. Not him.*

For the briefest moment, I falter and soften in his arms. In that moment, memory wins. The fire we once shared, the passion that once lay claim to me rises like a ghost between us. For one heartbeat, I forget the blood, the lies, the ruin.

And I miss him.

Gods help me—I *miss* him.

Vengeance floods my mind like a storm surge, washing away the momentary weakness with the brutal truth of my reality. My back stiffens against his roaming hands, my body recoiling in recognition...not of love, but of danger. A consequence of remembering the monster behind the mask and not the loving husband he appears to be for all the public to see.

His grip tightens, pulling me flush against him. The tension winds through my limbs, sharp and suffocating. A cruel reminder of the man he truly is. I brace myself, waiting for the familiar flicker of darkness that lives behind his eyes.

"I missed you terribly, *wife*," he hisses low, the word curling like poison around my ears.

I force myself not to flinch and to relax in his arms with all the grace left within me.

"As I you, my darling husband."

His eyes gleam, triumphant.

Sated with my performance, he turns and raises his voice for all to hear.

"Come! My men need refreshment." His voice rings through the courtyard, commanding attention. "Mideton, prepare a feast worthy of their loyalty. Every man who rode with in the queen's name shall receive gold for his service." He leans in, his lips grazing my ear, voice dropping like a blade. "And you, wife, will ensure the War Room is ready. We have much to discuss."

I slip my arm in the crook of his elbow as he leads me through the throng of hollow-eyed soldiers. Their haunted faces bow to their master and the *pretty little wife* at his side. The promise of warm food and gold does nothing to lighten the anguish carved into each man's face.

The air grows heavier with every step toward the iron fortress doors, pressing against my skin like a storm about to break. A storm that sets my frayed nerves on fire. A pulse of dread quickens in my chest, and I can't shake the feeling... *something is wrong with Olan.*

"Roimh..." I murmur, my voice tight with restraint. "Could I see Olan, please?"

He recoils from me as if my concern has somehow scalded him. He yanks free of me and strides ahead without a word. The iron doors close behind with a hollow clang, sealing me in silence and my own misery. But fear for my son kindles courage to an overwhelming blaze.

I follow, my breath unsteady, as I firmly ask again, "Please. Let me see him."

Roimh halts mid-stride and spins.

Crack.

His hand slaps across my face, the sound splitting the stillness like a thunderclap. My skin blazes while a frozen calm coats his voice as he speaks.

"*Your son* is with Drescher, where he will remain until his disobedience is properly dealt with."

A heat rises within my gut, swelling until it bursts past my clenched teeth.

"I *will* see my son."

His cold fingers snap around my throat as he slams me back into the iron doors, pinning me with cruel efficiency. I gasp for the sweet relief of air as his grip tightens. My eyes water, but I do not look away.

Rage meets rage.

Let him see it. Let him know I am no longer the girl who once loved him. I am the mother of the boy he will not break.

He sneers and spits on the floor. Like a coward, he releases me from his painful grip.

I gasp, fighting the urge to clutch my throat. I stand tall as he storms off, his footsteps echoing down the hall in retreat. My heart pounds, blood roaring in my ears. The gnawing urgency claws at my insides, growing stronger with each step I take. What will become of my kind-hearted boy under

Drescher's hand? I break into a run, heading straight for the War Room, to Mideton and his counsel. He will know what I must do.

He *must*.

He will show me the way.

Mideton waits patiently outside the large oak door of Roimh's study, a feather duster in one hand and what appears to be a small tea cake of chocolate raspberry. He offers it up with a familiar kindness, though his eyes linger a beat too long on the deep red marks blooming along my throat. I lift a hand in polite refusal, my voice still too raw...too broken from Roimh's grip.

"No sense in wasting a perfect good cake," he says lightly.

With a wink, he pops the treat into his mouth, raspberry juice staining the corners like war paint on a child. He licks the melted chocolate from his fingers with a loud, unapologetic smack. The absurdity of it softens something in my chest. I smile, Mideton's ability to shift heartache into a sliver of joy, if only for a second, dulls the ache growing inside me.

I step closer as he reaches for the door. A wave of warm, stale air brushes my face as the wood creaks open beneath his effort, the hinges groaning in protest.

The room is half the size of the Great Hall yet somehow feels larger...heavier...more suffocating. I shudder as I step into what Roimh affectionately calls his War Room, a space where both public decrees and private cruelties unfold.

A great mahogany round table sits stoically in the corner of the room. A clutter of maps is scattered across the weathered wood. Some are curled at the edges as if the parchment cannot bear the weight of his ambitions. Behind the table, an ancient map of Ravndal dominates the back wall; a silent warning of all that can be lost to blood and conquest.

Two tall windows offer little reprieve from the morning light. Instead, thin beams of sun cast long shadows that cling to the corners like ghosts.

Mideton follows, his gait light despite the years etched into his spine. He moves about the room with a practiced ease, as if dust and memory pose no threat to him.

I turn toward the table, carefully skirting the center of the room and the carved bear sigil mounted above the cold hearth. Its eyes, dark and hollow, seem to follow me. I busy myself with the maps, stacking them neatly, letting the quiet ritual soothe my fraying nerves. Anything to avoid looking at the man flitting about with his feather duster.

A blur of soft gray sweeps across the wall-sized map of Ravndal before Mideton finally speaks.

"Some of the councilmen have arrived," he says mildly. "They're in the library—smoking cigars, drinking brandy, being thoroughly entertained by Lord Tuathinne." He flicks a bit of lint from the corner of a map. "Councilman Rickon should here within the hour, milady."

My voice is weak and raspy as I speak, urgency breaking through the pain. I ignore Mideton's diplomatic tone.

"Mideton. What are they doing to my son? What has

happened to him?"

The feather duster halts mid-sweep. His shoulders tense and his head lowers, but he doesn't turn to face me.

"I wish I could stop it from happening," he murmurs.

The maps slip from my hands and scatter across the floor. Panic surges through my chest like a rising tide as I cross the room in hurried steps. Mideton finally turns. His eyes are heavy with guilt and the usual warmth in his expression is replaced by a grave scowl. My lips press tight, my voice cuts sharp and hoarse.

"Stop what, Mideton? What is he doing to my son?"

His eyes widen, startled, and his mouth opens...then shuts just as quickly. I reach for him, clasping his shoulder and giving it a gentle shake.

"Please," I whisper, my voice breaking. "Tell me what they're doing to him."

He covers my hand with his own, patting it softly. His nod is slow, reluctant.

"Olan..." His voice cracks around the name and my stomach twists. "He's being held. Questioned by Drescher for what happened at the border. Roimh believes the lad has pledged himself to the Laioses." He pauses, and the next words feel like a knife in my heart. "He is to remain under guard, with no contact, until Roimh deems him safe enough to return to the fold."

My legs nearly give out beneath me, my soul wailing for the innocence now stripped from my son.

"He's being tortured, then," I whisper barely breathing. "If Drescher is in charge, that means he's being tortured."

Mideton doesn't answer. He doesn't have to. The grief in his eyes confirms everything.

I collapse to my knees, anguish wracking my body. Mideton lowers himself with effort, gathering me gently into his bony arms. I cling to him as reason battles terror, desperate for some thread of hope...some illusion that Olan is merely being questioned, nothing more. But reality sinks in like a stone.

Drescher is neither honorable nor merciful. His cruelty is etched into the walls of this fortress. It's visible in the broken bones and burned skin of the younger Guard recruits. I shudder at the memory of the raven-haired boy, his screams echoing through the stone days after his tortured death.

Mideton tightens his embrace and presses a kiss to the side of my head. My tears soak through the collar of the scarlet tunic.

"Cia was seen at the border," he says quietly, "assisting the Laioses. They believe she's turned you both against the queen." He pulls back, just enough for me to see the fear lining his stern features. "You must be careful, Brynn. You're being watched. If Roimh senses anything...anything at all...he's been ordered to send you back to the Capital." He swallows hard. "Back to the queen."

I wipe tears from my eyes, though my chest still shudders with unspent grief. Mideton's lips thin, avoiding my gaze.

"What are you not telling me?" My voice is hoarse. "What else is there?"

He sighs heavily. "The servants have been instructed that you are not to see Ophele anymore. She is now under Lady Tuathinne's immediate care...until it is determined you are *fit* enough to be her mother."

"What more will he take from me, Mideton?" I choke through another flood of tears. "When will my brokenness be enough to satisfy his hatred for me?"

He pulls me into him again, his hand smoothing the back of my head. I breathe in his lemony scent and nestle into the comfort of his scarlet tunic, allowing my heart to pour out, raw and ruined.

"You will survive this, Brynn," he says softly. "You come from warriors. You may not feel their blood in you now...but it is there. You will rise. And may the Dagda have mercy on all of Agderia when you do."

I pull back suddenly, searching his face. My hand rests on his weathered cheek.

"You must be careful too, Mideton. Saying such things will have you beheaded."

He smiles and pats my hand as if I were a fretful child. "Don't you worry about ole Mideton. I've outlived far worse than Roimh. Now go on, get yourself ready for the meeting. He's requested your presence. I'll finish what's left here."

My chest deflates, forcing a sigh from my tired lungs. I quickly wipe the wetness from my cheeks and rise from the floor, carefully helping Mideton to his feet. He walks me slowly to the door, his energy now drained by the burdens of tomorrow. I kiss his cheek softly, murmuring my gratitude for his unwavering care. He squeezes my hand in return, a silent reassurance as the air thickens between us, cloaked in the weight of impending doom.

The suffocating cloud follows me down the corridor, clinging to my heals. It only retreats once I shut myself in the cold refuge of my chambers. But even here, I am not free. I move like a ghost, adrift in the fog of my own agony. How could it all unravel so quickly? As if the blood sacrificed beneath the full moon at the altar of Dagda had awakened something...some force of darkness now winding its tendrils through the cracks in my soul.

A prickling sensation crawls down my spine. I freeze, unable to shake the sense that I'm being watched. The air is thick...charged with something unseen, something wrong. I dress in haste, my hands fumbling in fear, more afraid of whatever malevolence lurks in the corners of my chamber than of Roimh's fury should I delay him before the nobleman.

My breath comes in shallow bursts as I run my fingers through my tangled hair. I try to smooth it, to compose myself, but the presence draws nearer. Closer. I stumble backward, toppling the chair in my panic. I lunge for the hidden drawer by the bed. The green handkerchief embroidered with gold thread flutters to the floor as I rip open the drawer. My fingers claw at the wooden seam, frantic to release the latch of the secret compartment.

I let out a shaky breath as the latch releases and pull the Rüin necklace free. The pendant is cool at first, then slowly warms, the metal tingling against my palm as I clutch it tightly...desperate to summon its protection from the depths of my soul.

A sharp *caw* draws my eyes to the frosted window. A raven takes flight from the stony sill, wings slicing through the wind as it disappears into the gray sky. With each beat of its wings, the oppressive weight in the room begins to lift, retreating like a shadow fleeing the sun.

The prickling along my skin ebbs slowly, but the fear coils tight inside my chest. I force myself to step away from the bed, though my trembling limbs betray my false courage. I stare blankly through the frost-laced window toward the distant town of Reik, my thumb brushing over the symbol of protection etched into the coarse metal of the necklace. With each pass, I recall Parela's voice, soft and steady, telling the story of the Laioses braids and the strength interwoven through generations.

Reluctantly, I loosen my grip on the pendant, letting it settle in my lap. I wait as the stillness stretches for some shift, some tremor in the veil, but none comes. The hearth crackles suddenly. I flinch with a sharp sigh at myself. The iron gate clanks against the stone, its echo carried by the wind, signaling the arrival of a council member.

I scramble upright and begin working my curls into two

tiny braids on either side of my head. I pull them back from my face with swift, practiced fingers. I fasten them with a strip of worn leather, letting them fall against the hair trailing down my back.

I retrieve the handkerchief at my feet and lift the hem of my royal blue skirt, exposing my thigh. With trembling fingers, I fasten Cia's necklace around it, double-checking the knots in the fabric and the strength of the hold. Satisfied, I smooth the skirt back into place, ensuring no trace remains as I cross the chamber to the mirror.

My fingers make quick work of the milky pearl buttons lining the front of my white bodice. Each pearl forged from the sandy depths of the Agderian Sea sit cool against my skin.

I stare at the reflection before me, but I don't see myself. I see a stranger. A woman suspended between two worlds, afraid of what the next step might steal from her. I am helpless. Broken. Alone. Shackled by the will of fate. My eyes blur and I shut them tight, unable to bear the sorrow that stares back at me.

Mideton's words echo through the silence, anchoring me.

You come from warriors.

I clutch onto those words, letting them settle deep within me. The blood of warriors flows in my veins. Courage and resilience stitched into every fractured part of my soul.

I open my eyes.

The sorrow is still there...but so is something else. A flicker of defiance. A spark of strength. I leave my chambers ready for battle. For that is what awaits me now, in the den of wolves.

I wait outside of the doors to Roimh's study, the chatter within growing louder with each passing minute. My pacing quickens, my nerves buzzing beneath my skin as I scan the corridor anxiously for his arrival. A servant passes, arms full of empty whiskey bottles, but still, Roimh does not appear. Panic prickles at my spine as I gather my skirts and hurry toward his chambers, afraid I have somehow missed him.

As I near the engraved wooden door, soft sounds drift through the crack. My steps falter. I press my hand to the wood, tracing the carved vines as I frown, puzzled. Who would he be meeting here, in private, just before the council?

I lean in, my ear against the door.

A moan rises from within. Soft. Intimate. Pleasured.

My blood goes cold.

Without thinking, I shove the door open. Everything inside me stills.

Renoa arches her back in ecstasy, her body grinding hard against my husband's lap. My breath catches bitterly in my throat as Roimh's hands roam her waist. Her head falls back, and when she spots me, her lips curl into a vindictive smile. Slowly, she presses his face into her chest like a final blow.

My vision blurs as I fight the urge to lunge. To grab her by that gilded hair and drag her across the stone floor until her birdlike face is smeared with the fury she's earned. She has taken everything from me. My child. My confidence. My peace. Now they mock me with this public desecration of what little dignity I have left. Years of dutiful silence. Of courtly submission. Of swallowing pain behind smiles. It all shatters at my feet.

I welcome the fire that rises to my tongue.

"Roimh, if you can pull yourself away from your whore... it's time for the council meeting."

Renoa's face twists in disgust at the insult. Roimh jerks his head up from her chest, eyes wide. I lift my chin, defiantly, refusing to flinch beneath his deadly stare. Let him burn in it. Without another word, I turn on my heel and walk out, back straight, shoulders high, leaving the door wide open in my wake.

There will be no more hiding behind closed doors.

Chapter 19

"What kind of Lord calls an urgent council meeting and then leaves everyone waiting? A complete fool," I mutter into my glass of whiskey before downing a generous gulp of the burning dark liquid.

The alcohol tempers the wildfire smoldering in my chest as I sit silently near the stained-glass window, the coldest seat in the room. My eyes drift toward the crest of Reikhaven mounted above the hearth. Ruby red and frost white banners curl like ribbons around tangled ivy, framing a polished metal shield. At its center, a single massive bear head snarls mid-roar, mouth open wide to display a maw of wickedly sharp canines. Brown and blond fur bristle as if it's ready to lunge.

I roll my eyes. Roimh, no doubt, sees himself in that beast...cunning, savage, unrelenting.

What a joke.

My gaze shifts to the men scattered across the war room, laughing too loudly, their cheeks flushed with whiskey and pride. "War Room." What a name. Like any of these pampered, posturing drunkards could conjure a strategy capable of winning anything but a tavern fight.

Seven noblemen—a mix of wealthy merchants and lesser blooded courtiers—make up the Council. It is not lost on me where their loyalties lie. This is no council; just a mouthpiece for the blood-thirsty queen—her voice disguised in the mouths of lesser men.

My gaze locks on Lord Tuathinne. What a pity he survived the battle just days ago. I resist the twitch in my hand and the urge to tear his dagger from his belt, then drive it through his balding skull. Instead, I lift my whiskey and swallow the burn. It distracts me from the pulse of fury I can feel building behind my eyes.

It was the Gaia's blessing that Cia and I made it back to Reik with hours to spare before Roimh's band of misfits. An icy storm raged behind us, just mere minutes after leaving the clearing, that hindered what remained of the small army Roimh commanded. Though Cia blew her cover by protecting Olan, I was able to remain hidden. Filtering through the smoke billowing from me and the chaos of the battle like a ghost. Those who did catch a glimpse of my face were silenced within the wrath of my flaming sword. Britta and Mideton are the only Laioses left within the walls of this bloody fortress and the last line of defense for Brynn. We will need to leave...*soon*. With that thought, I revert my attention back to the predator within the room.

He sits huddled with Rickon...Hilde's little lapdog...and

Sade, the Master of Secrets from the Capital. I study Sade as his hollow eyes slither across the room. The man has built his fortune on brothels and blackmail, his power woven from whispered sins and bleeding mouths.

Tuathinne's laugh cuts through the air, sharp and smug. Whatever Rickon said was pathetic, no doubt...but Tuathinne still grins, baring yellowed teeth in a way that wolves do before they bite. I watch his every movement. Of all the men here, he is the most dangerous. A bear among mice. Cunning. Cruel. A man who crosses lines without hesitation, who knows violence and savors it.

I slouch in my chair, letting the whiskey dangle lazily in my grip. I tilt my head just enough to look drunk. Just enough to let them believe I'm as useless as the rest.

The double doors swing open with a sharp clang, cutting through the noise and silencing the room. One by one, the men rouse from their whiskey-soaked stupor, trying to blink through the haze long enough to register who dares disturb their revelry.

And then I see her.

Standing in the doorway, bathed in blue and white, she looks like something pulled from myth and memory. The lamplight catches the auburn flame of her hair and the sea-glass depth of her eyes. My chest tightens.

She's thinner now. Hollowed. The softness once carried in her cheeks, her arms, her belly...gone. She looks ghostly compared to the last time I saw her, radiant and laughing at the Yultane ball. The difference is haunting.

And yet...she is still breathtaking.

Her porcelain skin made bright by the freckles scattered like embers across her nose and cheeks. Her lips, soft and full, hold the color of rose petals at their peak. And those eyes...gods, those eyes. A tangle of crystalline blues and greens. Untamable. Wild. There's light still buried beneath the shadow, and I would chase it to the ends of the world if she let me.

The braids woven into the textured waves of her hair mark her as a Laioses warrior...fierce, proud, powerful. She may not feel it, but I see it. She wears her bloodline like armor.

A heat coils in my gut. I smirk into my whiskey. If she only knew.

I throw back the rest of the drink, letting it sear through the growing ache beneath my ribs when movement catches my eyes.

Perri.

He crosses the room like a snake on the prowl, all teeth and calculation. He slithers to her side, hungry and possessive. He watches her like a spider ready to drain its prey. Rage rises, fast and hot. Before I can stop myself, my chair crashes to the floor behind me as I leap to my feet.

Shit.

The room goes still again. Perri freezes mid-step. Every eye turns to me. I lift my empty glass, offer a lazy shrug, and grin like a drunk fool.

"A little too much brandy, I'm afraid."

My apology earns a few chuckles before the men drift back to their conversations, the moment dismissed as easily as it arrived.

But Brynn's eyes linger on me. Curious. Wary. Watching.

I let my gaze soften and dip my head in quiet acknowledgment, lifting my empty glass. A smile tugs at her lips, soft and fleeting, as her cheeks bloom with a flush of rose.

Just for a breath, something warm passes between us.

And then it's gone.

Lady Tuathinne sweeps into the room, her eyes sharp as flint and aimed squarely at Brynn. I see the venom in them, the hatred coiled and ready to strike. Brynn stiffens beneath the glare, her softness vanishing beneath a hard, icy mask. My heart skips at the transformation.

"What was that about?" Sade mutters beside me, close enough to smell the musk of his cologne.

"Women," I say dryly, feigning indifference. "Petty things."

But inside, I feel anything but indifferent.

Roimh enters moments later, drifting toward his wife with the quiet menace I have come to know too well. The hair on my neck stands on end as he leans into her ear. I can't hear the words, but I see the damage. The color from her face drains like a sickness. She folds in on herself, shrinking. Withering. My eyes catch bruises around her throat, dark red and blooming like a necklace of pain, half-hidden by the strands of her hair.

The urge to strike him, to rip him from this world and

every memory she's trapped in, rises hot and hard.

I bite down curses as everyone begins shuffling to their seats, the room slowly settling into its formal shape. I fall back against the cold stone near the window, fists buried deep in my pockets. I clench them tight to keep the Draíocht from rising.

Roimh leads her like a lamb to slaughter, placing her delicately in the seat beside him. She wraps her arms around herself, holding tight as though bracing for a storm only she can feel.

I stare at her...at that broken posture...that fragile defiance.

I dig my nails into my palms, my jaw locking until I taste blood on my tongue, desperately willing the power inside me to stay quiet.

I continue watching her, ignoring Roimh as he brings the room to attention. Her chest rises and falls too quickly, her white-knuckled grip digging into the arms of her chair. My skin crawls at the hollow look in her eyes. Whatever he whispered to her...whatever threat he leveled...it's unraveling her, right here in front of everyone.

And none of them care.

Lord Tuathinne leans back in his chair, and my eyes snap to him at the movement. My blood simmers as I catch the perverse thrill on his face. The bastard is enjoying this... relishing in her panic like it's entertainment.

My gaze returns to her, more closely this time. Strands of auburn hair have slipped loose and beneath them, I catch another glimpse of Roimh's cruelty. Dark, finger-shaped bruises wrap like a collar around her throat. I taste iron as I grit my teeth, rage boiling up behind my ribs. I turn my attention to the true source of her terror.

"Welcome, gentlemen," Roimh says, voice slick and hollow. "I have called this meeting out of necessity and urgency. Lord Tuathinne and I rode to the border recently with members of the Guard. The horrors that lay waiting for us upon arrival have given cause for great concern."

Odd, how he neglects to mention Tuathinne's calvary of men and how he omits the staff that slaughtered the helpless and terrified, that sowed destruction into the very fabric of the Gaia.

He steps toward the carved wooden model of Reikhaven's territory, gesturing as if he commands something sacred. I fight the urge to slice his throat with the dagger in my boot. The men grumble among themselves, shifting uneasily. I drag my gaze away from him, trying to settle my fury before it sears through my control. I find myself watching Brynn again.

It would be so gods-damned simple to bring Reikhaven crashing down on his head, if only I wielded the full depth of the power born to me.

Roimh's voice drones on, painting lies as truth, twisting the horror into justification. My shoulders sag beneath the weight of it all. Without the fulfillment of the prophecy, I will never be able to save my people. And now...I'm not sure I'm willing to pay the cost it demands.

A sudden thunder of his voice snaps me from my thoughts.

"Sir Eowyn, Master of Ships. What say you? Will you agree to lend aid?"

I remain unmoved beneath the glare of his beady eyes. My voice comes heavy, dry as ash.

"Aye. Whatever you need, Lord Reikhaven...it is yours."

He smiles wide, though it doesn't reach his eyes. Nothing does. The rage flickering behind them remains...a wildfire waiting for dry brush.

"Good," he says. "It is settled, then. I will send word to the queen regarding the threat at our border. Reikhaven will prepare for the savages who dare trample Agderian soil." He nods toward Lord Tuathinne. "Lord Tuathinne and I will discuss any future endeavors while we await further direction from Her Majesty." Then louder, with false pride swelling in his chest, "Reikhaven will remain strong."

His eyes drift lazily to Lady Tuathinne, and his voice lowers to a purr. "It never hurts to prepare."

The room erupts in resounding agreement. Glasses rise high, toasting the queen's health with practiced fervor. I lift mine, my glass refilled and take another long swig of whiskey, letting the burn distract me from the sickness curling in my gut.

Lady Tuathinne crosses the room. Her hips sway with affected grace as she glides toward Roimh and Perri by the hearth. I arch a brow as she places a hand on Roimh's arm, her touch familiar and intimate. I shift, scanning the room. Where is Brynn?

There...still in her chair, stiff as marble. She doesn't move, doesn't blink. Her hands grip the fabric of her skirt so tightly her knuckles gleam white. Her brows are drawn together; her lower lip caught between her teeth. She looks shattered. Like something in her has broken so violently it cannot be hidden anymore. The color remains drained from her face, leaving her ghostly and brittle, as if one more breath might collapse her entirely.

Gods. What in the bloody hell did Roimh say to her?

My chest tightens. Rage crackles under my skin, and before I've fully registered the motion, I step forward...toward her. Toward whatever madness has her gripped in terror.

A hand clamps down hard on my shoulder, yanking me to a halt.

"Eowyn, is it? I don't believe I've had the pleasure of your company at any of these meetings before. "

I turn to find Rickon studying me, suspicion swilling in those bright blue eyes.

Without missing a beat, I sling an arm around his shoulder like we're old friends. Cia would be proud that I am playing the spy she trained me to be. My smile comes crooked, easy, and I let my eye drift lazily across his face, careful not to let the heat blooming in my palm betray me.

"Aye. That was my brother, Lanthe, who held the seat before me. Until death came knocking at sea." I tip my glass toward him, voice light. "Did you hear of that storm?"

I don't wait for an answer.

"Came out of nowhere. Tore through his fleet of merchant ships like they were driftwood. Smashed them right against the rocks near Vaniran."

Rickon's shoulders loosen a bit, though the edge of his gaze lingers.

"Ahh, yes. I heard a rumor of such," he says slowly. He leans in, voice lower. "Though it's said that storm was... unusual. Nothing like the people of Vaniran had seen before."

My ears prick at the subtle warning in his tone.

I laugh, low and carelessly, knocking back the last of my whiskey, letting the burn in my throat distract from the one rising in my eyes.

"As curious as believing any story a drunken fisherman spins," I say, sharp smile still in place. "But if you've got more tales, Audun Rickon, I've got another drink or three in me yet."

Rickon's sly smile sets my instincts on edge. I can't tell if he's swallowed the lie still bitter on my tongue or if he's simply playing the long game.

I set my empty glass down just as Brynn rises from her chair and makes for the door...quick, stiff, and utterly unaware of the lustful eyes tracking her every step.

Rickon leans closer, his voice a breathy rasp, thick with longing that makes my skin crawl. "She is quite beautiful, isn't she?"

My jaw tightens.

She reaches the door and pauses, her eyes finding mine.

The Draíocht surges beneath my skin, too hot, too eager, reacting to her gaze and the filth in this room. I take a sharp step away from Rickon, distance buying me a thread of control. Heat rolls off me in waves. I rub at my eyes, feigning a whiskey-induced headache to mask the fire burning there and force out a rough reply.

"Aye, Lord Roimh is a lucky man."

I don't wait for his answer. I turn on my heel and leave the room before I forget what restraint is.

Chapter 20

I gasp for air as if I'm drowning, dragged under by the crushing weight of the fortress closing in around me in waves. Blood pounds in my ears, hot and dizzying as fear leaks from every pore.

I round the corner and brace my palm against the cold stone wall, clutching my chest as my knees threaten to buckle. Sharp, breathless pants tear from my throat, my lungs burning...my vision swimming. Tears streak hot down my cheeks as the musty air coils tighter around my neck.

You will be punished.

Roimh's whispered words echo into a scream inside my skull.

"Brynn, my darling, are you okay?"

My eyes flutter, blinking rapidly as I try to focus...and see him.

My nightmare.

His rancid breath curls between us, thick with cigar smoke and whiskey. He presses forward, herding me back until I'm pinned against the wall, caged by his arms. His palms flatten against the stone on either side of my head.

I shrink instinctively, my spine grinding into the wall as if I can vanish into it. My whole-body recoils as his eyes roam with a hunger that makes my skin crawl. Every nerve within me screams in warning.

A greasy smile stretches across his face, sharpening the point of his chin as he leans in closer. He gleams, sick with satisfaction, as my body shudders against the stone. A cold dread seeps into my veins when I realize that he's enjoying this. Basking in the radiance of my fear.

I flinch at the brush of his hand; a whimper trapped in my throat as his fingers graze the fullness of my lips. I try to stay still, to bury the terror pounding in my chest, but my body betrays me. He breathes against my neck, hot and slow.

"You are my reward, *Poppet*. My sweet...delicious reward."

Bile burns its way up my throat as his fingers drift lower, tracing the curve of my breast.

"I cannot wait to taste you."

Rage ignites, erupting from my bones.

My hand meets his cheek with a slap that echoes through the stone corridor.

For a breath, everything stills.

Then he smiles.

Eyes darkening. Glazed over with pleasure.

He's on me in a blink.

My cry is cut short, a strangled gurgle, as his fingers dig mercilessly into my throat. He leans in, mouth brushing my ear with a venomous whisper.

"I like it rough...though I doubt you will."

My eyes bulge with panic. I claw desperately at his shirt, fingers searching for flesh, anything soft to wound. My kicks land wild and frantic, but he's too strong and his weight is a prison.

His tongue flicks ravenously against my neck.

A choked whimper slips free as his mouth descends toward my chest.

I close my eyes...not to hide...but to survive.

Then...he stills.

A low, murderous growl slices through the air.

"Release her. *Now*."

Warmth rushes in like a tide, wrapping around me like a shield. I gasp, wide-eyed, blinking away the black spots of my vision. A dagger gleams at Perri's throat. Its tip pressed just hard enough that a bright bead of blood rolls down his thick neck.

His grip loosens and my feet meet the floor. Air floods my lungs like fire. I cough, choking on the heavy scent of smoke and sweat.

"You will move from her now," the voice commands sharper than steel, "or face the death I am so eager to give... Lord Tuathinne."

Eowyn.

Perri's face darkens, eyes flicking between the blade and the heaving rise of my chest. Time stretches thin. My gaze clings to the dagger as it presses deeper, another droplet of blood blooms against his skin.

He steps back with a vicious sneer, grinding his teeth.

I stumble away, collapsing against the cold stone wall... shaking...gasping...alive.

My heart races as my eyes dart between Perri's rage and Eowyn's darkened face. The only softness in him lies in the deep dimple carved in his chin, everywhere else is sharpened steel. His jaw flexes with restraint and though heat rolls from his body, there is no warmth within him.

I cover my mouth with a soft gasp. The golden ring gleams in his fiery eyes.

Laughter drifts down the hall from Roimh's study, jarring me back to the danger that still surrounds us. *If Eowyn kills Lord Tuathinne in my presence, Roimh will have every reason to condemn me as well. And if I die, my children die with me. I will endure whatever I must to save them...even if it costs me my soul.*

The bruising echoes of Roimh's fingers give way to the fresh agony left by Perri's. I rub my throat, wincing as I press against the tender flesh. Urgency surges through me. I force down the pain, steady my breath, and clear my throat with a scratchy rasp.

"If you will kindly remove your dagger, Eowyn, Master of

Ships," I manage, voice hoarse but steady. "It seems Lord Tuathinne has complied with your order...despite his drunkenness."

Perri snarls as he spins to face Eowyn fully, a predator coiled for retaliation.

His smile is all teeth and malice as he looks between us. His eyes dance with dark amusement before settling on Eowyn's cold, unflinching glare. I hold my breath as the moment stretches taut.

A sickening chill surges through me, flooding my veins with ice. I shake uncontrollably, my chest burning with each frantic breath. My stomach turns as I watch his tongue glide hungrily across his lips. I can't breathe. My vision blurs and his shadowy smile is the only thing I can see as he saunters away, back to the laughter spilling from Roimh's study.

The world caves in.

I collapse to the floor, my knees slamming against the stone. Pain shoots through me, but I barely feel it. I bury my face in my hands, sobs wracking my body, grief pouring out in waves that will not stop. That will never stop.

Soft hands wrap gently around my arm. They pull, not with force, but care...urging me to rise. His fingers brush over mine, coaxing my hands away from my face, away from my only shield.

I lower them slowly, keeping my head bowed so he won't see the tears still falling. But his calloused finger lifts my chin.

He tilts my face until my eyes meet his. I try to look away, but I don't. I can't. His thumb brushes the tears from my cheek as he softly says, "Not here. Not in front of them."

I nod, silent and ashamed. I turn to leave, the hollowness blooms in my chest, spreading like rot.

I freeze as his fingers graze mine, so faintly I could almost pretend it didn't happen. But the warmth of him presses close behind me, and I draw in a shallow breath, barely daring to move.

His voice is low, unsteady.

"Why do you stay?"

I swallow the ache in my throat, my voice barely a whisper.

"Because I have nowhere else to go."

I do not wait for his reply. I've already chosen the fate laid out before me. His warmth fades the moment I turn the corner, vanishing like a dream. I am swallowed by the frigid air clinging to the shadow-stained stones. The corridor stretches before me, cold and silent, each step echoing with the weight of what I've endured.

I wrap my arms tightly around myself, pressing my hands into my sides as if I can hold myself together. The chill seeping into my bones is not from the air. No, it radiates from the hollowness inside me, from the fear that has finally settled and made itself a home.

I quicken my pace toward the only sliver of safety left to me. My room. My sanctuary. My cage.

Chapter 21

Hush child, close your eyes.
The spirit of the mist has come to say goodnight.
Hush child, stay tucked in your bed;
The darkness is coming among the bloodshed.
Sleep child, for the gods have heard your wails,
And fights for you beyond the vale.

My fingers gently weave through a thick strand of silky golden hair as I hum a lullaby from decades past to the sleeping child nestled in my arms. She stirs lightly, her lips puckering into a soft pout under the weight of her dreams. I tuck the strand behind her ear, pausing to trace its pointed tip with quiet wonder. I reach up to my own and wonder about the blood that binds us.

She snuggles closer into my warmth, seeking the safety I've promised her.

I study the dark lashes resting against her chilled cheeks, the delicate button of her nose reddened by the night air. I see myself in her...a child swept up in the pillaging fires of war, forced to fight for her own survival. Lost, but not forsaken.

Above us, the nearly full moon watches through the lattice of dead branches, like a beacon suspended in the impenetrable dark of the forest. A part of me refuses to let her go...refuses to say goodbye to the ghosts her presence awakens. It feels as if we are kindred spirits, drawn together by an unseen thread of fate.

A single tear slips down my cheek, the only outward sign of the sorrow I still carry for my mother, and for all that was stolen from me in the blood-soaked massacre of Fuath.

I quickly wipe the tear from my cheek and pull Lyla closer, savoring those final moments as the faint scent of smoky redwood drifts on the wind. He emerges from the shadows like a phantom, the fire in his eyes a mirror of the storm within him. I brace myself for whatever abysmal news he carries as he approaches the makeshift camp by the bay's quiet edge.

He lowers himself beside me onto the damp bed of dead leaves, his silence stretching into the sound of gently lapping waves beneath the brilliance of the galaxies above.

"What troubles you, brother?" I ask softly.

He glances toward me, his gaze falling to the fragile form of Lyla curled in my arms. Without a word, he pulls a golden coin from his trouser pocket, the size of his palm. Etched along the center of the coin with Rüin markings of a sea serpent with splayed tentacles. His thumb moves slowly across its surface, a gesture weighted with thought. With a flick of his wrist, he tosses the coin into the murky bay.

His voice cuts through the silence.

"We cannot keep her."

I nod, though it feels like tearing muscle from bone.

"She has the power of darkness in her voice."

A raven cries above us, as if voicing its own dissent. It lands in the tress behind with wary, watchful eyes. I sigh and gently smooth the child's brow with my fingertip, replying quietly, "So do I. And yet your father did not send me to the bottom of the sea."

His pale face jerks toward mine, wounded. I see the pain bloom there before he turns away. He clears his throat and speaks again, not to convince me, but to steady the war within himself.

"These are dangerous times, Cia," he murmurs. "I cannot bring Lyla into the clan...not with the prophecy hanging in the balance. There is already unrest as it is. The people will see her as a threat. A child capable of unraveling the fragile weave of the Gaia...while we're still under attack."

I bite my lip and look away, toward the dimly lit town of Reik in the distance. I force the sorrow back into its darkened prison before any more tears can escape. I will not cry. Not for a child I barely know. I will face this parting like I face everything else...a battle I must survive.

"Yes, I know." I offer him a faint smile. "Though I imagine Ronan will miss this one more than the others."

Eowyn's features soften. He leans close, offering his

comfort, and I rest my head on his shoulder, savoring the warmth that rises like a spark against the chill of the air. The lull of the night settles around us, and in the quiet that follows, I murmur sleepily, "What else has you so unsettled?"

He doesn't answer.

Panic pricks through the calm, sharp and sudden, banishing the haze of sleep from my mind. I lift my head quickly, searching the grief in his eyes.

"Is it Ronan?" I ask, voice trembling. "Is he okay?"

A faint smile touches his lips, and he shakes his head.

"No. Ronan is healing well. The burn from the fire is nothing but an annoyance now. The Cerwei healer was able to prevent any permanent damage. He waits with the warband for my orders just a few miles north of Reikhaven, on Agderian soil."

I sigh with relief just as the frigid tide rushes around our feet and steals what breath remains in my lungs.

The calm of the bay rises into a fervent symphony. Blackened sand and murky water churn in violent unison as if summoning the guardian of the sea with its frigid song. I hold Lyla tightly against my chest, willing the shadows to stand down despite the frantic thrum of my heart.

Suddenly, the bay erupts with towering white-capped waves that hurl the reflection of the moon into a thousand fragmented shards of glowing silver. Pandemonium reigns as the waves crash against the shore, rising higher than the deadened trees behind us. I am certain we are to be swallowed whole, claimed by the sea as penance for the blood on our hands.

The water groans, a somber roar splitting the air and from its depths bursts a creature no land was ever meant to know.

My breath catches, mesmerized by the fluorescent scales of turquoise and magenta that shimmer along the sleek length of its serpentine body. Barbed fins pulse with light, lining the ride of its head and spine, ending just before the massive, muscled man astride it bareback and fearless. The beast races for us on translucent fins that fan wide from each side like the galloping limbs of a phantom stallion.

A spray of brine mists the air as it quickly dives, painting a fleeting prism of color as it vanishes into the depths again. It leaves behind only silence and the stunned beat of my heart.

Eowyn rolls his eyes and crosses his bulky arms, unbothered by the spectacle of pageantry he summoned with the toss of a golden coin. I, however, stand frozen, scanning the waves that topple over each other like drunken giants... straining for any sign of the beast or the man astride it.

Lyla whimpers softly in my arms and I shift my stance as she buries her face into my side. Can I really hand her over? To someone I do not trust?

A sharp hiss breaks the stillness suddenly as a ball of murky water, no bigger than my hand, launches from the crest of a white-capped wave and hurls itself overhead with blinding speed. I twist to follow its path and watch in growing horror as it slams into the raven perched in the tree behind me. The raven shrieks, tumbling from the branches in a flurry of flailing feathers. It crashes to the forest floor, its black wings spasming, choking beneath the weight of the intruder's watery power.

Eowyn moves instantly, curses spilling from his lips as he hurries to the fallen creature. He kneels beside it, already muttering something beneath his breath. I am left standing alone in the ankle-deep water, exposed, vulnerable, and furious.

"Coward," I mutter under my breath, biting down the scream clawing my throat.

My eyes narrow as the sea hisses again, anger welling up from the dark pit inside me, demanding release. I shove Lyla gently behind me in the shallows, ignoring her frightened sobs as the frigid water climbs her legs. Shadows spill from my skin in dark tendrils that weave a curtain of black between her and the approaching threat. My fingers curl slowly around the blade strapped to my front.

A man emerges from the water, tall and terrible, haloed in moonlight. The waves fall silent around him, bowing to his command. He walks across the water as if it were solid earth, each bare step rippling only slightly. Never sinking. Never faltering.

His form is immense, his muscled frame making even Ronan seem small. Deep sun-kissed skin stretches over his broad shoulders and sculpted arms, taut across his chest and abdomen. Bright blue ink coils over his body like living script, telling tales of triumph and sorrow in the elegant sweep of every line. A crown of coral, sea star, and sun-bleached shells rests atop his head, tangled within a cascade of thick black curls that run down his back like woven rope.

A golden staff glows with icy Rüin markings, its surface humming with ancient power. Three dagger-like prongs jut from the top, pulsing with light...beating like a second heart in rhythm with his footsteps.

I can't tear my gaze away. Each of his movements is precise. Controlled. Dangerous. His scowl is carved like stone, merciless as his sea-green eyes find mine. I resist the urge to flinch beneath the weight of his cold and vast stare. His voice crashes across the bay like a lightning strike in a raging thunderstorm.

"Fools!"

I bare my teeth at his contempt. His sea-green eyes ignite, the edges glinting like emerald fire, as if my fury feeds something primal in him. He steps onto the bank, water peeling away from his feet in deference as the rising tension coils tighter between us. Eowyn's voice slices through it, taut and bitter.

"Kailiao. What is the meaning of this?"

The man doesn't answer. His gaze refusing to leave mine as he lifts a hand toward my face, slow and deliberate. I jerk back, teeth flashing as I snap at his fingers. He pulls away just in time, laughing as if the near bite has delighted him.

"I like your little friend, Eowyn," he purrs, his voice like the hush of crashing waves. "Feisty."

"Try to touch me again," I growl, "and I'll show you just how feisty I can be."

His laughter swells as he tosses his head back, the crown of shells catching the moonlight like wet bone. Darkness simmers beneath his grin as he looks at me again.

"I do love a challenge," he murmurs. "Especially one cloaked in shadow." His eyes flick to the swirling dark mass at my back. "Tell me, little phantom...what is it that you hide?"

Before I can spit back a reply, Eowyn stomps toward us, the heat of his fury boiling away the cold that clings to my skin. His voice is a sharp growl, heavy with warning.

"Gods-damned, Kailiao. Enough with your incessant flirting. What did you do to the raven?"

Kailiao shrugs with maddening ease. "You land-lovers are always too trusting. Proof enough lies in the black rot still streaming from that hideous thing's corpse. She controls everything this side of the border now...even the Gaia."

His eyes cut to Eowyn, gleaming with disdain. "Seems all that training with my father did little to chip away that thick skull of yours. Didn't he teach you to test *every* spirit?"

Eowyn flinches as if struck, jaw clenched. Whatever memory Kailiao stirred, it weighs heavily. I narrow my eyes and nod toward the behemoth before me.

"When did you train with *him*?"

Kailiao's grin returns like the tide...slow, inevitable, and infuriating. Eowyn cuts in before the sea-ass can indulge himself.

"Another time."

He turns to Kailiao with a frown that doesn't quite mask his urgency. "I need a favor."

Kailiao clicks his tongue, examining a grain of sand beneath his nail as though Eowyn's request bores him. "The Clan Chief of Tiene needs a favor from *little old me*? How positively charming." He drops his hand and leans forward, the grin still carved into his face, though it sharpens with something colder. "The Draíocht surges in waves now. The prophecy teeters like a blade on a string. The Breaking is upon us." His voice lowers to a murmur that dances with mockery. "So, mighty clan chief...have you come to barter with fate?" He licks his lips slowly. "Bring me the chosen one...and I'll give you what you seek."

Eowyn's hands curl into fists. They tremble with suppressed fury at the arrogance in Kailiao's voice. I laugh, sharp and incredulously.

"You would have us *deliver* the breaker of chains so your pitiful clan can steal the glory of restoring the Draíocht?" I glance at Eowyn, making sure his control still holds before turning back to Kailiao with scorn. "Has the salt and sand addled your brain, or were you born without it?" I nod toward the flimsy cloth around his hips. "That pathetic scrap must hide your incompetence as well."

His sea-green eyes flash with a dangerous glint, fury lurking just beneath the surface.

"One word from that perfect little mouth," he says coolly, "and I'll show you just how inept I can be, little shadow."

I don't give him the chance. I move like a storm...fast, fluid, and precise. The shadows fall away behind me as I close the space between us, my blade drawn in a single breath. The moonlight flickers on its edge as I press it gently against the cloth hiding his manhood, my voice a growl through gritted teeth.

"Speak again. I dare you."

Eowyn's voice snaps through the tension, thunderous and final. "Enough!"

He stalks forward, eyes locking on Kailiao.

"You would do well to remember...it was *our clan* that avenged your sister's death when the harbor burned. We found the slave merchant. Strung him up in the courtyard. Cut out his tongue and eyes...sent them to you as proof." His voice lowers into something bitter, something bruised. "A price that nearly cost us everything." He steps between us, chest heaving. "You owe us."

Kailiao's simmering eyes falter at the mention of his sister. For a moment, his bravado slips. He looks from me to Eowyn, grief flickering across his face in a silent, reluctant nod. I back away, slow and measured, keeping my blade in hand. Eowyn turns to me, and with a subtle glance, silently commands me to release Lyla from my protection.

Regret tightens my chest as I lower the veil of shadow, the smoke retreating back into my skin. The girl is revealed...tear-streaked, trembling, eyes too wise for her age. She steps beside me and slips her tiny hand into mine.

Kailiao's entire demeanor shifts as he stumbles back, muttering a curse with eyes widened in alarm. His gaze locks on Lyla as if she is something monstrous. Eowyn quickly places himself between us. His voice is quiet but resolute.

"We need you to keep her safe until we can reunite her with her people."

Kailiao's eyes flick between us, panic bleeding into fury.

"Have you *gone mad*? You bring a creature of darkness here and demand my protection?"

"She's a *child*!" I snarl, the shadows bristling behind my ribs.

Eowyn exhales hard, rubbing the crease between his furrowed brows He sounds tired. Older than his years.

"I wouldn't ask this if it weren't dire. She's being hunted by the queen...for her power. Either take her and protect her...or prepare to face her on the battlefield." He steps forward, his voice low and steady. "I've seen what she can do. With the queen's control behind her, she'll level everything we've built with a single scream."

He holds Kailiao's gaze, unmoving.

"As chief, every decision we make comes with consequences. What are *you* willing to gamble the lives of your people on?"

The green in his eyes flashes a promise of his simmering temper as he coolly replies, "One more word from that perfect little mouth and I will show you just how inept I can be, little shadow."

The Riacán Clan Chief stands silently, the wind tugging at the braids in his hair as he weighs the risk. For the first time, he looks like a man and not a warlord or pirate, but a leader burdened by the weight of consequence. He exhales sharply, stepping forward and lowering himself before Lyla's trembling frame. His rough hand hovers in the air, uncertain. When he speaks it's low and directed to Eowyn.

"Tala will take her for now. I'll offer my protection…until it's safe. But I want something in return for this risk."

Eowyn's face hardens, lips thinning. His voice crackles with heat.

"As you wish."

I roll my eyes so hard that I am certain they will fall out of my skull. The Water Clan is always bartering, always bleeding every favor dry. No deed is ever done without cost. No loyalty ever comes clean. Ronan was right. This eel of a man would trade his own shadow if it meant profit.

My fists clench as Kailiao reaches for Lyla's neck. He speaks softly; a whisper meant only for her.

"This will sting, but you mustn't scream."

Lyla wipes her nose with the back of her hand. Her lip quivers, but she lifts her chin with quiet resolve.

"I will be brave."

The three-pronged staff sparks to life in Kailiao's grip, each tip igniting in a brilliant, electric blue. His hand lightly touches the soft curve of her neck as the Draíocht surges down his arm, setting his tattoos aglow. Jagged waves of light flicker across Lyla's ghost-white face as she clutches my hand tightly, trembling violently. He lifts up his arm, the tattoos on his skin illuminating the ghostly expression on Lyla's quivering face. Her hand tightens in mine as she bites down on her tongue until blood seeps from her mouth. Her eyes roll back as she slips from my grasp and collapses into the sand.

I drop to my knees as Kailiao scoops her limp form into his arms. Three crimson, feathery gills pulse on her neck where his fingers touched her. The sight guts me.

Without another word, he turns and steps onto the sea as if it were solid ground, the waves parting around his feet. At the edge of the horizon, he glances back.

"I will come for my payment, soon," he calls to Eowyn. His gaze flicks to me and a wicked grin splits his face. "Until next time, little shadow."

I say nothing as the sea swallows them. I just watch, silent and aching, as they vanish into the depths. My lips barely move as I whisper a prayer to Fuath for Lyla's protection. Eowyn lays a hand on my shoulder.

"Come. There are things we must attend to."

A tear tracks down my cheek. I swipe it away and mutter through clenched teeth, "It can wait one gods-forsaken minute, Eowyn." His hand squeezes mine gently. "It's Brynn. Come."

Peace, joy, and prosperity...always just beyond reach. I feel the last of my strength unravel as I rise and follow him. My step falters.

At the place where the raven had once stood, only ash and smear of oily residue remain.

Damn the queen.

Damn them all.

We walk in silence toward the dead brush concealing the trapdoor, neither of us eager to speak. The Laioses have infiltrated Agderia with similar designs throughout the gods-forsaken country. Hidden rooms beneath taverns, where the revelry and drunkenness of patrons is clothed in shadows, carved out in secret over the years. The shadows feel familiar, even comforting, as Eowyn disappears down the ladder into the dark. I hesitate before following, the dread already crawling up my spine.

I shut the rickety door behind us. I can't tell if the unease gnawing at me is a warning from the Fates, or just the weight of everything we've lost pressing down again. It's getting harder to tell the difference.

The air down here is damp and stale, but I pull in a breath anyway to calm the storm building in my chest. Eowyn lifts a hand and sparks a small flame at his fingertip, casting the tunnel into a dance of shadow and light. For a moment, I'm distracted by the muffled sounds of laughter and music coming from above. The tavern is still alive. Even with the Guard crawling through the streets, the people of Reik are packed tightly, drinking and pretending that none of this is real. That their city isn't crumbling. That the Laioses haven't already bled it dry.

The flame dies in Eowyn's hand and the dark closes in.

Most people fear the dark. They think it's where all the monsters hide. I've seen enough to know better. The real monsters don't need the dark to do their work...they stand in daylight, smiling while they tear the world apart.

The dark doesn't frighten me. It never has.

It's what lives inside the light that should.

Three soft taps answer Eowyn's knock before light spills into the tunnel. A young barmaid hurries us inside an empty room and quietly places a draught of mead on the wooden table near the hearth. She doesn't meet my eyes...too busy sneaking flirty glances at Eowyn, who, as usual remains completely oblivious as she hands him a mug.

"Sarai, that'll be all," I mutter, sharper than I intend.

Her cheeks flush as she ducks her head and all but scurries out, probably thinking I'll dock her wages for daring to eye him. I snort under my breath. As if I'd punish a girl for doing what any warm-blooded fool might, given the way he looks.

I drop into the chair and shove a cube of cheese into my

mouth, then rip a chunk off the stale loaf of bread left behind. It's dry and hard, but it quiets the growl in my gut. Good enough.

Eowyn takes a long pull from his mug and wipes the mead from his mouth with the back of his hand. He eyes my less-than-graceful eating with a crooked smile and drops down onto the makeshift bed in the corner.

"Don't get mud on my quilt," I say, mouth full, tearing off another bite of bread.

He stares into the fire, eyes tracking the flames like they might whisper some answer he's been searching for. Gods know what battle plan he's working through in that lug head of his. I toss the last bit of bread at him, and it bounces off his arm.

"You're too damn skinny," I say. "Ronan's going to think I'm starving his baby brother."

Eowyn blinks back into the present with a half-smile, tearing the bread with his teeth like a damn buffoon. I tip my mug back eagerly, letting the mead soften the stale bread just enough to choke it down.

"What fresh disaster now?" I mutter.

The mug in my hand ices over, thin crystals spreading across the rim as my shadows lurch along the stone walls, dancing in furious rhythm to the news Eowyn lays before me. The promise made to that bloodthirsty wretch ruling Tuathinne.

He finishes grimly, "Kailiao's little display with the raven was enough for me. Queen Hilde has eyes and ears in every corner. It's too risky to send word to Ronan. I'll go myself before daybreak to gather the warband. I need you to find out where Roimh is keeping the children and the cleanest way in. Ronan's last missive said Tuathinne's forces were still camped along the forest border, but that may have changed."

He pulls a worn map from the chest at the end of my bed and spreads it across the table, smoothing it flat with a calloused hand. "We meet here, tomorrow night."

He taps a finger to a cluster of trees jutting from the Dark Forest toward the fortress walls. "Just get me a way inside; one hidden from the sentries posted on the towers and parapets. Then we'll take them all back, right under that bastard's nose."

A thrill shudders through me. I sip my mead with a crooked smile, letting the warmth of it settle in my chest. It's almost time. This wretched waiting is nearly over. Soon, we'll leave this gods-forsaken kingdom behind and return to Tiene.

Home.

I've missed it with every breath in my body. I miss the way the sunlight bleeds across the mountains, igniting the village in a fiery glow. The fellowship in the mead hall. The laughter. The feeling of Ronan's arms wrapped around me like armor. The brisk, sharp woodsy scent that drifts through the redwood forest.

I close my eyes, heart fluttering with relief and lean back into the chair. In the quiet, I listen to the rasp of Eowyn's whetstone against his Draíocht-filled blade and let myself dream of a life beyond the tyranny woven into every stone of this cursed land.

Chapter 22

The low red embers spark to life as I stoke the fire Britta built in my hearth earlier. The small flames offer little warmth as I change quickly into my nightdress, haphazardly untying the necklace secured at my thigh, and slip under the quilts to warm my icy feet. I remain rigid, clutching the Rüin mark in my hand until my palm aches, tensing with each sound of movement outside the sanctuary of my room.

I should be accustomed to living in constant fear and yet each time I feel as if I will drown in it. I wonder why I fight so hard to live when it would be easier to just give up and sink to the bottom of my misery. My entire life I have only survived, never have I truly lived. Renoa's merciless torture as a child, the pain of the queen's clawed nails digging into my fingertips every full moon, Roimh's broken promises and the hatred oozing from every word that crosses his lips. I do not understand their motivation, their need to break me, their incessant need to remind me of who is in charge. From the moment I was handed over as a gift to Agderia I had no choice but to bend to someone else's will. Even when it hurt.

I snuggle deeper into the covers, wishing the soft layer of quilts could protect me within their folds. Sleep calls to me, a weariness deep within my bones. I clutch the necklace once more, praying to the Dagda for my protection, and slip the necklace under my pillow—close enough to shield me without being detected. My heavy-lidded eyes close as I repeat Mideton's words over and over. If I say it enough, maybe. just maybe, courage will arise and save me before it is too late.

I come from warriors.

I jolt awake to the skin-crawling creak of my chamber door opening. My heart threatens to leave my body as I reach instinctively for the necklace under my pillow. In a panic, I fumble through the covers for the touch of cold metal, keeping a watchful eye for any movement despite the limited light coming from the hot coals burning in the hearth. Elongated shadows blanket the room in near darkness—shadows hiding the demon who has come to collect his reward.

My stomach turns violently at the smell of stale brandy and smoke filling my nose. I move quickly to the furthest part of the bed and draw my legs to my chest tightly, praying to the sleeping gods to keep me from his grasp. My mind races with a cascade of terror, as my eyes search frantically for him. I tremble as the smell draws closer to me, stifling a loud sob as hot needles of fear viciously stab me in the chest.

He uses the darkness of the room to his advantage, slinking closer like an animal stalking its prey. I am completely at the mercy of his desire. A conquest for his own taking. My throat burns angrily as I swallow bile. I can feel my fear, taste it, as if it too creeps with him. The roar in my mind swallows me whole as he steps into the pale light illuminating the end of my refuge.

"Let's play a little game, *Poppet.*"

His use of Roimh's nickname for me is like claws ripping down my spine. He inhales deeply, his purple-hued eyes dance with delight.

Desire weighs heavy on his tongue as he moans, "I do love the smell of your fear."

I have no time to react as he lunges for me with the fervor of a wild animal. He snatches my legs, pulling me toward him and forcing my body flat across the bed. I fight with the blood of a warrior rushing through my veins. I twist and kick wildly. I do everything I possibly can to loosen his hold on me, to free me from this hell. I desperately reach for the shadows just beyond my grasp.

He growls low with excitement as he digs his knees into my legs, pinning me in place—ensnaring me under the weight of his body. I am trapped. I cannot breathe. I cannot move. I cannot escape. My terror echoes across the stone walls as his nails claw into the flesh of my stomach, ripping the nightdress and exposing me to his greedy hunger. Teeth rip into the curve of my neck and I surrender to the numbness flooding me as he releases a throaty moan.

I shudder as his cold hand roams down the tattered fabric

of my exposed chest and stomach—his touch like icy slivers digging into flesh. I flail my arms frantically searching for my last ounce of hope tied to a leather cord. His hand travels further down and the dark walls of my room, my only sanctuary, closes in on me. His mouth devours my scream as bitterness coats my tongue with the taste of his sweat.

I close my eyes, shrinking into my own skin as hot tears roll down my cheeks. He positions himself on top of me as his cold hands roughly roam my body. My eyes fling open with horror and my mind thrashes—shrieking inside my skull. Biting flames engulf my chest, desperate for the air that does not come.

The cold skin of his cheek finds a home beneath my nails as I claw and fight with every fiber of my being to prevent the loss of my soul. The heaviness of his body frees me slightly as he sits up and touches the blood seeping from his face. My mind crumbles to ash as he looks at my rebellion forged in blood with sickening desire. I reach one last time into the darkness seeking the rough coolness of metal. The tips of my fingers burn, and I know I have found what I am searching for.

Ferocious anger explodes from within me as his wet tongue dances up my neck. I do not think. I do not feel. I just move with the wild beat of my heart and slam the jagged end of the Rüin marking into his exposed neck. The necklace vibrates in my hand as I stab him again and again until bright red blood pours from the tiny holes in his neck. A small smile creeps across my mouth as I watch the blood drip and splatter against my porcelain skin—staining it with his pain.

The room erupts with his roar as he slaps me hard on the mouth. I cringe under the metallic taste of my blood racing from my nose and down my throat. He jumps back from the bed, wrestling with my hand for the object of his torture, but I do not yield. He snatches me by my hair and my bones weep as my body hits the floor with a loud crack. My hand releases my only weapon, and I scramble back as it lands at his feet

I tremble as he calmly scoops the blood-soaked leather cord and dangles the necklace before him. Recognition crosses his face, and he spits at the ground in disgust, slinging the necklace into the coals festering in the hearth. The embers awaken, roaring to life, consuming the leather in its fiery thirst until the metal glows an icy blue. His eyes narrow at the sight with a vicious smile though he walks calmly to the table. I flinch as he stomps a chair leg free. I watch in paralyzing fear as he crouches at the hearth, twirling the splintered wood in the deep orange flames.

"You disappoint me, Brynn." The eerie calmness of his voice takes my breath away as he continues, "It is your duty to uphold the integrity of this land. Yet, you have disgraced your favor by drawing the blood of another lord, an ally, and *friend.*"

My bloody fingers dig into the stone floor as I painfully crawl to the door. He clicks his tongue in disgust as he turns to me with darkened delight. I freeze as he stands and shrink under the strained viciousness of his voice.

"I do wonder what Roimh will have planned for you when he finds out his pretty little wife..." He glances back at the Rüin marking engulfed in bright blue flames and turns to me with renewed fury. "Has allied herself with barbarians."

His face darkens grotesquely as the shadows close in around him. I whimper as shivers of shock run through me and I cower under the darkened gaze of his blackened eyes filling with evil intent. He holds the makeshift poker like a sword of suffering before him, the tip glowing hot. A familiar crack bounces off the stone wall as his boot hits hard against my hip. I flail across the floor, my chest heaving as I land hard on my back. I struggle for breath as his heavy boots thud slowly against stone.

He crouches down as he nears, and I frantically shrink from the hot embers that drop onto my naked skin as he toys carelessly with the glowing poker in his hands.

"Where, oh where, did you obtain such an enchanting little necklace, Poppet? Was it your little knight in shining armor, the one that interrupted our little game in the hall?"

I recoil at the mention of Eowyn and turn my widened eyes to meet his eager gaze. He croons with deepening delight.

"It seems as if our *Master of Ships* is not who he claims to be."

A wicked smile slithers across his face as he reaches down and pulls my leg rigidly straight with his freed hand. I close my eyes and sob as his hand moves up my thigh, ripping the tattered cotton fabric from my body. He holds my leg under the weight of his own and my tender flesh shrieks wildly at the heat nearing my inner thigh. I drown in his breathy growl.

"Scream for me, *Poppet*."

Chapter 23

Cia's soft snores fill the silence of the tiny hidden room as the crowd in the tavern below us drunkenly finds their way home with the waning night. I quietly place a fur blanket over her, and she cuddles up in the chair with a soft smile. She came to us half-starved and covered in filth a year after my mother's death. She was a comfort to my broken heart and quickly became far more than an outsider seeking refuge, but a sister in need of guidance and protection.

My father took great interest in her shadow-born power and as the sickness overcame his mind so did his manipulation of those powers; sending her off to spy within the Capital when she became "of age" despite Ronan's and my vehement protests. She returned to us covered in her own blood, her mind so fractured even her shadows seemed broken. Something terrible happened to her within those iron-clad walls, something she keeps hidden within the depths of her heart. It was then that Ronan and I vowed to never again let anyone else abuse her power for their own gain. I cannot help but think that I am following in my father's footsteps with Brynn—all in the name of fulfilling a prophecy.

I sigh heavily and fasten the leather sheath holding Tiene, the Sword of Flame at my side. I pause at the wall paneling concealing the room and listen for any movement in the guest room on the other side. Cia was clever when she commissioned renovations to the broken-down tavern when we first assimilated into Reikhaven. It gave her the perfect opportunity to remodel the upstairs bedroom, walling off a portion to include the hearth so that whoever found refuge in the hidden room would also find warmth during Reik's harsh winters. Her shrewd attention to detail came in handy when she built a faux hearth as an unsuspecting doorway that can only be opened from inside the hidden room. She planned every detail meticulously in case the Guard came sniffing around.

I take one more look around the sparsely decorated room and push on the paneling's unlocking mechanism. The door swings out with a quiet click and I step into the chilled air of what is now disguised as a storage room. I wait as my eyes adjust to the pale moonlight shining through the tattered curtains of the window to my right before making my way through the maze of stacked crates, mead barrels, and dusty bar stools.

My position as Master of Ships hangs in the balance after the incident with Lord Tuathinne, and it is only a matter of time before the Guard comes looking for me with questions I will not answer. I slip into the hallway like a ghost, utilizing the low light of the lanterns along the wall to my advantage. I carefully avoid the loose boards along my way though I am certain the sounds coming from each of the rooms I pass will mask any creaks and scrapes from my boots. Shadows envelope the stairs and I make myself home in their murky veil, watching...waiting.

Sasha moves fluidly through the tavern, a queen among her drunken patrons, refilling empty mugs and avoiding grabby hands. Sarai remains behind the long gray bar made of driftwood, undoubtedly placed there for her own protection by Sasha. She absentmindedly curls strands of her straw-colored hair around her finger in boredom. A man with rumpled vomit-stained clothes remains slumped on the stool, lost in his drunken slumber.

The purple-hued sky beyond the two massive front windows lightens with the rising sun, signaling my need to find a quiet corner to wait for the streets to fill with the hustle of morning. I lift the hood of my cloak and slink to the corner just beyond the low-burning hearth, preferring the soft crackle of the flames to ease my tension. Playing spy-master has never been my strong suit; according to Cia, my feet are too heavy and my movements too rigid.

I settle in the worn-down wooden chair as Sarai dashes to me, splashing the cooled mug of mead in her rush. Her eyes widen when she recognizes me behind the safety of my hood, and I quickly raise a finger to my lip. She nods conspiratorially and quietly places the mug on the table with a small curtsy. I wince at the gesture and look behind her to ensure no one saw her offering of respect. Sasha interrupts our exchange, handing the girl a broom.

"Go on girl, leave the gentleman alone and sweep off the porch before the morning rush."

Sarai obeys despite her pouting lips, and I give a silent thanks to Sasha for her quick-wittedness. I lean back in my chair, hoping the legs don't give out on me from the effort. I raise my mug to Sasha who winks and saunters away to the bar, leaving me in peace to eavesdrop on the drunken truths being whispered at the nearest table. One of Cia's girls sits on the lap of a dock worker, enduring his roaming hands. Her burgundy pleated dress swoops low, a distraction to hungry eyes as she leans across the table to the leather-skinned gentleman with graying hair.

I watch in amusement at her ploy as she looks to Sasha for a signal. Sasha lightly brushes the side of her nose, and the barmaid tilts her head with a flirtatious smile. The barmaid flicks her wrist softly and I jolt with the sudden rush of wind against my ear, their whispered voices now amplified as if I am somehow sitting in comradery among them. I have never met someone with the Draíocht of Nua in their veins, yet somehow Cia has found a Laioses gifted with the power of air. They are usually much less willing to help our cause despite their clan's betrayal centuries ago. I empty my head of all the questions racing in my mind and listen with feigned ignorance.

"Aye, I heard from a scullery maid at the fortress that they consume raw meat and blood like animals. He has them stationed throughout the forest where they are free to consume everything that walks and breathes."

The dock worker leans forward at the leather-skinned gentleman's claims and says, "Rumor has it, Lord Tuathinne is moving the rest of them to Reikhaven, a whole army of purple-eyed beasts, and Lady Brynn will be spending time away within the Capital's walls."

The barmaid teases, "Lord Roimh's consort will be most pleased to hear this news. I heard he doesn't even warm Lady Brynn's bed. That they sleep separately since she gave birth to that invalid daughter of hers."

The leather-faced man snorts, "A testament to that mongrel blood in the Lady's veins. The queen can dress her up like she is an Agderian, but we all know she is nothing but Laioses scum." He spits on the floor in disgust and continues, "No amount of charity she gives will ever change who she comes from."

The young dock worker licks his lips. "She sure is pretty. A man could get lost in those turquoise eyes of hers. I'd like a night with her, see if that Laioses blood really runs blue."

The leather-skinned man gulps the last of his drink and slams the mug on the table.

"Blue balls are what you'd end up with, or a cursed tongue. The woman is a witch. How else she did survive that attack on the harbor? Just walked out into the square with not even a burn on that delicate skin." He stands up on wobbly legs and leans forward with a malicious grin. "She deserves much worse than them bloody knuckles the Lord freely gives."

My fingers itch for the solace of my dagger as the flames in the hearth spark with renewed life. The barmaid's eyes dart to the hearth and then to my silent vigil, quickly flicking her wrist so that the voices silence to quiet murmuring. I lower my head, avoiding any curious glances that would reveal the heat burning behind my eyes as she stands up and finds refuge behind the bar with Sasha. The man drunkenly stumbles from the tavern as the dock worker scrambles after him, itching for more gossip the older man's loosened lips willingly give.

I toss a gold coin on the table and silently nod my thanks to the women as I leave out the door, mingling into the growing crowd setting up their wares among the morning dew glittering in the light of the rising sun. There is an uneasiness in the air. A sense of foreboding that prickles against my flesh, an urgency that I cannot explain whispering at the back of my mind. I stop mid-stride in front of a fish and scallop vendor scooping snow from his burlap sack onto a row of freshly caught cod. A flash of red in my peripheral is my only warning that I am being followed.

I disappear into the growing crowd, intentionally stooping so that my height does not betray my position to the guard stalking me a short distance away. I dare not look back as I slip into the safety of the darkened alley along the row of weathered shops leading to Parela's. I blend into the safety of the building's shadows; thankful the morning sun has not reached high enough to cast light upon my refuge. Cia finds refuge in the darkness. I, however, find it terribly unnerving, as if something menacing lurks beneath its blackened veil. Waiting. Watching.

My hand rests on the dagger sheathed at my side as the red cape nears the alley entrance. My head darts up as a window creaks open overhead with a flash of dimmed light from a burning lantern. I crouch low, avoiding the arc of light as the bald head of an elderly woman peers below. The lantern reveals a sly smile on her face as her gaze darts from me to the nearing guard. The guard pauses at the entrance, squinting as if it will somehow help him see me through the shadows. He takes a step toward me as the woman tosses a bucket of foul-smelling liquid from her perch.

The guard yells out curses as shit and piss rains down upon him, soaking him clean through. The sandy-brown haired man with scars across his face vomits as he snatches the drenched red cape clinging to his legs. The woman in the window snickers quietly and gives me a wink. With a half-smile I straighten and beat my chest once with my fist in a salute to her mischievousness. For all the vitriol the leather-faced man spoke in the tavern, it is a quiet relief to know that there are those among the townspeople that loathe Roimh's band of miscreants enough to risk retaliation. Regardless of Brynn's lineage, Agderia is just as much a part of her as her Laioses blood, and she will need their support in the war to come.

I step gingerly over the source of stench filling the alley and head for Parela's in search of a piece of history hidden within her shop's walls. I lower the hood of my cloak as the tiny bell clangs overhead announcing my arrival. Parela drops a swath of fabric to the wooden floor and opens her arms with a wide smile.

"Eowyn, my dear, what a sight for these old eyes of mine." She warmly embraces me like a mother welcoming a prodigal son. "Come, you smell as if you have rolled in a pig pen, and I cannot have your stench tainting my precious fabrics."

I stop her with a gentle hand as she turns toward the small table in the back of the shop.

"Parela, I need what my mother gave you to safeguard."

She turns to me quickly with a slackened jaw, searching my face with worried-filled eyes. She lets out a deep breath and silently nods. I follow her as she leads the way to the counter and the shelves of fabric stacked behind. She pulls an assortment of folded silks, stained with the color palette of a smoky fire, and places them neatly on the countertop.

"I did not expect it to be so soon," she somberly whispers before clearing her throat as if fighting off the emotion overwhelming her. She reaches for my hand softly and looks up at me with concern. "Is she strong enough to survive the breaking?"

I swallow hard and offer what little encouragement I can muster. With a gentle squeeze of her hand, I nod. "The Fates believe she is."

Her lips thin as she continues to search my face. "But do

you?"

I give her a half-smile though I am not sure I believe my own words. "I have no choice but to believe."

She pats my hand, blinking away the burden in her eyes and turns to the shelving of fabric. The back wooden panel of the shelf scrapes and she reaches deep into the hidden compartment. The Draíocht within me surges at the sight of the ancient bone in her hands as she gingerly places it on the countertop.

The origin of the bone remains a mystery so many centuries later though the rumors have abounded with its notoriety. Some speculate the bone is that of the winged protectors of the Dagda known as the Golith, while others vehemently claim it is made from the rib of the fallen Ancient, Eadom, and kissed by the god of flames, Tiene. How my mother, Thyra, acquired the sharpened bone remains a mystery—a secret she died with. I eye the twin flames that snake up the icy-blue handle and Parela firmly cautions with a heavy breath.

"It is said that the Gaia split her soul when creating the Dagda as her helpmate. The twin flames on the blade represent their connection to each other birthed from the power of the Draíocht. The flames reflect each other like a mirror, and their power only comes when each flame gives itself completely to the other. Your mother and father were fated to become this mirror...her death became the catalyst to his destruction. Twin flames are as damaging as they are powerful and can change the course of your life forever, no matter what the Fates decide."

The ethereal whispers of the past fill my mind as I lightly rub my thumb over the Rüin markings etched down the length of the blade. I feel the call of war drumming in the Draíocht rushing through me with my touch. My mother's gentle whispering overpowers that of the god's and my mind is sent back to the day that she gave it to me, covered in her own blood as death rattled in her lungs.

You will ascend to a higher calling, Eowyn. Give in to the thread of fate placed on your life, my darling boy, but do not lose your soul within the flames. With this blade, you will free us all from the grasps of an ancient darkness. Always remember, no matter what happens—believe in yourself.

The bitter memory fades quickly as I snatch my hand back, blinking until the room comes into focus again. Parela hisses and hurriedly wraps the blade safely in its tattered Rüin marked cloth of protection, silencing the whispers in my head. She busies herself with sealing the shelving compartment and placing the assortment of fabric back in its rightful place as I tuck the blade into my boot.

"Thank you, Parela. Your loyalty to Tiene—to me, is something I will never be able to repay," I scratchily say through my dried throat.

She keeps her back to me and huffs, "Aye, you have done more than enough to repay me, Eowyn. Keeping Tiene safe so that my grandchildren can grow, and flourish is all I could ever want." She turns to me with a bright smile. "I will remain here until the innocents are warned of what is to come and then I shall return to Tiene where I expect a full feast in my honor."

I laugh heartily and say, "I will ensure that the mountains will ring for days of your excellence."

Her eyes twinkle with delight and she teases with a sly smile, "Yes well, your soft bellied warband could use an old shield maiden to teach them the ways of war."

I chuckle and give her a quick kiss on her wrinkled cheek. "I would be honored."

She bats me away with a wave of her hand as she blushes deeply. I mockingly bow with a grin and head for the door. As the bell above dings one last time, she calls out from behind the countertop.

"Be careful, Eowyn. The path you walk is treacherous."

I secure the hood of my cloak on my head and walk out onto the street, the yoke of my burden settling heavily on my shoulders with her words.

I escape from the awakening town on the back of my horse just as other hoof beats thunder in a rush through the town square. The Guard barking orders to those gathered at the stalls echo far into the dark forest as the trees enclose around me. I had hoped Lord Tuathinne's drunkenness would have offered a reprieve for our encounter in the hallway, but alas I was not fated with such luck it seems. I say a prayer of protection for both Cia and Brynn as I make my way deeper into the forest and curse myself for my own hotheadedness. Threatening that bastard of a man so openly was a piss poor move in maintaining my own cover.

A war of my own wages in my mind. Brynn's desperation in that hallway was enough to send me over the edge. Her sorrow and pain continue to hit me square in the gut as my dapple-gray mare rides hard and fast. I welcome the stabbing frozen air against my face, a solace to the uneasiness in my soul. The prophecy is clear as mud, typical behavior of the Fates, but one thing my mother drilled into me from boyhood is that the breaking must happen.

It was easier before I met Brynn to put my people's best interest at the forefront of my actions. Watching her break and shatter in mind, body, and soul is something that I must do, yet I cannot help but feel as if I am no better than the man that finds joy in her pain. I grind my teeth against the guilt bubbling like acid inside me. I swore to the gods to die for this prophecy. I have bled for this prophecy. Thousands of innocent people depend upon me to see this through, to not interfere, to sit back and allow someone so pure of heart to die. It feels inhumane and I cannot grasp why the Gaia demands such a sacrifice to restore the balance that was snatched away when the Draíocht was tragically cut off from us all.

The eerie quietness of the dark forest settles deep in my bones, my skin prickles in warning as I make my way to Ronan's encampment. Something is amiss. I rein in the wildness of my mare and focus on my surroundings, watching for any sign of what has silenced the birds among the dying treetops. The stench of death reaches me before the sight of the clearing ahead and I quickly dismount, reaching for the sword of Tiene at my back.

The mare's eyes roll back in alarm, her nostrils flaring with warning as we reach the quiet clearing. I speak softly to her, urging her forward despite the pounding of my own heart. My eyes search quickly for any sign of movement among the trees scattered about. For any sign of life beyond the carnage that lays before me.

Sealskin tents and bedding have been cut into tatters and tossed about with little regard, blanketing the clearing. Beasts with slickened fur lay in pieces, their blood staining the warming ground in small puddles among the wreckage. I count the number of massive, long-snouted heads dismembered from their limbs and talons that are scattered about—eight in total. Each one paired off, the trail of their bodies enough evidence to know that they surrounded the encampment's four corners just before their hungered strike.

I let go of the reins and square my shoulders at the sound of a limb snapping beneath heavy feet. I call out my familiar whippoorwill song, anxious for Ronan's answer. Silence beseeches me and I angrily channel the Draíocht into my sword, its flames erupting with malice. Kailiao was right, damn my own ignorance. I caused this the moment I revealed their location in front of that bloody damn raven. I step into the clearing filled with self-deprecating anger. The tip of my sword kisses the earth as I walk, leaving a trail of fire and ash in my wake.

My body trembles with heated rage as I search through the wreckage for the bodies of my men—for my brother. Ronan has been my keeper since I could walk, my shield and armor. The one constant in my life that has believed in me, even when my own doubts shadow my clarity. My pulse quickens in the silence echoing through me and I fall to my knees before the rotting carcass in front of me. I lift my blade and slam it into the ground as the flames of my grief hungrily circle around me before exploding with a deafening roar.

I envy those who live a life unencumbered with the weight fated to them. A life filled with the luxury of never fearing that one mistake could collapse everything I have sacrificed for. Never having to calculate the risk of every move, never preparing for the worst outcome, nor anticipating what is yet to come. A life filled without the sting of death.

I choose not to hear the pleading voice calling out to me as I relish the burning against my skin and the thick smoke filling my lungs. Light and darkness courses through my veins until I become one with its power, the comforting song of its flames. I look up to the overcast sky above as my sorrow bellows its rage. I embrace the baptism of fire that darkens my soul and melts away my pain.

With the force of an ox, I am snatched back from the sanctuary of flames with the pain-laced bellowing of my name. I rapidly blink, my vision clearing as the Draíocht eases its torrent of power within me and the flames silence with my own disbelief.

"Ronan?" I croak through my scorched throat.

Smoke rises from his charred clothes as he beats the remaining flames from his body. I sit up quickly, guilt eating away at my conscience at the sight of raw skin beginning to blister on his arm.

"I—I thought you were dead. Ronan, I—I'm sorry. I—"

"Yeah, well I'm not." He grumbles, trying to mask the pain from the burns as he crouches before me. "If I hadn't come when I did, *you* very well could be." His large, burned hands clasp my shoulders, shaking me. "What would all this be for if you had burnt up the power in your blood? How many times do I have to save you from yourself? Your purpose is bigger than my life!"

I look down at the ground in shame and mumble, "I cannot do this without you."

He stands and shakes his head, walking away in disgust. He stops and turns his head to me, quietly murmuring, "One day you will have to."

I scramble to my feet as he walks to the scorched trees

beyond the clearing. I look around at the aftermath of my own power. Everything within the clearing has disintegrated into ash, the ground beneath my feet blackened with soot, the evidence of the prior attack lost to the flames I wielded. Just beyond the clearing stands my men, watching the exchange with paled faces and troubled eyes. I curse my weakness as they avert their gaze, and I wonder how I am going to keep their trust after witnessing my own proclivity for death in the face of great loss.

Ronan waits for me as Finnick quickly pulls a jar of salve from his saddlebag. The men go about salvaging what little supplies remain along the edge of the clearing. Muris watches my every move with growing suspicion in his eyes, and I have half the mind to gut him right there. Ornery bastard will use this against me when I least expect it; his grumblings of my ineptness at being clan chief a constant reminder that we are not as united as we should be.

I take the salve from Finnick's shaky hands as Ronan looks around at the men, his eyes narrowing on Muris' soured face.

He leans close and grumbles, "Not here."

I follow his gaze and nod. We walk further in the forest, leaving any curious ears behind. We stop under the scarce canopy of trees above and I quickly get to work on covering the numerous burns on Ronan's skin of my own making. He winces as I quietly apply the healing salve to his charred ear and neck. His low voice breaks the silence between us.

"Eowyn, you have to be careful. You cannot do that again.

No matter what happens, or you will lose this clan to the likes of Muris and those who support his claim."

"I know."

He clears his throat and continues with gritted teeth, "Declan is dead."

My eyes widen and my hand stills.

"I did not see his body among the slaughtered beasts."

Ronan sighs heavily and nods. "Aye, it was one of our own I am sure of it."

I growl, "How?"

"His throat was sliced soon after chaos erupted with the attack." Ronan's eyes dart toward the warband and he leans close, "There is no decay oozing from the wound."

My jaw clenches and I look out to the warband gathering together, waiting.

"Who do you suspect? Why?"

"Declan came to me just moments before the attack last night, asking for a moment away from the others. He had the evidence to back up his claim that we had an enemy within the camp. The men were drinking around the fire; too close for any listening ears. So, I asked him to keep it to himself until everyone was asleep and to meet me near the horses before the rising sun. He had left my tent mere minutes before the attack came. I did not see him again until Finnick found his body dragged beyond the clearing, his throat slashed from ear to ear."

I mutter a curse to the gods, my body shaking with anger. Ronan clasps my shoulders; his eyes filled with grief.

"He died without a blade in his hand."

Everything within me roars for vengeance, for the blood of the murderer who not only took an innocent life but took the promise of Declan's spirit finding a home in Elye.

"You've had one outburst today, Eowyn. You cannot have another. Control yourself."

I hiss and violently push Ronan's heavy hand from my shoulder, "I will control myself when the bastard is split from head to toe and his bowels blanket this gods-forsaken ground."

Ronan moves quickly, blocking the view of the warband with his towering body as he wraps his thick arms around me into a headlock. He whispers sternly in my ear.

"Your anger is justified but this is not. You are clan chief, Eowyn. We have to be smart about this. Your lack of control will do nothing but create division that we cannot afford. Heavy is the head that bears the sword..."

I still at the familiarity of our father's words, letting my anger stew in the embers aflame in my soul. Satisfied with my surrender, Ronan releases me, and I turn to him with narrowed eyes.

"We will honor his death as if he did hold a blade and I will be bloody-damned if the gods don't accept him into Elye," I icily say. "It is the least they can do."

Ronan grins heartedly and laughs. "That's the sanest thing you have said today, brother." He puts his arm around my shoulder in comradery, and we face the warband, united together.

We tread past the warband and Ronan begins barking orders as we separate. They work quickly to construct a pyre as I make my way to the sword standing vigilant in the center of the clearing. Not even the bones of the Werebeast remain, but still the sword remains upright, plunged deep into the ground. I look out at the men hurrying about their task of tree cutting and building. One of them has betrayed us. The thought turns my stomach.

We have all bled together and fought for a better life in the face of overwhelming adversity. Each man within my warband was chosen for their loyalty to Tiene, to the Laioses, and their willingness to wield their blade, to brandish their shield, so that peace will once again be restored. Betrayal is a bitter pill to swallow when it comes from the source that you once found love residing in.

Chapter 24

My teeth chatter loudly in protest of the piercing cold that seems to stab deep into my bones as I cower in the dark corner of my small, dank cell. What is left of my soiled nightdress lays against my exposed body in tatters. I cling to myself in a tight ball of arms and legs in my desperation for warmth. A low, pain-laced groan vibrates through me as the burned skin on my thigh breaks open with a nasty ooze.

Heavy footsteps move from the shadows of my prison, and I flinch with the violent rattle of the bars of my cell. I turn my face toward the slick, frozen moss-covered stone wall, avoiding Drescher's scowling face as he appears in the light from the broken window of the fortress prison. The cell doors rattle and I try to scramble further into the corner, the stone wall slicing bitterly into the flesh of my back.

I hold my breath, my heart racing inside my chest as his finger brushes against the matted hair dangling against my cheek. There is no warmth in his touch and only venom in his low voice.

"I knew you would betray us all. I knew it the moment I stepped foot inside this bloody fortress and saw the face of my wife's killer in your own." My eyes widen and my head darts to his. He grabs my chin roughly with a sadistic smile. "You have your mother's eyes."

I see stars as he slams my head against the stone wall and I try hard not to lose consciousness as he stands, satisfied at the sight of blood oozing down my temple. I dare not breathe or utter a whimper until the sound of his boots disappear up the stairs toward freedom. The heavy iron door closes behind him and I let out a soul-wracking sob. I am at the mercy of others who have never offered me an ounce of compassion. I am helpless. Alone.

The fear for my children is the only challenge to the death that I now pray for. I must survive long enough to ensure their safety. Long enough for Mideton or Britta to send word to Cia. Because even in death I know that my dearest friend will protect what my heart no longer can. She will avenge me by saving my children, protecting them from the ever-reaching hands of a man who knows not what love truly is.

Melting snow drips from the crumbling stone above me as I drift in and out of consciousness with the rising sun. I stare up into the holes of the roof, pleading to the gods for mercy that has never been offered to me. The sun casts shadows on the wall as the day gives way to evening and I wonder how much longer Roimh will stew. When will his desire to rid himself of me will finally come to fruition?

I have fought for life for so incredibly long. Fought for the promises that never came. For the love I thought would never die. For years I watched my hope shatter into tiny shards, and like a child, I took those broken pieces, clinging to them in hope that one day, just one day, those pieces would be made new. But death comes calling and I cannot hold on anymore. I am nothing but a ghost, lost and broken, in a world that listened to the cries of my heart and chose not to hear.

With each passing icy breath, I let go of the fear that comes before death, the fear of the unknown, of what may lay waiting for me on the other side of the veil. I fall into the pit of darkness that lay waiting in my mind and into the embrace of a restless dream.

I choke on the thick fog rolling through the window of the fortress prison. No not fog. Smoke. I scramble to my feet in alarm and cry out for help. Silence. There is only silence. I run to the bars of my cell and scream, shaking the iron in hurried desperation. The cell door swings open with a bang, and I wait, expecting Drescher to come through the heaviness of the smoke suffocating me.

A wolf with icy blue eyes enters my cell, and I scramble back in fear at the sheer size of the animal. Its long legs tower several feet longer than they should, its massive body overwhelming my own short stature. Its giant paws step toward me, the smoke rolling across the floor, parting with each heavy step. It stares at me with a sense of urgency that I cannot explain, as if it wants me to follow it out to my freedom.

I reach a shaky hand out before me as it lowers its head in quiet submission. My hand grazes over its soft, thick fur that glows white like the light from a full moon. I am lost in the glowing blue of its eyes when suddenly, I am flung out and through the prison walls with a violent shove from behind. I roll across the ash covered ground as the screams of the dying pound like vicious waves against my skull.

My chest heaves as I scramble to my feet, and I am blinded by the flames roaring around me. The fortress is on fire. Shadowy people scream and run in a frantic frenzy as the great stone fortress of Reikhaven crumbles around me. I scream out for my children, and I choke on the ash filling my mouth. I cannot see. I cannot breathe. I cannot move. The world upends itself around me and all I can do is feel the kiss of flames threatening to burn me alive.

Chapter 25

My shadows cling to me as I weave my way across the roughly shingled rooftops of Reik. A familiar calmness resonates through me as I leap from building to building, avoiding the guards littering the streets below. Roimh has prepared for this. He knows I am coming. My lips twitch with a smile. He just doesn't know the creature that's coming within me.

I jump to a mound of snow below the last shingled rooftop and roll into a crouch, slinking into the forest trees like a wild cat stalking its prey. Icy wind slaps against my face in resistance as I dodge through the darkened limbs of the forest edge. I keep sight of one of Slade's decorative carriages as it makes its way down the open road to the fortress. An unexpected gift that I just so happened to acquire with a little help from Sasha and the letter seal of Reikhaven that now bounces in the pocket of my pants.

I watch the clouds in anticipation, waiting for them to shift enough to dull the bright shine of the full moon. I go over every detail of the day in my mind. The layout of the prison, Roimh's study where the children are being guarded, and the position of Tuathinne's forces along the beach and just beyond the eastern wall of the Dagda's temple. I watch and I wait, but Eowyn does not show.

The clouds shift above as the gates open and welcome the carriage within its walls. I bite my lip, warring with my own impatience. I cannot wait. It's now or never. Brynn will just have to forgive me. I close my eyes and gather the shadows around me until I am hidden beneath their weight.

I make a mad dash for the opened field, cursing the tightening muscles in my legs as they scream in protest. I have become soft since arriving in Reikhaven. I should have trained more, spent less time playing madam and more time honing my craft as a spy for the Tiene Clan. My lungs burn angrily as I near the stone wall, my breath puffing out like smoke with each gulp of the frozen air.

I gaze up at the sky with a sly grin and thank the gods for the growing gray clouds that now blanket the sleeping moon. I move against the fortress wall, my fingers quickly searching for any gaps. I let out a single breath and center myself as I grasp a large gap above me. I hurriedly scale the wall and crouch next to the eastern tower like the snow leopard of Cerwei that waits patiently for an Elkan to appear.

My thighs burn as I count the guards, observing their pacing formations with a frown. There are fewer guards than I expected, only six patrol the space between myself and the prison doors. Two stand guard outside Brynn's cell, while the other four walk in steps of twelve before changing course. I search for Drescher among them with a sense of dread when he is not found. I quickly glance toward the now empty carriage for any sign of Sasha and the girls sent by an unwitting Slade. *Well, shit. Damn you Eowyn for leaving me to do this alone.*

I take a deep breath and channel my anger at the circumstances I did not anticipate. They prepared for Eowyn, but they did not prepare for me. A sinister grin bubbles to the surface as my narrowed eyes grow cold. I am Death, and I have come calling.

I grit my teeth and push hard from the stone wall with a leap to the ash tree towering a few feet in front of me. My shadows cocoon around me as I land silently on the barren limb. I grow unearthly still within their impenetrable black, slowing my heart rate with each deep breath until the darkness calms and centers me. I wait for the guard below me to move, counting the sound of his twelve steps crunching against the frozen ground. A few steps more and I leap to the ground, my stealthy descent muffled with the shadows beneath my feet.

With quickness, I release Ifreannach from my side and the blade hums in delight as it slices across the flesh of the guard's neck. The sounds of his trachea severing comforts me as hot blood splatters to the ground. My shadows move with their own will and loop around his lifeless body, softening the sound as he falls to the blood-stained ground. They billow back around me until I am nothing but darkness within a moonless night. I slink against the wall in quiet anticipation to the giant steel door that holds the future of Ravndal within its grip.

I make no sound as I emerge from their safety and into the light cast by the torches hanging along the courtyard walls that now light my path. I breathe in deeply, relishing the fear that now resonates from their bones at the sight of me. My devilish smile deepens as they draw their blades and firmly plant their feet where they stand. I teasingly toy with my own bloodied blade as I slowly walk forward, waiting for one of them to make a move.

The young guard on my left grasps at his courage and steps forward in a useless act of bravery. His longsword swings for my head and I crouch low with a spin before he can blink. Ifreannach slices effortlessly through the skin and muscle of his stomach, hungry for more. Before I can stand, he falls to his knees wide-eyed, grasping at his slippery insides that now spill forth from him and hit the ground with a sharp hiss.

I turn with a lazy smile to the remaining guard now frozen in his own terror. I quickly move across the ground with little effort and stab through his open mouth, stifling the scream that had begun to rise. I step over his lifeless body with little care of who he once was. I am judge and executioner, nothing will stop me in my pursuit to quench the bloodlust that flows in my veins.

The steel door groans as I open it slightly, allowing my shadows to filter into the pitiful excuse of a prison. My feet are feather light as I slip inside, moving like one with the darkness that permeates from my prickled skin. With each fluid step, the torchlight along the damp corridor of empty cells extinguishes into nothingness. The cluster of cells expands into an openness that smells of blood, a footprint left behind by the pain felt within the stone walls. I breathe in the fear permeating from the back of the prison with renewed anger.

The hum of a longsword meeting the frigid air beckons to me as a deep mocking voice calls out through the shadows.

"Come for the whore of Ravndal, have we?"

A flash of my blade is my only answer as I slice through the shadows toward his voice. I grit my teeth with a growl as his longsword swings wildly, seeking flesh. A clash of metal echoes throughout the prison rattling my ears as I brace myself against his strength. He relents and swings again as the moon suddenly illuminates the darkened dungeon through the holes in the neglected roof above.

I dodge his murderous swing for my head, pulling the shadows to me to conceal my next move. There is no time as Drescher's mammoth body sends me sprawling to the stone floor with a guttural roar. I roll quickly, grappling for my toothpick dagger as his sword hisses against the stone mere inches from my face. I flip to my feet with catlike agility and slash wildly at his stony face. The thirst for blood hums with overwhelming relief through me as he falls to his knees clutching the razor-like opening now pouring with a fury of blood. His moans of pain bring me solace as he hurriedly grapples at the flesh of his eye and nose that now hangs loosely.

The salty taste of his blood sends a prickle of excitement up my spine as I wipe the dagger clean with my tongue. I kick hard at his pathetic form and send him whimpering like a coward to the floor. I straddle him as I lower my mouth to his ear, my sword teasing the flesh of his stomach.

"You're Death's whore now."

I take my time as his flesh gives way to the slow strength of my sword. I relish the sound of his bloody gurgles as my blade inches deeper into his gut. I smile wickedly as his eye widens with fear of the fate I have bestowed upon him. His hot blood pools around us and I feel his heart slow beneath the weight of my body. A slow shuffling at my side interrupts my moment of bloodied triumph.

Brynn's voice shakes with waning strength. "Cia?"

The shadows rolling around me quickly retreat into my skin as I look up at her frightened face. The moonlight illuminates around her, revealing the shredded nightdress and the whitened knuckles gripping the iron bars of her cell. Drescher groans as my blade retreats quickly from his bloodied flesh. I stand quickly, grinding my teeth against the wave of emotion overwhelming me and hurry to free her before she collapses.

"Stand back," I gently say as I will my shadows around my hands and snatch on the brittle lock with the strength of the Draíocht flowing through me.

The iron door falls to the floor as if it is nothing but a child's toy. I gather her frail, trembling body in my arms as she buries her head into my shoulder with a heart wrenching sob.

"You came."

I soothingly brush her matted hair and quietly reply, "I will always come."

We stand in silence as she unleashes all the heartache and brokenness building inside. Each tearful sob beats against my heart and awakens a bitterness I thought I had long since buried. A bitterness born from the tears of another who was once ravaged and battered by the hands of predatory men. I hold her tightly and swallow back my own tears for a love now lost among my memories.

The throng of bells echo a warning through the night, and I am quickly reminded of the battle we have yet to face.

"We have to hurry."

She pulls back sharply from me, and her face whitens as her tearful turquoise eyes widen. "The children. Where are the children?"

I hang my head, unable to meet her gaze as I grit my teeth. "There is no time."

I scramble to hold her up as her legs give out from under her with another mournful sob. I wrap her limp arm around my neck and pull her close to my side, bearing most of her weight. I give no time for her protesting as I force her to move with me, hating myself for having to. We hurry down the corridor of cells and to the massive steel door ahead, the calamity of the night reaching a fevered pitch with each step.

The chorus of bells loudly greets us as we near the slightly cracked door. I quickly remove my cloak and wrap it tightly around her, silently cursing every Agderian who harmed her in such a way. The sound of running boots crunching in the snow draws closer and I grasp her hand in my own. I pray to the gods she hears the urgency in my voice and obeys, no matter if her heart screams to stay.

"No matter what you see or hear, you run. Run to the Dark Forest. Run faster than you have ever run before and do not wait for me." I peek through the crack of the door before embracing her once more. "You have brought more joy and happiness to my life than I ever thought possible. No matter what, Brynn, remember that."

"No one dies tonight, Cia." She squeezes me and steps back, offering a solemn smile. "No one."

A blast of cold air hits my face as I swing the door open wide. She grimaces slightly with a limp as we move out to the icy courtyard and the snowy path ahead. Within a breath, chaos erupts around us as five battle-worn men lunge for us. I push Brynn to the ground, avoiding the longsword aimed for her throat. She scrambles from the ground's cold grip, spitting dirt and ice as a frenzy of shadow meets steel.

One by one, men fall around us as I give in to the drumming of the Draíocht in my soul that sings the song of blood and death. A soft thread of shadow wraps around Brynn's hand, tethering her to me with renewed strength as we push forward and leave a graveyard of gaping throats and severed limbs behind us. Out of the corner of my eye I see guards pour from the barracks in various stages of undress. I laugh manically as they fall to their death in the snow, Sasha's poison pouring from their bloodied eyes.

I stop short as Tuathinne's assassins barrel through the garden gate, and I turn to Brynn, releasing the shadowy tether.

"Run, Brynn! Run!"

She hesitates, her eyes darting to the men drunk with bloodlust running headlong toward us, and I shout again, bracing myself to face them all. I swear loudly as the flesh of my arm meets the kiss of steel. I twist and turn, narrowly avoiding the sword thrust at my stomach. With each step I am surrounded until I am backed into a corner. I need a moment, a split second to scurry up the wall to my own liberation. Gods, I hope Brynn makes it to the forest.

An ugly excuse for a man lunges for me and meets the tip of my own blood-soaked sword. Where in the bloody-fuck is Eowyn? I grit my teeth and unleash the razor-like vine of shadow from the palm of my free hand. It hungrily stabs into the ear of one assassin and into the ear of another like a whip with deadly precision. I curse the gods, the Fates, and everything in-between. If the Draíocht ran freely through me, I wouldn't even be in this mess. With just a feeble swish of my hand every single one of these bastards would be on the ground screaming in the void of their own nightmares. Damn that good for nothing bitch, Queen of Darkness. Damn the bloody-fucking prophecy. Damn them all.

I twirl the blade of my ancestors in my hands. I am not going to die today. Not at the hands of the filthy Agderians. I spit on the ground and give the guard swinging a blade for my head a teasing smile. I feint left, avoiding his blow. The stone behind my head sparks at the blade's hit. This is my moment.

I lunge for the guard, kicking him back hard into his companions with the strength of the Draíocht. He topples into them in a heap of flesh and steel. Without a moment of hesitation, I scale the wall and reach the top before the men have time to untangle themselves from each other. I launch myself from the wall and tumble to the ground. My shadows cushion me as I land, rolling through the snow. I scramble to my feet and run headlong for the forest that beckons ahead.

Chapter 26

The burn on my leg gnaws at me viciously as I run for the Dark Forest that looms beyond the road to Reik. Cia's wet cloak clings to my legs against the wind but still I run. Hope roars through me at the sight of the outline of trees ahead as freedom beckons urgently for me. The sound of hooves thundering behind me nearly collapses me as fear burns wildly in my chest.

The crack of a whip slices through the frozen night air and I scream in agony as leather pierces my back. Burning pain overwhelms me as I fall to my face. My fingers claw into the frozen dirt as I pull myself back to my feet and attempt to sprint to the trees that now scream for me. The whip cracks like lightening before it coils around my neck, biting into the skin of my throat as it sharply tightens and slings me back to the ground. My feet fly into the air in front of me and I hit the ground with a bone-crushing thud. I claw at the leather around my throat, desperately gasping for shallow breath. The creak of a saddle is my only warning before my broken body is dragged against the earth like a wild animal.

I fight for consciousness, my skin ripped and shredded raw from the frozen ground, screaming in agony as we enter through the iron gate of the fortress. The whip imprisoning my neck slowly releases as we come to a sudden stop. I gasp for shaky breath as the rawness of my flesh meets the cold air. My desperate instinct is to shield my neck with my hands, but I am unable to muster the strength to even touch the imprint of brutality against my skin.

Voices call out vile threats and accusations around me, but I do not hear them. I am stuck falling into the murky depths of suffering. I am hauled to my feet with a vicious snarl from the guard who had given me wildflowers one summer. Henrick. Is that his name? I blink back tears as the world spins around me and muddles my thoughts. Strong hands tighten around each arm as I am forced forward, my feet dragging against the ground with each step. My head hangs heavily as if the weight of my life has finally come to for its reaping.

The ancient whisperings, silenced after my haunting encounter at the Temple of Dagda, now awaken with a vicious roar as we near the room of my impending execution. It is as if the gods themselves are in my head, fighting for me when I have given up every will to fight on my own. This is the end. The end of my suffering. The end of my hope.

Hope has done nothing but leave me in a bottomless pit chained to disappointment. It has left my heart bleeding into my soul until all the light within me has been smothered by the cold hands of grief. Hope has not saved me, instead it has held me prisoner, tormenting me with unmet expectations. Now hope has tired of me and now all that is left is for me to mourn my own death.

Commotion rises from Roimh's study as the door bangs open suddenly. I lift my weary head as a coldness rises in my chest and chills me to the bone. Olan fights against the guards holding him in their grasp, his terror-stricken face looks at me with surprise and wilts at the sight of my own imprisonment. He is so thin, his lips so cracked. A fresh bruise darkens his face. I snarl in anger at the torture my child has endured and thrash against my own captors.

"Mamma?"

My heart seizes in my chest and my whole body stills at the familiar soft whimper coming from the study doorway. I turn to see my beautiful girl trembling in the arms of Renoa who looks upon me with a snake-like smile. The necklace I had gifted her for Yultane dangles delicately against her chest.

Perri suddenly appears in the doorway, thundering sharp commands. "Load them in the wagon. I want guards on the boy at all times until we reach the forest." He pushes Renoa forward, who then looks upon me with silent triumph as Ophele begins to cry and Olan begins to scream in vain. "Come Renoa, let us be done with this."

I try to lunge, to kick, and buck wildly. I try to fight and claw my way to them. I gnash my teeth and snarl viciously. I scream until my lungs give out and my throat bleeds raw, but nothing I do brings me closer to them. I am held against my will within the strength of the guards surrounding me. I am haunted with their cries that echo through the corridor as I am forced into the study to meet the man I once loved and the fate that awaits me.

I am thrown to the floor like I am trash, easily discarded, as we enter the low-lit room. My bones rattle as I smack hard against the floor and I groan with the impact, every muscle in my body aching as my adrenaline wanes. I reach for the chair leg in front of me to hoist myself up. Roimh snatches it from my grip, and it clatters against the wall in a heap of splintered wood. I am met with a swift kick to my side. I crumple into a ball of pain, clutching my barely healed ribs with an agonizing sob. There is no warmth in his voice as he kneels on a knee next to me and looks with disgust upon my face.

"This is the fate you chose when you whored yourself to that Laioses scum." His fingers grasp my face hard, forcing me to look at the darkness of his eyes. "The queen has learned of your treachery. She is quite displeased, so much in fact that she has given me liberty to break you in more ways than one." He savagely slings my face into the floor and rises. He moves to the war table in the center of the room and affectionately fingers the leather coiled on top. "Seeing as you have whored yourself, I am unsure of our children's legitimacy. Considering that *boy's* fondness for betrayal and the obvious impairment of the *other*, it seems as if they have no ounce of Agderian virtue running through their veins, but only that of their bitch of a mother." He turns to me with a darkened smile that haunts his face grotesquely. "The queen has petitioned for me to rid any suspicions of their bloodline."

My heart thunders as my mind races over the veiled threat. I gather what little strength remains within me and shakily rise to my knees and ask with a quivering voice. "What have you done?"

He holds the coiled leather whip up in the air as if inspecting it for his veracity and turns to me with a wicked smile. His eyes dart to the window overlooking the darkened forest beyond and coldly proclaims, "There are many ravenous beasts that venture in the darkness. The queen gave her permission with only one request—that you survive the breaking you are about to endure."

Bile rises to my throat and my mind crumbles. I clutch my chest tightly as my heart shatters into a thousand pieces. My children. He is going to kill them. Perri's voice echoes in the back of my mind. He is taking them to the forest to die.

I gasp for breath, but it does not come. I am lost, falling into a darkness within my own soul and do not see the blow that comes. The whip cracks and my flesh screams of fire and blood. One after another the blows come, slicing into my skin. In his frenzy, I am nothing more than an object to satisfy his thirst for pain.

Chapter 27

The sinking moon above sneaks behind an overcast gray sky as I make my way quickly across the open field that leads to the forest ahead. I search among the clearing for any sign of Brynn, and a sense of foreboding prickles against my spine as I reach the tree line. There are no visible tracks in the snow as I run anxiously along the forest border. There is no sound besides the nervous whinnies of the horses tethered a few yards deeper into the forest. I take a deep breath and close my eyes, willing the sounds of the night to reach me.

I try desperately to break through the iron wall within, placed firmly between myself and the free flowing Draíocht that lies just beyond its impregnable stone. If I had just a sliver of access to that churning essence, I would be able to hear through the darkness for miles using the full power of Fuath. I scrap and claw, looking for any weakness in the stone to no avail. I rub the sharp headache stabbing my temples in frustration and look back to the fortress with a sickening feeling. Something terrible has happened. I can feel it in my bones and that bloody hell of a place is the center of it all.

I test the Draíocht remaining in my blood and frown. I need rest. A day to recharge the measly supply of power that I am offered by the shadow god, Fuath. There is no way I will survive another onslaught of Tuathinne's forces. I look to the fortress again and grit my teeth. I will just have to take a chance. After all, the fate of the Laioses now befalls upon me since Eowyn is still missing. I push the fear from my mind over his absence. He knows how important tonight is, for him not to show means something terrible has happened and I cannot face that crisis without settling the one unfolding before me.

I swear loudly, hoping the Gaia hears my disdain for her passive interference for her own future. With Brynn dead, Ravndal will be destroyed and there will be nothing to stop the blood-sucking queen from ravishing the Gaia with cruel pleasure. I sigh heavily, mustering the strength to take on the fortress once again on my own while regret screams loudly in my mind. Regret that I did not just take Brynn against her will the first chance I could, to avoid all this bloody mess. Regret for allowing love and loyalty to cloud my own judgment. My instincts knew that waiting was wrong and yet I ignored them for the chance to continue building a friendship that was doomed from the start.

I break from the trees in a run, the muscles in my tired legs anger with each quick movement as I make my way toward my own death along Reik road. The rumble of a wagon alerts me just in time and I dive for the waterlogged ravine along the road, pulling the shadows to me to mask my presence and shield me in darkness. I watch with bated breath as the wagon moves swiftly down the road.

Lord Tuathinne sits in the front next to one of his soldiers and nearly topples out of his seat to look toward my hiding spot. I am nearly certain he can somehow see through the shadows when he smiles, drawing his sword. I tense, my hand hovering over my own blade and wait for him to order the wagon to halt. To my surprise he instead swings the butt of his blade at the hooded figure in the back of the wagon, silencing the fearful whimpers of his captives.

I remain still, offering up a silent prayer filled with regret for the women that had accompanied Sasha. Their fate is now interlaced with the cruelty of Tuathinne and the darkness that lives within his soul. I wait until the wagon veers off for the narrow forest path that butts up against the shadowy side of Reik before I move again. The momentary rest does nothing but aid the cramping that is now forming in my legs.

My body craves rest, my mind filling with a heaviness that accompanies an excessive use of the Draíocht, but still I push forward. As I come closer to the fortress I am startled by the sudden appearance of crimson red sails along the shoreline of the cliffs. I move stealthily through the clearing and toward the cliff edge. Something is amiss.

I creep along the cliff, squinting my eyes to see the chaos unfolding along the sandy shoreline below. Tuathinne's soldiers board two warships, as the captain of each ship bellows out orders too faint for me to hear. I frown at the sight of Sasha's dark hair billowing in the breeze, chains of indigo wrap tightly around her arms and neck. I shudder in remembrance of what those chains do to someone with the blood of the gods.

My mind floods with questions as Renoa emerges from the shadows, accompanied by what can only be her henchmen. The group of men part to make way for her as she makes her way through the sand and up the gangplank. Each man holds what looks to be a burlap sack over their shoulders as they follow closely behind her. I chew on my bottom lip trying to work out what any of this could possibly mean and why Perri would leave Renoa to head toward the forest.

My heart stops suddenly in my chest at the abrupt sound of agony-laced screams filling the silent night. My eyes dart toward Sasha whose head hangs low as another scream erupts. I look quickly toward the fortress and bile rushes to my throat with a sadistic burn as another scream slices through me. I sprint toward the sound, abandoning all sense of my own salvation.

The Draíocht angrily hums within me, and I pull hard against the wall blocking the flow within. Another scream erupts and I can feel my blood running cold with the trickle of Draíocht pushing through the cracks of the stone wall within. I push the shadows that race with me forward and they dash across the ground like the shadowy tendrils of a sea monster, searching for the source of the pain and suffering in each scream. Memories of my childhood cloud my vision and haunt me with each hurried stride of my legs. Images of the army that ransacked my village, the screams of my mother and the coldness that I felt at my own helplessness.

I near the fortress gate when silence unexpectedly slams into me. Something is wrong, very wrong. My chest tightens with the malicious grip of terror as the fortress gate comes into view. At the foot of the wall, just outside the closed gate lies a crumpled body. A body with long auburn hair.

No, please no.

A wind rises around me. No not a wind. An ethereal voice that sings through the chilled air like that of a warm breeze. A voice that hums with the Draíocht that now races through my body. The voice of the Gaia.

A shout along the parapet above the closed iron gate of the fortress rings out as I approach.

Bloody-damn, it's a trap.

A black cloud of arrows rains down around me. The shadowy tendrils racing in front of me slam together and form a wall of black around me. Together we dodge and weave as the voice of the Gaia sings louder into the night, guiding me to the naked body lying unearthly still against the frozen ground. I brace myself for the next onslaught of arrows, unsure of how much more my shadows will be able to take shielding me.

I look up in surprise and watch men fall one by one where they stand along the parapet above the closed iron gate. I slow my pace and quickly look for any sign of movement overhead.

To my disbelief it is as if the entire fortress has been lulled to sleep with the Gaia's song. Relief briefly floods through me as I look up to the overcast sky offering my thanks, promising to withhold my grumblings of her indifference for at least a fortnight.

Unsure of how long the men will remain under the Gaia's spell I move quickly to the blood puddling against the white icy ground around her. I gasp in horror at the sight, nearly stumbling over my own feet in complete shock of what is left of her. Every single inch of her porcelain skin is covered in deep lacerations that blood continues to flow freely from. Her face is unrecognizable, the flesh split into a dozen or more tiny cuts. I fall to my knees and softly lift her face to my chest. I rock back and forth as anguish deep in my soul comes forth in a frenzied torrent of tears.

A soft moan slips through her split lips. I look down wide-eyed and cry out with a mix of relief and disbelief.

"You're alive! Oh, thank the gods. You're alive!"

Through some act of fate or the gods themselves, she is alive! I lay her head gently down onto the ground and hurriedly look for any glimpse of the cloak I had given her earlier. A slew of curses erupts from my lips at my own willingness to believe the bastard would have any sort of humanity. He left her out here to die, shaming her even in death by not discarding the cloak with her body. I bite my lip, contemplating a mad dash for the stables and decide against it. The cost of clothing her against the chill a price I am not willing to pay if the men above awaken from their stupor.

My stomach turns as I lift her into my arms, the metallic smell of her blood overwhelming me as I struggle under her deadened weight. I breathe deep, fighting against waves of nausea to center myself and pull from the remaining depth of my Draíocht. I call to the shadows with a gentle smile as they dutifully answer the song of my heart. From the pores of my skin, clouds of thick black billow around my arms and intricately loop around the brokenness of her body.

Her arm slips from the safety of her exposed stomach, and my knees buckle at the sickening sight etched into her skin.

Whore of Ravndal.

I scream out in anger and sorrow. He has taken everything from her and branding her as if she had a choice in the matter is more than I can mentally take. Memories of my past, of a life within the Capital walls flood back and it takes everything within me to push forward—to not turn around and die fighting my way into the belly of the beast. I take a step toward the forest, willing myself forward. They will all die. One way or another they will meet the kiss of Death. It is the only hope that I can hold onto. The only promise that allows me to leave.

With each step I can feel my power waning as the Draíocht slams against the wall that stifles the flow within me. My skin burns hot, my nose dripping with my own blood as my mind explodes with a painful warning. I continue to push myself, the shadows farther than the Draíocht will allow until each step I take with her in my arms causes my body to scream in agonizing pain as if it is being ripped apart from the inside.

The shadowy tree line of the forest is but mere inches from enveloping us both in their safety, but I cannot hold on any longer. I collapse to the snowy ground as fire fills my lungs and I scream, writhing in torment, gasping for breath that will not come. Brynn topples out of my arms and lands hard into the snow. I grapple for her bloodied hand, afraid to let go—afraid to succumb to the darkness erupting in my head. Thundering hooves erupt from the forest as the world around me grows dark with the rapid beat of my heart.

Chapter 28

My skin tingles with a silent warning as we ride hard for the tree line along the Dark Forest. I anxiously look up through the thick covering of the towering trees above for any glimpse of the moon to determine how long Cia has had to wait. I grind my teeth knowing there is no way Cia would have waited. She would have run headlong into danger if it meant saving someone she loved. I look to my side and try to make out Ronan's face in the darkness that seems to permeate the forest.

I wrestle with the guilt of leaving Cia and Brynn to fend for themselves while knowing that this warband—my warband— needed to mourn their brethren and maintain their faith in their clan chief. Declan was a good warrior and a better brother. A young, soft-spoken man who carried more wisdom than his age should have allowed. It was his patience and willingness to teach that earned him the honor of training the lads in Tiene the art of bearing a blade. It was his lethal precision, with any weapon given to him, that awarded him a position within the warband. I push the regret and bitterness over his untimely death to the back of my mind as we near the meeting place within the forest.

Hope springs forth as I make out the outline of two horses ladened with supplies tied to blackened trees. That hope fizzles as we near unhindered. There is no wall of shadows warning us away, no foul-mouthed filled assaults of my failure bursting forth. There is just an impending symphony of doom orchestrating within the silence of the forest.

The icy ground crunches like bone under Ronan's bulky form as he scrambles from his mount. With a flick of my wrist, my band of men silently draw their weapons and spread out into the shadows of the forest. Ronan's movements are near frantic as he searches the onyx-colored mare's saddlebags. I scan the open field beyond the tree line for any sign of movement as a whisper of a desperate curse breaks the silence and chills me to the bone. I gently urge my mare forward, its ash-colored tail flicking with nervous energy as Ronan turns to me with a shadow-borne dagger in hand.

"She's gone." His rough voice rattles with worry as he looks back toward the quiet of the Fortress.

My eyes flick to the ancient stone triumphantly standing guard as my teeth grind with bitter regret. Smoke fills my flaring nose as I silently unsheathe the sword of Tiene from my back and move from the covering of the blackened tree line. I failed Declan, I will not fail again.

I close my eyes and breathe deeply, savoring the smoke

filling my lungs, as the sound of hooves against the frozen ground fill the void behind me. I crookedly smile as the heat within my eyes greets the cold air with a blood-thirsty roar. I raise my sword, the Draíocht within my veins racing for the hilt, when a pulse of air rushes for me and I nearly topple to the ground with its violence. Chaos erupts behind me with a thunderous shout as my gray dapple-colored mare rears up with a shrill whinny. I grip the saddle horn as another vicious pulse of air whips toward us, forcing the frightened mare back into the covering of the forest.

The Draíocht within me surges with a rapid crescendo and I leap from the horse before I burst into the flames that vehemently beg for release. Ronan's muffled shouts are drowned beneath the shrill scream of my mind as I fall to my knees. I quickly release the sword from my grasp, my fingers digging into the frozen soil. The buildup of Draíocht threatening to consume me releases into the Gaia with a wicked roar, incinerating the ground until all that is left is a blanket of ash.

The sweat from my body ices over as the Draíocht within me settles into a soft warmth and I am overwhelmed with the distinct smell of damp juniper leaves and blood.

Cia.

My pulse quickens and I scramble to my feet wide-eyed, my instincts suddenly alive with knowledge I should not bear. The warband's pale faces are a blur as I stumble wildly through the trees, afraid that I will lose the scent of her—the calling, that now drums with the beat of my heart. Ronan's shout does nothing to deter my pursuit, and I shove my own voice warning against my recklessness aside as I run headlong for whatever lays awaiting me several hundred yards from my grasp.

My blood vigorously hums as the smell of Cia's shadows overpowers my senses. *I am getting close.* The sound of hoof beats closing in behind me pulse against my ears as my feet slide against the frozen ground at my sudden stop. I reach behind me for the sword of Tiene and mutter a curse at myself for leaving it behind. I quickly pull Thyra's blade from my boot, savoring the surge of power it brings and step into the clearing. Nothing could have prepared me for the bloody sight before me.

I have no time to process the thick black ball of shadow swirling protectively above the amount of blood staining the icy slush of the ground a sickening crimson before Ronan bursts forth behind me with a shout of anguish.

"Cia!"

I grab his burly arms, and he wrestles free from my grip, running headlong for the shadows that now move like spiky tendrils across the ground. I run after him as the warband dismounts behind us, drawing their weapons with bewilderment. Ronan ignores my pleas to stop and roars at the wall of black that greets him.

"You know me, let me see her!"

The wall of shadows begrudgingly eases away like a fading

fog, revealing the true horror beneath. A collective gasp echoes behind me, followed by unsettled murmurs too quiet to make out. He gathers her limp body in his arms, blood staining his flesh as he smooths the hair from her face. He clutches her body to his chest with a gut-wrenching sob of relief.

"She's alive! Brother, she's alive!"

His joy does nothing to penetrate the coldness growing in my bones. My lungs struggle for breath as I gaze down in stunned agony at the person left lying in her own blood. The dagger in my tightened grip shakes as I grapple against my growing wrath at the exposed depravity of her mutilated flesh. Ronan rises to his feet, the shadowy tendrils moving lazily behind him as he makes his way to the crowd of men waiting in silence. I do not move as the slush beneath my feet melts with the heat radiating off my body. The golden glow of my eyes turn toward the fortress and the bastard with a death sentence hanging over his head.

"Eowyn?" Finnick's youthful voice calls from behind me.

I blink, the war raging fire and brimstone in my heart stifling, as I slowly turn toward his out-thrust hand. I quickly grab his offering of a fur cloak, and the smell of singed hair billows between us. He lowers his head swiftly, avoiding the sight of Brynn's torture. I secure the dagger into my boot and leave the puddle beneath my feet with a splash as I move to cover her nakedness with my warmth.

She groans in pain as I scoop her broken body gingerly into my arms. The promise of Roimh's death seals itself in my heart at the sound. I lean down and gently whisper a solemn vow into her ear.

"I will always keep you safe."

A deep ominous warning of bells slowly creeps across the clearing from each of the fortress towers. I abandon my concerned gaze from her battered face to see movement along the notched battlement of stone above the closed gate. The fire within me sparks to life as a cloud of arrows darkens the glow of the full moon above. My eyes burn with the flame of a thousand stars as I stare at the fortress of stone with teeth bared in unnaturally wicked defiance. I quickly judge the distance between us and take several footsteps back, listening to the war song of swallow tail arrows penetrate the blood-stained ground before me.

Ronan's voice thunders toward me and snaps me out of the lure for righteous vengeance. I look down once more at the shallow rise of Brynn's chest and pull myself from the fight I vehemently long for. Smoke plumes in wispy clouds behind me as I make my way to where Finnick stands holding the mare steady.

I briskly command, "Remove the saddle. I'll ride bareback."

Finnick nods, wide-eyed and quickly unlatches the belts, slinging the saddle over his shoulder. With Brynn tucked safely in my arms, I swing my legs over in one swift movement and grab the mare's ash-colored mane. I glance over the weary faces of my men, my eyes lingering over each one, gauging how much fight was left burning in their bones. I say nothing, my own weariness now eating away at my voice, and take off into the forest as the sound of shallow tail arrows sing through the night their bitter warning.

We ride hard, a lethal unit closely flanked, until the dead trees blanket us in an impenetrable canopy of night that not even the moonlight can find a way through. I do not slow our charge into the sanctuary of darkness until the quiet trickle of a running creek greets my ears. My voice is heavy and quiet as I bellow a simple command to make camp. The horses paw nervously at the ground as if sensing the filth that finds solace within the death that walks within the darkness. Murmurs of discontent, of the beasts that stalk the shadows, rattle among the men.

My temper simmers beneath the surface, begging for release. I swallow hard, grinding my teeth against the impetuous desire. Ronan looks to me for direction and I simply shake my head. Rebellion festers among the group and I will not allow my own weakness to unravel the sacrifices we have made to get here.

They all remain saddled as my feet vibrate against the dampened ground with a heavy thud. Silence thickens around us until all that remains is the steady flow of water from the creek and the sound of crimson leaves crunching beneath my feet. I quietly place Brynn against the trunk of a dying ash tree, frowning at the sight of her blueish colored lips and sunken black eyes. I crouch before her and gently smooth a tendril of bloody hair from the deep gash across her cheekbone.

I straighten slowly and stiffen my back as I turn to the countless eyes watching me warily. With a voice as hardened as the iron in my sword I bellow a simple command.

"We *will* make camp."

I wait, forcing the Draíocht down, driving the growing desire to make them fall to their knees and tremble beneath my fiery power to the depths of my soul. If I cast away my integrity, their free will, by succumbing to oppression, then I will be left with the corruption of my heart and the ashes of my people. No, I will not rule with a tyranny that demands silence in favor of obedience under the guise of justice. I will not become my father.

Ronan is the first to move, my ever-faithful brother. I watch as one by one they begin to unsaddle their horses. My eyes flick to Finnick who shrugs off his father's clasp to join the others rolling out the fur bedding from their saddlebags. Muris' balding head steams with his anger as he looks around at the allegiance weaving itself through every mundane task. Ronan places Cia, who too remains lost to unconsciousness, next to Brynn and clasps my shoulder with an approving smile. I let out a sigh of relief and relax under the strength of his hand.

Muris leaves the safety of his saddle and saunters across toward us with narrowed eyes and a withered face hardened with fury. My fingers curl into a tight ball as the Draíocht eagerly begs for a reckoning. With clenched teeth and tension coursing through my rigid body, I coldly ask, "Is there a problem, Muris?"

His wrinkled hand tugs on his braided beard and briskly responds, "You need to place sentries if you are going to make us stay in this gods-forsaken place."

A storm of fury brews and my anger thunders within my bones as I take a step forward. Ronan's hand clasps hard on my shoulder, his strength like that of oxen as he holds me back from pummeling the sneer from Muris' leathered face. The smell of flesh burning fills the air around us—*Ronan's flesh.* I hurriedly grasp for self-control; my internal struggle building like the clouds of a thunderstorm until it drenches the fire within my blood. Ronan quietly tears his fingers from my shoulder; their outline now burned into the fabric of my tunic. Muris' lip twitches slightly at the sight and I can feel my self-control slipping just as a moan from the ash tree breaks the growing tension between us.

A familiar voice exclaims, "Are you two done playing king of the forest or do I have to get my own bloody damn water?"

Ronan and I both whirl around with overwhelming surprise. Cia sits up on her forearms, her eyes darting between the three of us with a sheepish grin. Ronan nearly chokes on the sigh of relief he utters and runs headlong for her, squeezing his bulky arms around her tiny frame.

"I'll place the sentries." Muris grumbles to no one in particular.

I glance at him, eyes still dancing with flame, and wickedly grin. "Good. You can be first watch then."

I watch the bulge of his eyes and reddening face with

roguish satisfaction. He retreats, licking his wounded pride and barking orders to the men who gather curiously to see Cia's resurrection.

Her voice cracks, scalded by the burn of the Draíocht, and I turn my attention to her growing concern.

"How is she?"

Ronan kisses her forehead lightly and softly reassures, "She lives."

She smiles with feigned relief, her eyes telling a story of pain and sacrifice. She quickly glances away and gently commands, "Ro, please get me water."

He grumbles at the idea of leaving her but slowly obeys, looking behind him every few steps as he makes his way to the creek bed where the horses now water. I move closer and crouch before her, studying the furrow of her brow, the quiver of her lips.

"I pushed too far trying to save her. I nearly burnt myself from the inside out."

My jaw tightens with disapproval and we both glance to where Brynn lays. My voice is firm, a little too firm. "You cannot do that again." I look toward Ronan as he makes his way back to us with a delighted smile behind his scraggly beard. "It will kill him."

Cia musters a smile as Ronan gently offers the flask, his face brightening like that of a thousand suns at the touch of her fingers against his own. Their simple show of affection stirring the familiar ache within my heart that I have tried desperately to silence. I quickly glance at Brynn, watching the slow rise and fall of her chest as Cia empties the flask with a quiet shiver. Ronan takes a seat next to her, his hands fidget with the desire to pull her closer but instead he maintains his distance as the whites of her eyes begin to blacken with streaks of anger. I take a deep breath. Cia's moods are as volatile as her shadows, shifting as quickly as sand, and based on the soft glow of white in the flecks of her darkened eyes I am certain to meet her wrath for my part in her near demise. Her low voice rakes deep against my spine as if Death has come calling.

"You didn't show." She looks at Brynn's bloodied face and her head snaps back to face me, her eyes now shining as bright as a full moon. I brace myself. She lunges for my throat as Ronan wraps his burly arms around her in a tight squeeze from behind, catching her mid-air. Her finger shakes with rage as she points at me with a voice filled with venom.

"She wanted to leave! We were going to bloody damn leave! Then you didn't show! You gods-damned didn't show!"

I hurry to my feet as she wrestles free of Ronan's grasp. Her tiny fist swings hard and hits me square in the jaw as I stumble. I see the flash from her boot too late as she leaps on top of me. The cool touch of blade slices lightly into the flesh of my throat, just enough to draw a drop of blood. She turns her head and snarls viciously at Ronan who approaches cautiously to rescue me from her blind rage as the warband circles with weapons drawn.

"I will gut him right here if you move another step!"

The vein in my neck beats precariously against the pressure of her blade as I holler for them all to hold. She turns to me, her face like stone and streaked with tendrils of black against her fawn-colored skin. There is a hidden depth of pain in her voice, behind her gritted teeth as she whispers, "They discarded her as if she didn't matter. They left her naked and exposed to all who dared to watch. They carved *Whore of Ravndal* in the soft of her belly, over her womb. Did you see her skin brother? Did you see the way it was flayed to the bone? You could have stopped it. You could have taken her a year ago, a bloody damn fortnight ago, but instead you chose a prophecy over a gods-damned person!"

The self-control I had tried so hard to muster melts beneath the rage that boils hot in my gut. I move before her shadows can react, grabbing the wrist possessing the blade tightly and with my free arm I loop and wrench her arm back against her shoulder blade. Within seconds my legs wrap around her hips and within a heartbeat I twist, flipping her to the ground and forcing my body on top.

She struggles under my weight as I quickly pin both of her arms above her head, pushing them painfully hard into the frozen ground. The fiery glow of my eyes against the white glow of her own reflects a cosmic war of will and heartache.

"People died for that prophecy. Good people. Your people. That gods-damned witch killed every last one of them for that prophecy. Seven of the thirteen men here have lost someone to that prophecy. You lost your entire clan to that prophecy. She *had* to break. I did what I was fated to do, and I will continue to. *You* of all people should know that." I lower my head to her ear with a malicious whisper. "Do not tell me you do not crave it, little sister. The growing urge that breathes in your veins. The need to feel complete. Tell me. Is the call of the Draíocht why you feel so guilty, that you, too, waited until she was broken?"

The black tendrils drain from her face and tears flood her eyes. The fire in my own blood drains at the sight of her defeat and I release her wrists, slowly moving to the side as I stand. The warband disperses quickly, each one avoiding our cold war. All but Muris, who annoyingly watches from his post as sentry with folded arms and a wicked smile. I offer my hand in an effort of peacekeeping, and she spits at it, flipping herself up to her feet. She storms off with a scowl, snatching her curved blade to her side. Ronan and I remain still, silent, as she marches past us and shoulders Muris hard in his upper arm before saddling a black speckled mare. I watch her blend into the night, kicking myself in frustration for allowing it to get this far.

Ronan turns toward me, and I can hardly stand under the gaze of sympathy and sorrow building behind his eyes. His footsteps are as heavy as my heart as he makes his way to me. He pulls my forehead against his own, before his voice, laden with emotion, breaks out silence.

"Heavy is the head that bears the sword."

I sigh deeply and mutter, "And strong is the Draíocht that

flows through the blood."

His hand squeezes against the back of my head with a brotherly love of reassurance. "Tomorrow is fated, not finished."

I smile with the memory of our mother teaching us those very words as boys, before our father's madness. How we clung tightly to those words when the world seemingly upended for us both with her death. I am not sure why the Fates chose me to lead the people of Tiene instead of Ronan. He is a mountain of a man, able to kill an ox with his bare hands. Slow to anger, incredibly patient, and respected among all people. As lads, it was Ronan that was favored for the succession of Chieftain. A fierce warrior who is as fair as he is wise. I have always been short-tempered, impatient, and prone to make rash decisions, even before the fire in my veins roared to life. The Draíocht awakening within me only fuels my lack of self-control.

When the Fates chose me and the Draíocht awakened, the elders of the clan were forced into a decision that they were not willing to make. Muris said as much the day of my ascension. Making Ronan my second was my first decision as Clan Chief and one that has helped maintain a balance of peace among the elders ever since. He has always been my shield, my protector, my voice of reason when the flames burn too bright. His simple reminder comforts my aching heart, and I am able to regain the footing needed to continue pressing forward.

We let go of each other's embrace. He moves to the center of the camp while I settle next to Brynn. Ronan's deep voice echoes through the quiet of the trees as he brings the warband together in a jovial mead hall song. I look away from the stillness of Brynn's body in shame as Cia's words come back to haunt me. *Whore of Ravndal.* I clench my fists and hang my head, feeling the weight of my own decisions pressing me deeper into a grave.

Chapter 29

The darkness within me does not settle as Eowyn's words chase me deeper into the forest. Exhaustion begs for the solitude of sleep, but I know even then I will be haunted by my own doings. My heart finally gives up the fight and I swing off the horse to the ground, collapsing to my knees among the deadened leaves of the decaying ash trees. Tears well in my eyes and I let out a guttural scream into the void of my sorrow.

My shadows attempt to soothe my pain, but I brush their efforts away with a flick of my hand. Nothing can comfort me now, I must feel this, to remind myself of my own humanity. I cannot lose sight of that thread of morality like before. For it is when I am numb to my pain that He comes calling and I cannot allow the past to wage war for a foothold in my mind. As if in response, my senses are overwhelmed with the smell of salty orange blossoms—of *her*.

She was beautiful, like sunshine and light summer rain.

She was the balm to my cold, dark heart and I was in love with every part of her. The way her golden eyes would shine with mischief as she stole apples right under a vendor's nose with a simple sleight of hand. The sweet smell of her honeyed breath against my lips after a night of drunken debauchery in the belly of the Capital. The softness of her raven-colored hair and the feel of her perfumed deep golden skin against my fingertips.

I grasp my stomach, my fingers tracing the deep scar across the softness of my skin. I am immediately overwhelmed with the flash of images in my mind. Of a darkened tower, the burn of the blade ripping my flesh open, and Aliera's screams of agony. I was too late then. Too late to save the only person who had ever loved my darkness fully until Ronan. I ran from that tower like a coward, leaving her to suffer a fate much worse than death. Tonight, I nearly suffered the same fate. I nearly lost someone who had become the balm to my darkness all for the sake of a prophecy I only half-heartedly believe we will win with.

I wipe the tears from my eyes and slowly stand, allowing the shadows to nuzzle against my cheek.

"Come along old friend, we have fate to attend to."

My shadows happily spring forth and take the shape of phantom woodland creatures no bigger than my hand. I softly laugh as they frolic ahead with each step I take. A gentle reminder of my childhood and the presence they have always maintained in keeping me safe no matter how lost I have been in the wilderness. Guiding me to Tiene and the man I now call home.

I slip past Finnick unnoticed, something I will have to berate him about tomorrow, and follow the path to Ronan's soft snores. Being near him, feeling his warmth, smelling that earthy scent of pine and rain is exactly what my soul needs. I offer a gentle smile to Eowyn as he remains at vigil over Brynn. He glances my way solemnly, an unspoken truce growing between us as I lay my head against Ronan's chest and drift off to sleep.

The warmth of the rising sun settles on the camp though there is no light other than that of the small campfires scattered about when Brynn's pain-laced scream awakens me. I scramble to my feet, dagger in hand as the camp comes alive with the clang of swords and shields. I blink the sleep from my eyes and nearly topple over Ronan trying to get to her. Eowyn stumbles backwards, his face ghostly white and panicked. She looks at me wild-eyed and I reach to softly rub the hair from her broken face. She thrashes wildly and the cuts across her chest and arms begin to drip blood anew as she cries out. My voice breaks with the weight of her fear.

"Shhh, you're okay. You're safe. I promise. You are safe. I am here."

She blinks rapidly, her eyes focusing on my face and not the fear that clouds her mind.

"Cia?"

I quietly sob a sigh of relief. "Yes, it's me. I am here."

She moans in pain as she lifts her shaky arm and reaches

for my hand. I grasp it as tightly as I can without causing her pain. She falls apart at the touch, her voice a symphony of grief and agony.

"He...he wouldn't kill me. I begged and begged for him to kill me."

I glance up quickly at her proclamation as Ronan mutters a curse. Eowyn's grief-stricken eyes dart to my own and the pain in his face is as if her words have stolen his ability to breathe. I quietly wipe the tears from her cheeks, trying my best to console her, though I am certain that nothing I say will ever take away the suffering of what she has endured. Her eyes widen and she chokes on a fresh sob as she tries and fails to rise from where she lays. I can taste the saltiness of her panic before she even speaks.

"He...took them. Cia! He took them!" She begins to shake uncontrollably, clawing at my arm to pull her up. Her face whitens as I help her sit up, the wounds across her body cracking open with each violent move she makes. "He's going to hurt them. He told me he would just start over. Cia! He took them... "

Her eyes widen as she takes in the darkness around her and the decay of trees canopying us from above. She gasps, her body going completely still as her eyes dart between Eowyn and Ronan. I hold my breath, watching as she takes in the sight of Ronan's braided beard, the blue markings etched into the bald sides of his head, and the Elkan antlers secured at his sword's sheath. She swallows hard and turns to me with a fearful whisper, "Here...he brought them here."

In an instant, a coldness sweeps over me as dread settles deep in my bones. I can hardly catch my breath as I look at Eowyn, searching for some kind of solace to give her. His own fear is etched in every line across his furrowed brows and clenched jaw. Minutes pass between us and our silence is filled with the painful outcry of a mother who has lost the very thing she lives for—her children.

I flinch as Ronan's voice breaks through the barrier of grief surrounding us and roars orders through the camp. In an instance, the men watching sympathetically from a distance come to life without hesitation. Wee ones in a forest riddled with darkness is one thing we all as a clan will rally behind. The Laioses may be everything the queen claims, but we do not tolerate harm toward children, no matter their lineage. I call after Eowyn with my own demands.

"Go to the pack horse and look in the saddlebags. Bring them to me." I quickly turn to Brynn and slowly help her to her feet. I tuck the fur blanket tightly around her and soften my voice. "Come, let's get you dressed in something warmer. Then we will go find them." I muster a reassuring smile despite my own fear prickling my spine. "Finnick is our best tracker. We will get them in no time, you'll see."

She smiles weakly back at me though her eyes tell me she does not believe a word that I am saying. Eowyn's return interrupts my pageantry of pleasant smiles and gentle reassurances.

"Open that one. Yes, that one. Hand me the woolen tunic. No, not that one." He lets out an exasperated huff as I continue to bark orders. He gathers the clothes in his arms, kicking the saddlebag out of the way. Brynn sways as I release my grip on her and move to meet him. I quickly grab the clothes and nod toward Ronan's blanket. "Grab that and hold it up." I look at Brynn apologetically. "I would use the shadows to hide you, but I want to be well rested once we safely recover the children. You are in no shape to care for them and well you know how rambunctious Ophele can be."

She nods weakly, reaching out to hold my arm to steady herself again. Satisfied she has accepted my little lie, I get busy helping her into the woolen tunic, breeches, and fur-lined cloak. Each movement brings soft cries and moans every time the lashes marking her body pull until I am sure that I will choke on the lump forming in my throat.

"Do you smell that? It smells as if hair is being burned," Brynn exclaims through labored breath.

My head darts to where Eowyn stands, a tendril of smoke pluming from each hand. I mutter a curse under my breath; Ronan is going to be furious his favorite blanket is burned.

"Hmmm. I don't smell anything," I proclaim loudly before hurriedly crouching and placing the boots at her feet. "Here, put these on. They are a little big, but they are all I could snatch on short notice." I look up at her with a wink as I help her slide the boots on. "Though, I am not sure what we are going to do with *that* hair."

She slightly grins awry and teases, "You should see yours."

I stick my tongue out in response and stand, turning to Eowyn. "Okay, we are done now."

He gathers the blanket in his arms and Brynn drops her gaze immediately to the ground. He walks cautiously toward her, his voice as smooth and sweet as honey.

"I am going to wrap you in this blanket, if that is okay."

Her head shoots up, eyes wide with fear, her body jerking with tension. Eowyn immediately stops advancing, respecting the distance between them and looks to me. There is a softness in his approach that I have never seen in him before, and I watch in awestruck wonder at this side of him he rarely allows to be seen.

"That's okay. I am just going to give the blanket to Cia then and she can wrap you in it. Will that be, okay?"

Brynn nods quickly, avoiding his gaze as he hands the blanket quietly to me. I lean toward him, keeping my voice low so that any of the men scurrying around do not eavesdrop.

"She has a nasty infection within the burn on her thigh. She will need it cleaned and dressed by the healer once we are in Ravndal."

Brynn suddenly erupts in a storm of bitter tears. I hurriedly move from Eowyn and wrap the blanket around her, unsure of what has caused the abrupt well of emotion. She clutches to it tightly like it will somehow protect her from her memories and hauntingly whispers, "Perri...He branded me. To force me to always remember the night he almost..."

I am unable to control the shadows that seep from the pores of my skin as a feral rage unleashes within me. I mutter a storm of curses toward the bastards who have taken a piece of her that she will never get back. The faint smell of charred wood and ash wafts into the air around us and I quickly glance at Eowyn's darkened face and the flames that burn bright in his eyes. I tense and position myself as a shield in front of her, not trusting the wrath that scorches the air around him. He does not move, he continues standing there, holding space for her to work through the emotions she is drowning in. The race of my heart slows with the soothing sound of his gentle voice.

"Brynn. I know you have been lied to, and that I have been part of that lie, but I need you to understand me when I tell you that *nothing* like that will ever happen to you again. You are safe here." He nods toward me with a half-smile. "Cia and I will *always* make sure of that." He looks behind him, as Ronan approaches with our horses. "Now, we are going to go find your children, but you will need to ride with me if you are okay with that. Your wounds are fresh and there is a highly probable chance that you will collapse from the pain that riding will incur." He turns toward us and pretends not to see her grab my arm tightly. "Cia will be right beside us with Ronan, my brother."

She meets his gaze, and I am certain I see a slight wince as he studies the full effect of Roimh's wrath. Her troubled eyes dart to mine and I tap her hand with a reassuring smile. She frowns slightly, the color of her face as white as snow, but she nods in agreement. Ronan brings the horses forward with the nod of Eowyn's head and I do not venture far once she is atop the mount's bare back. I squeeze her hand tight as Eowyn reaches for the reins and swings his legs over, settling in behind her.

She slumps to the side, passing out from the movement of the horse pawing the ground impatiently. Eowyn quickly grabs her before she topples off and melds his body into hers, setting her head against his chest. I unleash a sliver of shadows from within, wrapping them together as one. The men fall in line behind Eowyn as I take my place atop the black speckled mare. Eowyn's voice commands the atmosphere as he addresses the warband.

"Fan out. Look for a blond little girl and a sandy brown-haired lad. Do not go alone. We stick together no matter what. If you cannot find them before sundown, head to the border. Remember, we are Tiene, and we make the darkness flee!"

The warband erupts in a war cry before splitting into groupings. It is only then that I notice the absence of Declan. I turn in the saddle to Ronan, my brow furrowed in confusion, and he solemnly shakes his head. I have no time to question the circumstances of such a loss before Eowyn leads us swiftly toward the known path to the border. Brynn's whimper of pain is the only sound between us.

Chapter 30

I am unable to garner any sense of peace in my soul with each gasp and whimper she makes in the safety of my arms. Her fingers dig sharply into my skin with each gentle sway of the horse, but I don't mind the pain. It is but a small penance for my part in her suffering. Roimh may have been the executioner of her pain, but I might as well have handed him the whip. I had played a dangerous game by allowing her to stay and not whisking her away the night she collapsed in the temple of Dagda.

I justified it then, telling myself that I was giving her autonomy, a voice in deciding to leave of her own accord, that she was not ready to come willingly. I was a coward, hiding behind the guise of honor while lusting for more of the power wailing for freedom within me. Whatever creature the queen had conjured within that temple had been desperate, forcing her hand in such a way to risk Brynn's life and I had done nothing to stop it. Instead, I chose to stalk within the shadows like a ravenous beast waiting for the first scent for a sweet release.

She slumps further into the crook of my arms, fighting to stay conscious with each beat of her heart. I glance down, gazing at her battered face while the war between my mind and soul rages for a foothold. A war that has been waged since that very night she collapsed in the snow along the garden path. The night that I held her in my arms like this, longing for a fate that will surely never come. I look ahead, shifting my focus and allow the wildfire that pulses with life in my veins to drown out the hopeless dreams of my soul.

The Draíocht within me continuously burns with a solemn promise, an ancient oath passed down within the bloodline of the gods—to protect the Gaia and all who honor her. That is my purpose, my fate in this world, anything else is but a distraction from the duty in which I have been called to answer. The crunch of dying leaves beneath the mare's hooves seem to answer in agreement. The Gaia is dying; this forest is evidence enough of it and if the queen is not stopped in her perversion of the Draíocht there will be nothing left but the dark creatures that stalk the night.

The Witch of Agderia holds no qualms of the corruption she creates with the desperate blood thirst that comes with her power over life and land. Those born with the blood of the gods are offered up like sacrificial lambs. My mother warned our father of her power, of her desire to possess all those born with

Draíocht running in their veins, of the need to protect the child born of light despite the years of civil war within the clans of Ravndal. She spoke of unity among the Laioses and how the Draíocht would never run freely, never destroy the darkness birthed at the queen's hand.

Most of the Laioses history was destroyed in the burning of the Cerwei temple and the murder of the priestesses that protected the ancient scrolls when the queen rose to power. People will always rise from the ashes. It is in the taking of their history, rewriting it until the truth is somehow lost within the remnants of those ashes, bringing about true destruction. Silence their past and you will have authority over their future.

I was but a wee one, not long after learning to walk, when Queen Hilde brought a plague of darkness to the land and with it came the death of Oéngus, the Clan of Light. An entire clan, wiped from existence, as if they were nothing but dust within the lush valley of hills they called home. With the Clan's death, the Draíocht awoke within countless children across Tiene after generations of lying dormant. I was the only one to survive the Threshing, a curse placed upon our bloodline that burns a child from the inside out once the flames of Tiene ignite in their blood.

I do not know much of Tiene's earliest history, only that of what was passed down through the Elders over campfires and clan meetings. After setting fire to half the village with the grief over my mother's death, I was sent off to Riacán, the Clan of Water. It was there that I truly learned of the power bestowed to the gods and the price of inheriting that power. When I returned, I understood two things: the Gaia must be protected at all costs, and the darkness cannot possess the Draíocht, or we will all perish.

As I grew into my power so did Hilde's power and despite the clan's best efforts, the strength of the Laioses continues to wane. The clans now live in a tentative cold war, forced into a guarded sense of peace for survival. Neither clan fully trusts the other, but we all share the hope in a prophecy spoken by the Priestesses of Cerwei long ago. A hope for a future, for prosperity, and a life untethered to the sorrow that comes with the darkness of death.

I glance down at Brynn, whose pain is etching tensely across her face. I question my own sense of duty that has been ingrained within me since childhood. I can feel the Draíocht break free of the chains holding it back with each trauma that she suffers, and I question how much more will she have to break for the prophecy to be filled? Can I watch someone so innocent, so pure of heart, suffer to the point of death so that we might all live? Will I be able to stand by and allow it to happen anymore?

My fingers soothingly brush the softness of her clenched jaw. If she breaks anymore, whether it be physically or mentally, only an act of the gods will ensure her survival. I cannot help but feel a sense of understanding beyond my own comprehension, that it is exactly what the prophecy means by her breaking. That the gods or Eadom himself will use her to create what the Dagda once was, an embodiment of the Draíocht—a living and breathing weapon capable of mass destruction.

My mare's ears pin back flat, and my inner thoughts quickly silence as a branch snaps like bone in the distance. I narrow my eyes, searching for the source as the cool shadows unwrap around my waist and shoot off, probing into the dark path ahead. Brynn lets out a quiet whimper as I hold her tighter against me and pull the sword from my back with my free hand. Cia and Ronan close in tight, drawing their own blades to attention.

The hair on the back of my neck stands, my instincts echoing the Draíocht's warning that something watches me. I quickly look to Cia, who tightly nods to me in agreement. *She feels it too.* Her shadows pour out of her skin, lashing through the brush and trees around us like a whip, searching. The mare freezes suddenly as the forest goes unnaturally quiet. The Draíocht within me surges out of my control, the markings on my sword hum to life with an icy-blue glow just as a flash of white darts across my left side.

Cia's shadows let out a shriek that chills me to the bone. She nearly topples from the force of their return into her body. Her face is pale, her eyes wide in true fear, as she glances uneasily from me to Ronan. The shadows shrink from no one, dead or alive. Not until now.

I grasp onto the tether between the Draíocht and the sword in my hand, forcing the Draíocht to pour into the Rüin markings along the blade. The skin within my hand tingles with anticipation as the sword comes to life with hot bright flames that illuminate the darkness slowly growing around us. The Draíocht lets out a piercing wail within my mind and I nearly collapse from the force of its howl. Cia lets out a cry, grabbing her head as Ronan watches us in bewilderment, unphased by our sudden turmoil. The creature steps on to the path before us and the Draíocht's wail of pain suddenly silences. The flames engulfing my sword instantly extinguish as if the tether between blade and power have been sliced in two. No one breathes, no one moves—horse and man frozen in place under the gaze of its piercing blue eyes swirling in starlight.

The wolf-like creature is the largest beast I have ever seen roam the Gaia, like something out of a child's nightmares. The top of its legs sit level with the top of my mare's head with paws twice the size of my head. Its thick coat is blindingly white, and I fight the urge to shield my eyes from its purity. The ground trembles as it takes a step toward me and lowers its massive head until we are eye level with each other. I feel the Draíocht within me falter into submission and I grapple with the reality of what is before me. Have the gods awakened? Do they walk among us again?

The creature bares its sharpened teeth as if it has heard my own musings. Brynn stirs, her body growing overwhelmingly hot in my arms. The beast's gaze shifts from mine to the woman in my arms, eagerly licking its massive jaw. I am trapped under the weight of its ethereal power, unable to move or speak to quiet her as its gaze shifts deliberately back to me and I am suddenly overwhelmed with images of my mother slowly dying until I am again a boy of five holding her weakening hand. Her voice faltering under the grasp of Death.

A child, chosen by Eadom, born of Light,
Shall bear the weapon forged in fire,
And broken in blood.
The Chosen shall unite the Laioses,
And bring Death upon all who bear His name.
Guard the Chosen until the darkness breaks—
And what was lost shall restore again.

Remember the prophecy, my sweet boy. Remember what you are fated to do. Only then will we survive. Promise me, Eowyn. Promise me you will, for the Gaia and the Draíocht burning in your blood. You will ascend to a higher calling, Eowyn. Give into the thread of fate placed on your life, my darling boy, but do not lose your soul within the flames. With this blade you will free us all from the grasps of an ancient darkness. Always remember, no matter what happens— believe in yourself.

My mother's blade burns hot against my skin as the memory fades from my blurry eyes. The beast closes its eyes and tilts its head back to the sky. With an earth-shattering howl that ripples toward us in forceful waves, the wolf leaps on its long, powerful legs into the air before us. I watch in complete disbelief as the white of its fur turns black and its body becomes an unkindness of ravens, circling toward the canopy of trees above.

"What in the bloody hell was that!" Cia cries out in a mix of shock and dismay.

Ronan's mouth hangs open and I shake my head, unable to grasp any sense of thought or words to explain the insanity of what just happened. We do not sit for long grappling in our shock for reality, when a familiar birdsong echoes through the trees. My heart drops in my chest and Cia's face tightens with foreboding worry.

They found the children.

Chapter 31

With strength I did not believe I could possess, I fought the agonizing pain and waves of nausea from the moment Eowyn placed mc on the back of his horse. I drift between consciousness; a sea of thick canopied trees made of decaying limbs and the tender concern hidden behind the flecks of flame in his eyes. The horse's abrupt stop and the tightening hold of his strong arms jolts me from my pain-induced slumber. I awoke to a dream of blinding white and icy-blue eyes towering above me that transform into a sea of feathers the color of the darkest night. I'm lolled back to the dark corners of my mind by the mournful sound of birds filling the air.

I slowly blink awake to Cia's hushed voice, concern burrowing deeply across her face, though I cannot make out what she is saying. A thick blanket of fog rolls across the ground where she stands just beyond the row of trees ahead. I close my eyes hard and open them, trying to clear the blur coating my vision. My heart races as I watch the strength in her shoulders sag with the weight of what the wrinkled bald man dressed in furs tells her. Just beyond them is a clearing where several warriors, all dressed similarly in furs with various lengths of braids in their hair and bearing scars of battles on their skin like trophies, stand in somber vigilance.

She turns, her face downcast to the ground, unable to look at me as she makes her way to us. Eowyn's grasp tightens protectively around me as if to shield me from whatever dreadful news Cia bears. I am certain that I will choke on the dread burrowing its way down my throat and into the pit of my stomach with every heavy step she takes toward me. I dig my fingers into Eowyn's warm skin and stiffen my spine straight as she looks up at me with overwhelming grief.

I whisper, "Take me to them."

Cia glances at Eowyn and shakes her head slightly. I know deep down in my heart that it is her way of protecting me from whatever brutality lay waiting for me in that clearing, but I do not care. My sorrow wails within me and I cannot bear to remain behind the shield of her protection. The mother within me, the one who nurtured and loved with a never-ending love, cannot bear it. I must hold them. I must kiss their innocent little faces one last time.

"Take me to them, Eowyn. Now. Or so help me, I will crawl to them with what little strength I have left," I vehemently command.

There is a heartbeat of silence and in that moment, it feels as if the world might collapse around me with the heaviness of that stillness. Cia steps back as he picks up the reins and pulls me closer to him so that our bodies are flush with each other. I breathe in the smokiness of cedar and a crackling fire as he squeezes his legs into the mare's ribs. My physical pain numbs to the pain now erupting in my soul as salty tears fall from my face. My broken body screams with the rushing pace as we break through the trees, but my soul screams louder.

Freezing water splashes as we emerge from the forest and into the clearing littered with islands of dead grass patched across the marshy dark water like chess pieces. The sun shines bright upon us within the crisp blue sky overhead, a vast contrast from the darkness of the forest. Eowyn pulls hard on the reins as we near the center of the marshland and I grab hold to the mare's ash-flaked mane to keep from toppling over its head. It is only then that I see them.

Two small shapes laid neatly upon a frozen island of grass now stained deep crimson with their blood. It is as if the sun itself could not bear to look upon the violence inflicted upon such innocence, the snow still inches deep beneath their still bodies. The sight of them laying there so lifelessly knocks the breath out of my lungs and my body threatens to collapse as my blood ices over. Eowyn lifts me gently off the mare and my legs give out from under me, my knees sinking into the pool of muddy water beneath me. I let out a gut-wrenching sob as Eowyn places his hand softly on my shoulder and whispers, "We don't have to go any further. You shouldn't see this."

I fight against the bile rising to my throat and I lift my head to look upon him coldly. A gentle wind stirs his brassy red hair and a lock tumbles down from his braid. He looks upon me with a tender concern that I have never experienced before, but I feel nothing but the coldness that creeps into my heart with every dreadful beat. I push past the acrid taste on my tongue, tearing my gaze away from him and to the small red mounds waiting for me in the snow.

"I am their mother."

I weakly rise, leaving fragments of my soul to drown in the marshy soil and make my way to where my bludgeoned heart lays waiting. My strength to continue living weakens with every step I take. My knees buckle as the smell of death greets my shaking body, and I falter under the weight of it. I collapse to the ground, what remains of my soul screaming until my throat burns raw at the horrific sight of their mutilated bodies.

Blood—their blood, coldly soaks through the woolen fabric of my breeches, baptizing my skin with its touch. Bile rises from my stomach, and I fall to my hands, heaving what remains of me. Emptiness radiates in my chest from the chasm of darkness where my heart once beat. I beg for the comfort of Death, for this indescribable pain to cease at the hands of a mercy that will not come.

Ophele's blond curls are now soaked red and splayed in the snow like a broken crown. The necklace she proudly wore around her neck hangs haphazardly over what remains of her fragile skin. The chain sinks deeply into the gaping slash across her tiny throat. I close my eyes and turn my head, unable to look at the missing flesh of her mutilated face, but I am haunted by the brutality of her death even in my memories. Her button nose, pouty lips, and turquoise eyes now replaced with the evidence that she has been feasted upon by the demons that stalk the darkness of this forest.

I quickly open my tear-filled eyes and what is left of my mind shatters. *Olan.* His body is a shield across Ophele's chest, even in death he protects his sister. Splinters of my mind cut through every inch of me and burrow into what is left of my soul at the sight of his back cut open and ribs flayed out like wings. His head is twisted grotesquely to the sky so that the muscles and bones in his face greet the sun.

I tilt my head up, my blood-stained hands clutch my chest, and I scream in agony—breaking under the weight of my suffering. The world shakes violently beneath me and answers my piercing anguish. Still, I scream. My eyes burn with a white-hot pain that blurs my mind beneath a fiery blue blaze. I burn from the inside out as the icy blue fire rushes through me and consumes me. Still, I scream. The earth upends itself, pelting me with its ricochet of soil and rock as my body rises from the ground. Smoke fills my lungs, the flames devouring me and I burn within its relentless roar.

Part 2

A child, chosen by Eadom, born of Light,
Shall bear the weapon forged in fire,
And broken in blood.
The Chosen shall unite the Laioses,
And bring Death upon all who bear His name.
Guard the Chosen until the darkness breaks—
And what was lost shall restore again.

Chapter 32

Brynn

I fall through a myriad of fluorescent colors, plummeting through glowing shades of purple, green, orange, pink, and blue until I hit the ground hard. I hesitantly peek out from my burning eyes, bracing myself for what lays waiting for me as my mind awakens in an unknown world. I open my eyes wide as shock rolls through me and scramble to my feet. I look around in wonder, the death scene of my children no longer before me. I quickly look down at my hands, puzzled by the softness of my skin. I no longer bear the cuts of Roimh's whip nor the stain of my children's blood.

What once was marshy land is now powdery white sand that reflects like crystals in the bright sun above. I shield my eyes as I look above me, and I am breathlessly taken aback by the swirls of soft pink and peach against the violet sapphire sky. The sound of waves crashing gently lulls me with their peaceful song just beyond a thick fog that stands guard along the sand. A sense of peace, something so foreign to me, wraps softly around me like a warm blanket on a stormy night. I cannot help but want to remain in this place, where heartache ceases and misery is without company.

Where am I?

A raspy voice calls from beyond the fog, "You have come at last."

I squint my eyes and search for the voice, swallowing hard against the lump in my throat as something terrifying steps from beyond the veil. A creature, both man and beast, greets me with a smirk. Elkan antlers, covered in Rüin markings and draped with silver moss sit atop his head. A robe of black drags behind him as he walks, leaving a trail of shadows that rise like wisps of smoke and turn the glistening sand into darkened silt. I eye the shadows dancing along the engravings of the towering scythe in its hand nervously as the raven perched on its shoulder cocks its head and laughs at my obvious discomfort.

"W—what do you want? Who are you?"

The creature lifts its long bony, gloved hand toward its face as it replies, "You begged for me, did you not?" His eyes glow white, like that of the brightest moon on a clear night, cast haunting shadows across his heavily scarred face. His hair reminds me of spiderwebs glistening in the sun, though the strands are much thicker, like spun thread that tapers well below his broad chest. "I have come for you at last, my dear Brynn."

My skin crawls at the emphasis of my name and I take a hesitant step back. I wanted peace. I wanted to be reunited with my children. I did not want to be dragged off by some creature of Hel into the billowing fog that now builds like thick smoke behind him. My eyes dart to each side of me, searching for a way to escape, to hide. He watches me closely, waiting for me to make a move. His fingers tap impatiently against the scythe, the scratch of sharpened nails against metal sending shivers up my spine. I hold my breath as he slowly turns to the raven perched on his shoulder and heavily sighs.

"It seems, she is not as ready as she once thought." He turns his face to me with a deep scowl. "What a pity."

I flinch as the raven hisses at me in disgust. My heart races as I fight the urge to fall to my knees in fearful submission. He raises a hand, splaying his wicked fingers toward me and opens his mouth to reveal a blackened tongue laced with words of warning.

"A life for a life. A soul for a soul."

One by one he pulls his fingers back toward him and my lungs painfully tighten with each vengeful movement. The beat of my heart slows as each finger closes into a fist until I am desperately scratching at my throat for release.

"Do not summon me again, my darling, unless you are willing to pay the price now owed to me."

He drops his hand, and I choke on the air refilling my lungs. My heart thunders wildly in my ears as I double over holding my chest. With tears staining my cheek, I gasp for more of the precious salty air surrounding me. I raise my head to nod an agreement to his terms but all that remains is a trail of darkened silt imprinted upon the sand.

"Hello, daughter of Eadom."

Bloody Hel.

I quickly stand straight and whirl around to greet the light, hollow voice behind me. I stumble backwards, my mind grappling for a grasp on what is happening as a woman emerges from the air before me. She is clothed in a sheer robe spun from living vines and delicate leaves that glisten with dew. The fabric clings with her every movement as tiny flowers bloom and fade within the vines with every breath she takes. Her skin is a luminous shade of pale blue that is kissed with the shimmer of light as if she is made of nothing but diamonds and mist. She glows softly like moonlight against water. Her hair is a cascade of soft ivory waves that fall down the length of her back like running water. Tiny, iridescent pearls nestle like morning dew in each strand and capture the sunlight so that it looks as if she bears a crown of divinity. Her brilliant amethyst eyes are like the purest jewels as she stares back at me in silent amusement at my shock.

"W—who are you?" I ask timidly.

Her soft smile magnifies the amethyst glow of her bright eyes. "I am who I am. The beginning and the end."

She glides across the sand with bare feet, and I'm lulled into a sense of comfort as she draws near.

"What is this place?"

She looks slowly around her and gently says, "We are neither here nor there, as it is with all who face the sting of Death."

My spine tingles with her words and I look hesitantly behind me as if I will somehow find Death and his raven staring at me from the veil of fog. She gently touches my chin and pulls my face back toward her.

"You have already chosen, daughter of Eadom. Now you must see."

I swallow hard and breathily ask, "What must I see?"

She softly brushes a tangled strand of hair from my brow and smiles brightly, placing a finger against the center of my forehead.

"Everything."

I am blinded with light at her touch, and the echoes of her voice fill my mind as images begin to flash before me. I shrink within myself as my children's bodies flash, but as quickly as the picture comes another follows behind it. Cia, much younger than she is now, with long raven-colored hair, stumbles into a land of golden mountains. Blood pours from a wound in her belly. I reach out to her when she quickly disappears and is replaced with Eowyn. He is just a boy engulfed in flames. Tears pour down his face as a village catches fire, with the enormity of his grief. Children, no bigger than Ophele play together in a field of wildflowers. One with curly auburn hair braided down her back and the other with short, tousled copper hair. The light blinds me from seeing their faces as a woman with bright copper hair runs toward me with a wailing bundle of linens in her arms. Behind her a village set in hills turns to dust, the screams of the dying rattle me to my bones. I try to close my eyes but still the images come with an urgency I do not understand.

War and famine litter the ground with broken bodies and blood. There is so much blood that the grass suffocates under the weight of it, turning black with its stain. One by one trees begin to decay, flowers wilt, and all that was living and breathing succumbs to the violence inflicted upon it. A flash of deep indigo eyes and a sinister smile, peers out from a prison of bones with each horrifying image of malice. I shrink from its gaze as another image flashes and I am thrust forward until I stand within an arching doorway.

Before me stretches an alabaster-marbled courtyard, bursting with an overwhelming abundance of blush-colored snapdragons, lavender peonies, and white hyacinths. Their delightful scent wraps around me like a blanket on a warm spring morning. Impossibly high archways rise from massive pillars engraved with golden vines that shimmer with opulence, forming the four walls of the courtyard. Violet wisteria cascades from above in delicate clusters, creating a whimsical ceiling of blossoms.

I turn my attention to those gathering at the center, dressed in silken fabrics befitting royalty. A man—taller than Eowyn and broader than Ronan—stands at the center of the courtyard, his presence impossible to ignore. His skin glows as though fire flows just beneath its surface. His hair, a crown of flickering flame, moves with a life of its own, crackling softly and casting shifting light across his sharply defined features. His eyes blaze like twin embers, glowing orange with hints of gold at the center, fierce and unrelenting. Rüin tattoos smolder faintly across his forearms and chest, flickering in and out of view, his expression continuously caught between fury and joy. Every breath he takes seems to radiate heat, the air around him shimmering subtly with warmth. When he moves, it's with the coiled grace of a wildfire barely restrained —raw power wrapped in the form of a man.

I watch with bated breath as the man made of flame embraces another with bright sea-green eyes that glow with soothing wisdom and an unsettling depth. He seems untouched by the warmth of the flames, his skin shimmering like the sea with the man's touch. His water-glistened torso and back are etched with flowing blue Rüin tattoos—elegant, wave-like markings that seem to ripple subtly with each breath he takes, as though they're alive like the waves of the sea. His black hair cascades in damp spirals down his back like sea grass drifting in a strong current. A crown of polished shells, coral, and a sun-bleached sea star rests atop his head. His voice, when he speaks, carries the soft cadence of crashing waves and distant thunder though I cannot make out his words.

The man of fire steps back and turns toward the doorway where I stand, eyes narrowing. I step back, trying to remain hidden, unsure if he can see me or just feel my presence, when a jolt of familiarity strikes me. That strong jaw, that furrowed brow...

I wait, counting the beat of my heart until he turns back to the group, satisfied with whatever has disturbed his turbulent peace.

The woman with golden hair that gleams like sunlight against her ivory skin stands at the center of the gathering, laughter dances from her lips like a birdsong in spring. She bears high, delicate cheekbones with soft full lips, the color of rose petals at daybreak. Her eyes, a piercing turquoise blue, seem to hold both warmth and command, and glow faintly beneath her long lashes. There is a quiet power in her gaze, as if she sees not just the world before her, but the truth beneath it. Her beauty is captivating as if she is the essence of light itself.

My breath catches as another figure appears behind the woman, resting starlit hands on her shoulders. He is taller than all the others, radiating an authority the others—despite their daunting power—do not. He is the most beautiful man I have ever seen, so much so that it nearly hurts to look upon his chiseled face. His skin is luminous, bearing light unlike fire or the sun itself, but of the stars that dance within a midnight hour. His eyes are a swirl of starlight in an endless sky, and I cannot help but feel as if I stand in the presence of an ancient divinity.

I avert my eyes just as a pair emerges from the shadows. Silence blankets the courtyard in their wake, as though joy itself has been snatched away in an instant. The starlit man bristles at their approach, and the other men instinctively step forward, shielding the golden-haired woman. Curiosity claws at me. I step closer, needing to see the source of such tension. My heart stutters when I realize—the woman cloaked in shadow is the golden-haired woman's twin. Unlike her twin, this woman's presence seems to drain the warmth from the air with an overpowering coldness that makes my soul shudder. Her straight hair spills down her back in a cascade of obsidian waves laced with threads of silver. Shadows cling to her skin and trail behind her in tendrils that shift and curl, responding to the shift of her mood menacingly. She reminds me so much of Cia with skin kissed by the fading light of the sun and eyes like darkness rimmed in haunting pools of moonlight. Like my dear Cia, she carries a weight of secrets and sorrow hidden within the darkest corners of her soul.

The man who accompanies slowly removes the hood from his head and I am struck by the deep pit of indigo of his eyes that hold a stillness only found in the void of light. His face cut with sharpened lines along his jaw and cheekbone like that of stone. A jagged scar runs across his face, like a crack within the firmament. Like the starlit man, there as an ancient divinity within his presence and that of his shadows. Unlike the woman's, these shadows coil tight around him, shifting against his skin like oil on water, a deliberate fluidness in his movements.

I hold my breath, frozen on the threshold, as I wait for the inevitable clash between darkness and light. Movement from the balcony distracts me and I look up to see the woman with blue-hued skin overlooking the exchange grimly. I nearly shout at the sight of the person who protectively steps to her side. The Dagda.

He strides forward with an immense, unshakable power, like that of a mountain come to life.

The engravings of him within the temple at Reikhaven an accurate representation of the long-plaited haired man, yet those engravings do not bear the scarred flesh of his thick muscles nor the weathered look in his face. I marvel at his golden chestnut eyes and cool umber skin that shines just as brightly as the woman who he stands beside. His beard is thick and unruly, braided with feather, bone, and bits of forest floor —small emblems of life. He stands with a wisdom that is interwoven with the fragments of life and time.

A roar echoes from above and I shield my eyes against the bright sun to see a white leopard jump from the ash trees surrounding the courtyard. I watch with fascinated wonder as the fur of the leopard transforms into the tawny-colored skin of a woman. She moves across the courtyard with a fluid lethal silence only born from instinct and power. Her wild amber eyes, rimmed in kohl, accentuate a feline femininity that is breathtakingly dangerous.

A man with dark, tousled hair, streaked with silver hurries through an archway with a cloak of deep bronze balanced across his parchment-like skin filled with an assortment of *scrolls that bear the markings of Rüin symbols and stars. Out of all those before me, he favors the Dagda the most in both features and the aura he bears. All except for his mismatched eyes; one a deep, bottomless brown like that of rain-soaked soil and the other a clear, crystalline gray that seems to reflect the depth of his soul. His ink-stained fingers lightly drape the robe over the nakedness of the shapeshifter as he looks up to the Dagda with a small smile.*

A gust of wind bellows from behind me like that of a storm forming restlessly untethered. I am pelleted with warm sand as a man steps from the swirling ball of wind forming within an archway nearest the doorway where I stand watching. His skin is like dust and windswept stone with dark eyes flecked with storm clouds of blue. His eyes are a shifting canvas of clouds and air. His mischievous smile and short stature are a stark contrast to his companions as he joins the others gathered amid the center of the courtyard. The tension within the scene before me lightens with his arrival as the woman with golden hair steps to the center of the courtyard.

The man bearing scrolls steps forward, his voice heavy with measured elegance as he begins to recite from the Rüin marked scroll. As he speaks, the alabaster begins to glow an icy blue in a perfect ring of seven interconnecting circles. The man's cadence increases as the glow becomes threads of blue lifting from the ground and encircling the woman with golden hair. Just as the threads of sparkling blue begin to burrow in the woman's ivory skin there is an ear-piercing scream from above and lightning crosses the sky with a vengeful wrath.

The group of people scatter as a lightning bolt slams into the marble, sending chunks of stone raining down as chaos ensues. I watch in horror as the alabaster stone beneath the golden woman's feet turns bright red, a golden blade made of bone protruding from the soft flesh of her neck. I scream in terror as the sparkling blue thread lashes out angrily toward me as if I have somehow caused this turmoil. I shield my eyes as its blinding light races for me.

In an instant the light disappears, and I am once again standing alone upon sand. Familiar whispers, spoken in the ancient language of Seidré, blow faintly in the breeze like a ghost I have heard before. I take a step forward and the ground gives way beneath me. I fall through the shimmering pearlescent sand. No. Not sand. Stars! I am falling through a sea of stars, their delicate brilliance cascading around me like a snowfall made of light and fire.

I reach out, desperate to touch their light, to grasp something solid, when a terrifying roar echoes from below. A roar that cracks through the dark abyss beneath me. I drop my trembling hand as something colossal stirs and rises. I watch in captivated horror as it emerges from its cavern of darkness.

A monstrous serpentine leviathan, with scales of obsidian, coils upward. My mouth opens wide with a scream that does not make a sound as its twin slitted eyes, glowing with a venomous violet light fixes its gaze upon me. Its eyes are each *the length of my body and seem to only magnify the seething hatred that now burns against my bones. The creature growls low at my presence, and it feels as if the air around me groans in pain.*

I grapple for the stars around me as it opens its mouth wide, revealing sharpened fangs that drip with shadows. I am certain it could swallow a fleet of Tuathinne's warships in one gulp. A mix of shock and horror coils tightly around the breath in my lungs as wings, the color of an impenetrable black, rush out from each side of its scaly serpentine body.

I brace myself for impact when suddenly a blinding bright light from above, like that of a falling star, plummets toward the beast. I raise my arms to shield my eyes from the inferno of white as it slams into the beast. The sea of stars around me tremble and quake with the force. My descent slows until I am suspended a breath away from the battle of light and darkness.

I watch with a racing heart as the serpentine creature writhes, shedding its monstrous skin. I choke on my fear as a man carved from darkness steps from where the creature once breathed. Feathered wings birthed of night lash out from the man's back in untethered fury. Within seconds he slams into the light of the fallen star with a brutal roar. I tumble backwards within the void of weightlessness, floundering to maintain control as a man steps from the blazing light.

His wings are of the purest white, each feather burning with golden power as he meets the man of darkness with a violent clash. Their battle is a dance of light and shadow that shakes the stars like Elkan bones in a death rattle. Two ancient beings fight in a dance of dominance for control of the darkened abyss below. Their bodies twist and spiral as an icy blue thread of power unwinds between them, an intricate ribbon of fate as they tumble downward together. Suddenly, the winged being of light gains control and with a final strike plunges a glowing golden dagger of bone into the heart of the one born of night.

I scream as the blue ribbon of their power rockets upward and violently slams into my chest. All at once I am hit with a blinding blue fire that sears my skin and floods my mind with revelation all at once. I claw at my chest, my throat, my mind as I burn from the inside out until light envelopes me and I am no more.

Chapter 33

Brynn's cry of brokenness shatters the air, her grief like shards of glass splintering through the atmosphere. I stand frozen in sickening awe as chaos unravels around me. Above me, the sky fractures and darkens as the sun fades into the void of the eclipsing moon. The trees that encompass the marshy clearing explode into ash beneath the sheer force of her anguished scream as if they were made of fragile glass. The ground splits open with a sickening groan, jagged cracks spidering outward from where Brynn suspends just feet above the soil.

I brace against the next wave of sorrow, powerless, as Ronan and my warband drop to the ground, thrashing in agony. Blood pours from their ears and noses, their cries of pain drowning beneath Brynn's immortal wail. The horses rear, their eyes rolling wildly as they try to flee the shuddering earth beneath their hooves. I look for Cia who stands in equally horrified awe when I fall to my knees with a bone breaking crackle of flame from within.

The Draíocht surges past the impenetrable wall from within, tearing through me like wildfire until I am engulfed in the crackle of flame and smoke. I smile at the familiar scent of smoky redwood as the fullness of the Draíocht burrows itself within the fabric of my being. My soul sighs in relief at the wholeness it has longed for finding its home at last. I look up through my burning eyes and see the source of my freedom. Her body convulses within the air, swallowed by searing flames of an icy-blue fire that devours her completely in its unnatural fury, a beacon of light in the dark.

I look around me, astonished at the vibrancy of the world as if I have finally been given the eyes to see the Gaia in the way it was created. Colors and sounds once dulled now carry a vitality that breathes into the very essence of my being. I blink slowly, trying to acclimate to the newness of my sight. I look up to where Brynn continues to burn and the Draíocht rushes through me as if commanding me to action.

My voice rumbles with unyielding authority, cracking through the chaos with a roar, "Cia! Put her out!"

I spring into action, darting toward where Ronan lies groaning in the mud and muck. My hands find his shoulders, and I drag him from the horse threatening to pound his body into the ground. My gaze flicks to Cia as shadows, thick and roiling, begin to spill from her skin in an unmeasurable abundance. They form two great clouds that churn hungrily and consume the warmth hanging within the air. She turns to me and flashes a wild grin as her shadows surge toward Brynn like an impenetrable wall of darkness.

The icy-blue flames devouring Brynn snarl as they approach, licking higher as if to resist the dark grasps of the shadow's storm. Cia grits her teeth, her tiny frame shuddering with a violent flinch but still she pursues. Her eyes gleam an unnatural white filled with defiance and a guttural growl escapes her pursed lips. The air trembles beneath the roar of her power as shadows begin to rise from the ground and coil up her leg like obsidian serpents. Shock rolls through me as I realize she has called upon the darkness of this forest to strengthen her. Tendrils of black surge from the surrounding forest and weave through the air, encircling those icy-blue flames. Cold sweat drips from Cia's brow as each tendril of black devours and smothers the fire until all that is left is an unearthly stillness.

Brynn's body, now free of flame, falls to the ground just as Cia crumples. Ronan bolts from my side toward her as the shadows begin to retreat like storm clouds back into her flesh. My stomach drops and panic takes hold of me. I sprint toward where Brynn's unmoving body lies.

Shock clenches the breath in my lungs as I take in the sight of her. Her body, her clothes, every inch of her bears no mark of the flames that consumed her. Not a thread of her clothes, nor a strand atop her head has been burned. Instead, her entire body glows like the flawlessness of starlight. The cruel remnants of Roimh's torment and the scars of her past are now erased.

I slowly kneel in the bloodstained snow beside her and fight the tremble in my fingers as I press them to her throat. Relief floods through me as I feel the slow pulse awakening beneath my fingertips. My joy is short-lived as my skin sizzles against hers and sweat begins to bead across her forehead. Dread coils sharply in my gut.

My breath catches as I lift her shirt. Across her ribs and stomach, angry sores bloom like bruises lit from within. They glow faintly, pulsing with the power now bestowed upon her. My heart tightens. She survived the ascension, but her body was not made to bear the burden of being chosen. My mother's voice, soft as breath, whispers through the wind as if carried on the ashes of my memory.

With this blade you will free us all from the grasps of an ancient darkness.

The Draíocht surges toward my leg to the bone-blade hidden in my boot like a tide to the moon. Heat floods the bone, too hot, too fast. I hiss through my teeth, stumbling back as the leather of my boot begins to melt against my skin. I quickly draw the weapon and the Draíocht pulses with a sharp shock that races up my arm at the touch. I cannot grasp what is happening. It is as if the Draíocht moves with a will of its own, wild and unbound, no longer obeying my command. It chooses my every move as if the power itself answers to a call of fate.

A voice erupts in my skull, like cracking embers wrapped in a mountainous thunder that sears my mind with its power.

Forged in fire and blood. Twin flames, woven in soul and flesh. Bind whom fate has chosen to power Tiene's flame.

I fall to my knees, gasping as fire floods my veins. Ronan's shout roars above the thunderous cracking against my bones. I close my eyes against the pain, my mouth opening, but no words come. There is only smoke. My mind begs for the God of Flames' mercy, but mercy has no place among the flames.

The Draíocht seizes my hand and my fingers tightly close around the golden hilt of the bone-blade now glowing bright blue. My arm moves on its own accord and the top of the blade cuts deep across the wild beating in my chest. Blue blood, the color of the Draíocht's purest form, spills from the wound. An unrelenting voice overcomes my own as I speak the threads of fate into existence:

"By fire unbroken and blood undone,
By the fate of the gods and the bones of men,
Bound together in flesh.
Shielded in flame."

I collapse under the weight of the words as silky threads of flame flow from my chest and burn into the nape of her neck. Her body arches, a gasp escaping her throat, as the thread of our fate converges into one. I am mesmerized as the flesh along my chest closes, leaving behind swirls of shining white now tattooed against my skin. I softly brush back the strands of hair against her neck. There, shimmering against her skin, lay the same shining markings.

A sharp crack lands across the back of my head as Ronan's palm connects. His voice bellows through the air, trembling with a mix of fury and disbelief, "What have you done?"

Heat continues to hum beneath my skin as I bewilderedly look up at him.

"I—I don't know," I stammer.

Ronan's chest heaves, his eyes wild with panic as he shakes me by my shoulders with a growl, "Show me."

I drop the bone-blade as he pulls back my tunic. His eyes lock onto the white flame-mark that glows faintly against my skin like moonlight etched in fire. His hands fall away as if burned and he takes a step back, shaking his head. I swallow hard, his disapproval stinging sharper than a blade. I swallow against the burn in my throat.

"I didn't choose this."

He stares at me blankly and turns his gaze toward the faint light pulsing at the name of Brynn's neck. His jaw tightens as he hauntingly replies, "And now you are bound to her. If she fails—you burn with her."

I pull the tunic back over the mark and coldly retort, "Then I will burn as the Fates have deemed, brother."

Ronan whips around, his jaw clenched. His silence is far louder than any words uttered. He turns again, stalking off with sagging shoulders and heavy steps. Cia hesitates for only a breath, her moonlit eyes flicking between me and Brynn. She gives me a gentle half-smile as if she understands the line that I have crossed. She spins on her heels and follows him, smoky shadows curling protectively around her ankles as she moves.

The marshy clearing falls into a tense quiet as the eyes of the warband watch me with reserved hesitation. I square my shoulders, rising to my feet and raise my voice.

"Gather the horses...whatever's left of them."

The warband snaps to attention at my commanding tone. I glance around at the cracks still gaping in the earth and the mounds of ash where trees once stood tall.

"This will have drawn attention. Whether it's scouts from Reikhaven or the creatures lurking in this gods-forsaken forest." My gaze sweeps over their bloodied and rattled faces. "We ride for the border. *Now*."

They scramble to obey despite being rattled and they remain efficient. Whatever disgruntled opinions they may hold are spoken in hushed tones among each other. Muris doesn't move; his narrowed eyes watching me closely. Suspicion is written across every line of his weathered face. He says nothing. My patience snaps as the quiet between us tautly stretches.

"Gather what is left of the children's bones," I bark, voice sharp as a blade. "Their mother will want to bury them."

Without flinch nor a word, Muris turns away and steps across the ash-drenched ruins to carry out the order. I exhale slowly through clenched teeth, the tension between us remaining coiled tightly within my chest. Finnick and Igor approach, struggling to keep hold of my wild-eyed mare. She is soaked in sweat, her nostrils flaring as if she is still caught in the storm of fire. I cast one last glance at Brynn lying motionless on the ruined earth and regrettably move to help tame the fear within the mare.

The mare bucks and jerks the reins in Finnick's hands and he stumbles back, swearing under his breath. Igor tries to close in, but I lift a hand to stop him.

"Let her go."

They hesitate, glancing at each other in confusion. I give a wry grin and nod. They both step back, giving the mare room to breathe. She backs away a few steps, her rolling eyes watching me as her hooves stamp restlessly in the ash-slickened muck. She's trapped in the nightmare of Brynn's making. I look up to the sky as the world brightens slowly and the sun reemerges to its given form. I step forward, slow and steady. No reins. No commands.

"Easy, girl," I murmur, my voice low and rough from smoke. "It's over now."

She tosses her head with a hard snort but doesn't bolt. I raise my hands slightly, palms open. Finnick and Igor watch with fascination as I whisper my own misgivings.

"You felt it, didn't you? The shift." The mare steps to the side, her ears flicking with the twitch of her muscles. I turn my back to her, softly saying, "I felt it too." She paws at the ground, and I wait in silence for her quiet surrender. Minutes pass as I allow her fear to settle. Slowly but surely, she moves toward me and nuzzles my neck. I smile, placing a hand just below her jaw and reach for the reins with my other.

Finnick and Igor stand aside gawking, their mouths hanging wide as I walk slowly to Brynn. The mare follows behind me as if she didn't just try to trample them into the dirt moments before.

Finnick calls out after me with a boyish eagerness lighting his voice, "I need you to teach me *that*."

I chuckle and call over my shoulder, "I will once you get a little more wet behind the ears, wouldn't want you snapping that twig of a neck."

Igor's laughter and Finnick's grumbling protest fades behind me as I kneel beside Brynn, scooping her into my arms. As I lift my head to stand, a flicker of white moves just beyond what is left of the tree line.

A shout erupts from one of the men, sharp and alarmed, "Movement!"

A hiss of steel follows with a chorus of blades being drawn in perfect unison. I rise fully, tightening a protective hold against Brynn. My eyes lock on the trees as my mare stamps behind me nervously. From the shadows, it emerges. The warband freezes, not a breath rising between anyone. I remain still as the massive wolf with its blindingly white coat steps into the clearing.

"Hold," I command roughly.

The Draíocht stirs affectionately within me as the wolf's

piercing blue eyes, swirling within a sea of starlight, settles their magnificent gaze on me. The warband shifts behind me, their unease rippling through them with every labored breath. I remain calm, unmoving, as the wolf lowers its head in silent reverence. It is as if it knows the sacrifice that has been made here. The thread of fate set in flesh and now it stands as witness to the prophecy finally fulfilled. I subtly lower my head in acknowledgment of the deity cloaked beneath the wolf's form. In the blink of an eye, its form begins to unravel. With a rush of air, a flurry of ravens burst forth, their feathers black as night. They swirl upward, their wings slicing through the stillness of the clearing, weaving into the shadows of the forest's edge until nothing remains.

Chapter 34

The rumble of pounding hooves jolts me awake, my head throbbing miserably with each lurch. Around me the blackened forest blurs, its twisted limbs clawing past and intertwine like bone until they choke out the sky. Fatigue weighs unbearably heavy within every inch of my sore, aching body. I blink rapidly, my eyes wide and wild, trying to gather my shattered thoughts through the fog clouding my mind.

Was it all just a dream?

A foreign warmth stirs deep within my gut. Powerful. Alive. It rumbles through me like a beast awakening from an ancient sleep. My mind reels, too disoriented to grasp what now hums within my veins. A vicious snarl tears through the darkness around us. I flinch violently at the sound of its hunger. His breath is smoky and warm as it brushes against my ear.

"Don't scream."

I clench my jaw, a scowl tightening across my face as I dig my fingers, harder than necessary, into the flesh of his arm wrapping around me. His breath is hot in my ear.

"Do what I say. When I say it. We are being hunted."

I roll my eyes and am suddenly aware that I no longer care to remain obedient. Something burns inside me, coiled like flame, fierce and unyielding, that refuses to bow. No, whatever has awakened within me will not remain silent and I will not make myself small for anyone. I square my shoulders in defiance and lean away from his hard body. He shifts forward, his lips grazing my ear again.

"Understood?"

Anger flares, quick and hot. Without thinking, I snap my head back, slamming it into his jaw. Pain explodes through my skull, white-hot and blinding. I grit my teeth, refusing to show any weakness. Eowyn groans, tightening his hold against me. A snicker rises closely from my left, cutting through the thunder of hooves. Heat floods my cheeks as I attempt to focus on the dark ribbon of road ahead.

The nightmarish snarls close in behind us when an unnatural wall of black thickens around us. I can barely make out the ears of the horse we ride as it solidifies around us. A hiss slices the air, followed by a shout of warning from our right.

"Eowyn! They're here."

My blood turns to ice as the howls erupt in a frenzy. I instinctively shrink back into the unwelcome warmth of

Eowyn's chest. A low growl builds in his chest, a sound I can feel within the pulse of my blood, just as the first of the creatures tear through the veil of black fog surrounding us. I scream as elongated teeth snap for my legs.

Eowyn's blade flares to life, a scorching brand of fire as he defiantly swings wide against the dark. The flames throw shadows that dance across the trees and in that flickering light I see what hunts us.

Their long snouts and pointed ears are that of a wolf and yet they race at us upright and towering on hind legs as tall as our horse. Short arms tipped with jagged claws lash violently through the air. His blade comes down and the wolf's head rolls cleanly from its shoulders, sizzling as it hits the ground. The pack howls, shrieking with rage as they lash at us in a flurry of claws and teeth, their eyes glowing red with vengeance.

A guttural snarl is my only warning as one lunges for my boot. My stomach twists at the sight of sharpened bone jutting from its paws like claws, curved and gleaming like razors dipped in a dripping obsidian. They slice through the dark, merely inches from my foot with terrifying ease. Eowyn's sword hums with fire, its song sharp and furious as it slices clean through the bone.

We tear through the dark, racing for the faint glow of a clearing ahead as a beast lunges for Cia. Eowyn's blade arcs wide, flames snarling with a bitter symphony. Thick black blood sprays into the air and hits the ground with a hiss. I clutch the horse's mane tightly as the stench of rot and death invades my nose. Droplets of its blood splashes against my arm and sears my skin. The warmth coursing through my veins recoil, screaming in revulsion at the corruption of the blood's touch.

Shadows pour from Cia's skin like living smoke and coil protectively around her. They strike out with silent fury like onyx vipers, slinging the massive creatures weightlessly through the air, clearing our path. She turns atop her black-speckled horse, eyes glowing like a beacon of twin moons, and raises a hand toward us. A ribbon of darkness bursts forth, snaring the throat of the creature leaping for us, its claws mere inches from Eowyn's side. With a single flick of her wrist, she yanks back. The beast's neck snaps with a sickening crack of splintered bone.

Still, they come. Red eyes blazing in the dark, gaining ground on either side of us. My heart pounds in my chest, each beat echoing louder than the thunder of hooves beneath us. The fire in my veins surge, fierce and untamed, building from the inferno churning deep in my gut. The ancient power stirs with a wild madness until I am certain I will burst into flame.

I glance ahead, gritting my teeth as my vision blurs with the light urgently beckoning beyond the Dark Forest. The first of Eowyn's men burst through the veil of darkness and into the sun. Their horses launch together over a ravine as if they bear wings. Just a few more yards. Just a few—

A vicious growl vibrates through the air, and my blood runs

cold as a blood curdling scream rips through the forest near the clearing. I watch in horror as a beast tears a rider from his saddle, its claws forcefully digging into the rider's leg and peeling the flesh like parchment. I nearly choke on the mix of panic and fury rising in my throat.

Cia's shadows lash through the darkness, furious and unrelenting. They strike against the beast still mauling the boy, wrapping around the beast's torso with a dark song of vengeance. With a sickening screech, the creature is yanked into the air and hurled violently through the clearing. With widened eyes and a pounding heart I watch the beast agonizingly twist its body under the strength of the sun, smoke erupting from cracks in its slick skin as fire rages from the inside out.

Relief surges through me as Cia and Ronan break through the tree line and into the light only to die out as my breath catches in my throat. A beast lunges from the edge of the forest and slams into Cia's mount just as it leaps over the ravine. The horse crumples mid-air and tumbles into the chasm of earth below. Ronan roars, his hand thrusting out in desperation. Cia reaches for him, her lithe body twisting as a tendril of shadow whips from her arm. It lashes around Ronan's outstretched wrist, and he swings her through the air. She lands hard in the saddle behind him.

Across the ravine, Eowyn's men unleash a fury of flaming arrows that rain down around us. We are seconds away from freedom when a beast slams into our mount, sending us airborne. Eowyn grapples for me, his fingers brushing mine as claws swipe inches from my throat. I slam hard into the earth with a bone-jarring force, my lungs aching for breath as I skid across the rocky path. My heart pounds as I scramble to my feet, red eyes surrounding me.

The fire inside me surges, clawing its way up my spine, begging to be released. I instinctively raise my hand, willing the power to burst forth as I have seen Cia do but nothing happens. No fire. No power. Just silence. Panic grips me. I can feel it, burning like wildfire in my veins, coiling tightly in my gut, my chest, like a dam desperate to break. A low growl inches closer, and I step back, trembling, my hand dropping uselessly by my side.

The blade of fire swings violently over my head and Eowyn's voice thunders, "Run!"

I push my heavy legs to move, breath ragged and lungs burning bitterly. Red eyes flash behind me, too close. I force myself to run harder, faster despite my fatigue. A warm tug, like a tether of smoke and flame, shifts within me and I am drawn to where the rider fell. I stumble toward the carnage; drawn by something I cannot name. My heart hammers against my ribs with recognition of who lies bloodied on the path.

His blond-hair peeks through the blood pooling around him. His face, so similar to Olan's, contorted into a painful grimace.

"Finn?" I whisper breathlessly.

The horse he rode is torn to pieces. Its insides ripped out and devoured. Blood continues to pool beneath my feet as I move closer. The musky smell of fear overpowers the metallic smell of blood. I gasp as his outstretched hand twitches.

"Help. Please help me," he pleads weakly.

My head whips behind me as the beasts growl and stalk toward us, salivating at the mouth. I fall to my knees and grasp frantically for his arms. Blood soaks into my pants and my stomach turns at the familiarity of it. I struggle to pull him from the weight of flesh and bone. I lift what I can of the horse's remains and he fights to wrestle himself free. I wrap my forearms underneath his armpits and pull hard. I fall back into the bloody muck as he slowly frees his leg.

I scramble to crawl across the blood to where his body lies. His left leg is badly contorted, bone protruding from his ankle. I vomit at the sight of his right leg. What flesh remains on his thigh hangs in strands, a gaping wound of decay. Black oozes from the exposed muscle and tendons. His blue eyes look at me and his face begins to pale with shock.

I hold his head in my lap and smooth the hair from his brow. He looks so much like Olan, or at least how I imagined Olan would have looked...if he'd had the chance to live. My heart staggers at the thought and I bite back tears. The beasts close in on us, but I don't care. Finn is dying and there is nothing I can do to save him. I lay over his body protectively and pray for Eowyn's gods to intervene.

I feel the piercing of sharpened bone against my skin. I

scream as they dig deeper, snatching at the muscles over my ribs savagely. I reach desperately for the fire within me, sobbing as it flees from me like drifting sand. The smell of decay fills my nose and the world around me spins violently.

Chapter 35

I slash my sword of flame against the snarling head of the Werebeast lunging for me. The blade hisses, spitting fire as it cleaves through the rotting flesh and black muscle, the stench of decay boiling off its hide. Another charges, and I twist, spinning on my heal, slicing clean through its ribcage.

There are too many.

This isn't a stray pack.

This is a trap.

I pivot again, narrowly avoiding the poisonous claws aiming for my head. The Draíocht surges inside me like a thunderous storm. My veins burn as my nose fills with the sweet smell of smoky redwood born from Tiene's flames. I reach deeper than I ever have into the pit of power erupting inside of me. My eyes ignite like twin embers as the flame bursts forth in a violent wave. Wildfire screams from my body, a searing storm of fury and godly power, devouring the beasts in a single breath. The air crackles with what remains as ash rains down where they once stood.

Pain lances through the shimmering scar on my chest as Brynn's scream tears through me in violent waves, shaking me to the marrow of my bones. A deep guttural growl erupts from somewhere deep within as I watch the Werebeast rake its claws down her back and leaves her flesh hanging loosely in strips.

Rage blinds me.

I hurl the sword of Tiene with everything I have as I begin to run, the Draíocht cracking at my fingertips. The flaming blade arcs through the air and slams into the beast's torso. It howls, twisting in agony before crumpling into a heap of charred flesh and bone. Flames erupt in my hand as I hurl balls of fire toward the pack. I drop to my knees, sliding across the scorched earth until my fingers close around the hilt of my blade, the steel still thrumming with embers. With the blade secured in my grasp, I reach for her, my fingers brushing against the blood-slick skin of her back.

The Draíocht answers, erupting in a tower of blue and amber flame that bursts forth and ignites the dark canopy-covered sky above. The twin flames spiral upward wildly, twirling together in a dance of light and flame. Wildfire cracks the earth open with a violent shake. Werebeasts scream, consumed in the inferno as they turn to ash before they can flee. Blue flames lash outward, searing across Finnick's body where he lies motionless beneath her. The ground sinks with a thunderous roar, as we fall into a deep crater at the heart of the destruction.

I pull Brynn to me, her body still shimmering with blue flame, and cradle her head in my lap. My breath catches, the Draíocht within her...it's too much. I can feel it; how close she came to burning herself from the inside out. Her breathing slows, the beat of her heart slowly syncing with my own. The icy blue in her eyes fades into the soft turquoise as she stares wide-eyed into the distance, lost in her own turmoil. I smooth the hair from her damp, bloodied face and whisper with soft urgency.

"You're safe now, Brynn."

Finnick sits up, a crooked grin tugging at his ash smudged face. He watches me cradling Brynn close, my hand steadying the tremble still coursing through her.

"She's pretty amazing, isn't she?"

I glance down and study the storm barely quiet beneath her softening face. I softly smile. "Pretty amazing indeed."

She stirs, eyes blinking as reality sharpens. She scrambles from my lap and abruptly throws herself in Finnick's arms with a choking sob.

"You're alive! Oh, you're alive!"

The lad freezes like a rabbit caught in a snare, his face turning a deep crimson. I chuckle, letting the warmth of the moment settle briefly over the wreckage around us. Brynn sharply gasps and pulls back from Finnick. Her fingers tremble as they hover near his leg.

"Your leg! It's...but...no, it was shredded. There was bone and muscle...and blood. There was so much blood!"

I crouch low and squint at the limb I had watched nearly torn from his body. My brows knit in disbelief. There's nothing. Not a scratch. No sign of decay eating away his flesh. The shredded fabric of his breeches the only evidence of the Werebeasts mark of death. I meet Brynn's stunned gaze with my own surprise. *How is this possible?*

She reaches out and cups Finnick's face gently. Her voice is barely a whisper, her breath catching with the weight of her words. "You were dying. You were dying and they were coming. I couldn't stop them..."

Suddenly she springs to her feet, spinning in frantic circles, her hands reaching behind her back. Her panic bleeds into the air, the frantic energy stirring the ashes at her feet.

"Brynn—" I move toward her, hands calmly raised. "Brynn, breathe. You're alright now."

She whirls to face me, chest heaving, eyes wild with fear as a flash of memory crosses her face. Her expression is like that of a wounded animal backed into a corner. I cannot help but wonder if this is an echo of what Lord Tuathinne stole from her as she tries to hurriedly cover her exposed flesh with the tatters of fabric hanging in ribbons against her skin.

"I just need to see your back. I promise not to touch you."

She wraps her arm around herself protectively and turns her back to me. The green wool of her tunic has been shredded, the blood-soaked fabric clinging to her skin. I step closer, careful not to spook her, my voice is steady and calm.

"I see blood on what's left of your tunic. Can you lift it for me?" She spins around; her jaw clenched as fire flickers behind her stare. "I just need to see if you're hurt," I gently add.

She bites her lip, torn between instinct and reason. A war between old wounds within the soul and the budding trust between us. My blood hums with the burning rage for what Tuathinne took from her. What he did to her. He will not die quietly for it.

Her wary eyes flick toward Finnick and then back to me. I force the fire in my chest to simmer beneath and nod once, keeping my voice level, never taking my eyes off her face.

"Finnick. Turn your head."

Brynn exhales shakily and turns, lifting what's left of her tunic. I let out a hushed sigh of relief at the smooth pale flesh bearing not even a single scratch from where the Werebeast clawed her skin open just moments ago. She drops her shirt quickly and whirls around, arms folded tightly.

"Well?" she briskly asks. "Am I dying?"

My lips slightly tremble, struggling to hide my amusement. "Not today, it seems."

She exhales in sharp relief, her shoulders slumping slightly. With his head still turned, Finnick lets out a low whistle to lighten the mood. Brynn misreads his motive and glares at him, nose scrunching.

"I'm not some prize to be gawked at. I'm nobody."

Finnick turns toward her with a sheepish grin, ignoring the barbs in her tone.

"I'm Finnick," he says. "I'm nobody too."

Her glare falters, and the corners of her lips twitch. The freckles across her cheeks crinkle as a reluctant smile overcomes her. In an instant I know he has won her over.

She turns to me in a flurry of words. "Something... something is inside of me now. I...I think it is the same power you and Cia have. The Draíocht? I don't know how I have it. I thought I was dying in that marsh at the foot of my children and then I saw things...so many things that I do not understand. But there was this power, this icy blue light that kept hunting me. And then I woke up here." She lowers her voice, her eyes falling with shame. "I tried. I really did try. But every time I reached for it, willed it to come forth, it ran away from me."

I frown, and the hurt in her eyes deepens. This is going to be a problem. If she has no control over the Draíocht then she is truly volatile—a bomb waiting to ignite. And when she does, she'll burn herself out.

My gaze drifts toward Finnick, toward his perfectly healed leg. None of us should have survived. I don't possess the Cerwei Clan's Draíocht, and as far as I know, neither does he. But somehow, she does. I shift uneasily.

"I don't have the answers you are looking for."

She follows my glance toward Finnick. "Does he have Draíocht? Is that how he's healed? Is that why I'm healed?"

Finnick heartily laughs, oblivious to the tension building. "I wish I had Draíocht. That would be a gift indeed!"

She turns back to me, searching my face for answers. "Then how?"

I don't answer. I look instead around the crater and the pile of ash surrounding us. My throat dries when I look back at her. She stares at me, and I feel the weight of it. For the first time in my life, I feel as if I have bitten off more than I can chew. The gods, the priestesses, and their game of riddles. Nothing could have prepared for the what ifs that now seem to dictate my actions.

Without another word, I climb from the crater and leave her questions behind. The moment I reach the edge, I freeze. Splintered trees lay waste for miles around. The canopy above is shattered and sunlight pours through massive gaps. Ash swirls around me with each step I take. Nothing is left. Not even the remains of my mare.

I whistle low, the sound echoing through the destruction and the forest. I crouch at the lip of the crater, peering down through the haze of smoke and swirling ash.

"It's safe. You can come out."

Brynn stares up at the ledge, jaw clenched, eyes wild with defiance. Her hands grip the slick, scorched earth as she starts climbing despite the faint tremble of exhaustion in her arms. She gets halfway before her boot slips, sending a clatter of rock and dirt skidding beneath her. She mutters a curse under her breath and tries again. Finnick stands just behind her, brows raised as his eyes dart between us. She slips again, more dirt tumbling as she lets out a frustrated growl. *Stubborn.* I sigh.

"Do you want a hand or not?" I call down with slight amusement.

"No," she snaps back through ragged breath. "I've got it."

Her boots scrabble beneath her, her fingers clawing into the crater's wall like a wild animal. Her muscles shake and breath hitches as she grunts with the wane of adrenaline.

"Brynn." My tone softens. "Asking for help isn't a weakness."

She doesn't look up though her body stills with the slump of her shoulders. I quietly extend my hand over the edge and wait for her to make up her mind on whether to trust me. Without looking at me, she slowly and reluctantly reaches up. Our hands clasp as I grip tightly and haul her up as Finnick boosts her from below.

She stumbles onto the ground with a hiss of pain and drops to her knees before me. Ash streaks her cheeks in a mix of sweat and tears that she refuses to acknowledge. She shoves herself to her feet before I can say anything. Finnick climbs up behind her with far less trouble and lets out a low whistle as he looks around.

"*Gods...*"

Brynn looks around and whispers, "What happened?"

"You," I answer without hesitation.

She whirls on me. "You don't even know if it was me."

I shrug. "Pretty sure this is what being the source of Draíocht looks like."

She glares and storms off, heading in the wrong direction.

"Wrong way," I call out behind her.

She freezes, fists clenched, and stomps past me in the right direction.

Finnick scratches the back of his neck as she brushes past. "She's got some fight in her at least."

I grunt in agreement. Waiting for the distance between Brynn and I to grow before I follow. She stalks ahead through the blackened wreckage, her shoulders still tight and fists still clenched. I shake my head and let her have the illusion of control by leading us. Finnick follows behind her, humming some half-forgotten tune, his boots crunching over soot. The lad doesn't know how close he came to death or maybe he does, and just is too afraid to care. I will have to talk with him later, just to see where he is mentally.

My eyes stay on Brynn as they break through the line of smoldering trees and out onto the jagged cliff overlooking the shimmer of the ravine beyond. *Tiene.* Even from here, I can feel it calling. *Home.*

Brynn slows to a stop at the cliff's edge; arms crossed tightly across her chest. I step beside her, the breeze tugging at my tunic. My heart is caught somewhere between dread and relief. The ravine stretches wide beneath us; the depths lost to shadow. Across the chasm, small, distant shapes rush to the edge. I can practically hear Ronan furiously demanding answers. Brynn's chin lifts slightly, her eyes fixed on the far side.

"Do you think they saw?" she asks softly.

I nod. "They saw enough."

Her shoulders tighten, her jaw clenching as if she is holding back a flurry of words. She hugs her arms tightly around herself and I cannot help but feel the vulnerability oozing from her every breath. A flicker of sympathy stirs, and I turn toward her when her eyes widen at the sight of shimmer peeking from my tunic. She hesitates before pulling the gap in the tunic further to the side.

"What is this?" she asks breathily.

"It's evidence of an unbreakable vow."

She snatches her hand back and looks up at me wide-eyed. "What? Why? Have you always had this?"

My voice is heavy with smoke. "It is recent." I rub my forehead in exasperation as her eyes narrow. "I was going to tell you once we got to the village. Once you had time to... adjust."

She glances back at Finnick, who looks afraid of what is going to happen next.

"One of you better tell me right now."

I sigh. "When you were...reborn so to speak. The Draíocht was too much. That power in mortal flesh is too much. You were dying. The Fates...Tiene...well he sort of took matters into his own hand, though I was willing."

Her face twists with my words. "A blood oath? Aylah spoke of blood oaths and how damning they could be for everyone involved. Why would you do that? Why would you bind yourself to me? What about your men, your clan?"

My eyes simmer with fire, "Because your life is valuable... with or without the Draíocht."

Her jaw slackens.

Finnick pipes up quickly, "You have one too!"

She raises her arm before her. "Where is it?" She twists her body to see behind her.

I point toward her neck but dare not move closer.

"It curls behind your ear and runs down either your back or shoulder. Before you ask...I wouldn't know which seeing as you have clothes on."

I leave her to interrogate Finnick as I scan the horizon and depth of the ravine below, unsure of how we will safely cross. I look down at the long sharp rocks jutting from the ground in all directions below, a small stream of water flowing through them. I squint my eyes toward the small figures waiting on the other side and in that moment, I am overwhelmed with defeat.

I glance back at Brynn. She hasn't moved though her hand still hovers along her neck. The wind tosses her hair into her face, but she doesn't bother brushing it away.

"You shouldn't have done it," she says, her voice quiet.

I furrow my brow. "But then you would be dead."

She turns to face me fully, her eyes narrowed, blue fire

sparking faintly behind the depths of turquoise. "I was dead. That was the whole point, wasn't it?" she snaps. "I was supposed to be. My children are gone. And now I am some bonded weapon with power I cannot control and no say in how or why I was chosen. You should have let me die."

I bristle, the Draíocht stirring restlessly in my chest. "You think I wanted this?" I ask tightly. "You think I made that choice lightly? That all of this doesn't weigh just as heavy on me? All these years I have had one responsibility above all. Protect the prophecy, restore the Draíocht, and bring peace to Ravndal...to my people."

Her eyes flare and she spits venom in her words. "Were you protecting the prophecy when *he* was beating me? When he took my children from me? When he made me a prisoner wrapped in fine silks and gold? Where were you, Eowyn, when I suffered quietly behind ancient stone and closed doors? Or was all of that part of it? At least, Cia tried! She tried to help me, to keep me from suffering. If it weren't for her, Perri...he would have...Were you supposed to just let me suffer until I couldn't anymore and then swoop in like some gods-forsaken savior and bring me back to *this*!"

"The Fates...the Draíocht made the call. I just answered."

Her laugh is bitter. "How noble."

We stare at each other in silence. Finnick shifting nervously behind her, wide-eyed. She closes her eyes and hangs her head low. "What if I burn everything...everyone. What if this power inside me doesn't stop?

"I'll stop you," I say simply, though my heart clenches with the brokenness of her words. "With this blood bond, I will help you. You are not alone in this, Brynn. Not anymore. Cia and I will help you."

She looks up at me, tears brimming beneath her long lashes and whispers, "You bound yourself to a broken woman."

I step closer, just enough for my words to calm the storm of grief wailing within her. "No, I bound myself to a survivor."

I clasp my hands tightly behind my back, resisting the urge to gather her close and turn back toward the edge, praying to the gods that they will show us a path across—*and soon.*

Chapter 36

The ground had trembled beneath my boots. It started as a low hum, like the forest itself was holding its breath. Every man in the warband fell silent, eyes pinned across the ravine. Ronan had lost his mind with grief and Muris...I will never forget the grief-stricken wail when he realized it had been Finnick, his son, who had succumbed to the Werebeast. We all stood along that embankment grieving when twin flames, one blue, the other amber, shot into the sky like spiraling spears thrown by the gods themselves. That wild, glorious surge of power slammed into us like a wave.

We fought, all of us, on whether to wait, or continue to Tiene. I, of course, won the fight after threatening to disembody them all as they slept.

Now we all stand here, fighting again, this time over how to get them across the ravine unharmed. Muris is surprisingly silent as he maintains focus on Finnick standing next to Brynn as if the lad is but a mirage playing tricks on his heart. So many questions. So few answers. My eyes flick to where Eowyn and Brynn stand, an obvious fight unfolding on their side as well. My patience wears thin as Mahurin demands we take our chances going through the land of Golith.

"Enough," I grumble through clenched teeth. They all turn to where I stand, resting my shoulders lazily against the mare's rump. I rub my thumb across the tips of my fingers, eyeing the tendrils of smoke that plume out. "It is simple. I will build a bridge."

"You will build what?" Mahurin's gray eyes study me incredulously.

I roll my eyes. "A bridge."

Ronan sighs, "With what, Cia?"

I smile prettily at him. "My shadows of course."

Ronan goes to protest as the men erupt with further argument, completely ignoring my idea. I push myself off the mare, moving to where Muris stands.

"He's real you know. Not a mirage or a stygar," I say softly.

Muris breaks his gaze and looks at me. "Aye, I will trust it once I feel his heart beating."

I snort and stalk to the edge of the ravine as the warband's disgruntled argument continues behind me. I close my eyes, allowing the Draíocht to rise within me. My skin tingles as the shadows respond to my call. They writhe beneath my skin like smoke in a bottle, thick and familiar. I savor the feeling as I raise my hands out before me with a sly grin.

The shadows spill from my fingertips like ribbons of ink, twisting into the air and diving down into the chasm below. Like serpents in a dance, snapping and coiling, they rise and stretch outward, level with the other side. The warband grows silent behind me as the shadows weave an intricate arched web of darkness. Ethereal black tendrils twist into roots and interlocking branches that build a path of obsidian glass over the death that waits below.

Chapter 37

I take a step back as Eowyn stares down into the ravine below. The sunlight shines warm against my skin, but all I can feel is the weight of our words and the heaviness of everything I don't quite understand pressing down on me. His words continue to echo through me. *Blood oath*. Aylah had spoken of them as if they were vows filled with heartache and destruction. Something to avoid all together, no matter the cost. My fingers graze the lines now etched into the flesh of my neck, and I can feel the hum of Draíocht sealed within.

I glance at Eowyn wondering if he too could sense it when I feel a shift in the atmosphere. A strange, dense humming of chilled power carried through the wind. The hairs on my arms rise and I loudly blurt out, "Can you feel that?"

Eowyn turns his head toward me, a boyish grin on his face as he nods.

"What in the gods'..." Finnick breathily murmurs beside

me.

I look to where he watches and I take an instinctive step back. Shadows twist unnaturally toward us. Tendrils of black, solidifying as they connect in midair and gleam under the sunlight above. I stare in stunned silence as the last wisp of shimmering black anchors into the ground near us. My eyes follow the path across the ravine, and I suddenly feel an echo within my blood that I cannot explain, calling me.

Eowyn lets out a slow breath beside me as if he has been holding it this entire time. "Looks like we've been summoned."

Finnick does not wait and bounds across the path fearlessly. I notice Eowyn's lips tighten at the sight and I briefly wonder what troubles him about Finnick's courage. He steps forward, but I remain still. This bridge should not exist and yet it does, somehow built through shadow and Cia's fortitude. Eowyn offers his hand, and I fleetingly consider taking it but swat it away as I take a step forward.

Each step feels as if I might fall through at any moment. The shadows shift beneath my boots, and I can feel their heartbeat of power breathing beneath my feet. Below, jagged rocks glisten with mist and water. Eowyn's voice rumbles behind me.

"Don't look down."

I glance quickly over my shoulder. "I'm not looking down... just merely glancing is all."

He chuckles softly, but my nerves stay stretched taut as I continue to gingerly step forward. We make it halfway across the bridge when it begins to ripple beneath my feet. I stagger, my arms flailing and Eowyn's hand is instantly at my waist, steadying me.

"Easy."

I look down at the shadows stirring like ink beneath my feet. I let out a breath through gritted teeth. "I'm fine."

His hands let go of me and for a split second I consider begging him to bring them back. I force my gaze ahead, where the warband waits. Ronan stands above the others, his arms crossed tight against his chest. Cia stands at the edge, her hands extended. Shadows, lighter than normal, emerge and fill any gaps as we make the last few steps across.

Relief floods through me as my boots touch solid ground and I nearly burst into tears from the sheer joy of keeping my balance. The shadows unravel behind us, seeping sluggishly back into Cia's skin as she staggers for us. I catch her in my arms before she falls to the ground at our feet, her body trembling in my arms.

"You're alive," she breathes, tears shining the soft glow of her eyes. "Oh, you're alive!" She clutches me tight and pulls back, the white flecks in her dark eyes seem to dance as she looks between me and Eowyn. "Gods be damned...You did it."

A shout fills the air, interrupting our reunion.

"My boy! My boy!"

I look up as Finnick embraces his father, the weathered faced man with scars that nearly outnumber his wrinkles. The joy among us all is short-lived as Ronan approaches furiously.

His eyes bear into Eowyn as he halts mid-step, not even a glance my way.

"What the bloody hell happened out there?"

Eowyn steps forward, slightly shielding me. "Enough, brother. We need shelter, water...and a way to Tiene. We lost two horses and the Draíocht within the three of us is spent."

Ronan's jaw tightens, his temple throbbing as he stares down his brother. Cia lays a hand on his arm. He glances down, his anger fading into concern at the slight tremble in her fingers that betray her exhaustion. Eowyn nods toward the open horizon.

"We will make camp just beyond the reach of darkness." He looks up to the sun slowly sinking in the sky. "We leave now." He turns toward the men standing around and commands, "Mount up."

The soot-stained men immediately fall into action as they adjust saddles and check gear. I am amazed at their fluidity and how quickly everyone works. Cia remains at my side, looping her arm through mine. She attempts to cheerily soothe my nerves.

"Water, shade, and maybe a night of peace will do us good."

I nod, unsure of what to say or how to feel. Our friendship has changed in a way, just as I have. Before, we were Audun Cia and Lady Brynn. Now, I am standing in a foreign land, my old life severed. Who I was once before is now made new. I close my eyes and tilt my head to the sun. Reikhaven is so cold and dreary, even the darkened forest holds no warmth, but here in Ravndal...the warmth seems to explode all around me. I inhale deeply, even the air is lighter. There is life here, so much life. The weather, the land, the sun, it is all so different. So bright and vivid. Nothing at all like the stories describing Ravndal as a land of ash and bone.

"Igor!" Finnick calls out. I open my eyes and see him jogging toward the lad sitting atop a chestnut mare. "Looks like you're stuck with me. Don't worry...I only nearly died once today."

"Twice," Igor mutters.

"Details, details." Finnick grins and swings into the saddle behind him.

Chuckles ripple through the band of men. Cia pats my arm and moves to Ronan. He offers her a hand in silence. She takes it, settling in behind him on the saddle, holding tightly to him.

Eowyn approaches and holds out his hand to me. "You're with me."

I hesitate for a second and bite my lip as all eyes turn to me. I place my palm in his and he lifts me onto his mare. Without another word he climbs up behind me in one smooth motion, his arms lightly resting against my waist as he takes hold of the reins. The warband waits for his lead and we take off for the waves of copper and gold-colored dunes ahead.

Hours pass in silence, broken only by the bickering of Igor and Finnick, the creak of leather, and the muffled thud of hooves against sand. The heat lingers like a suffocating blanket long after the sun has turned the sky into a haze of crimson gold. Sweat pours from every inch of me and I desperately long for a nice, cool bath. The dust mingles with my sweat and clings to my clothes and skin, settling heavy in my throat with every breath I take.

Eowyn hasn't spoken since we left the ravine, but I can feel the tension in the stiffness of his body. I say nothing, allowing our silence the space it needs. Finnick begins singing off-key behind us and his voice cracks halfway through a verse with a throaty wheeze. Undoubtedly, a result of Igor's waning patience. I stifle a giggle and look toward Cia.

I frown slightly as she leans into Ronan's back, her eyes closed. I worry just how much the use of the Draíocht has taken out of her. Ronan's hand sits lightly over hers at his waist, a gentle gesture of protection that warms my heart. I sigh loudly, rolling my shoulders to relieve the pain twinging in my sore muscles. The silence between Eowyn and I grows too loud.

"How do you use the Draíocht?" My voice comes out throatier than I intended.

He doesn't answer right away, and I sigh again, leaning forward slightly.

"It's something you don't command," he says quietly, "It's something you carry. It's a part of you, both physically and mentally, and oftentimes emotionally, but it also has a will of its own. You just have to learn how to wield it. It takes practice."

I lean back, my muscles finding comfort in the hardness of his chest and quietly murmur, "I hate that."

He chuckles softly. "Yeah, I did too."

We top the last dune just as the sun begins to set, bathing us in its celestial light behind us. I squint my eyes and look for any sign of shade or water Cia promised.

Sand.

More bloody damn sand is all I see.

Eowyn pulls on the reins and swings off the saddle. I look around skeptically, wondering if the rest of the group sees what I am obviously blinded to. The man they call Mahurin swings off his saddle and rummages through a saddlebag. The thick veins beneath his muscular arms bulge as he pulls an Elkan antler, covered in Rüin markings, from the leather bag. He catches me staring at him and his thin upper lip twitches in amusement. The wrinkles around his almond-shaped eye deepening as he winks at me. My cheeks grow hot, and I avert my eyes quickly.

I lean against the saddle horn, silently rubbing the sore muscles in my legs as Mahurin hands the hollowed-out antler to Eowyn and steps back. The Rüin markings along the length of the bone glow an unearthly blue as Eowyn raises the horn to his lips and blows. The ancient guttural sound pulls at the Draíocht within me like a tide calling to the waves. I grip the saddle horn tighter for balance as my body pulls toward the fading note of Eowyn's final blow.

A low hum pulses through the cooling wind and vibrates

like a heartbeat beneath the surface of the sand. The air thickens and my skin prickles as the sand begins to shift beneath us. My eyes dart to Eowyn. He doesn't flinch nor does he even glance back. Instead, he simply walks to the horse and gathers the reins.

"What's happening?" I hiss, my voice tight and quiet.

He looks up at me, a smug smirk tugging at the corner of his mouth. "Just watch," he says, nodding toward the horizon.

Blue light glows faintly beneath the crimson sand, a soft shimmer that swirls and pulses in time with the hum in the air. I clamp my mouth shut and roll my eyes, masking the uneasiness rising in my chest. He swings back into the saddle behind me and nudges the horse forward without any hesitation despite what the horn has started.

The sand ripples and begins to gracefully spiral downward into the glowing blue just beneath the surface. As it does, the making of a hidden basin slowly reveals itself. Towering sandstone cliffs begin to rise, kissed with the pale pinks and golds of a sunrise. In the center, crystal-clear and overwhelmingly enticing, sits a large pool of water that reflects the dying sun like polished sapphire. My throat dries at the sight, my scorched skin longing for its cool touch. Trees rise along the water's edge, tall redwoods that stretch into the sky. I watch mesmerized as spirals of deep green vines rise from the damp soil and drape the trunks in spirals of blooming violet and pale blue flowers.

Shade.

Blessed, glorious shade.

We descend slowly into the basin, far slower than I would like. The horse gingerly makes its way over soft white stone that crunches delicately under its hooves. Every inch of me aches to run straight into the water, to drink until my belly aches and my bones find relief. Around me the others dismount, groaning and stretching the stiffness out of their muscles. Eowyn dismounts with ease, a soft smile smoothing the hard lines of his face as he takes in the damp earth and the fragrance of wild blooms permeating the air. He glances up at me, the soft smile turning into a knowing smirk.

"You going to sit up there all night?"

I grind my teeth, trying to swing my leg over without wincing. He catches me, his firm hands steady against my waist as I nearly topple to the ground with my feeble attempt. I hiss through my teeth and clutch his arms, willing my legs to hold me, as he sets me to the ground.

"Easy," he mutters, his voice low and amused.

I scowl, my knees slightly buckling as I quickly drop my hands to my side. Ahead, Finnick and Igor launch themselves headfirst into the clear water. Their joy is as infectious as the laughter echoes through the sandstone cliffs and I cannot help but giggle. Eowyn's eyes catch mine and something shifts behind them as a flicker of longing crosses his face. He quickly looks away and stalks to where the others gather without a word.

Cia silently appears beside me, her footsteps barely making

a sound over the soft white stone. There is a slight shift in her expression, the smallest crease between her brows as if she is attempting to put a puzzle together, but she says nothing. She reaches out and lightly taps my elbow.

"Come. Let's wash the grime off," she cheerily says with a grin.

I look back as she leads me away, Eowyn's back still turned against me as he flicks his wrist over the layers of wood someone has piled up, lighting the campfire. A reflection of stars dances in the ripple of water as we near the edge. I kneel beside it, relishing the cool surface against my fingertips and splash my sand-kissed face vigorously.

We sit in silence, watching the men unload the saddlebags and prepare what smells like a feast of charred beans. I run my wet fingers through the knots tangled in my hair and glance at her. She sits with her back resting against the redwood's trunk, her hands draped loosely over bent knees. The violet flowers blooming in the vines are like a crown atop her head. Her eyes are shadowed with exhaustion but still they burn bright in the flecks of white as if the Draíocht still beckons within her.

Her voice cuts low through our quiet. "You bear it now."

I blink at her, startled. "Bear what?"

Her eyes trace the curve of my neck. "The mark. The blood oath."

My hand lifts instinctively, fingers grazing the flesh behind my ear where the Draíocht pulses faintly. I nod though my throat tightens. "Eowyn...sort of told me. I'm still trying to understand it all."

Her mouth tightens and she looks at me, grief softening the lines in her face. "You were dying. After the ascension. When you became the source of Draíocht...like the Dagda. But you are not a god, Brynn. And the power was...is too much for your body." She looks out toward the campfire, smoke and sparks of ash rising in the air. Her voice lowers. "He did what had to be done to save you. And I think...he would have done it even if the gods weren't involved in that decision."

"I didn't ask for this," I whisper. "I didn't ask to be chosen as the source. For the oath. Or..." My voice cracks. "To walk out of that marsh and leave my children behind. They were innocent...so beautifully innocent and I couldn't save them."

Cia's hand stills. The silence between us, thick and painful. The weight pressing into the hollow parts of my soul, unbearable.

"I should've told you sooner." Her voice trembles. "About the Draíocht. About who I am...who you are. I should've come clean the moment your nightmares started. When the voices began whispering. I should've done more...but I was so fearful of what the cost would be. You were enduring so much already with Roimh." She looks down, her shoulders sinking with the weight of her regret. "I was afraid I would lose you when I have already lost so much."

I inch closer and I rest my head on her shoulder. My voice is soft, but firm. "We will get through this...whatever this is. Together. No secrets."

She leans her head against mine and quietly grumbles, "Ronan's going to be a pain in the ass. But he will come around."

I nod, quietly whisper. "Thank you, Cia. For always seeing me."

We sit again in silence, but this time it feels different like a balm over open wounds. A place of healing carved into the sand and far from the noise of uncertainty.

Chapter 38

The fire crackles at the center of our makeshift camp and casts shadows that dance along the pink within the sandstone. I take a gulp of crisp water from the clay cup in my hand and take a seat beside Ronan. The soft white pebbles crush into sand under my weight. Around us men eat and chatter nearby. Finnick is already through his second bowl of beans and humming something utterly obscene with each bite. Igor snorts into his drink. It is a hearty comradery of fellowship we desperately need.

I glance at Ronan, the clay bowl in his hand remaining untouched. He stares into the flames, his face drawn tight as he absentmindedly traces the rim of his cup with his finger. I peer out across the quiet water to the bank where Cia and Brynn sit close together against a redwood tree.

"It's a lot to take in," I say, glancing sideways at him.

His voice is harsh, but quiet. "The crater. The fire. The

oath." He shakes his head and glances at me. "She's dangerous."

I continue watching Brynn, unable to meet his face. "Aye, but there's a quiet softness in her." I nod across to Finnick, his head tilted to the sky in a hearty laugh. "After everything she has endured, she still threw herself over the boy."

He exhales deeply, shoveling a wooden spoon into the beans. "And you? The oath? You know the consequences of it. The pull it gives to those bonded. If her allegiance changes, Eowyn."

My jaw tenses. "There wasn't time. It was that or let her die." I shake my head and turn my head to him. "And you know what I'd choose."

He studies me for a moment, then slowly nods. "Aye. You're reckless as ever."

I snort and grin, clapping his shoulder. "It's why I keep you around."

His rough-edged laugh rumbles and eases the tension in my chest. He leans back on his elbows as the women step into the ring of firelight, their hair still damp and skin rosy from the chill of the water. Conversations quiet as heads turn.

Brynn's eyes flicker over the group as she straightens her shoulders. Despite the tired, sun-worn lines on her face, she carries herself with a grace that blooms in every movement. I watch as the men take her in, noticing those who look with curiosity and others who look upon her with reservation. Finnick picks the song back up, a subtle unspoken kindness given to her, and the men join in again with equal vigor.

Cia heads straight to Ronan, curling up into his lap with a heavy sigh and steals his bowl before he can protest. She greedily scoops the rest of his beans into her mouth as he wraps his arms around her waist and gently kisses the top of her head. I rise and meet Brynn halfway, pressing a warm bowl into her hands.

"Here," I murmur. "Beans fit for warriors."

She raises an eyebrow. "So, terrible then."

I grin. "Completely."

She laughs, the green of her eyes glimmering as she settles beside Finnick. He slings an arm over her shoulders as if they are old friends.

"Did I tell you," Finnick bellows, "how this frail thing pulled me right out of a carcass like I was sack of grain and whispered sweet nothings into my ear..."

Brynn interrupts, lifting her cup with a grin. "Pity your first time in a woman's lap was so...*underwhelming.*"

She takes a long sip of water, hiding a smirk. I catch her gaze as everyone erupts in a roar of laughter. Something gentle and unguarded flickers in her eyes. My heart twists unexpectedly in my chest. I lift my cup toward her. She nods, a quiet smile blooming across her face behind hers.

The night wears on and one by one the band of men drift off to their bedrolls placed haphazardly near the fire. Cia sleeps curled against Ronan, his hand stroking her hair.

The fire crackles, sending embers like dying stars into the

sky. Only Brynn and I remain awake. She stares into the coals, quiet and distant. I lean against the cool stone behind me, content to just watch her in the firelight. Neither of us speak, but something unspoken fills the void between us and I wonder if she feels it too.

Chapter 39

A hand clamps down firmly over my mouth. I jolt, eyes wide, panic flaring as I thrash against the grip. Eowyn's face comes into view, pressing a finger to his lips. I stop fighting his firm grip as he leans closer. His voice is barely audible.

"We're under attack."

He slowly releases me. I suck in a ragged breath as my heart thunders frantically in my chest. I sit up slowly, the first sliver of light, warm and golden, grows across the horizon. I scramble to my feet as the men move around me in a tense silence. Bedrolls vanish and are replaced with a flash of blades. I look around me with confusion. I do not see any imminent threat lurking within the camp.

Cia appears at my side, her twin blades already drawn. She crouches quickly, yanking daggers from her boots and thrusts them into my hands.

"Put one in your boot," she hisses urgently. "Keep the other ready. Do not leave my side."

I fumble with the weight of them beneath my clammy fingers, but I obey without another word. Eowyn unsheathes his blade, though he chooses not to ignite it. Instead, his tightened gaze sweeps across the basin for any slight movement. I still do not understand what is happening when the wind shifts and blows across my face. I scrunch my nose at the sulfuric stench. My stomach lurches and the Draíocht suddenly ignites within me in a violent fervor.

An ear-piercing screech rings out and I nearly drop my blade to cover my ears. Without warning, the sand in front of me bursts to life and I am staring into deep indigo eyes set in the contorted face of a nightmare. Its body is forged of compacted obsidian sand with skin that is layered in jagged ridges that ripple and move. A grin spreads across its thin lips and sharpens its narrowed nose cruelly. Rows of needle-like teeth glint at me hungrily as the creature's mouth stretches wider.

My legs refuse to move as the creature glides soundlessly across the sand toward me. Cia becomes a blur, her blade flashing as it slices through the top of its head, splitting the creature in half. Its shriek rips through the air like a soul torn from a body as it explodes into a cloud of sand. I watch in horror as the grains of sand coil together in a twisting whirlwind, reknitting the creature back to life. The Draíocht surges to my fingertips, crashing against the fear that anchors me to where I stand.

Cia snatches me from the creature's path. I slam hard against the trunk of a redwood, the bark splintering against my back. With the next rapid breath in my lungs, I am swallowed by a tunnel of swirling shadows that curl protectively around me. The dagger in my hand trembles as I watch the fight unfold through slivers of dim light within the shadow's shroud.

The basin erupts in blasts of sand as more creatures begin to rise from the depths below. Eowyn's voice cuts through the chaos as he roars commands, his blade swinging wildly for the creature at Cia's back. Her blades are a blur of shadow and steel as she spins in a calculated dance through the creatures gliding toward me. Finnick and Igor stand back-to-back, working together in one fluid motion as they fight against the wave of creatures advancing from the south of the basin. With every slice and every shriek filling the air the creatures continue to reknit themselves back together. I hear the song of the Draíocht hum to life as Eowyn's blade ignites. He moves like a storm, his blade like wildfire, scorching the sand with malicious fury.

"Take the head!" Ronan's voice thunders close.

His ax arcs through the air and severs the demon's neck with one brutal blow. The creature collapses in a heap of flesh and bone. Ronan stumbles back, his face pale with sudden recognition as the head rolls across the sand at his feet. Mahurin falls with a choking gasp, crumpling to the ground just beyond my feet. Bright blood blossoms across his chest like a crimson flower of death. The creature crouches over him, its claws twist and pull, digging deeper into Mahurin's chest until it wrenches his heart free with a sickening snap.

"No," I whisper.

A scream tears violently from my throat as rage blinds me. I lunge through the shadows before I realize that I have moved. The creature turns; its indigo eyes gleaming with cruel delight as it lifts Mahurin's still-pulsing heart toward its' monstrous mouth. I slam into the creature like a wild animal, driving the blade again and again into its throat as sobs wrack my body, my grief shaping into a living entity within me that howls with fire and fury. The creature snaps its teeth, biting wildly for flesh even as its body begins to unravel, but still, I do not stop.

I brace my hand against the sand, my strength nearly gone. Flames engulf my palm as soon as I touch the ground, the air around me pulsating in waves of Draíocht. I drive the dagger into the creature's jaw and wrench hard, severing its head. Smoke curls from my palm as I breathlessly rise, the severed head in my hand. Blood and grit cake my face as I lift my chin and find everyone staring at me. Eowyn stands frozen mid-step, his gaze locked on me and the wild fury that still burns behind my eyes.

For a long breathless moment, no one speaks.

Chapter 40

My heart pounds in my ears against the silence that stretches across the ruined basin. My breath is shallow and ragged. My hands tremble, one still tightly clutching the dagger and the other stained with blood and ash. The last remnants of the severed head scatter with the breeze. The rage built upon the foundation of my grief slowly buries itself deep in the hollow ache of my soul. The Draíocht that once flooded my veins now simmers gently, no longer an overwhelming storm of power, but a single ember deep in my gut. There is a part of me that longs for its return. For it to rise and burn through the pain that accompanies my sorrow.

Eowyn doesn't move. He stands a few paces away, his sword lowered, chest heaving. He watches me with those burning gold eyes as if I am both divine and truly terrifying. I am not sure why it matters to me what he sees when he looks at me, but a part of me wilts under it.

Cia steps beside me, her curved blades still slick with blood. I flinch at her cool touch as she gently tugs on my elbow.

"Come," she says softly. "Let's get you cleaned up."

I glance down. My tunic is soaked dark green and clings to my skin. Blood, Mahurin's or the creature's, soaks me. My stomach twists and I quickly release my grip on the dagger. It falls to the sand with a dull thud. I lower my head, unable to meet the watchful eyes of the warband and allow Cia to guide me. I cannot help but notice they step back as I pass. As we round the bend of the basin, Eowyn begins barking orders and the men rally together, retrieving belongings as quickly as possible.

Cia eases me down onto a flat-topped stone at the water's edge. She crouches in front of me, her eyes searching my face with a quiet intensity. All I can do is blink and stare off into a distance I cannot see.

"I'm going to scrounge up something cleaner for you to wear," she says gently, squeezing my hand. "I'll be right back."

As her footsteps fade, the silence swells like the black waves of the Agderian sea. I sit motionless, though I feel everything all at once. I stare at the rippling surface before me, the faint pink sunrise painting a pretty picture across the water. That is until it gets to me. My haunted reflection is barely recognizable. My cheekbones are sharper, my face hollower than I remember. A faint glow rims my irises like trapped lightning that deepens the shadowed heaviness that clings beneath my eyes. Splattered, drying blood covers my skin like a blanket and my wild curls cling to it in damp, tangled strands.

I close my eyes, and I see them. My children. The soft faces I kissed goodnight. Olan's wry grin when he realized he had won the game of chess. Ophele's button nose scrunched in laughter, the kind that could soften the hardest of hearts. I see their small hands reaching out in that marsh, slick with their own blood.

I wasn't enough.

I was never enough.

My eyes flutter open and I lunge for the water, scrubbing at the dried blood beneath my fingernails. I scour my skin, desperate and wild. My fingers rip through the knots in my hair, yanking free the strands matted to my face. Every gasp is sharpened, every breath an agonizing blade. I claw at the soiled tunic, tearing it from my body. My modesty surrenders to my frantic desperation as the sun bathes me in its warm light. I sit back on the rock, drawing my knees to my chest and allow my silent tears to fall.

Cia returns with hurried footsteps; a tunic folded tightly in her arms. She stops short when she sees me, and her breath catches softly. A flicker of sorrow crosses her face as her lips tighten. She peers past me and across the quiet water. I follow her gaze. Eowyn stands at the far bank, his shoulder squared as he watches me. The mark on his exposed chest coils across like lightning. His gaze never leaves mine, though concern shadows his face like a storm barely held at bay. Behind him the others linger near the horses, all purposefully turned and pretending to busy themselves with their gear.

She crouches behind me and drapes the tunic over my shoulders. Her voice is too light to be casual.

"He said it would suit you better than him today."

The fabric smells of him—smoky chestnuts and fresh dew lingering in the woody richness of forest air. I slip the tunic over my head, breathing in the warmth until it settles the jagged edges of everything I feel. Cia sits behind me, crossing her legs and begins to work her fingers through the wild strands of my hair with practiced precision. Her fingers weave the braids with quiet reverence, starting at my temples and pulling back into tight rows that cling to my scalp.

"Has Eowyn ever explained why they braid their hair?" she asks quietly.

I snort. "Eowyn doesn't say much about anything. He's all moody scowls and narrowed eyes."

Her hands still as she bursts into loud and sudden laughter.

"Aye," she says. "He is all self-deprecating, carry the weight of the world on my shoulders so my tongue is too heavy to actually talk, kind of man."

I smile. "I've noticed."

She chuckles, her fingers resuming their work as she binds my hair into a warrior's crown. Three thick braided ropes fall heavy to my waist, each fed from intricate braids that frame my face.

I blurt out, "It was actually Parela, the dressmaker, who told me about the braids. She said they were for protection. A symbol of balance and power." I hesitate, my voice softer as I glance back at her. "She also told me to see through the shadows. That didn't make any sense at the time, but now…"

Cia's hand stops mid-air, leaving the leather strip to dangle in her grip. "Parela is Laioses, a Tiene elder. She was once a shield maiden with Eowyn's mother."

I sit in stunned silence as my thoughts churn. So many secrets. So many half-truths whispered with kindness. I sigh and teasingly say, "She was always rather feisty. I would've liked to see her square off against Birdie."

Cia chuckles, tying off the last braid. "Birdie would just fling that ugly blue dress of yours at her."

I laugh full-heartedly, the memory of that gods-forsaken dress burned into my brain. Cia grins as she stands, brushing off her breeches. "There. You look like a true Laioses now." She offers a hand. "Come on. Let's show them what resilience looks like."

I offer a genuine smile and follow her, trying not to fidget with the braids out of nervous energy. Ahead, Ronan and Eowyn stand close, their voices low and strained as we approach. I don't mean to eavesdrop, but the urgency in their tone catches my attention.

"We burned his body. I said the rite." Eowyn mutters. "There's no way it could be Declan."

Ronan's voice is clipped. "It was him. His eyes were black, but it was him."

Eowyn's expression hardens. "Still no sign of Muris?"

"Nothing," Ronan casts a glance toward the southern rim of the basin. "His tracks just vanish."

"We can't afford to wait," Eowyn says under his breath. "I'll send a raven to Cerwei. We need to know what these things are. Warn the other clans."

Cia clears her throat and both men look up. Eowyn's gaze finds mine, the gold in his eyes flaring for a breath before he quickly looks away. Ronan offers a small nod and a half-smile before sweeping Cia in his arms. She giggles, pressing her cheek to his chest, her fingers toying with his braided beard.

"All those years braiding yours finally paid off," she teases. She glances at Eowyn and mischievous smirk. "Say she looks pretty, Eowyn."

He rubs the back of his neck and mutters, "You look...nice, Brynn."

My cheeks flush as Finnick strides up behind him and jabs him in the arm with a whistle. "You can ride with me, Brynn. I'll whisper sweet nothings to you all the way to Tiene."

Eowyn scowls and shoves Finnick half-heartedly. "She's riding with me," he grumbles.

Finnick throws his hands up in mock surrender. "Touchy. Must be serious."

A low chuckle ripples through the warband, but I catch the flicker of tension still clinging to Eowyn's jaw. I lower my gaze quickly, fighting against the heat rising in my cheeks. My soul still aches with loss but there is something about him—this unspoken tether between us that stirs. His protectiveness, even before in Reikhaven, from the moment our paths crossed, has settled strangely in my bones. It's not possession, not like Roimh. No, it's something steadier. Something that asks nothing of me but simply...stays. I glance up at him just as he glances down. For a brief second the flicker in his eyes softens. Not a flame, but warmth.

Something I could *almost* trust.

The moment breaks as Ronan hoists Cia effortlessly onto Mahurin's bay-colored mare. His movements are effortless, and I am certain Cia allows it because it's him. There is no way she would allow anyone else to do such a thing. The others follow suit, murmuring quietly as they mount. Finnick pauses for a brief second and surveys the south as if he needs one last quiet search of his father. Eowyn steps toward me, hand outstretched.

I place my hand in his warm and steady grip. He lifts me as if I weigh nothing and settles me in front of him. I feel the solid wall of his chest at my back, the rise and fall of his breath. I ponder the reasons as to why his presence grounds me in an unexpected way, even the Draíocht seems to calm within me when he is near. He gathers the reins, and we depart from the basin, leaving the ghosts behind to haunt the sand.

Ahead, Ronan leads with Mahurin's body wrapped and slung over his horse like a solemn sentinel. Cia rides behind him with her spine rigidly straight and chin high. No one sings this time. No one speaks. The warband solemnly grieving their loss as we ride.

The sun stretches high above us, and I swelter beneath its unrelenting gaze. My tunic is a thin, soaking strip of fabric, between the flesh of my back and Eowyn's bare chest. We chew on dried meat that is as tough as it is tasteless. I take a small sip from the Elkan-hide waterskin Eowyn offers me. Stopping, Eowyn insists, is not an option considering what else might stalk us across the never-ending dunes.

I hand the waterskin back to him and throatily ask, "Did Mahurin have family?"

Eowyn shifts slightly behind me in the saddle. "Aye. It's why he joined the warband. Said they were what he was fighting for. A better life for his sons."

My throat tightens. I blink hard, trying to the sharp burn in my eyes.

"I'm sorry." I whisper. "I was too late. I am always too late. And then I just...lost it."

His hand flexes subtly on the reins. "It's not weakness, Brynn. What happened back at the basin," his voice is low and even, "You protected us. You protected yourself."

I remain quiet, chewing on his words. I feel the weight of his thoughts settle in the space between us when he softly adds, "You don't have to trust all the pieces of who you are, Brynn. Not right now, at least. But I hope one day you will be able to see yourself, who you are becoming, the way Cia sees you." He hesitates for just a breath. "The way I see you."

I shift in the saddle and force out a breath, quickly changing the subject.

"Finnick...I'm worried about him."

Eowyn's arm tightens slightly around my waist. "Aye, he masks it with humor, but he feels more deeply than most. He'll hold it together...the warband. But I've got my eye on him. He won't drift too far."

I bite my lip, casting a worried glance at the back of Finnick's sandy-blond head. "Does he have family?"

Eowyn sighs, "Muris was his only blood. But he has us. He has me." He pauses, then adds. "Finnick's got a way of sticking with people. Even when he's not around, he somehow still...is."

The Draíocht prickles against my spine, as if alluding to something I am not equipped to understand. I quietly nod and lean back against him, my tired shoulders seeking refuge against the comfort of his chest. We ride on in silence as the sun sinks lower behind us, casting a faint golden glow against the endless stretch of sand. We crest another rise, and the wind shifts without warning. It swirls past my face, no longer dry and scorching but cool, almost gentle. The faintest scent of wildflowers and damp stone steals my breath.

My skin prickles as the Draíocht sparks to life like a bolt of lightning racing through my veins. I grip the saddle horn tightly, flinching with each strike of power. My breath quickens and my body trembles in a sudden panic. Behind me, Eowyn chuckles softly.

"It's okay," he murmurs. "It's just the boundary. Keeps out the uninvited." We reach the top of the dune, and he reverently exhales. "Welcome to Tiene."

Chapter 41

I gasp loudly, the sound escaping my lips before I can stop it. Before me stretches a landscape alive with vibrant color. All my life, I was told Ravndal was a place of terror. A wasteland, unforgiving and barren. A place where beauty went to die and nothing kind could ever take root. However, what unfolds before me is a masterpiece painted by the Gaia herself. Each hue, each curve of earth a radiant defiance against every lie told.

The dunes give way to a sea of lush grass that rolls in waves and sways gently in the cool breeze. Towering on the horizon are two mountains that rise like giants cloaked in flame. The fading sunlight ignites their peaks in a shimmering dance of golden amber. They each glow as if forged in the heart of an eternal fire. Whispers stir deep within the Draíocht at the sight, and a vision suddenly flashes behind my eyes.

A boy with storm-gray eyes.

A girl with sea-glass green eyes.

Both laughing, innocent and full of joy.

They chase each other down a hill blanketed in wildflowers, the petals delicately clinging to the girl's long, curly hair. The memory slips away before I can grasp it, dissolving like sand between my fingers and leaving only an ache that comes with loss.

Finnick's voice cuts through the haze as he launches into song. The warband joins him in roaring harmony, even Eowyn's deep voice bellows the chorus with vigor. They sing of home and of love waiting beyond the mountains kissed with flame.

The sea of grass grows thicker, its blades brushing the stirrups as we ride through the gently rolling hills. Towering redwood trees rise ahead, ancient and proud, into the deep blue sky. Their trunks are far more massive than those within the basin, their deep crimson bark shimmers faintly in the fading sunlight. Above, a dense canopy of leaves, the color of blood and flame, rustle with the cool breeze. An abundant array of flowers flanks the narrow dirt path that winds ahead, their vibrant colors like paint across the forest floor. We pass beneath the arching limbs of the redwoods, and the earth comes to life in the fading light.

Everything glows. Not brightly, but with a soft, almost ethereal shimmer. It is like the forest itself exhales the essence of Draíocht with every breath of life living within it. The moss carpeting the forest floor glistens faintly as if covered in dew that captures a morning light. The deep, saturating green of the leaves are veined with threads of golden light. Flowers painted in every imaginable hue bloom with brilliant golds, deep reds, and the purest blues. Some bear soft translucent petals that seem to capture the light like glimmers of glass while others only absorb the light along the petal's edge and along the flower's stems.

"Mesmerizing," I exhale softly.

Eowyn's lips graze my ear, and he faintly whispers, "Welcome home."

His words settle into my chest like a spark catching flame and my stomach flips beneath the weight they carry. *Home.* I have longed for this...a place of belonging, for peace, for a place that I could simply *be*. But just as the warmth begins to build within me, a twinge of guilt snatches it away. How can I feel this...hope, this joy...when the ghosts of my children haunt the hollow spaces of my soul?

I cannot stop the tear that slips free from my watery eyes and trails down my cheek. Eowyn flinches as it splashes against his arm, and without a word he gently pulls the reins. I lower my head, hiding my grief-stricken face as the others glance puzzled by the sudden stop. Eowyn moves from the saddle and walks ahead to where Ronan waits, his sharp eyes study me with quiet concern. Cia leans down toward Eowyn's hushed murmur, her gaze flicking to me, sympathy softening her features. She nods once and dismounts, handing the reins to Ronan. Eowyn lifts a hand and signals to the rest of the warband to continue ahead. He returns to my side and helps me dismount before he leads the mare toward Ronan. Cia crosses the distance swiftly, her expression unreadable, but her steps are steady and sure.

Cia reaches me without a word and places a steady hand on my arm. Her touch is gentle, grounding me despite the well of emotions bubbling to the surface. She doesn't try to pull me into an embrace or whisper assurance I am not ready to hear. Instead, she just stands with me, a pillar of strength amid my anguish. I cover my face with my hand and let the raw, small and broken sob I tucked tightly inside of me...free.

I stand in the middle of the glowing forest and unleash everything I had walled up tightly inside of me.

The anger.

The hurt.

The betrayal.

The unrelenting sorrow over a future I will never hold.

I release it all in bitter, silent tears that scream with my agony. The hollow ache inside me doesn't vanish...but it quiets. The sharp edge of grief softens and settles into a dull, bearable echo. Still there, always there. But not all-consuming. I wipe the tears wetting my cheeks and look up to Cia.

"I thought if I could just endure a little longer...if I could just give more of myself...Roimh's heart would soften. That he'd see *me*. I regret every day not leaving sooner. Not trusting you. Myself." My voice cracks. "The future I thought my children would have...it's all burned to ash. They should be here. They should be filling this forest up with exclamations of wonder, with their laughter. And instead, they lie in a cold marsh, an entire world away from me." I swallow the sob clawing up my throat. "How do I live knowing that? Why won't this terrible ache inside me stop? How do I learn to feel joy again...without guilt? To feel peace? How do I...be happy?"

Cia squeezes my hand, firm and steady. "This sorrow you carry will never truly leave you," she says softly. There will be days...like now...when it cuts as sharp as a blade to the soul. But with time, that pain becomes something you can carry." She pauses, "You will learn to hold on to the love you have for them, not just the ache of their absence. And when joy finds you...and it will...let it interrupt your grief. Let it remind you that life is meant to be lived." She glances toward the others. "You are not alone in this, Brynn. We will stand in the gap for you...even when you are too weak to stand."

I squeeze her hand gently with a silent thanks, blinking back another wave of tears.

Ronan clears his throat and calls out lightly, "Welcome to the family, Brynn. We are all a bit..."

"Unhinged?" Cia cuts in with a smirk. "Emotionally unstable? Prone to violence?"

Ronan rolls his eyes. "I was going to say complicated, but sure...let's go with that."

Eowyn lets out a sharp laugh as Cia playfully winks.

"You'll fit right in."

I breathe out a soft laugh, a flicker of joy stirring as sadness loosens its grip. Cia grins, squeezing my hand before stepping aside. Eowyn approaches quietly and offers his hand. He helps me into the saddle, settling close behind me. No pressure. Just presence. Ronan waits for Eowyn to pass, allowing Mahurin's body one last moment within the ethereal light of the forest.

We round a gentle bend and the air shifts, carrying with it a scent of hearth smoke and warm honey. The forest begins to thin ahead, its vibrant light fading into a softer, muted glow. Ahead, the warband waits, like toy soldiers against the towering wall of redwood trunks. Their sharpened tips crown the palisade like a row of spears, a silent warning to any who might threaten the lives within. Along the timber, Rüin markings carve intricate paths across the wood, each one glowing faintly as we draw near. They pulse like a heartbeat woven into the wooden grain.

My eyes widen as I take in the towering gate before us. A serpentine body coils around the frame of each door; its scales carved with such precision they seem to ripple with movement. Massive wings stretch across the panels; their span nearly lost in the shadow of the trees. The creature's eagle-like head rears back in a silent cry, its carved eyes gleaming with power. Lightning spirals from its throat to its hooked talons, glowing with the same rhythmic pulse as the Rüin markings. It feels alive—as if the creature still breathes through the power of the Draíocht.

"Golith," Eowyn murmurs behind me. "Once fierce protectors of the Dagda. Guardians of the Draíocht."

My brow furrows. "Once?"

"Aye," he says darkly, spitting at the ground. "Extinct through betrayal. A great loss to the gods...and to the war against the Darkness."

My gaze lifts at the faintest flicker of movement above and my breath catches. Camouflaged among the redwood trunks are men and women, bows in hand, cloaked in bark and shadow. They blend so seamlessly that I am certain I only saw them because they wanted me to.

Their eyes are sharp.

Watching.

Measuring.

My heart thunders in my chest as Eowyn reins in, his shoulders squaring. The warband instinctively close rank behind him. There is a heaviness in the air...a charged reverence that beats with anticipation and quiet revelation.

The Clan Chief of Tiene has returned.

Chapter 42

I cannot help the smile that tugs at my lips as we enter through the wooden gates of Tiene.

Home.

Children race, barefoot and bold, up the dusty trail like embers loose from the forge. Their laughter carries with the slight breeze and settles like a balm against the iron weight in my chest. A horn should have announced our arrival as it has many times before. The silence is a sharp reminder of Mahurin's absence in the warband.

I gaze out at the timber-framed homes stretching along the hillsides like sleeping beasts roused by smoke. Their wooden-shingled roofs slope low, held up by carved beams that are etched with clan sigils and soot from generations of those who walked among the dirt path before us. Doors creak open as men and women begin to emerge; their eyes wide with hope... expectation.

But their hope curdles quickly into confusion as they take in our numbers. I draw in a deep breath, the weight settling deeper in my chest. My arm tightens slightly around Brynn's waist as we pass beneath their quiet stares.

The mead hall awaits us...as do the elders.

The silence sharpens as we pass. A hush that spreads like smoke down the hillside as more of the clan emerges and takes in our battle-worn faces...the shrouded body draped over Ronan's horse. Eyes widen. Mouths press into thin lines. A few turn their faces away. Others clutch their children tighter.

Eila emerges from the mead hall, her hands still coated with flour. Strands of hair cling to her damp cheeks, her apron streaked with ash and dough. Her eyes land first on Cia riding Mahurin's horse. She frantically scans us...counting. Her gaze settles on Ronan. On the bundle swaying behind him with each step. Of the blood seeping through the shroud.

Her legs buckle as she falls to her knees, a hand covering her mouth in silent despair. I pull my mare to a halt a few feet before her and swing off with a dull thud against the dirt. She looks up at me, her eyes hollow with the weight of blood and the darkness that follows a warrior's death.

I crouch down in front of her, meeting her grief-stricken eyes and gently say, "Mahurin was fierce to his last breath. He held the line so that we could live." I pause, searching her face. "He did not suffer. Not in vain."

Her hand trembles against her apron, but she nods faintly, swallowing the grief that words cannot ease. Her eyes dart to

Brynn, flashing with something sharp and dangerous. A cold fire born of pain and fear. She says nothing, but the silence is enough. Her grief giving birth to misdirected anger.

The crowd presses in around us, murmurs rising like a fast-kindling flame. A few women step forward to lift Eila, cradling her sorrow as they help her to her feet.

I look back at Brynn as the weight of every unspoken blame gathers like storm clouds around her. I rise slowly and nod to Cia. Her jaw tightens as she moves through the crowd, her eyes already on Brynn. Without a word, she takes the reins of my horse in her hand and guides Brynn away from the side-glances and growing suspicion erupting through the crowd.

I turn toward the mead hall. It rises before me like the spine of an ancient beast, its curved roof like the broken belly of an overturned ship. Carved into the roof's peak at each end are twin Golith heads, their snarling mouths open in warning. Time and weather have darkened the wooden slats to a deep, smoky brown that only seem to highlight the Rüin markings carved into the ribs of the hall like scars. Its wide doors remain open, dark and waiting. The fire within flickers dimly, casting long wavering shadows against the walls as I step through the threshold.

The warmth of the hearth greets me, but it does little to thaw the chill burying deep in my bones. The air is thick with smoke and silence, not even a scrape of a spoon or the whisper of a breath greets me. Just the fire...and their eyes.

Five elders sit in a crescent along the far end of the hall

beneath crossed beams that still bear the banners from the Great War. Runa, the eldest among them, sits at the center wrapped in fur and thick silence. Her braided hair is like the frost of a deep winter; her eyes sharp enough to gut a man. They say nothing as I approach. No welcome. No condolences. Only waiting.

I stop a few paces before them, my eyes meeting Runa's and say, "It is done. The prophecy is fulfilled."

A murmur passes between them, soft as wind rustling bone. Runa does not flinch. "Who carries the blame?" she asks, voice low but steady. There is neither cruelty nor kindness in her tone. Only the weight of truth.

I let the question hang between us like a blade before answering.

"We all do." My eyes sweep coldly over each one. "The woman you fear...she did not run. She did not falter."

Another pause. Longer this time.

Runa's eyes narrow. "And yet Mahurin is dead."

A voice cleaves through the quiet like a thrown ax.

"Where is Muris?"

Anval, thick shouldered and iron-eyed, his braided beard tucked into his belt, leans forward on the bench. His gaze sears into mine as the air thickens.

"He left with you. Where is he now?"

My jaw tightens, hands curling into fists at my sides. "Gone. Taken by creatures made of sand within the

Wasteland."

"You're sure of that?" Anval's tone drips with suspicion. "The girl has Mahurin's blood on her hands, should she not also have Muris' as well?"

"Enough." The word burns in my throat. "Mahurin died protecting her. All of us. He stood against the darkness when others would have turned to run."

"Protecting her," Anval spits. "Again, we bleed for that girl."

I step forward, smoke rising from my bare chest like fog off a lake. The Draíocht coils under my skin, barely leashed. "You weren't there," I say, voice low and dangerous. "You didn't see what came at us in that basin. You didn't see what she became to stop it. If Mahurin were standing here, he'd say the same."

Silence slams down like a hammer. Behind me, the flames flare high into the open sky in a fiery warning. Runa slowly lifts her hand. The movement is gentle, but it stills the air, stills the Draíocht burning within me like the pull of the tide.

"That's enough, Anval," she says, her gaze still on me. "Let the wind carry its stories. We deal in what is known." She leans forward and pointedly asks, "What say you of the blood oath etched into your flesh. What have you done, Eowyn?"

The heat in my chest tightens, presses against my ribs like a second heartbeat. I do not look away, matching her pointed gaze.

"I do not have an answer for what the god's decree. For what the Fate's weave."

The fire behind me snaps once, sharp with judgment as

Runa leans back slightly, studying me as if weighing a stone in her palm.

"And yet your hands are scorched. Your breath still smokes with power."

"I gave what I had," I say. "To hold the oath. To hold her."

"To hold her…" she echoes, a note of something colder, more measured, threading through. "Then what stands before us, Eowyn of Tiene? The boy who left our gates with a warband? Or something else?"

I don't flinch. "I stood between Death and what lives. Call me what you will."

Her eyes flicker with something unreadable. "And the girl?"

I exhale. "She carries the burden now. The Draíocht has chosen."

The elders shift, the sound of their movement like old bark groaning under heavy snow. Runa's expression does not change, but she nods slowly.

She gestures to the bench at the side of the fire pit. "Sit. There is more to say. And we will not meet the end of this story with only half of its truths."

The weight of every eye settles on me like a stone in a riverbed as I lower myself onto the bench. Some searching, others already damning. The oath burns beneath my skin, etched in blood and fire. I do not know what the rest of tomorrow will bring but I know the line I stood on, the line Mahurin died for. Let them question me. Let them doubt her. The truth will rise like smoke, slow and choking. It will sift through with a reaping and by then, it may be too late to breathe.

Chapter 43

Despite the darkness, I stare out at the homes dotting the gentle, rolling hills of the valley with quiet fascination. Brilliant vines coil up wooden beams that burst with violet blooms like a protective weave over their timber frames, while steep roofs slope low as if bowing to the land itself. Flowers spill from every sill, every garden, every crevice of the valley in wild bursts of pinks, golds, and indigos. Their scent carries in the breeze with a sweetness that clings to my throat.

The golden mountains cradle the valley like ancient gods half-asleep, their snow-laced peaks still glowing with the light of the rising moon. A silver stream runs through the village, curling between mossy stones and whispering grass, mirroring the peaks in its trembling surface. Overhead, the sky stretches vast and endless, shrouded with the light of endless stars.

Torches flicker along winding dirt paths, their flames cradled in glass orbs shaped like blooming thistle and roses. The scent of smoke and honey-baked bread drifts from open windows, where little eyes peer out curiously at me. Carved totems stand tall at the edges of each garden, shaped into wolves, foxes, or Golith wings. Their eyes inlaid with stones that catch starlight and shimmer as if they watch over each home. The breeze carries heat but never burns, the earth beneath my boots seems to hum with reverence. As if the village itself remembers every footstep, every name, every wound ever spilled upon its soil. Everything feels alive and achingly familiar.

Standing just beyond the mead hall, atop a hill near the mist-shrouded forest rises a grand timbered home with steep gabled roofs that reach skyward like folded wings. At the tip of each peak snarls the carved head of a Golith, their weathered jaws frozen in mid-roar as if guarding the soul of the structure itself. The home is hewn from dark, weather-worn redwood, its planks etched with swirling Rüin markings and symbols that seem to pulse with silent history. Vines crawl up its sides and blanket the stone steps that lead to the massive arched door of iron-bound redwood. Warm light flickers from lanterns up the steps, casting golden halos over the violet blossoms that greet the moon.

Tall, sweeping windows flank the walls, divided by curves and tendrils of dark wood woven together like the branches of an ancient tree. They stand open, golden light spills like honey from the mountains and pours into the rooms that face them. I inhale sharply, my mind alight with memory of those windows, the morning sun, and the warmth on my cheeks. A child's memory. My own.

"Cia," I whisper. "I…I've been here before."

She stares at me, brows furrowing, her nose wrinkled with disbelief. "That's impossible. Ronan would have told me."

I bite my lip, the sense of familiarity clinging to me like mist. The memory won't loosen its grip, vivid and unrelenting, as we step through the threshold.

I glance upward to the timber-framed ceiling, where narrow openings in the high rafters reveal scattered stars. Moonlight filters down in silver shafts, casting soft pools of light across the wood-planked floor.

At the center of the great room, a stone-lined fire pit blazes, sunken into the floor and surrounded by worn leather chairs. The flames crackle steadily, throwing warmth into the air like a living heartbeat.

Cia interrupts my thoughts. "The first time the fire sparked to life was when Eowyn awakened the Draíocht. An eternal flame, living so long as he breathes this side of the veil."

The scent of burning redwood and herbs wander freely through the open room, curling through the air like smoke-laced memory. Animal pelts drape over the backs of chair and strewn across the floor, their soft, wild textures contrasting against the hard edges of wooden shields mounted along the walls. At the center of each shield lies the same symbol. Three interlocked mountain-shaped knots, bold and angular. From the base of the knot rises a column of fire, three flames spiral upward, tapering and curling like serpents caught dancing in the wind.

I inhale sharply. I have seen this before. Carved into the Wheel of Fates.

"The Flames of Tiene," Cia says, her voice low with reverence. "The unyielding strength that binds the past to what is yet to come."

Banners bearing the flame crest hang between tall timber columns, their fabric swaying gently in the cool draft slipping through the open eaves. A wide, stone staircase curves upward, its railing carved with spiraling Rüin markings that glint faintly in the firelight. I reach out, fingers trailing the grooves and, in an instant, I am no longer here. I am a child again, racing up the stairs, laughter echoing behind me like a shadow.

Cia leads me upward, and we step into the second-floor loft. The air is quieter here, more still. Sleeping chambers line the hall, each tucked behind heavy redwood doors. Their iron handles are worn smooth from time and use.

"Eowyn will insist on you taking his room," Cia says, gesturing to a door just before the end of the hall. "But don't worry...this is my room."

I nod toward the door opposite hers. "And that one?"

"It was Eowyn's, growing up. Ronan made him take the larger room once he became clan chief. That one hasn't been used for years."

"Finn..." I pause, clearing my throat. "Finnick, might do well to stay there now that Muris is missing, don't you think?"

A smile spreads across her face. "I do believe that would be a rather kind offer."

She moves to the last door at the end of the hall and pushes it open. "This will be where you stay. At least for now. Don't mind the mess…I'll have someone come clean it tomorrow. Eowyn is…not exactly known for his domestic skills."

The door creaks open on thick hinges, and cool air spills out to greet me. Ash, old wood, and a faint hint of lavender greet me as I step into the room. The room is large, carved from stone and timber in a way that feels as if it belongs here. A broad bed sits low to the ground, draped in furs worn soft by years of use. The pelts spill over the edge like waves, pooling onto a thick sheepskin rug that stretches across the creaking wooden floor.

Near the river-stone hearth sits a small table, cluttered with scrolls, half-filled ink pots, and loose sheets of parchment curled at the edges as if long forgotten. Above the bed, mounted into stone hangs a broad shield emblazoned with the Flame of Tiene. The symbol is dark with soot and age, its carved lines catch the flicker of firelight, like veins of molten gold, as Cia lights the hearth. In an instant, warmth wraps around me and lulls me into a sense of safety.

One great arched window frames the weathered stone opposite the hearth, open toward the mountains. The view stretches into snow-dusted peaks, sharp and watchful beneath the moon. A window seat sits buried in more furs and blankets, some folded while others are tossed aside, as if someone had spent many nights there watching the mountains and the hills of wildflowers that sway with the breeze.

Cia interrupts my thoughts with a small nod. "I'll get you fresh clothes and something to eat," she says softly. "Rest. You look like you need it."

She slips out, leaving me alone in the warm hush. I cross the room slowly, brushing my hand across the edge of the table. I move to the window seat when my gaze lands on a stack of loose sketches buried beneath a bear fur blanket. Some remain unfinished while others are shaded with careful attention. A tree. A stag. A burning flame. But one makes my breath catch.

A little girl.

Drawn in ink and memory, she sits beneath a redwood tree with her knees pulled up to her chest. Her face is turned toward something just out of frame. Her hair is loose, tangled, the curls unmistakable. I blink, stunned, the parchment trembling in my hands. My fingers tighten, my knuckles pale as my blood pools at my feet. The lines are faint but drawn with the careful hand of someone who knew me. Not guessed. Not imagined.

The curl of my hair, the slight tilt of my chin, the little scar above my brow from the attack of my village at birth. This isn't fantasy. It's memory. And it's not *mine*.

The door groans open behind me.

I freeze, the sketch still in my hands.

Boot steps...measured, unhurried. I turn slowly.

Eowyn stands in the doorway, shoulders broad, posture

rigid. He glances at the paper in my hands. His expression gives nothing away. Not at first. But there, behind his eyes, something shifts. A flicker of flame that flares sharp and bright.

"How long have you had this?" I rasp, my voice fraying under the weight of disbelief.

He closes the door with a quiet click. "A long time."

I rise slowly, stepping forward and hold the drawing out between us. "This is me. I was...what four? Five?" My throat tightens. "Where did you see me, Eowyn? When?"

His jaw flexes, but he says nothing.

I press further, my voice sharper now. "You knew me. Back then. Before Agderia. Before Reikhaven." I shake the sketch, hand trembling. "Why didn't you say anything? Why didn't Cia?"

He looks away, as if the stones in the hearth are suddenly more compelling than the truth unraveling between us. "Because it wouldn't have change what happened."

I take another step, closing the space between us. "*What happened*?"

He exhales, slow and deliberate. His gaze lift to meet mine. There's no fire in them. Only exhaustion. Regret.

"You came here. My mother...she raised you, after your village was destroyed by Hilde's greed. You were no older than three. But when she died...the night our clan was attacked... you vanished. The village was in chaos. Fires. Blood. And you were just...gone."

My heart pounds in my chest, each word crashing into me.

"My father built the defensive wall we rode earlier through, right after that night. He used my blood to bind the Rüin markings to it, for protection. Years passed. We searched. All the clans did. Some believed you dead. Others...hoped." He swallows hard. "It wasn't until Cia was sent to spy in Agderia that we learned the truth. That you hadn't been taken by beasts or burned in the wreckage. You had been...sold. To the queen. For the price of immortality."

I stagger back as if struck. "No. No. That's not what happened."

My voice breaks as the memories crash against the edges of my mind, unformed and jarring.

"Hilde's scouts found me. After the attack on my village. She saved me. She took me in as her own. I would remember this place. You."

I collapse to the floor, my knees buckling beneath the weight of unraveling truth. The sketch slips from my hand, forgotten. My arms wrap around myself, trembling. The wooden floor presses into my skin, but all I can feel is heat... burning behind my eyes...rising in my throat.

"I would remember," I whisper, rocking. "I would remember. I would remember."

The door creaks open.

"I brought bread and..." Cia's voice is light, warm with effort.

She stops mid-step, her eyes landing on me, crumpled on the floor, arms wrapped around myself like I might come apart at the seams. Everything about her shifts. Her breath catches. Her smile vanishes. Her gaze snaps to Eowyn, sharp and flashing.

"What did you do?" she asks through clenched teeth.

Eowyn doesn't answer. He stands still, the sketch fallen at his feet like a crime exposed. Without breaking stride, she shoves the bundle of clothes and bread hard into Eowyn's chest. He lets out a grunt, barely catching everything. She drops to her knees at my side.

"Hey. Hey, I'm here," she whispers, her voice laced with alarm and care. "Brynn, look at me." Her cold touch finds me, steadying the fire building inside. She wraps her arms around me, drawing me into her bottomless chill. She picks up the sketch slowly, her eyes scan it once and her head snaps up to Eowyn with fury.

"What the bloody hell is this?" she hisses.

He doesn't answer. She stares at him as if she will strike him down where he stands.

"Get out."

I feel Eowyn's sorrow though our eyes do not meet. A pity that burns worse than rage. He sets the bread and clothes down on the nearest bench and turns for the door. His steps are slow, heavy, as if something in him sinks with every pace. His hand touches the doorframe when Cia's voice cuts clean through the silence behind him.

"And tell Ronan," she snaps, venom in every syllable, "to find comfort with the pigs tonight."

Eowyn pauses, just for a breath, but doesn't turn. He disappears into the hall, leaving the quiet behind and the ghosts of our past.

Chapter 44

I guide Brynn like she's made of cracked glass. One hand clutches the small of her back, the other wraps gently around her wrist. She doesn't lift her feet; they instead drag, her gaze locked on some fixed point in the void of her mind. I can feel the Draíocht pulsing wildly inside of her, desperate to get out, to relieve the tension coiling tightly within the marrow of her being. I fight against my own power flaring to life with each pulse.

"Come on. Just a little more," I say, though I suspect Brynn doesn't hear me.

I sit her down on the edge of the bed and begin to undress her carefully, like dressing a child after a long illness. The tunic is stiff from travel and dirt, clinging in places it shouldn't but Brynn doesn't resist. She doesn't help. She just stares.

I swallow hard as I ease the fabric off her shoulders. My hands tremble slightly as I pull the new linen tunic over her head and let it fall around her like a shroud. My mind races, desperate for answers I do not have. Why won't she snap out of it? What has happened?

I help her into the bed and tuck the blanket around her, brushing a loose curl from her cheek. Her skin is aflame.

"I don't know how to fix this," I murmur, my voice cracking like a snapped twig. "But I will not leave you in it."

No answer. No flicker of recognition. Just that empty, gaping silence that fills the room like smoke.

I stare at her for a long moment as she finally closes her eyes and I feel something rupturing deep in my chest. When her ragged breathing eases into a soft, peaceful slumber I back away slowly and close the door with care, as if the sound might undo her completely. I fight against the tears, the fear as I make my way down the cold hallway. I top the staircase when I see them. My rage rises like a scream.

Ronan and Eowyn stand below, deep in hushed conversation. Ronan grips the banister with white-knuckled hands, his brow drawn tight. Eowyn's jaw clenches as he says something too low for me to hear, his voice clipped with intensity and guilt.

"You broke her," I hiss.

Their heads snap up.

Shadows leak from my fingertips like spilled ink, slithering across the floor and twisting up the stair rail without an ounce of control. The lantern beside the steps sputters violently and bursts in a shower of sparks.

Ronan steps forward, hands raised. "Cia…"

"Don't." My voice is sharp as shattered glass. "Don't say my name. Don't you dare say *hers*."

The shadows hiss and twist around Eowyn, drawn to the quiet way he watches me, the way he doesn't defend himself. A part of me wants him to. Wants a reason to hurt something. Someone.

"I trusted you," I growl. "Both of you. And now she's in there not even breathing right." The shadows stretch up the wall behind me, violent and alive, licking toward the beams overhead. "You *tore* her open. And you just stood there. Watching her bleed."

Eowyn's voice is steady, too steady. "It was not my intention for her to ever see that sketch. Her memories…they drastically differ from ours." He glances at the shadows building around me. "Hilde…or *something*…has altered her mind in such a way that she cannot decipher the truth."

Ronan shifts beside him. "Cia…I would have told you. I was going to tell you. But then she didn't remember me on the beach…she didn't remember Eowyn. We thought it best to wait…just until we understood why. You promised her no more secrets and this was one I knew you couldn't keep. Not without hurting her."

The shadows thicken at my back, climbing like ivy up the walls. Eowyn's gaze narrows. "Cia…your control," he says slowly. "You have none. Did something happen when I left that room?"

I blink. The walls are blackened with shadow. The hearth dims under their weight. The floors groan. My shadows lash in wide, uncontrolled arcs, weaving around beams like vipers. And then I feel it.

A pull. A tearing rush from within.

I spin on my heel and take off down the stairs, boots slamming each step as I try to hold it in, to hold it together... just long enough to make it outside.

I barely make it through the doorway before it happens. The moment the cool night air touches my skin, the dam inside me breaks. A scream tears from my throat, ragged, furious and grief laced. The shadows *erupt*.

They explode from me in all directions, not like smoke or mist, but like thousands of jagged spikes piercing the air with a terribly violent precision. They spear into the ground, the trees, the sky...warped shards of anguish I cannot contain. The ground trembles beneath the force of it, a low groan of protest that echoes across stone and soil. The light of the torches around the village flickers once...twice...then snuffs out entirely as I collapse to my knees.

All around me, the spikes stand like a forest of black glass... trembling, humming...*alive*. They pulse with my heartbeat, as if they too, are trying to survive this moment. As if they are all that is left of me. I press my forehead to the ground and gasp for breath, trying to gather what I've shattered but the shadows don't retreat. They watch. Waiting. And for the first time, I do not know how to call them back.

Footsteps thunder behind me, quick and urgent.

"Cia!" Ronan's voice cuts through the air, hoarse with alarm.

"Stay back." My voice is sharp, guttural, not my own. I lift my hand without looking, fingers trembling. A wall forms across the doorway behind me, jagged and serrated like a mouth of teeth. It carves through the stone and wood around the frame, barring them from crossing.

Ronan skids to a halt just behind it. "Cia…"

"I said *stay back*!" I whip around, my eyes wild, my chest heaving. The shadows tremble around me, hissing like they've taken on a mind of their own. They coil around my limbs like armor. Ronan's voice is calm and steady.

"You're not alone in this. We are here. Let us help you."

I turn away, lowering my hand though the spike wall remains. I stay on my knees beneath the silver hush of the moon, its light spilling across the ground in soft patches. My chest still heaves, shadows twitching around me like living ash. They quiet into a soft murmur, slowly ebbing into a thick fog. Crickets begin their nightly song again, tentative at first then builds into a full chorus. A cool breeze carries the scent of redwood bark and crushed wildflowers. I breathe it in like it's the only thing keeping me tethered to this world.

My fingers curl into the Gaia, letting the ancient pulse beneath her surface calm the rapid beat of my heart. I don't know how long I sit there, only that the Draíocht slowly quiets. It curls back into the edges of me, no longer screaming and sharp...just silent. And in that silence, I come back to myself.

I look up as Ronan places a hand on my shoulder, the spiked wall that once divided us is now reduced to a faint shimmer of shadow that thins like mist in the moonlight. My voice comes out slivered, barely more than a breath. "I don't know what happened."

Ronan offers a faint smile, the kind of smile he gives when words can't mend the break.

Eowyn's voice cuts gently through the quiet. "When you touched her earlier...did you feel anything?"

I hesitate. The sensation returns in a rush...an overwhelming surge that leaves me breathless and shaking.

"She was so hot when I touched her skin and that heat radiated deep inside me. I didn't pull. It was like fire pouring into me in an overwhelming flood. Like it had nowhere else to go."

Eowyn's expression darkens. "The Draíocht."

Ronan stiffens. "You think it..."

"I think it was protecting her," Eowyn interrupts. "Or maybe all of us. I felt it, the shift." He rubs his chest over the blood oath absentmindedly. "Brynn's body couldn't contain what she felt. Grief like that..." He trails off, shaking his head. "The flame would have taken her whole."

"She didn't burn," I whisper.

"No," Eowyn agrees. "Maybe because you were there. Maybe because the Draíocht saw you and chose to give her ruin to someone who could carry it."

"It nearly ripped me apart," I say, voice cracking. "It didn't ask permission."

Ronan's hand tightens on my shoulder. "It never does."

Eowyn's voice softens, "It trusted you."

A hollow laugh escapes me. "Then it's a fool."

"No," Eowyn says, firm. "It's desperate. The Draíocht isn't just power...it's instinct. Protection. Memory. When she shattered, it did what she couldn't. It survived."

"But why now?" I ask, barely louder than breath. "Why this time? Why did it not do it when her children died?"

Eowyn swallows hard, his jaw tensing. For a moment, he doesn't answer. The breeze shifts, rustling the wildflowers and cooling the sweat on my skin. He speaks quietly, but each word lands with finality.

"I was the tether then. Tonight, I was the reckoning."

The silence that follows is brutal. Ronan looks over at him sharply, as if he's only just realized it too. But Eowyn doesn't meet his gaze. He keeps his eyes on the horizon, where the valley dips into shadow and moonlight.

"I held her grief then," he continues, voice rough. "Took it into myself and didn't let go, not even when it burned. But this time...she didn't reach for me." He finally turns to me. "She reached for you."

I shake my head, heart hammering. "I didn't..."

"You didn't have to," Eowyn cuts in gently. "The Draíocht knew. It saw who stood with her when everything else fell apart. Who helped her walk when she forgot how.”

Ronan finally speaks, his voice heavy. “So, the Draíocht acted on its own.”

Eowyn nods. “It’s not just inside her anymore. It’s watching. Choosing. Reacting.” I follow his gaze and gasp.

A faint glow pulses from my finger, soft as breath and pale as frost. I lift my hand slowly, my heart stuttering. A crescent moon is etched just beneath the skin, the same pale opalescence that marks him.

Ronan shakes his head, helping me to my feet. I slump in his arms, fatigue overtaking me as I murmur. “I guess this is what the prophecy meant by uniting the Laioses.”

He steadies me with a grim nod; his hand braced at my back as if he too has just begun to grasp the truth. “Not just uniting them,” he says quietly. “Binding them.”

The words settle between us like smoke. In the silence that follows, I understand what we’ve begun.

Not a rebellion.

Not even a war.

But an ascension.

Chapter 45

The morning air hangs thick with smoke and sap as the villagers gather along the faint red sands of the beach. Mahurin's body lies atop a pyre of cedar and wildflowers, wrapped in the war-worn cloak he wore the day he fell. His sword rests in his hand as if still guarding those he loved the most. Rüin markings carved into driftwood slats frame his head and feet...symbols of protection, strength, and passage.

I stand at the front of the gathered crowd, hands clenched behind my back. My formal leathers feel stiff, too tight across the shoulders, as though the weight of leadership has begun to settle in. Others flank me in silence...Cia to my right, Ronan to my left. Finnick stands just behind Runa with Igor. All dress in solemn shades of ash and smoke. The villagers bow their heads, but the grief isn't quiet. It simmers, a low, pulsing thing that feeds on confusion and fear.

Runa nods, and the warband advances. With one final

farewell, they shove the raft farther into the bright blue water of the cove. It creaks as it floats, a cradle of flame not yet born. From behind me, Finnick raises a long horn etched with clan Rüins and flame. It is the first cry of farewell. The mournful crowd answers with a warrior's call. Their fists pound their chests in rhythm, voices rising in grief and fire. I lift my voice so that all can hear.

"From the marrow of battle, you came. To the marrow of the Gaia, you return. Ash to ash. Fire to flame. May the gods remember your name." I raise my palm. The Draíocht unfurls, curling from my fingers in a ribbon of flame. It flickers with something older than fire, older than breath. The flame arcs across the air like a burning star and lands silently on the pyre boat. Cedar and wildflowers erupt in flames of gold.

"May no spirit bar your way. Let fire guide him. Let smoke carry him. Let the sea open its mouth and speak his name. Mahurin of Tiene...Son of Ash, Son of War, Keeper of Hearth and Blade...Your fire is not forgotten. May your enemies kneel in your shadow." Softer now, almost to myself, I say, "Flames of the Old Blood...light the way."

The village falls silent as the tide claims the fire-bound vessel, the smoke rising like a banner of mourning toward the sun. The crackle of flame fades beneath the rhythm of waves. One by one, the villagers begin to drift away in silence, their heads bowed in a mixture of mourning and uncertainty. The warrior's call lingers like an echo carved into the bone of the mountains, but now there is only the sea, and the woman he left behind.

Mahurin's wife kneels in the sand long after the others have gone, her shoulders trembling. Her sobs break the hush...raw, unhidden, and infinite. I remain still, the weight of her sorrow anchoring me. A murmur of shifting voices draws my gaze, and I turn to see Brynn standing atop a hill.

The light of the rising sun frames her in a wash of gold. Her hair whips like a bright banner in the salt breeze, her eyes glinting wet like two glass shards reflecting the blaze below. She doesn't move. Doesn't flinch. Only watches, shoulders square and mouth drawn in a line so tight it is as if she is carved of stone.

I step up the hill toward her, each footfall heavy with ash and meaning. Brynn doesn't look at me. Her gaze remaining locked on the sea, where the fire still flickers across the waves like a dying star. Before I can speak, a voice cracks the stillness behind us.

"You!"

Mahurin's wife storms up the slope, her eyes bloodshot, her hair clinging to her damp cheeks. Sand sticks to her skirt and knees from when she'd knelt. Grief has carved her into something half-feral. She doesn't stop. Doesn't hesitate.

"You think you can stand up here and watch like you didn't bring death into our homes?" she cries. "You led him to ruin. Cursed him!" She stands chest to chest with Brynn, trembling with rage.

Brynn remains still, unmoving, jaw clenched so tight it's a

wonder her teeth don't shatter.

"You are death," the woman hisses. She spits at Brynn's feet, the sound wet and awful in the quiet.

Finnick surges forward like a flame catching wind. Igor grabs his arm as Finnick growls, "Watch your mouth!"

Ronan's expression darkens as Cia steps beside Brynn; her face carved from ice. The crowd closes in, voices rising. Hands reach to pull the widow back, but not before her arm lashes out. Brynn doesn't flinch. Her head turns just slightly from the slap, as if welcoming it.

"Enough." The word splits the air like a bell of war. "Enough!" I bellow again, louder. My voice carries over the village like thunder. Silence falls. Even the sea seems to hold its breath.

Mahurin's wife stares at me, stunned. Runa's eyes fix on mine, reading every line of my face. The warband stands ready, breath held. Brynn's shining eyes flick toward me. Tempered. Waiting.

I step forward, my voice carrying unmistakable steel, like a blade drawn from a scabbard.

"We are born of flame. The kind that devours the dark. They think we are broken. Ashes scattered to the wind. But I see warriors. I see roots sunken deep in sacred soil. We will not crumble beneath the weight of loss. We will not turn our blades on our own kind." I look to each of them, unflinching. "Mahurin's spirit walks with us now. And if the gods have ears...let them hear us rise. Forge your axes. Sharpen your resolve. We will not fall in silence. Freedom rides on the coattails of the sun. And we will meet it with fire in our hearts and fury in our bones. For freedom isn't given. It is taken." I turn to Ivar, the blacksmith, my voice ringing, "Ready the forge. We begin to take back what was stolen. Tonight."

There is a long beat of silence that follows my words when Runa steps forward. Her stern mouth bends into a rare smile, pride gleaming in her dark eyes. She nods once, sharp and certain, and the crowd begins to shift. Murmurs of approval rise like sparks on wind as the valley begins to roar with defiant agreement. Cia flashes a grin, her expression equal parts impressed and mischievous.

"Well," she mutters, bumping shoulders with Ronan, "looks like someone found his fire."

Ronan huffs a quiet laugh beside her, shaking his head. "Took him long enough."

My eyes find Brynn. She doesn't speak. Just watches me with a gaze so soft it steals the breath from my lungs. There's no fire in her look...only quiet awe as if she is seeing more or remembering a part of me I'd nearly forgotten. I turn from her slowly, raising my voice one last time.

"Ready your shields. Sharpen your blades. Cia, Ronan... begin training anyone who has not yet been tested by war. Test their strength. Teach them to endure." Both nod at once. Ronan shouts orders, Cia pulls off her cloak as if she's been waiting for this. "Finnick." My voice lowers just enough for him to hear. "Meet me at the house. We'll need to speak before the moon rises." Finnick nods, the fire still flickering in his eyes. I lean in and whisper to Brynn, "You and I...need to talk."

It's not a request. Her eyes narrow just slightly, curious and unreadable. She nods as Runa lifts her voice.

"Those not training will prepare a feast for tonight. We eat as we once did...together."

The crowd cheers, a hum of purpose igniting the air. Above it all, smoke from Mahurin's funeral pyre curls into the sky high and wide, a banner of flame, grief, and glory. A beacon. Not just for what was lost. But for what must come.

Chapter 46

We walk in silence, the kind that stretches long and taut between two people who have said too much or not nearly enough. The ground is still cool beneath my bare feet, damp from the morning dew. With every step, the valley begins to stir around us. Mist clings low to the hills like breath yet released and the rising sun spills gold across the wildflowers, turning the green fields into a sea of gilded fire.

It is breathtakingly beautiful and yet I feel nothing. Just the weight of too many eyes. I press my hands to my sides to stop their trembling. Something in me has unraveled. Each time death brushes past...I feel it more. The *power*. Wild. Seething. Hungry.

What once responded to my fear now only pulses with my rage.

I can feel it even now, humming in my bones, curling in my chest like smoke. I don't know how to quiet it. I don't know if I want to. Control is slipping. Not all at once. Just...thread by thread.

Eowyn walks beside me, silent as the dead. I catch glimpses of him through the corner of my eyes. The square of his jaw, the tension in his shoulders, the way he keeps his gaze forward like he is afraid to look at me too.

Maybe I deserve it. Maybe we both do.

We crest the final hill just as the forge's smoke begins to rise again in the valley behind us. Hammers strike in the distance. A village awakened with the preparation of war. And I...I'm still trying to remember who I am in it.

"You're losing control. I can feel it through the bond."

I stop. My jaw tightens.

"You think I don't know that?"

He turns to face me fully now; his eyes shadowed beneath the weight of everything unsaid. A slow, deliberate sigh escapes him.

"You've been through more than most could survive. I know. But what's inside of you now...it's not just yours anymore. It answers to no one."

I look down at my hands. They don't even look like mine anymore. Not after what I've done with them...the blood they have spilled.

"What if I can't control it?"

"Then you'll burn out everyone you love before you even know it's happening." He pauses. "And then you will burn yourself out." He stops walking, lowering his voice. "Last night...while you were sleeping...Cia nearly burned out just from touching you."

He gently lifts my hand. His fingers brush the side of my pinky, and something stirs in my chest. A slow ache.

"She's bound to you now," he says quietly, "like me."

He turns my hand over, revealing the faint mark now etched into my skin. The crescent moon, small and silvered like ash, glows faintly. I gasp, snatching my hand back.

His voice becomes gentle, just barely. "Tomorrow, we leave for the Temple of Tiene. You'll learn what the fire inside you is. Where it comes from. And how to keep it from consuming everything. Including you."

I study his face. There's something else he isn't saying. Something buried beneath his words. Fear? Grief?

"Why now?" I whisper.

He hesitates. "Because we don't have time for later. The clans need you." He releases a breath. "*I* need you."

I look away, heart lurching painfully at the edge of that confession.

"We'll go at dawn," he adds. "I'll ride with you. Finnick too. But we won't go inside. That part...that part is yours alone."

We stand in the hush between breaths as the sun crests the eastern ridge and pours across the valley. Golden light spills over the hills and catches on the smoke rising from Mahurin's pyre. Eowyn turns and walks again, slower now, as if he is dreading what comes next. He finally speaks, avoiding my gaze.

"You truly do not remember our past?"

I stop cold, my breath catching. I rub the tip of my fingers absentmindedly.

"My dream last night..." I swallow, the words bitter. "There were the blood pricking ceremonies. A man with indigo eyes. Pain in my head after each one...like something clawing at the inside of my skull. And her...Hilde." My voice breaks. "She was shifting through my mind like paper. And the man...he told her what to look for. How to change it all."

Eowyn stops in his tracks. Slowly, he turns to face me again. The sunlight halos around him, casting his features in gold and shadow. But it's not the light that makes him look older...it's the sorrow. My throat tightens, but I say nothing. I don't trust my voice not to shatter.

"I would've died for you back then," he says, breath shallow. "I know we were just children...And I almost did when you went missing."

He's so close now I can feel the heat radiating from his skin. The fire between us isn't from the Draíocht. It's older than that. More human. More dangerous.

"I will not let her steal one more piece of you," he says, quiet and sharp as a blade drawn in the dark. "Not again."

I don't move. Neither does he. The silence between us pulses, alive and breathless. I feel it first in my fingertips...a tug, a trembling, as if the fire inside me is reaching out to him...like it knows him better than I do.

His hand lifts slowly, hesitating for a heartbeat before brushing a loose strand of hair from my cheek. The touch is feather-light, but it sets everything inside me aflame.

"Brynn..." he says, almost like a question...a prayer.

I lean in.

I don't know who moves first, maybe both of us, but suddenly we're close. Too close. His forehead rests gently against mine, and for one long, aching breath, the world disappears. The scent of ash and wildflowers clings to him as his hand cups the side of my face, rough and warm... grounding. I let my eyes fall shut.

"Well, this is cozy."

Finnick's voice slices through the air like a whip.

I flinch, stumbling a step back as if the fire between us has burst into an open flame. Eowyn pulls away too, his jaw tightening as he turns toward the voice. Finnick stands a few paces off, arms crossed with one brow arched in smug amusement. He makes a show of glancing at the rising sun.

"Hope I'm not interrupting anything urgent," he says, the corner of his mouth twitching.

I cross my arms instinctively, cheeks burning.

Eowyn's voice is clipped, as if he is trying to contain his own desirous fire. "Brynn made the suggestion to Cia last night that you move into the house. Get your things." Without another word, he turns and heads to the house. Finnick watches him go, then glances sideways at me with a lopsided grin.

"So," he says. "That wasn't intense at *all*."

I don't answer. I brush past him, the fire still smoldering under my skin. Not a single part of me knows what to do with it.

Chapter 47

The morning air hums with the scent of embers and damp earth. Somewhere beyond the hills, the firelight glints off the edge of the sea, but here...here it's quieter. The kind of quiet that comes before change.

Brynn is different. I can feel it in the way her footsteps echo too softly, in the way her emotions press against my skin like heat trapped beneath glass. The bond between us, whatever the Draíocht made of it, pulls taut when she's near, vibrant and tabled like a thread trying to remember its origin. I glance up toward the hill where she stands with Eowyn. I should look away, give them their moment, but I can't. I know what it costs her to be seen and what it will cost her if she ever lost him again. To lose whatever is igniting between them. I look across to Ronan, knowing full well what it would cost me if I ever lost him.

Ronan strides through the early fog, beard wind-blown and

cocky as ever.

"You gonna stare at them all day or help me train an army?"

I snort, stretching my shoulders. "I figured you could handle it on your own."

He glances toward the crowd forming below us. The entire village save for those too old to lift a sword have shown up. Some older and battle-tested, but mostly the young...wide-eyed and uncertain. Each of them bearing a fire waiting to spark.

"Hope you brought real blades."

Ronan's grin sharpens. "What do you take me for?"

The warband appears, laden with blades from the forge storehouse, each of them distributing weapons one by one. Swords, spears, and axes gleam with sharpened edges. The smell of steel and smoke dances in the breeze.

Ronan pulls the ax from behind his back, his voice booming across the valley like thunder.

"We live by the sword or die by it," he calls. "Might as well start now."

By mid-morning, the training field crackles with movement. Recruits line up in uneven rows, some trembling beneath the weight of the weapons in their hands. Ronan and I take turns demonstrating the basic forms: stances, footwork, and striking zones. The warband fans out around the field, adjusting grips, correcting posture, barking the same drills over and over until muscle remembers what the mind cannot yet grasp.

"Watch the hips," I shout, stepping into a fluid parry as Ronan advances, his ax slicing low. I pivot just as his blade whistles past, our weapons clashing in a practiced arc. Sparks fly.

"That's where the intent shows up first."

Ronan smirks. "That's not the only place intent shows up."

I snort and slam the hilt of my sword into his chest. He stumbles back, laughing as the recruits burst into hoots and jeers.

We fall into rhythm, instinct guiding every strike. I lunge too wide and he catches me in a hook, nearly knocking me off my feet. He feints low, and I spin with a growl, knocking the ax clean from his grip. It lands with a thud in the grass. The field erupts in cheers and whistles, laughter crackling like fire in the air. For a moment, the weight of grief is replaced with adrenaline, sweat, and the joy of movement.

Ronan picks up his ax and shakes his head. "You always fight like you've got something to prove."

I grin. "And you always act like you don't."

A whistle sounds from the side of the field. Finnick leans on a post, his eyes scanning the field with lazy amusement. "Get a room or finish the round!"

I roll my eyes. "You're just jealous because no one claps when you don't miss a target."

"Not true," he says, sauntering over. "Igor claps. Sometimes."

Igor shrugs with a grunt. "You're very enthusiastic."

Finnick feigns offense and draws his blade, taunting me with a fight. I grin.

"Oh, you want to lose in front of everyone today? Bold."

"I live boldly," he says, twirling the blade like a showman. "I also die dramatically, so let's keep things balanced."

He lunges, and I parry without hesitation, steel ringing out across the field. We fall into an easy rhythm. His strikes are more flourish than force, mine sharp and efficient. Ronan leans on the top of his ax, smirking.

"You've gotten fast," I admit as I duck a sweeping arc.

"You've gotten meaner," he counters, eyes glittering.

"Not mean," I say, slipping behind him and nudging his leg with my boot, making him stumble forward. "Precise."

Finnick pivots, grabs my wrist and twists. I laugh and hook my leg behind his knee, dropping low. With one sharp twist and pull, he crashes onto his back, blade flying from his hand. I plant my boot on his chest and lean on my sword like a staff. "Lesson one, little brother...don't bring flair to a knife fight."

Finnick stares up at me, wheezing dramatically. "I...I see the light."

He reaches up and I haul him to his feet, brushing dust from his shoulders with mock care. Ronan calls out, waving the next group forward.

"Back to work. We're not fighting for sport."

Finnick limps off with a grin. "It *was* for sport until Cia ruined my dignity."

"Like you had any!" I shout after him, grinning wide.

I turn back to the recruits, blades flashing in the light of the sun. I'm halfway through correcting a recruit's stance when I feel it, a subtle ripple in the air...a tug of something familiar. My head lifts before I even register why.

Brynn.

She stands toward the back of the crowd, half in shadow beneath the swaying arms of the grove of cedar trees. Sweat glistens on her brow, catching in the wild strands of hair that have slipped free from her braid. Dirt streaks the cuff of her tunic as she works the stances with Eowyn, her movements tense and deliberate.

I shift my stance, eyes tracking the recruits as they mimic the forms Ronan and I demonstrated. The young ones are sloppy and hesitant...chaos wearing the face of discipline. I gauge how many morning training sessions we will need before we are fluid and precise like the warband. I can feel Brynn's frustration like a distant thunder, too faint to name but familiar all the same when my spine prickles.

I catch the glint of Ronan's blade too late for thought, but not too late to move. He's making a point, showing the value of a surprise attack.

I pivot hard and fast, throwing out my arm just as he lunges. My blade meets his with a sharp clash and I hook under, using his momentum to send him sprawling flat on his ass. The recruits freeze. A stunned silence swells and then laughter breaks out as Ronan groans. I plant the tip of my blade in the dirt next to his head and grin down at him.

"Surprise attacks only work if your opponent doesn't already have eyes in the dark."

He blinks up at me, mock wounded. "You ever get tired of being right?"

"Not once."

From the edge of the crowd, I feel her before I see her. Brynn's eyes on me. Wide. Unblinking. Like she'd known too. Like the Draíocht whispered it through her skin. For a second, we just look at each other. Not speaking. Not smiling. Just that breathless awareness humming between us.

Ronan grabs my ankle and yanks me down with a curse. I hit the dirt with a yelp and laugh.

"You were saying?" he teases.

I flip, fast as breath, and drive my knee into his chest, pinning him with a smirk. My dagger kisses the side of his neck, playful but sharp.

"Yield, yet?"

Ronan's breath catches, but his grin stays wide, eyes sparkling with mischief. Without hesitation, he reaches up, gripping my tunic and yanking me hard against him. The world narrows to the fierce press of his body and the searing heat of a sudden, fiery kiss. I kiss him back with a grin and a growl, both of us laughing into each other's mouths like fools in the sun. When we finally break apart, I lean my forehead against his, breathless and flushed.

I look past the noise of training, past the sweat and grit,

past the broken world we're trying to mend. And for the first time in too long, I feel it...that flick of belief that maybe, with enough effort and a little luck or fate, we might just win this.

Maybe we already have.

Chapter 48

The afternoon sun warms the valley, casting long shadows across the stream where I sit, washing the dirt and sweat from my skin. The water is cool and clear, swirling around my fingers as I scrub away the grim of the day. My hair is tied back loosely, strands escaping to cling to my neck. The ache in my muscles is steady, familiar, but nothing compared to the weight pressing inside me...the voice growing louder with each passing moment.

A soft rustle behind me makes me glance up.

"I thought I'd find you here," Finnick says quietly, settling beside the bank. His eyes scan the water, careful and steady, though they flick to me with quiet concern every so often. There's a calm in his presence, an unspoken tether between us that feels older than words, bound deep in the Draíocht itself. For now, that's enough. Though, lately, I find myself questioning *why* it exists at all.

We sit in silence for a while, listening to the soft gurgle of the stream as it winds around smooth stones and tangled roots. Sunlight filters through the canopy in gold-dappled ribbons, catching on the droplets still clinging to my skin. A breeze stirs the tall grass behind us. Finnick doesn't rush the quiet. He never does with me. I draw my knees to my chest, wrapping my arms loosely around them, and I glance at him from the corner of my eye.

"Thank you," I murmur.

His brows lift slightly, "For what?"

"For stepping in earlier." I pause, swallowing. "You didn't' have to."

He exhales slowly, the corner of his mouth twitching. "Of course I did."

I nod faintly, staring at the water until it blurs. Another silence drapes between us, heavier this time. When he speaks again his voice is quieter than before.

"I should've done more for you," he says. "Back in Reikhaven. I knew what he was doing to you. Everyone knew. The Guard would make bets on how quickly you could heal."

I look up startled by the rawness in his tone. His gaze is fixed on the current like he wants it to carry the weight of his words away.

"I told myself it wasn't my place. That I'd do more harm than good. Told it to myself so much that I started to believe it." He turns to meet my eyes. "I'm sorry, Brynn."

My throat tightens. I look down at my hands, flexing my

fingers as if the memory lives in them.

"It wasn't your burden to carry," I say, but my voice trembles. "But thank you. For saying it."

The stream murmurs between us as a bird calls somewhere deeper in the woods though the sound feels distant.

"I think about them every day," I whisper. "My children."

Finnick doesn't speak. He just listens, and that makes it easier.

"I see their faces when I sleep. Hear their laughter where there is none. I know they're gone. I know it. But some part of me still waits for the sound of small feet, still wonders if they would've loved the wind here...the flowers..." My voice breaks. "I miss them so much I can't breathe some days."

I draw in a shaky breath. "And the longer I sit in it...this grief...the louder something else becomes. There's a...voice. In the back of my mind. It's been there since the ascension. Since the power woke inside me."

I swallow hard.

"It's not mine," I say quietly. "It's...older. Hungry. And when I let myself fall too far into sorrow, that's when I hear it most. Whispering like it belongs to me. Eyes like indigo fire. Watching from behind my eyes."

I turn to look at him, my voice low. "I think it wants me to break, Finnick. Not just stumble...*shatter*. I think it waits for that. This voice...this thing...it doesn't care about love. Or hope. It offers relief. From the pain, from the guilt. All I'd have to do is let go."

He studies me, his jaw softening into a kind smile.

"You won't," he says firmly. "You never have. No matter what you have endured, you've always shined brighter. And that is something the darkness can't take from you."

I try to smile, but it falters. "Sometimes I'm afraid I will let it."

He nods slowly, voice sure. "Then promise me something. When that moment comes...when the choice feels too heavy... promise me you'll choose light. Even when it's the harder path."

I close my eyes, holding the words like a lifeline. A vow. A warning.

When I open them again, I reach for his arm, gripping it with sudden urgency. "Please don't say anything to Eowyn or Cia. I'll tell them. Once things settle. Once the tension in the village eases."

Finnick squeezes my hand once before leaning back in the grass, eyes tracing the orange-rimmed clouds drifting above.

"You know...ever since that day with the Werebeasts... when you pulled me back from death...I've always been able to find you."

I look at him, brows furrowed in quiet curiosity.

"I don't mean just track you," he says, still watching the sky. "Though I *am* the best tracker Eowyn has." A smile tugs at the corner of his mouth. "Back in Reikhaven, you'd vanish like mist in a crowd. Reappear only when you wanted. But now...it's different."

"Different how?"

He shrugs slightly. "I don't know. Sometimes, it's like I *feel* where you are. A hum in my chest that grows louder when you're near. And other times...I hear something. A whisper, maybe." He pauses, thoughtful. "I thought I was losing my mind at first."

I don't respond, but the silence between us settles with weight. The Draíocht stirs inside me, like a string being gently plucked.

Finnick turns, fixing me with a mocking expression. "Or maybe I'm just dangerously obsessed with you. Could be that."

I snort, shoulders relaxing. "You're impossible."

"And yet, here you are...choosing to sit with me instead of walking straight into Eowyn's waiting arms. I'll take that as a win."

I laugh, loud and unguarded. "That obvious, huh?"

Finnick snickers. "You two couldn't be more obvious if you tried. Makes me feel *naked* watching you dance around each other." He pushes up on his arms, more earnest now. "You know, Brynn...love doesn't have to come wrapped in pain. It can come softly."

I splash water at him with a grin. "Says the one too young to know anything about love."

Finnick flashes a wicked grin, pressing a hand to his heart as he stands. "But my heart is hopelessly devoted to you, Brynn of Oéngus."

I laugh and shove him hard enough that he topples

sideways with a splash, limbs flailing as he crashes into the shallows of the stream.

"Brynn!" he sputters, surfacing with water dripping from his sandy-blond hair and a betrayed look on his face.

But I'm already running, the laughter spilling from me unfiltered and unburdened. My chest aches from the joy of it... rare, fleeting, and bright. I sprint barefoot up the path toward the house, the soft earth cool beneath my feet.

Eowyn stands on the porch, arms folded loosely across his chest, watching the stream with a raised brow.

"You push him or did he finally confess his feelings and faint?" he calls as I approach.

I try to compose myself, but a giggle escapes as I double over, catching my breath. Moments later, Finnick trudges up the path soaked through, water trailing from his sleeves and boots.

"She's unhinged," he mutters, flinging droplets from his hands like a scorned cat.

Eowyn's lip twitches with a smile. "Noted."

My breath hitches, the warmth lingering on my cheeks. Eowyn steps closer, his voice lower...more thoughtful.

"Happy looks good on you, Brynn."

I blink at him, caught off guard and blush all over again.

Before I can answer Eowyn, the porch boards creak behind him. A woman steps out from the shadowed entryway, arms crossed and eyebrow raised with amused disdain. She carries herself with the kind of authority that doesn't need announcing. Her sharp-angled face, long dark braid laced with streaks of copper and auburn, and eyes the same mossy green remind me of Parela.

"You finally decided to bathe, Finnick?" she drawls, surveying his dripping clothes. "We were starting to worry."

Finnick groans, sloshing up the last few steps. "I *was* clean until someone pushed me."

"Ivar said you smelled worse than the pigs." Eowyn chuckles beside her, but the moment softens when her gaze shifts to me. Her posture eases and her arms drop to her sides. "You must be Brynn."

I nod, still catching my breath from running. "And you're...?"

"Veera, but you may call me Vee as my friends do," she says, offering a faint smile. "Parela is my mother."

My breath catches. "I...she...helped me. Saved me, really."

"I know," Vee says gently. "She sent letters about you. Of a star that didn't know it was burning. She said you'd come when the world needed you." I lower my gaze, unsure of what to say but she steps closer. "She also said you'd need this."

She places a small bundle wrapped in deep blue cloth in my hand. The gold twine around it is fraying, as if it's been carried a long while.

"She sent it months ago. Said it was for a moment such as now."

I stare down at the bundle in my hands, my fingers

trembling just slightly as I trace the worn gold twine. Parela's presence seems to still cling to the cloth. Months ago, she sent this...before she could've known I'd make it here. Before I even knew I *could.* Something swells in my chest. Grief and gratitude tangling into a knot too complex to name.

Vee smiles. "You've got friends here." Her eyes dart between Eowyn and Finnick. "Even if some smell like a goat pen in midsummer."

"Vee," Eowyn groans.

"Don't Vee me," she says, patting his arm. "You took my husband away to work in that forge, let me have my fun." She turns to me, eyes crinkling with warmth. "Welcome to Tiene, Brynn. Don't mind the others in the village. We've been waiting a long time for our freedom and now that it is here, some of them have become a little too complacent. Now if you'll excuse me," she adds, already heading toward the path. "Runa will have my hide if I burn the bread."

I smile, tucking the bundle under my arm and step toward the door, brushing past Eowyn. He smells of redwood smoke and freshly squeezed lemon. I glance up at him just once, a glance that lingers longer than I mean it to. He offers a gentle smile that stirs a fire deep in my fluttering heart. I step inside before I'm swallowed whole.

The house is warm, shadowed and quiet. I climb the stairs slowly, each creak of the wood echoing in the hollow space of my chest. In the room, I pause at the window, watching the rays of the setting sun spill over the valley like honey. I sit on the edge of the bed and with steady hands, begin to unwrap Parela's gift.

I lift the dress from the silk wrapping and the room seems to quiet around it. Its icy blue color is so bright it mirrors a soft glow. The fabric is weightless in my hands, sheer but luminous, as if stitched from mist and starlight. Tiny stars scatter across it in delicate embroidery, no larger than grains of salt, but they catch the light with every movement, shimmering like constellations drawn onto silk.

I quickly snatch my own tunic and over-sized breeches off, eager to see what the dress will look like on me. The bodice curves gently, simple and unadorned, allowing the fabric to speak for itself. There is no belt to cinch it...only the natural fall of the gown as it skims my body like water flowing over stone. When I move, it ripples like a reflection disturbed, elegant and fluid. Along the arms and lower skirt, it turns near translucent, hinting at the shape of my limbs beneath, like moonlight slipping through frost-covered glass. The sleeves cling just barely to my arms, weightless and fine.

The neckline plunges immodestly, lined with wispy lace so intricate it looks grown rather than sewn, each vine-like thread curling downward. The bodice offers no armor, no corset, only the quiet strength of silk and lace laid bare over skin. The hem trails behind me in a soft sweep, dusting the floor like fog, light pooling around my feet. I feel as if I look like a vision carved from myth...soft, untouchable, and divine. A goddess of light, reborn not in fire or fury, but in silence and starlight.

A soft knock raps at the door, followed by the familiar creak as it opens a sliver.

"Brynn?" Cia's voice drifts in, light but uncertain.

I turn, the gown catching the last rays of golden light pouring in from the window. The shimmer of stars flickers across the sheer fabric as I move, my hair loose around my shoulders as the door opens wider. Cia steps inside and stops abruptly.

Her breath leaves her in a stunned exhale. "By the gods…" she whispers. "You look like something born of the heavens. Like the goddess of Oéngus herself just stepped into the world."

My cheeks flush as I glance down at the shimmering fabric, suddenly aware of the way it clings, the way it reveals and veils all at once. Cia crosses the room in a heartbeat, reaching for my hand.

"Come. Let me help you with your hair. Make Eowyn forget how to breathe."

I laugh softly, the sound cracked. "It's just a dress."

"No," Cia murmurs, guiding me to the mirror. "It's not. Tonight, they'll see who you are. Whether they deserve to or not."

I touch my hair softly, smiling at my reflection of the broken woman now made anew as Cia drags a chair across the floor. I sit down dutifully as Cia's fingers move through my hair with practiced care.

Long waves of auburn spill like fire-warmed copper down my back, each curl thick and gleaming, gathered into an elaborate cascade of braids and loops that weave together like an ancient sigil. At the crown, two twisted sections frame my head like a circlet, joining at the center in a delicate knot. The braid thickens from the knot with each twist, threading through soft coils and loose tendrils that dance along my spine. The strands curl with a wild elegance that brush the curve of my lower back. Small strands frame my face in gentle wisps of curls kissed by amber and flame.

Cia grins at me when she is done, her eyes shimmering with pride. I catch my reflection, barely recognizing the woman looking back. The power in my eyes, the light in my bones. I cannot help the flutter that stirs in my stomach at the thought of Eowyn seeing me like this.

I rise from the chair, my dress sweeping behind me in a whisper of light. I remain barefoot, desiring the grounding coolness of the Gaia outside. There is something sacred about feeling the pulses from the valley itself as if it, too, watches and waits. Cia gives me one last look, mischief in her smile, and spins on her heel, striding down the hall.

"Eowyn!" she calls, voice echoing with playful command. "To the foot of the stairs. Now."

There is a shuffle from below, scraping of chairs and Ronan's muffled murmuring. I step out into the hall, my pulse racing as I reach the top of the stairs. Finnick leans lazily against the wall, sharpening a blade that doesn't need sharpening. Every eye turns toward me. The air freezes with silence. Even Finnick forgets to pretend he's unaffected. I shift my gaze to Eowyn.

He stands at the bottom of the stairs, caught in the shaft of golden firelight. His eyes are already on me, storm-dark and wide, stunned in a way that steals my breath. I feel his gaze like a touch across my skin, slow and reverent, tracing the fall of the sheer gown, the threads of starlight woven into its folds, the bare skin of my collarbone.

My stomach flips.

He doesn't smile. He doesn't speak. He just looks at me as if the gods themselves had stitched me back together from ash and flame. Like he is too afraid that if he breathes, I'll vanish.

His lips part. "Brynn," he says, like a secret, as if my name on his tongue has become something holy.

I begin to descend, barefoot and trembling slightly, each step slower than the last. The wood is cool beneath my feet. The firelight shifts across the silk at my ankles. I don't look away from him.

"By the gods, we're all doomed," Finnick mutters somewhere off to the side.

I barely hear him as Eowyn closes the distance between us like a man pulled by gravity. His hand lifts slowly, hesitantly, and the oath seared into the flesh of my neck begins to burn with a quiet, aching warmth at the nearness of him. My breath catches. His fingers hover just near my skin, as if asking permission without words.

"My stomach's about to collapse in on itself," Ronan groans from behind him. "Can we please walk and swoon at the same time?"

Cia snickers, wrapping her arms around Ronan. "He has a point. Starvation makes a poor audience for romance."

Eowyn exhales softly, his jaw ticking once, but he doesn't look away from me. Not even as the moment breaks around us like a tide pulling back to sea. I finally breathe, though my heartbeat thuds behind my ribs like war drums. We both turn, just a fraction, as the others begin to file out toward the door. We follow the group, spilling out into the warm amber dusk, laughter echoing. Eowyn lingers beside me at the doorway for one heartbeat longer, his voice low and barely audible.

"You look like starlight that refuses to burn out."

Without waiting for a response, he joins the others. I remain still for a moment, the echo of his words burning through me brighter than any oath.

Finnick heralds our arrival to the mead hall with rambunctious vigor. Igor appears from nowhere and unceremoniously shoves a full mug of mead into Finnick's chest.

"Try using this to shut up," he grumbles.

Finnick grins and lifts the mug in salute. "To silence, then."

The cool earth beneath my bare feet grounds me, steadies the fire still burning within. The mead hall doors stretch open like a warm mouth, music and laughter spilling out into the crisp night air. Even from a distance, I can feel the glow radiating inside. Bright with firelight, roasted venison, and the scent of warm bread thick in the air.

A hush falls as we step over the threshold.

Dozens of villagers crowd the long tables, seated along benches or gathered by the hearth. Tankards of mead hover midair, conversations taper into silence as one by one, heads turn toward the doorway. Toward me. Their eyes widen, some with uncertainty and others with awe. I inhale slowly and lift my chin, offering a faint smile.

Finnick makes a show of bowing low before me. "Your Majesty of Ember and Starlight," he declares.

I laugh and shove his shoulder, catching the glimmer of mischief in his eye.

Cia slides in beside me, the edge of a grin tugging at her lips. "Told you they'd stare," she murmurs, low enough for only me to hear. "They'd be fools not to."

Ronan doesn't wait. He reaches for her hand and pulls her onto the dance floor, spinning her like its second nature as the musicians strike up a chord.

I feel him, silent and solid. I don't need to look to know it's him standing at my side. My breath hitches as the thunderous rhythm rises through the floorboards. Palms clap against tables, feet stamp in time, mugs rise high.

Someone presses a mug into my hands before I can refuse it. I lift it to my lips. The mead is sweet and bitter, burning just enough. And all the while, I feel the weight of Eowyn's nearness, like a hand pressed to the small of my back. Like fate, pulling me in.

The music slows, slipping into a haunting rhythm, low and

pulsing, with pipes that echo like a memory from another life. A circle begins to form at the center of the floor, boots scuffling back, benches scraping. No one says a word, but they clear the space with reverence. Eowyn turns to me, his hand never reaching, but his gaze never leaving.

"Walk with me," he says softly.

We step into the center, the entire hall leaning forward like they're holding their breath. The pipes swell. The drums follow.

Eowyn circles me, slowly, his eyes fixed on mine. The firelight flickers across his face, carving the sharp angles of him into something wild and beautiful. I turn with him, letting my bare feet glide across the dirt floor. My breath slows to match his.

We never touch. But the air between us feels alive...charged like lightning before it strikes. His chest rises and falls in time with mine. Our bodies twist and turn like twin stars caught in orbit. Not touching but impossibly bound. Around us, the music builds into something ancient. Something sacred. My fingers brush the air between us, and he flinches with it. That invisible thread. That spark. The mark seared into my neck burns softly, glowing beneath my skin. We move together in perfect rhythm, like we've done this before. A dozen times. A hundred. In another lifetime, another world and I am drowning beneath what I don't yet understand.

Eowyn pauses for half a breath, his expression unreadable, then slowly steps back. The music ends on a low note, leaving the room suspended in silence. It is only then that I see it. The glow between us...soft and spectral. Threads of Draíocht suspended in the space like frost-lit spider silk, weaving between our bodies without ever touching. Pale and silver-blue, the power humming faintly like it remembers something I've forgotten.

It curls around Eowyn's fingertips, trails down my collarbone, and coils between us in slow, spiraling arcs that are both delicate...intimate. As if it too...had danced. Eowyn holds my gaze a moment longer as the glow pulses once and then fades. Whatever passed between us, he knows. Has known. I stand in the stillness, my heart pounding, the taste of the Draíocht like winter wind on my tongue.

Chapter 49

Eowyn extends his hand, this time not to dance but to lead. I take it, unsure if my legs will carry me. My skin still hums from the power, from the weight of the villagers' silence. As we pass through the crowd, they part for us...not with suspicion, but something closer to reverence. Heads nod. Hands touch hearts. I don't know what to do with any of it.

At the head of the room, Eowyn pulls out the high-backed chair beside his own. I sink into it without thinking, only then realizing how ravenous I am. A tray of roasted meats, fruits, breads, and bowls of honeyed cream are passed down. I reach for the bread first, tearing it open with shaking hands. Eowyn leans close, his voice just low enough for only me to hear.

"Are you alright?"

I nod, mouth full, and glance at the others talking in low voices. Cia, Ronan, and Finnick trade jabs between sips of mead. It's loud but safe. Warm. Real. I turn back to Eowyn.

"What was that?" I ask softly. "Back there...between us."

He doesn't answer right away, his eyes searching my own.

"It's called the Dance of the Draíocht," he says at last. "Few have ever seen it. Fewer still have felt it. It happens when fate...unfolds itself, even for a moment."

The words settle into my bones like prophecy.

"Well." Runa stands before us, arms crossed, chin tilted as she studies me. The firelight halos her hair in light, but her stare is sharp as a dagger. "That was...something."

I don't answer. I'm not sure if I'm meant to.

She takes a step closer, eyes narrowing as if she's reading more than my face. "There's a saying among our people," she says, her voice quieter now. "Only the gods dance with Draíocht. When mortals do it...something always burns."

Her gaze flicks to Eowyn. She gives him a slight, approving nod, then walks off without another word. I exhale slowly, the heat rising in my chest again...not fear, not quite desire...just...weight.

Dinner passes in a blur of laughter and refilled mugs. I sip mead gingerly, my head already swimming as Finnick recalls an outrageous story about being mistaken for a traveling bard. Someone plays a hand drum; others clap in rhythm. For the first time in longer than I can remember, I feel full. Not just in my stomach...but in my soul. The night wears on when Eowyn rises and offers his hand again.

"Come. You'll want to see this."

We step out into the cooling air. The wind carries the scent of cedar smoke and honeysuckle. Those still awake and not slumbering in their mead cups gather in a wide ring around a towering wooden structure along the beach. Firewood is woven with flowers, herbs, and crimson ribbons. Children dart between legs, laughter spilling into the night. I look up to the full moon, stained red like blood and reflecting in the cove beyond the beach. At the edge of the crowd, a hush falls as Eowyn steps forward alone.

He rolls up his tunic sleeves and lifts his palm to the sky. A slow, deliberate breath escapes him. One that draws the air still and pulls every eye toward him. He begins to move, his body flowing the precision of something practiced but never performed. His limbs cut through the dark like blade through silk. With each twist of his fingers and turn of his wrist, fire flickers to life at his fingertips, trailing behind him in ribbons of gold. He dances not for spectacle but for something older. Reverent. A call to the ancient god of fire and fate.

Flames arc from his outstretched hand, skimming the earth, curling up the sides of the wood pile. Sparks scatter like seeds. The fire catches, not in a burst, but a breath. It grows like a heartbeat, pulsing outward in rings, igniting layer by layer until the entire pyre blazes with warmth and light.

Cheers erupt from the crowd. Music rises like a heartbeat, but I cannot look away from him. The way the fire kisses his skin. The way he makes it answer.

Gasps ripple through the gathered villagers as the celebration stills. Heads bow. Hands press over hearts. From the trees a thousand points of light begin to rise. They drift upward in a great hush, swirling above us like constellations torn loose from the sky. I stand frozen, wonder caught in my throat.

"Fireflies," Eowyn murmurs low in my ear, sending a heat up my spine.

He lifts a finger, and I gasp as one lands on it. The small body glows from within, a pulsing ember. Flames shimmer through its delicate wings, casting a soft, golden warmth across his face. Eowyn's eyes catch the light and wildly gleam with tenderness. The firefly lifts, joining the others in the dark. He turns back to me, his fingertip grazing my jaw.

I can't move despite my body begging to melt into his.

A hand catches my own.

Finnick.

Grinning like mischief itself.

"One dance," he says, "before I lose you to fate."

He whirls me away into the thrumming crowd, laughter spilling from my chest as he pulls me into the rhythm. Drums beat like thunder and flutes rise in wild joy. The fireflies swirling above us like stars reborn. He spins me...once...twice... then lets go.

I tumble backward...right into Eowyn's waiting arms.

He catches me like he was always meant to. His hands find my waist, steady and warm. My breath leaves me all at once. The music fades. The fire blurs. All I can see is him. His eyes aren't on my lips, but on my soul...unafraid. As if he's already memorized what he'll find in me and still chooses to stay.

My fingers curl into the fabric at his shoulder. I don't move. Neither does he.

"You burn," he murmurs. "And yet I move closer."

It's not a question. It's an answer to the pull we have been pretending not to feel. I lift my chin. My voice comes low, hoarse.

"So do you."

His mouth meets mine. Soft. Sure. A whisper of a beginning.

The Draíocht flares suddenly between us, wild and alive. It crackles like lightning just beneath my skin, rushing from my lips to my fingertips, pulling at something deep in my core. The kiss, once soft, shudders with a tremble of power neither of us can control. My breath catches. His hand lifts to cup my cheek, but we both freeze as a halo of pale fire coils around us, shimmering silvery-blue and brilliant shades of orange.

We pull back, but the Draíocht doesn't.

It stretches between us like threads spun from the stars themselves, delicate and dangerous. His eyes widen with fire, his jaw tight. Not in fear...but restraint.

His thumb brushes the soft line of my jaw as we stand there, suspended in something greater than either of us. The taste of the kiss lingers, the Draíocht still alive between us.

Not threatening.

Not tame.

Just waiting.

He leans in once more, his forehead resting against mine, voice barely more than breath.

"I would burn the stars to choose you in every life. Even if it ends us."

The earth groans beneath our feet. A sound ancient as bone.

And then...

the darkness answers.

Chapter 50

A blast of sound and flame rips through the night. The bonfire shatters outward in a roar, sending sparks spiraling like dying stars. Screams rise. The fireflies scatter in a thousand streaks of panicked flame. A shock wave knocks me back and Eowyn reaches for me, shielding my body with his.

Too late.

Smoke rises from the Rüin fortified wall.

The Draíocht howls inside me.

Something tears open in my chest, a white-hot pull like lightning down my spine. I clutch my skull as pain detonates behind my eyes. The world spins. My vision fractures into shadows and flame as they spill through the valley like a plague.

Not men. Not beasts.

Things.

Their bodies are forged from cracked obsidian and bleeding stone, animated by veins of pulsing indigo light that shimmer just beneath their skin like molten iron. Joints grind and crack with every unnatural movement. Some crawl on all fours, claws gouging deep furrows into the earth. Others stand nearly twice the height of a man, hunched and grotesque, with skulls that stretch too long, too narrow.

The ground trembles again, and something massive groans beneath it. A deep, guttural creaking, like the forest itself exhales rot.

The roots come.

They split the soil in violent tendrils, tearing through the grass like spears. Thick, gnarled coils of bark twist into limbs and claws, dragging themselves upright. Tree-creatures, their trunks charred black and leaking sap the color of decay, rise with hollowed-out torsos and faces carved by hatred. Moss dangles like rotted hair.

There is no time to think, no time to breathe when all across the hillside the once-beautiful wildflowers, once perfuming the breeze, suddenly burst open with a hiss. From each flower, creatures pour forth, insect-like things cloaked in petals and wings of glimmering decay. Their skin is translucent and glistening, veined like leaves dipped in acid. They fly fast and erratic, stingers dripping with venom and slicing through the air like razors. One lands on a woman's face and burrows into her eyes. Another swarms a child, its mouth unfolding like a bloom filled with needles.

The air is a sickly-sweet smell of rotting sweetness and of burnt honey that chokes me until I am dizzy. The creatures wail with the same cry that rises from the earth...a scream of the Gaia's death song. The Draíocht surges.

It moves before I can think, before I can speak. My hands fling wide with no command of my own and the power flares... raw, wild, alive. A blinding pulse of light carves a barrier between a child and the snaring claws of a vine-creature. The beast recoils with a shriek as the girl stumbles into my arms, sobbing. I don't remember moving. I don't remember deciding.

"Go!" I rasp, forcing her to her feet. "Down to the boats!"

Around me, the villagers scatter like leaves in a storm. Eowyn's orders echo across the valley, hoarse and fierce. Women and children too young or too old to fight arc ushered toward the cove, toward the longships rocking violently in the rising wind. Cia and Ronan move like twin blurs through the madness, shielding the weakest with blades, bodies, and shadows. Runa's ax swings as she cuts down a root-beast lunging for a boy's throat. Ivar drags Veera out from beneath a fallen timber and shoves her toward the water.

"Get them across!" he roars, already turning back to fight.

A tangle of limbs and antler bone leaps from the trees, lunging for a fleeing mother.

I scream.

The Draíocht answers.

A burst of flame coils from my hands and consumes the creature mid-air. My arms tremble with aftershock. My vision tunnels. I stagger back, breath hitching. I turn just in time to see Eowyn drive his flaming sword through the chest of a massive beast made of twisting roots and thorn. Blood and soot streak his face. A second creature rears up behind him.

I run without thought, without care for the power surging or the fire beneath my skin. I run because I see him. Because he's still standing. Because I have to get to him.

He turns.

Our eyes lock.

The sky splits.

Lightning rains down around us, wild and unrelenting. The air explodes in a cascade of blue and gold light. Thunder cracks the sky in two, weeping with violent fury. The ground quakes beneath my feet.

Still, I run.

The Draíocht answers me, scorching the earth in my wake, each step a spark of light and flame. My power surges, sears, and screams beneath my skin.

I am the storm.

I nearly reach Eowyn when the battlefield stills in eerie silence, as if even the creatures know. I skid to a halt, breath ragged, chest heaving. The storm within me falters, flickering silent as my gaze follows the others'...to the top of the hill.

Framed by smoke and a blood-streaked sky stands Muris, cloaked in betrayal. Clutching a twisted staff of indigo stone that pulses with a light not born of this world. I turn my gaze like the others, to the top of the hill.

No one speaks. No one moves.

He didn't vanish in the Wastelands.

He didn't die with Mahurin.

He brought this.

The blood.

The fire.

The beasts.

He brought it all to us.

To *me*.

His voice booms across the battlefield, carried by the wind like a curse.

"You will never unite the clans, girl," he says, his eyes locking with mine. "You were born to bleed."

He lifts a dagger of obsidian, its edge gleaming with unnatural glint. Within a heartbeat the dagger spins through the air, aiming straight for my heart.

Time fractures.

A body crashes into mine.

"No…"

The word tears from my throat as he hits the ground with a sickening thud, the dagger buried in his chest.

Everything halts.

My breath won't come.

The Draíocht thrashes inside me, a wounded animal, a scream of light, fire and agony begging to be unleashed. My knees hit the sand. I press trembling hands to his chest.

Blood. So much blood.

It spills over my hands, warm and endless. His eyes flutter.

"Stay with me," I whisper. "Please...stay."

Finnick's eyes are wide with shock and fear, his entire body trembling. His mouth opens to speak, but only a wet, gurgling cough escapes. Thick congealed blood spills from his lips. His chest rises and falls in harsh, uneven rasps. He's suffocating. Drowning in his own blood.

I clutch him to me, my voice shattering against my sobs.

"Shh...shh. It's okay," I whisper. "I'm going to fix it. I'm here. You're okay, Finnick. You're okay."

My body trembles with anguish, wracked by sobs as my hand burns around the jagged blackened blade lodged in his chest. I try to pull it out and he cries out...his scream choked and broken through gasping breaths.

Bright red blood spills from his nose, then deepens... darkens...turning a sickly black. He strangles on it, thrashing in my arms.

"Finnick!" I scream his name, wiping the golden strands from his sweat-slick face. My voice splinters. "Stay with me. Please, stay with me."

I call the Draíocht in desperation, pulling from the fire within. My hands ignite with light, glowing hot with hope. But the moment the black blood touches them, it stings. Burns. The Draíocht recoils with a shriek from him. It refuses to pour into him.

"No, no...take it. Take it!" I force the pulse of power

through my palms, tears blurring the edges of everything. "I'm begging you," I sob, lifting my eyes to the skies. "Please. Give me the power to save him. I'll pay the price. Just let me save him."

But only silence answers.

I clutch his face to my chest, rocking him like a child, like something sacred I'm not ready to let go of. My tears fall freely now, hot and heavy, soaking his cheeks, his hair, my trembling hands.

The light fades from his eyes.

All the grief I've held back.

Every scream I swallowed.

Every wound I buried.

Every hope I dared believe...erupts at once.

I drown in it.

My head tilts back and a scream tears from my throat. A sound no human should ever make, a song wrenched from the marrow of a shattered soul.

The mountains around us quake as if they too are grieving. The ground splits in jagged lines. Massive red boulders shear from the mountains, crashing to the ground with earth-shaking force. The sky bruises, roiling with storm.

Still, I scream.

The Draíocht pulses around me, wild and unhinged, caught in my grief. Lightning slashes across the heavens, striking the peaks in blistering white arcs. Wind howls like the voice of the gods, whipping around me, lashing my hair into my face.

I can't breathe. I can't stop.

His body begins to flake...soft...crumbling...like dried leaves caught in a storm.

"No," I whisper, holding him tighter. "No. Don't go. Please...don't go."

But he's already slipping through my hands.

Ash swirls around me, catching in the wind like fine black snow. His weight vanishes, his warmth gone. My arms close around nothing but air and grief. I fall forward onto the ground with a broken sob, clutching the remains, my body wracked with tremors.

The darkness in my heart cracks wide open. It spills out, swallowing everything.

And I let it.

Eowyn shouts, but his voice is a ghost. Lost. Silent. Meaningless against the roar of my heart. I cannot hear him. I cannot hear anything but the emptiness inside me collapsing. The sorrow within me rises like a tide, hungry and relentless, and I submit to it completely. There is no strength left to fight it.

I weep uncontrollably, choking on sobs that won't stop. My upturned hands tremble before me...empty...hollow...where Finnick should be. Where he was just moments ago.

He was my friend. My family. My brother.

He is what is good in this world. What is pure.

He protected me from the moment he met me.

He saved me from myself when the grief consumed everything.

And now...now he is nothing.

Nothing but ash against my flesh.

The wind whips around me but I don't feel it. The ground trembles with aftershock but I don't notice. I'm frozen in the moment...my world ended.

Eowyn's hand clamps down around my elbow. He jerks me upright with a force I don't have in me to resist. His eyes... golden and fierce...are rimmed with sorrow he does not speak. He doesn't have to, I see it in the way his jaw locks, in the tremble behind his strength, in the way he refuses to let me go.

I stagger behind him, blind to the burning valley we leave behind, to the death littered across the stone. I can't feel the earth beneath my feet. My body moves but I am somewhere far away...still on my knees in the ash, still holding him. Still screaming.

Cia meets us at the edge of the trees, her shadows unraveling like thread from a broken spool. They pour from her like smoke and wrap around us, sealing us in darkness. Her face, usually so bold, is drawn and pale...her eyes a flicker of disbelief.

Frightened faces blur around me. Their mouths open and close but I cannot hear them. I do not want to. Ronan's voice barks orders like a war drum in the distance, rallying the wounded, forcing the broken to keep moving. His fury and pain are weapons now.

But mine...mine is a hole so wide it will never close. A scream still echoing in my soul.

My body shakes hard though I cannot feel it. Eowyn's muffled voice fills my ears and my heart beats angrily against his words.

"Brynn! Look at me. Brynn. Please! Brynn. Come back to me! Please!"

He kisses my lips hard, my eyes, my cheeks...tears stream down his face. I smell the familiar smokiness of him as he pulls me to his chest, sobbing, but I feel nothing. Not his warmth. Not the pain. Not the weight of his arms trying to hold me together. An unbearable cold leeches into my bones, a frost that numbs everything it touches. Even the memory of love.

He pulls me back, his golden eyes searching desperately for mine.

I look away from the flames and down at my ash-covered hands. My voice is as cold as I feel.

"Finnick is dead."

The words hang like a curse in the air.

The world around me crumbles. My knees buckle. My soul breaks open. I fall through myself, down and down into the deepest, blackest part of me. I no longer scream...I don't have the strength. There is only silence now. A vast, endless quiet inside my chest.

The sorrow is too wide to hold. Too sharp to bear. My heart feels like torn paper in a storm. I sink into the murky depths of it, pulled under by guilt...grief...and fury, until no light shows above.

A voice...

It coils through the darkness...

Ancient.

Patient.

Cold.

A silken blend of whispers and wind.

Of lullaby and warning.

A voice velvet-smooth and full of promise.

"Hello, Daughter of Light. I have been waiting."

Acknowledgment

Writing this book has been the journey my heart didn't just want...it desperately needed. What began as a quiet act of survival, a way to breathe through the weight of my own life, has grown into something far greater than I could have ever imagined. Every word, every perseverance, every moment of beauty has caught me by surprise. To share this story now feels like offering a piece of my soul to those willing to hold it.

First and foremost, thank you to my children for enduring the "crazy music" I played to help with inspiration, for the weekends you let me vanish into my writing, and for the unconditional love that reminded me why I kept going.

Thank you to my family and friends for always believing in me, even when I didn't believe in myself.

Ashley, thank you for always being my Cia. You reminded me I was loved. That my voice mattered. You gave me the courage when my own had been buried by others.

Amber, I couldn't have made it this far without you. You started out giving me guidance, then becoming my editor, and now you are bound to me as a life-long friend. You fought for this book, for my voice, and for me when I couldn't do it alone. I am forever grateful.

Shelby at Maple Projects, thank you for the amazing cover design. You brought to life my transformation, a phoenix's rise made tangible. I am constantly astounded by it.

A special thank you to G.W. Prouse for always being an encouraging message away, providing wisdom, and the kind of support that never falters.

To my readers... whether you stepped into this story early on as a Beta Reader or are opening it for the first time...thank you. If you too, live among ashes, I hope these pages remind you that you can rise, that your scars hold strength, and that your voice can set the world on fire. This book is as much yours as it is mine.

-Whit Jordan

About

Whit Jordan is a passionate storyteller who loves weaving rich worlds filled with complex characters and emotional journeys. When not writing she enjoys spending time with family, reading all the indie fantasy books she can find, the week of faux-fall the South Georgia heat brings once a year, and drinking copious amounts of iced salted caramel lattes.

This is Whit Jordan's first published book. She draws inspiration from her own personal experiences and the worlds created in her mind to escape reality. She believes that stories have the ability to transform, heal, and unite us all.

Connect with Whit Jordan and follow the FIFAB series on Instagram at WhitJordan_Author.